DIRT

A guerrilla lecture about the high cost of dying ...

A nose ring removed the hard way ...

An unemployed couch potato with a trust fund ...

A pair of ex-cons with a plan ...

A sharp-dealing funeral director ...

A common blackmailer ...

An uncommon hearse ...

A twice-dug grave ...

A silver cross ...

A steel .45 ...

Happy hour at a morticians' convention ...

Lessons in longevity ...

Poor impulse management ...

A vanishing wristwatch ...

Remedies for a black eye ...

A small shoebox of mementos ...

The TherMAXX 2500 Human Reduction System ...

And a tenacious young reporter who knows

  that for every hole,

  there's a pile of dirt somewhere.

Quince Bishop
habitually semi-employed loafer unwillingly thrust headfirst
   into a mystery

Joel Moss
unscrupulous head of Palm Grove Cemetery

Billy Guilder
groundskeeper at Palm Grove and ex-con, trying hard to
   keep his nose clean

Carl Rosen
career armed robber with his own plan

Melanie Roth
Quince's perpetual ex-girlfriend and newspaper reporter

Maria Casteneda
founder and leader of the SoCal Valley Memorial Society

Gerald Kinghorn
porn-loving pawn shop proprietor with a son gifted in the
   art of refrigeration repair

Detective Timms
hard-working, no-nonsense Santa Monica detective

Arlen Maxwell
aging actor who is both landlord and life counselor to
   Quince

ALSO BY SEAN DOOLITTLE

Burn

DIRT

SEAN DOOLITTLE

UGLYTOWN
LOS ANGELES

Second Edition

Text copyright © 2005 by Sean Doolittle. All Rights Reserved.

UGLYTOWN AND THE UGLYTOWN COIN LOGO SERVICEMARK REG. U.S. PAT. OFF.

Library of Congress Cataloging-in-Publication Data data on file.
ISBN: 0-9758503-0-X

Find out more of the mystery: UglyTown.com/Dirt

Printed in Canada

10 9 8 7 6 5 4 3 2 1

IF ONLY I had kept my first copy of Sean Doolittle's *Dirt* in what book dealers call "fine" or "very fine" shape, I probably wouldn't have to worry so much about my retirement. I figure by the time I can break into my paltry 401-K without penalty, that true first edition of *Dirt* in mint condition will be worth as much as, say, an early Elmore Leonard, or a copy of Carl Hiaasen's Tourist Season. So close to easy street, so far. It was ever thus.

The thing is, what rigid soul could read Sean Doolittle without dog-earing him? And, if one is a writer, hating him, just a little. Here is a sampling of lines that caused me to crimp and covet my way through *Dirt* when it first appeared in 2001.

Cruel? Perhaps. But cruel she had coming.

Still, there was something about listening to her describe the putrefaction stages of dead human tissue that filled him with a peculiar discord.

The second thing you must have is an acute sense of observation. I stuck my middle finger in the corpse's anus, but I licked my index.

Bording ath hoe. (To appreciate this surly greeting, it helps to know that the speaker is a two-bit punk who had "a nose ring removed the hard way.")

I could go on, but I'm not getting paid, by the word or otherwise, and I've probably taken the edge off your appetite. So where did this guy with the drier-than-dry voice come from anyway? Short answer: just outside Lincoln, Nebraska. The coastal snobs may call it flyover country, but there's a case to be made that these vast open spaces have their own version of hardboiled. After all, where else can your childhood elementary school be flattened by an F-4 tornado in less time than it takes to do the "one times" on the multiplication table? (This really happened to Sean not so long ago.) Where else do they hand a 14-year-old kid a machete and turn him out to—well, what exactly did you do with that machete, Sean?

"The job was a regular summer thing before I was old enough to drive myself to some other kind of job," Sean wrote when I asked him to jog my memory about this anecdote, shared at a conference in Omaha. "The common slang for this was 'cutting cane.' It consisted of walking milo and bean fields (on a crew) with a machete, which we called a 'corn knife,' chopping out shattercane and other weeds. Milo is better-known to the rest of the country as sorghum, although I didn't know it at the time."

A corn knife, shattercane, milo, sorghum. It's hard not to wonder if Sean might have forgotten more material than most of us are ever given. Plus, there are all those meth labs in Nebraska, but maybe that's just a nasty rumor started in my crack-besotted hometown.

Dirt, at any rate, is set in Los Angeles and you could read it for the details about the funeral business alone and feel you had gotten your money's worth. But it provides much more, the kind of sophisticated caper tale that can derail the most experienced novelists. A character in a Gail Godwin novel, a college writing instructor, once observed that the most difficult thing for a beginning writer to do is to get a character to stand up, cross the room, open the door and leave. Imagine trying to get a diverse cast of characters with varying agendas to converge on an L.A. cemetery and a Seattle hotel in a wholly satisfying climax. Now imagine doing it *drunk*. (I'm not saying Sean was, but he has admitted to proofing his copy in barrooms.)

Seriously, Sean was far from a beginner when he wrote *Dirt*; it just happens to be the first novel he published. A longtime short story writer—his varied body of work spans almost three decades, from "The Great Popcorn Caper" to the Dagger-nominated "A Kick in the Lunchbucket"—he had written two novels, both of which made the rounds in New York. With *Dirt*, Sean turned west, toward the Los Angeles-based UglyTown, a press that proves small is indeed beautiful.

It has been a felicitous partnership, leading to a second novel, *Burn*, which more than delivers on the promise of *Dirt*. I'm sure monographs and dissertations will one day focus on Sean and UglyTown, separately and in tandem. But, for now, just be grateful for this second chance to get in on the ground floor.

Me, I've started telling people I knew Sean when he was cutting milo with a corn knife. You know—what you Easterners call a machete.

Laura Lippman
Baltimore, Maryland
July 2004

This book is for Jessica,

for giving me a hundred reasons to wake up every morning.

The inevitable push out of bed is also appreciated.

Dying is a very dull, dreary affair.

And my advice to you is to have nothing whatever

to do with it.

—*W. Somerset Maugham*

DIRT

THE TROUBLE didn't seem to start so much as it simply landed, like a hunk of blazing debris.

Quince Bishop hadn't even been paying attention. In fact, right up until the moment all hell broke loose, he'd been thinking about how depressingly generic the morning seemed.

A tent, a hole in the ground. An assemblage of folding chairs on a rolling green lawn. A head bowed here, a handkerchief clutched there, bright bunches of flowers all around. Rain showers earlier in the morning had left the cemetery turf fragrant and marshy, and the mound of excavated earth still looked damp beside the grave.

But now the sun was high. The sky was blue, the air was crisp, and the breeze coming in from the ocean was warm. And for the most part, his good buddy Martin's was no more or less ordinary than the next funeral.

Rhonda, Martin's wife, had asked Quince to sit up front with the family. Quince felt awkward here, but he could never have declined. Rhonda Waxman now sat two chairs to his left, next to her mother, who held Katie on her lap. Katie had turned four in September. Martin's boy Nathan—six—sat on the other side of Rhonda, fiddling listlessly at the crease of his pint-sized Dockers. Rhonda kept her arm around his small shoulders. Otherwise she sat straight, wearing a dark yellow dress Martin had liked. Every few minutes, Quince caught a glimpse of her hand as the corner of a linen handkerchief slipped beneath glossy black sunglasses.

"You know, if you keep staring at it like that, I'm afraid that box might levitate."

He'd been gazing absently at Martin's casket while they all waited for the service to begin. It took Quince several moments before he realized the whispering man on his right was speaking to him.

Quince whispered back: "Sorry?"

The man, who had been introduced at the wake only as Pastor Mike, winked kindly and tapped his bare wrist. Quince understood; he tilted his watch so Pastor Mike could see. Six minutes until showtime. The minister responded with a low thumbs-up, which he shielded from view with his prayer book.

Then he leaned in further and whispered something that caught Quince off guard.

"Are you okay?"

Quince glanced at him. Nodded.

Pastor Mike wore an expression of understanding on his elastic, friendly face. He joined Quince in watching Martin's casket for a minute or two. It was buttoned up and gleaming in the sunlight, suspended by canvas straps above the rich black hole.

"Makes you think," Pastor Mike whispered.

Quince just nodded again. What could you say?

Practically everybody who'd ever met Martin Waxman would tell you: he was one of the good guys, through and through. Quince had gone to work for him five years ago, writing software manuals for Martin's development firm. He'd been a terrible employee, and Wax had the good sense to fire his ass on several occasions.

Eventually, Martin got over the habit of re-hiring him again, which really was the best thing for everybody concerned. But despite such natural obstacles as managerial relations and office protocol, the two of them had been fast friends from the beginning. They'd never found a good reason not to stay that way.

All things considered, Quince supposed he probably liked Martin Waxman as well as anybody he could think of. Hell, he'd truly admired the man. Martin was one of the good guys. And he'd died towel-drying his hair, two weeks before his 36th birthday.

It was miserable from every angle. The whole situation put Quince Bishop in a roving, reflective, cliché-addled mood.

Dammit, here was a guy who had done everything right: never smoked, drank only in moderation, ate smart, played vicious racquetball at least two times a week. He'd loved his family, done things for others, and never assumed he was entitled to anything.

And still, Quince's friend Martin had somehow managed to crump decades too soon. From an undetected coronary thrombosis, and not two months after a clean yearly physical. Three days ago, Martin Waxman had been a successful independent software developer from San Pedro. Today, he was leaving topside a young wife, two small kids, and a lease on a new Q45.

Quince found himself watching Nathan and Katie, wondering how they'd remember this. He'd been Nate's age when his own parents had died. His older brother Paul had been eleven. Quince wondered if Nate comprehended more or less of this than he had, at the time.

He wondered what Martin would have told his son, had he known it was his only chance.

He wondered what else Wax would have tried to squeeze in under the deadline, had he been granted a glimpse of this in advance.

Then he looked up and wondered what the hell was going on.

But by the time Quince realized something was wrong, it was too late to matter anyway. His good buddy Martin's funeral was already in shambles. And cratering fast.

Nobody saw them coming.

One minute, Pastor Mike was saying something that Quince couldn't quite hear. The next, several things seemed to be happening all at the same time.

First, the funeral director appeared. His name was Joel Moss, and he wore a sharp navy suit with a plum-colored tie and matching boutonniere. At precisely ten o'clock, Moss smoothed his way over to the family row. He placed a light hand on Rhonda's shoulder, asking in gentle tones if she were ready to begin.

At roughly this same moment, Quince noticed a commotion developing at the back of the tent. A few heads turned curiously.

Pastor Mike stood. Quince joined reflexively. Beside him, he heard Nathan Waxman say, "Who's that?"

Quince followed Pastor Mike's eyes.

"Christ," said the funeral director. He disappeared.

And all together, as if collectively cued, everybody in attendance looked toward the sudden hissing sound.

Later, Quince would tell the cops that he had absolutely no idea who the assholes with the road flares were. He only knew that there had been four of them. And that they'd appeared suddenly, as if they'd dropped from the palm trees, all wearing hooded death's head masks, black leather gloves, and loose black clothes.

"Wake-Up-Now! Wake-Up-Now!" The interlopers chanted these words in unison as they descended upon Martin's funeral.

Even in his confusion, Quince noted that the foursome did not appear to be moving with what he would have called crack paramilitary efficiency. If anything, they seemed distracted by the volatile spew of the sizzling flares they carried. But their sensational entrance served its purpose. Having secured the undivided attention of the crowd, they managed to flank the tent in sibilant pairs.

"This is probably going to be unfortunate," Pastor Mike said.

Quince barely heard him above the noise.

"Wake-Up-Now! Wake-Up-Now!" The protesters pumped their flares above their heads with each incantation of their rally phrase. Blue smoke now hung above the gravesite in acrid clouds.

"What's happening?" This came from Rhonda Waxman. She seemed to be reaching everywhere at once: Katie, Nathan, her mother, Quince's arm. "What's going on?"

Quince had no idea. Several feet in front of them, one of the activists jammed his flare into the mound of grave dirt as though he were staking land. While the others positioned themselves, this apparent leader stepped behind the podium and began orating into the microphone.

"Greetings, consumers," he shouted, his voice swallowed

by the morning. The guy peered at the mic, tapped it, then began searching around behind the podium. In a moment, he'd successfully flipped on the sound system with a piercing yowl of feedback.

"Greetings, consumers!" he repeated, his words now ringing over the PA as he unfolded a piece of white paper and smoothed it on the lectern in front of him.

"We are here," he announced, "on behalf of the native peoples of the Amazonian regions. Each year, peaceful citizens of the rain forest lose their lives and livelihoods to ruthless mahogany loggers. I am referring to the same brutal thugs who, through reckless harvesting practices and outright violence, helped make this upmarket sob-fest possible today."

Quince noticed that Joel Moss had returned, his salon cut tossed by the breeze. And he'd brought help. Moss gestured wildly to a cemetery groundskeeper who wore a work shirt and heavy construction boots. At the funeral director's coaxing, the larger, tougher-looking man attempted to rush the podium. The remaining activists fended him off by making broad threatening sweeps with their flares.

"All," continued the man at the microphone, leveling a clenched fist at Waxman's casket, "so that the indulgent and the self-important can rot underground in style! And so that the Death Traders," now turning the fist directly on Moss, "can go on boosting …"

A pause.

"… boosting exorbilant profits at the expense of the living!"

While Rhonda Waxman began to sob beside him, Quince thought: *exorbilant*? As if by way of punctuation, Skull Punk ripped the microphone from its stand and reached Martin's

26

SEAN DOOLITTLE

casket in three big strides. He slapped the lid dramatically with his hand, shouting, "We find this unacceptable!"

In the next fluid motion, the tree crusader vaulted aboard the coffin itself. He seemed unaware of the distinctly metallic-sounding scrape produced when something—maybe a pebble caught in the sole of his Doc Martens—screeched across the casket's showroom finish. Quince saw the other protesters glance at each other. To their credit, they covered their apparent confusion quickly, supporting their speaking member with an energetic vocal outburst.

The leader called: "We at the SoCal Valley Memorial Society support the efforts of the global anti-mahogany campaign!"

And then he plummeted.

Quince watched the whole thing with gloomy fascination. He watched Skull Punk slip, struggle for balance, and finally lose his footing on the casket's slick, domed lid. The gardenia and orange blossom wreath skidded out from beneath his feet, and the voice man went down like a great black bird shot from the sky.

He landed hard on his back, flailing with a leg. Somewhere in the pinwheeling flurry of motion, his foot connected with one of the winches mounted on either side of theinterment rack. This was followed by a fast ratcheting sound.

With a sinking sensation, Quince watched the head-end of Martin Waxman's casket drop like a steel beam.

The guy with the microphone banged his head, spun, and toppled off into the dirt behind. Everyone gasped; there came a terrible wrenching sound. Martin's casket rocked and lurched, finally thudding to rest at a sideways cant, propped nearly on end, half in and half out of the hole.

Rhonda Waxman screamed. Pastor Mike quickly

maneuvered himself between her, the children, and the morbid scene. The other skull people looked at each other again.

Then they scattered.

Quince reacted without thinking. Maybe it was reflex; perhaps the adrenalized chaos of the moment just got the better of him. Or maybe it was the simplicity of the sudden, sweeping indignation that enveloped him on Martin Waxman's behalf.

He truly didn't know. But as he approached the beginning of his third decade, Quince Bishop had compiled a sobering laundry list of his own character deficiencies—the personal shortcomings which, he believed, routinely combined to produce the many awful decisions he seemed to make instinctively.

The moment the mahogany activist jumped his friend's casket, Quince was swept away by a fast tide of problem #3: poor impulse management.

He hit the guy high and hard, and they toppled over the mound together. The guy grunted heavily. Encouraged, Quince forged onward, hindered only by the fact that he didn't have a clue what to do next.

Quince Bishop just wasn't an action-oriented person by nature. And he realized quickly how little he knew about proper tackling.

His trouble: all form, no landing. Quince felt in control of the situation as he rode Skull Punk down the opposite side of the dirt pile. This changed when they hit solid ground and Skull Punk's bent knee punched squarely into Quince's diaphragm.

He felt his breath leave his body in one long, sickening *whoosh*. There came a moment of panic; Quince struggled to keep some kind of leverage by tightening the hug, but he was restricted by his suit coat. As the guy squirmed to get out from under him, Quince realized he might actually lose consciousness soon.

There just wasn't a choice. He had to roll off until he could coax a rattling breath into his lungs, which gave his opponent more than enough time to scramble to his feet. When Quince opened his eyes, the lone activist was sprinting for a lush green hill that sloped up and away.

Somehow, Quince caught him again just before he reached an artfully-placed cluster of tall, slender date palms. Quince managed to snatch the back of the skull hood with his fingertips.

Wheezing, he yanked.

And just as the mask started to come off in his hand, Quince was blessed by a stroke of pure dumb luck. He heard the guy yelp. Instinctively, Quince increased the tension. The guy dug in his feet and pulled the other way.

Standing there, facing each other, Quince could see that the fabric of the hood had somehow gotten snagged up in the thick silver nose ring the guy was wearing. Quince tried to reel him in, not sure what he'd do once he did. The guy held his ground. Quince felt his grip slackening and wound the mask around his wrist; the guy lowered his head and bent at the knees. The protester's nostril distended radically.

Sensing that what he essentially faced here was a scared, overzealous kid, Quince spoke in a soothing voice.

"C'mere, you little scumbag."

And a kind of understanding seemed to settle over the mahogany activist's face.

Quince could see him considering his limited options. The two of them locked eyes. Toward Skull Punk, Quince projected a single thought: *I dare you*. Privately, he thought: *He won't*.

By the time Quince realized he was wrong, it was already too late.

Appearing to have weighed his choices earnestly, Skull Punk took a deep breath. He closed his eyes. He balled his fists. And he threw all his weight backwards against the mask. In the same motion, the protester opened his arms wide and tugged his head toward the sky.

Everyone in the funeral party heard the high glottal scream split the morning air.

By then, the groundskeeper, who'd rushed the tree people, had loped across the lawn to offer aid. When he appeared at Quince's side, sheer moments too late, Skull Punk was already cresting a gentle rise a hundred yards in the distance. Another second or two, and he'd reached the six-foot stucco wall which bordered the grounds. Skull Punk leapt, scrabbled, strained mightily, and finally dumped himself over, disappearing from view. Quince looked at the groundskeeper. The groundskeeper shrugged supportively.

And when Quince finally walked back to the funeral tent—muddy, panting, carrying the empty skull mask with the bloody nose ring still attached—a dozen people had already gathered to see.

Moss rushed over. He looked harried, frantic, at an utter loss.

"What rain forest?" the funeral director pleaded. He wore a helpless expression on his face. "This casket is solid copper. Forty-eight ounce!"

"Yeah," Quince said. Handing over the mask, he added: "You can see the dents from here."

WITHIN the quarter hour, two SMPD cruisers converged at Palm Grove cemetery in Santa Monica. The blue-and-whites were followed closely by a Channel 11 news van, a camera crew from the television tabloid *Inside L.A.*, and an unmarked Oldsmobile sedan.

The detective who drove the Olds accompanied Rhonda Waxman, her mother, and the kids across the grounds. Moss, the funeral director, showed them through a service door to the main building, steering them into the carpeted, air-conditioned quietude of the funeral home's chapel.

Meanwhile, back at the grave, the four responding officers had broken into teams. One pair tried their best to set up a line and cordon the media behind bright yellow tape, while the other worked to calm and disperse the bewildered funeral crowd.

Quince tried to be useful without getting cornered by anybody with a microphone. Commotion ruled. For a while, he helped the cops move people toward their cars, noting disconsolately how much Martin's eternal resting place at Palm Grove currently looked like the bleary aftermath of a rousted lawn party. Pastor Mike volunteered to run interference while the cops worked the area, which he accomplished by tossing fluffy quotable marshmallows to the accumulating clot of press folk. Behind the yellow line, pens scribbled and tape rolled.

When he was tapped, Quince spent ten minutes giving his account of the situation to the detective, Timms, a broad-shouldered man with knowing eyes and a wrinkled sport jacket that stretched at the seams. He wore his badge on a clip at his belt. Quince told him all he knew, which was nothing. Timms thanked him for his cooperation and moved on.

And in the sudden vacuum he left behind, Quince found himself standing purposeless. He watched the detective make his way over to the groundskeeper, who was now standing with his hands on his hips, scrutinizing Martin's upended casket from a variety of angles.

A voice behind him said: "You're going to need to get that suit cleaned."

Quince knew it was Mel before he turned around.

"Hey," he said.

"Hey yourself," said Melanie Roth. She reached forward to brush a dried crust of grave dirt from one of his sleeves.

Quince had been starting to wonder if she'd made it to the service at all. She'd declined his suggestion that they ride together, and he hadn't seen her arrive.

But here she was, in chunky but sensible heels, wearing a short-sleeved blue summer dress and a small box purse on her hip. Mel wore the purse slung from the narrow peak of the opposite shoulder, bandoleer-style.

"You look nice," he said.

Mel squeezed his hand, appraising him. "So are you okay, or what?"

"I'm fine."

"What a mess." Mel stood on tiptoe to pick a leaf out of his hair. "Poor Rhonda."

Quince tilted his head, appraising her in return.

"What's wrong?" she said.

"When did you do that?"

"Do what?"

"Your hair," he said, still surprised. She'd gotten it cut short, and she'd lightened it. Where it had once been covered, the back of her neck was still pale.

"Oh, for crying out loud Quince, last week, I don't know. I look like Tinkerbell. Seriously—are you all right? What on Earth got into you, anyway?"

Quince repeated that he was fine, didn't have an answer for the second question, and thought to himself: *she did it again*. He could always count on the clockwork regularity of this particular pattern of Mel's. This was how he always knew things were truly over between them once again: one day, she'd show up with a completely new haircut.

Couldn't help but like this one. On Melanie, it looked breezy and great.

"Have you seen Rhonda yet?"

Mel shook her head. "No. Do you think the kids are doing okay?"

"They're all in the chapel now." He gestured behind him, toward the low building with the clay tile roof. "Probably use the company, if you're up for it. Katie loves you to pieces."

Mel's eyes wilted. "Okay. Of course. I need to talk to that cop over there first, then I'll go."

"Timms? What for?"

"Timms. Is that his name?" She dipped into the purse and retrieved a little notebook of her own. She unclipped a pen and scribbled TIMMS on the first page. When she noticed Quince watching her, she sighed. "I'm covering this for the paper. Don't look at me like that."

"Like what?"

"I called on the cell and talked this assistant city editor I know into letting me on it. For pete's sake, I'm already here."

"Great," Quince said.

"Don't." She looked him directly in the eyes. "Don't even say it."

"I didn't say a word."

Mel was a lifestyles writer for the *Times*, but for months now she'd been struggling for a chance to work hard news. Her problem was that she did a great job and was as dependable on a deadline as any writer around. Naturally, the Living section wanted to keep her, and nobody else had any good reason to start a fight about it. All things being equal, the metro desks seemed to believe they had better things to do than get into some internal recruiting scrap over a lipstick writer.

So far, it had been one career-stumping brick wall after another for Melanie. This, then, was a certifiable coup; a classic Mel Roth end move. Under any other circumstance, Quince would have been proud of her.

"This isn't a break, Quince," she told him. "Martin was my friend, too."

"I know that."

"Just look over there. Tell me I won't do better by him than *those* vultures."

He didn't doubt her. But as Mel jerked a thumb behind her, indicating the yapping collective still surrounding Pastor Mike, Quince noticed for the first time the trim, tallish blonde guy in the double-breasted suit.

The guy was standing with his hands in his pockets about twenty yards away. He fixed his gaze politely in another direction: the unmistakable posture of somebody waiting for somebody to finish talking with somebody he doesn't know.

Quince said, "So who's your date?"

"This isn't a date, Quince. It's a funeral."

"I don't mean it like that. I'm just asking."

"His name is Colin," Mel said.

Quince looked again. "Colin" was sun-streaked and moisturized and looked like he lived on a Nautilus machine. Quince could actually see a bulbous knob of triceps through the guy's suit coat.

"Underwear model?"

Mel gave him a hard look.

Oh, he knew. It was an idiotic thing to say. But he couldn't help himself; the words just made a break for his lips and escaped before he could chew them down.

"Colin owns a brokerage," Mel told him.

Of course he did. Quince nodded appreciatively. Thinking: *jerk.*

"He was one of Martin's investment guys," Mel said. "We got to talking last night at the wake, and we just decided to come together. It's no big deal."

"Hey," Quince said. "He sounds swell."

"Enough," said Mel.

Quince held up his palms innocently.

"Look, I'm on," she said. Behind him, Timms had finished with the groundskeeper. "Are you sure you're all right?"

"I'm fine, Mel. Quit asking."

Mel eyed him clinically. "I'll call you tonight," she said. "Okay?"

Quince nodded.

Mel said, "Okay."

Then she walked past him, toward Detective Timms. Quince watched her go, thinking again that he really liked the new hair.

By lunchtime, Joel Moss wanted nothing in the world more than a long hour in a quiet room with a cool washcloth draped across his brow. He had a headache that began somewhere in his retinas and radiated all the way to the soles of his feet. Joel truly could not remember experiencing such a merciless throb. And it was barely noon.

After Timms had finished talking with the Waxman family in the chapel, the two of them had retreated to the quiet of Joel's private office above the mortuary.

"So besides this," the detective was saying, holding up the skull mask with one hand, "there were no actual assaults?"

"Not unless you count Mr. Waxman," Joel said. "I'd call that assault."

"Of course."

"It's downright repugnant, is what it is."

"I wouldn't argue," the detective said.

Moss released a long breath through the nose. "I apologize. It's been a long morning."

Timms nodded. "I expect it has." With the knuckle of an index finger, the detective nudged the blackened highway flare sitting in the middle of Joel's desk. Charred powder sifted onto the blotter. "I guess it's safe to assume that this explains the reports of explosives we received?"

"It would appear that the facts were somewhat over-stated," Joel said.

Oh, it was priceless, really: in the thick of the moment, somebody in the funeral congregation apparently had dialed the SMPD's emergency line on their cell phone and reported an armed vigilante attack.

"Again. I really do apologize."

"It happens," Timms said.

"But one of my guys got burned," Joel told him. "If that makes any difference."

"This would be…." Timms flipped through his notepad. "Guilder?"

"That's right," Joel said. "Billy Guilder." Fishing a short bottle from the top drawer of his desk, Joel carefully sorted six Excedrins and a Zoloft into the palm of his hand.

At that moment, as if by telepathy, the office door opened. The one and only Billy Guilder stuck his head inside.

"Oh," he said. "Sorry, coach."

"Billy." Joel tossed back the caplets, reached for the glass of water on his desk, and gestured with his free hand. "Come on in."

Joel's groundskeeper stepped inside and closed the door behind him. As always, Billy Guilder seemed fundamentally uncomfortable in the office, like a coyote that had wandered in from the canyon by mistake. He was all cropped, sandy hair and lean, ropy muscles and hands that were entirely too large for his body. A pair of knucklebound Vise-Grips hanging off the ends of his arms.

"How's that arm?" Timms asked him.

"What. This?" Billy bobbed his head unimportantly at the scatter of angry, raw, dime-sized burns on the paler underside of his forearm, which he'd used to shield himself from a swinging flare. "No biggie."

Timms nodded. For the first time since he'd met the man, Joel noted that the detective seemed privately amused.

"Detective," he said. "About these SoCal Valley thugs. Is there anything you can tell us about what might happen from here?"

At this, the big detective offered a look of weary professionalism. Joel recognized the look immediately. He knew just how the detective felt.

"I'll be honest," Timms said. "This isn't really my area. We'd turn a terrorism call over to the FBI."

"I assume by your tone that you don't feel this qualifies."

Timms smiled kindly. "Under the circumstances, what will probably happen is, one of our guys will follow up with...." He checked the notebook. "SoCal Valley, is it? See what they have to say for themselves. At the least, I'd say you're looking at trespassing, maybe protesting without a permit. I'll remind one of the guys outside to check that out, if it comes to that. Mr. Guilder here probably has an assault case, if he wants one. Otherwise ... I guess there's probably some kind of code about disrupting a burial."

"You bet there is," Joel told him. "Plus destruction of property inside a cemetery. And that's state time we're talking about."

"So you may decide you want to press charges there."

"Oh, are you kidding me?" Joel said. "I want these tree-hugging cretins locked up. I sincerely do."

Timms nodded along. "Don't worry. I'll be leaving you in good hands."

Joel rose from behind the desk and extended a hand of his own. "Thank you, Detective. You've been a great help on this. I appreciate it—I really do."

"Not a problem," Timms said, and shook Joel's hand. As

he turned to leave, he clapped Billy Guilder manfully on the shoulder. "Stay out of trouble, now."

Billy Guilder grinned. "All the time."

With that, Detective Timms showed himself out the door.

When the cop was gone, Joel sank back into the tall leather chair and pressed the heels of his hands into his eyes. Sometimes, on days like this, he swore he could practically feel the last of his worthwhile years slipping through his fingers like sand.

Billy Guilder said: "Some morning, huh?"

"You can certainly say that again."

"SoCal Valley?" Billy sounded as though he were trying very hard to conceal some boyish enthusiasm, no doubt activated by the crazy excitement of the morning's festivities. "That's that chick Maria Casteneda, right? One's always dogging your ass? Butt, I mean. Sorry."

Joel dismissed Billy's casual vulgarity, though he'd counseled his groundskeeper about it on many occasions. "Oh, it's her all right. The one and only."

Billy grinned. "Guess you musta really torqued her off this time, huh?"

Joel couldn't bring himself to respond. Maria Casteneda and her little group of muckrakers were beneath him, for one thing. For another thing, he simply didn't have the energy.

"Hey coach," Billy said. "You want me to, like ... get you anything?"

Joel finally took his hands away from his face and leaned back in the chair. He swiveled, propping a Kenneth Cole on the corner of his desk. "That's okay, Billy. Thanks. I'm fine."

Which was increasingly true, in fact, thanks to the powerful prescription mood elevator now wicking its way into Joel's bloodstream. Even the pounding headache began to recede behind a wall of pleasant white noise. Joel Moss rolled the chair over to gaze out the big corner windows, which overlooked a six-foot privacy fence. The fence surrounded his struggling new bentgrass putting green directly below. In a minute, he saw Timms on the ground level, leaving the mortuary through the employee exit. The big detective walked straight across Joel's rain-logged putting surface with his size-11 shoes. Moss watched the trail of foot-shaped depressions, thinking, *that carpet is never going to fill in*.

But to be perfectly honest, Joel practically didn't care. It was this new prescription; it just had to be. As always, his therapist had warned him not to expect extreme or immediate results, so Joel had voluntarily doubled the prescribed dosage. He thought: *I am absolutely, positively getting a refill on this stuff*. Little Tic Tac-sized miracles, every last one of them.

"So," he said. "What's going on out there?"

Billy Guilder shrugged. "Most of the people are gone. Cops are still hanging around. And that cat Bishop. Man, did you get a load of that guy? Now him, I like."

"He's something, all right." Joel thought: *a lunatic*. "We're sending him a fruit basket."

Billy Guilder seemed to think that was a nice idea. "Hey. You know what you could do? Have 'em put quinces in there. Those little pear-lookin' things, right? Like the dude's name."

"That's clever, Billy," Joel said. "I like that."

Then he took his foot down and squared his elbows on the desk. Enough chit chat. He needed some peace and quiet, and quick. "Where's Carl, anyway?"

"I think he stopped by the head," Billy said. They spoke of Carl Rosen, Palm Grove's newest employee. "Should be along."

"You guys got Mr. Waxman situated?"

Guilder hesitated.

"Billy?"

"See, that's kind of the problem."

"I don't understand."

Before Billy Guilder could reply, the office door opened again. Carl Rosen entered, stone-faced. Possibly annoyed. Joel honestly couldn't tell. He did note, however, that Rosen was wearing his usual work attire, about which Joel had already spoken with Carl several times, as his manner of dress was completely inappropriate for the workplace. Today? One of those half-sleeved guyabera shirts, like you could buy off the rack again; chinos with holes; no socks, and those sports sandals, the kind with Velcro ankle straps. He looked like a deranged tourist.

At Carl's entrance, Joel took a moment to collect his thoughts, appraising his two groundskeepers.

Since the second wave of staff reductions in July, Billy and Carl Rosen comprised the sum total of Palm Grove's grounds team. Together, they handled the duties formerly shared by a six-man crew.

The two of them were definitely load-haulers, of that there was no doubt.

They also were the only two ex-cons Joel Moss had ever met in his life. Like almost everything else about the family business, the whole thing had started out as his dad's idea.

Around a year and a half ago, Joel's father, Walter Moss had gotten inspired after seeing a *Dateline* feature story about a "scared straight" program somewhere in the midwest. The way his dad saw it, they were in a unique position to do something similar at Palm Grove. Within a few months— against Joel's strident recommendations to the contrary—

DIRT

Walt Moss had set up an experimental program of his own with the California Department of Corrections. Under the trial agreement, Palm Grove would give selected new releases a much-needed leg up; these former inmates would repay the favor by playing a much-needed role in the regular world. By Walt Moss's eyes, the concept was not so much an effort to scare anybody straight as it was an example of community service in its perfect form.

Joel had his own ideas about how bloody perfect it was. Bringing known criminals onto the company payroll! The very notion was Walt Moss in a nutshell: a big-hearted, well-meaning, indescribably horrendous business strategy.

But at the very least, it always promised an interesting trade. Take Billy, the program's first beneficiary. Joel's father had hired him a little over a year ago.

Billy Guilder was a forty-year old collection of misdemeanors and relatively benign felonies. He'd spent most of his life on the wrong side of the rulebooks; for whatever reason, the inherently rigid nature of most civic and social law codes had always been extremely difficult for Billy Guilder to comprehend. But he was basically harmless, and even Joel had found it difficult not to warm up to him, in a supervisory way. Billy was a likeable fellow who followed directions, worked like a horse, and never questioned anything.

This Carl Rosen, on the other hand, came from an altogether different breed of criminal. Nothing in Joel's experience had equipped him to relate to the Carl Rosens of the world—and quite frankly, Joel Thomas Moss had no desire to expand those horizons now.

Carl Rosen was a genetic thug, plain and simple. But that wasn't the worst. The worst part about Carl Rosen was that his presence was Joel's own dumb fault entirely.

He'd put himself in a pinch, and that was the long and the short of it. Over the course of the past six months, Joel had restructured Palm Grove's overhead until the wheels practically fell off the gurneys.

He'd had little choice. Joel Moss had loved his father dearly, but the man had left Palm Grove's finances in terrible shape. No matter how he'd sliced it, Joel couldn't classify the situation as anything better than dire straits. He'd whittled the staff to the quick himself, in a blind white heat of economic frugality.

The cutbacks had certainly whipped his P&L sheets into line. But within a few weeks' time, Joel realized that he'd left himself hopelessly understaffed. And facing the holiday season.

Under the circumstances, he'd come to recognize a beauty in his father's social rehabilitation program he'd never considered before.

Parolees like Billy Guilder were the best source of cheap labor you could find this side of an INS raid. Better still, Joel realized he held over these strikeouts 100% omnipotence— a complete, unquestionable authority he knew he'd never wield over any regular employee. For heaven's sake, they were on *parole*; they couldn't give him any grief, and they had almost no room to complain.

So he'd placed a call to his father's former coordinator at the CDC. Three weeks ago, they'd filled his order with Carl Rosen, whose parole had recently been transferred to Los Angeles County, where he now sought work.

A hundred times since, Joel had chastised himself, thinking: *maybe going with such a hardcase wasn't such a fantastic idea.*

But the truth was that Joel had barely glanced at the man's profile sheet at the time. He'd simply gotten desperate for help, told corrections he needed somebody pronto, and snapped up the first guy under 65 they offered.

As a result, he now found himself stuck with a middle-aged career offender whose rap sheet read like the glossary of a criminology textbook. Where Billy Guilder came across as the easygoing, salt-of-the-earth sort, Carl Rosen looked like exactly like what he was: a guy who had very recently spent nine years at San Quentin for armed robbery. His third fall for that particular offense.

Rosen could have been anywhere in his forties, but only in the way your forties looked if you were a dock worker or a hardened felon. He was about average height. Much, much better than average build. But his was not the athletic, sculpted physique you get from a club and a personal trainer; this was the thick, functional bulk that comes from years of pounding a prison yard iron pile. He wore his longish dark hair swept back and a Vandyke goatee threaded with gray. This, coupled with hard dark eyes that noticed everything. Or nothing. You'd never know which. When he wore shirts like the one he was wearing today, cloudy gray prison tattoos were visible on both cabled forearms and the knuckles of both hands.

In short, the man scared Joel half to death.

And those sandals. One way or another, those hideous fungus traps had to go.

"So fellas," Joel said. "What's the problem, again?"

Billy glanced at Carl Rosen, who stood like a golem in the corner, hands shoved deep into the pockets of his chinos.

Billy shrugged. "See, that rack is tweaked. We can't get them apart."

"Can't you just leave the rack in the hole and work the casket out?"

Billy shook his head. "It's really bent."

"Try using the front-loader."

"Did that." This from Rosen in the corner.

"They just pulled up together," Billy added. "And it tore the hell out of the grass."

Moss closed his eyes. He could see the footage on the six o'clock news: a big mangled lump of metal swinging lazily, six feet in the air. He didn't even want to imagine the ruts the tractor had left in the rain-soaked lawn.

At this point, Carl Rosen muttered something else. Joel didn't hear what he said.

"What? Sorry, Carl—I didn't catch that."

"Said it's too hot for this shit." Carl's tone of voice was like an empty metal bucket dropped on a pile of gravel. "Just torch it already."

Joel looked at Billy.

"We were thinking we could cut the rack with a blowtorch," Billy explained. "But that lid's copper. I'm thinking it'll go fast."

Joel found himself kneading at his temples. The headache was coming back again. He drummed the desktop, considering the irony as the pads of his fingertips tattooed the mellow wood: solid mahogany.

"Go ahead and do it," he said. "I told Mrs. Waxman we'd replace the casket anyway."

"I can rent an acetylene rig this afternoon," Billy said. "I know a guy who'd give us a rate."

"Fine," Moss said. Then he sat forward. "Wait. That's a Carbondale box, isn't it?"

Guilder shrugged.

"Yeah," Joel said. "It is. An Ambassador, I think."

Maybe this didn't have to be a complete loss after all. Joel was thinking of the market-leading casket maker's no-hassle return policy on premium models. That, and the removable interior panels on all the Ambassador Royales.

"Let's hold off on the blowtorch idea," he told them. "Billy, see if you can't find a work-around." Later, he'd have Guilder remove the used satin lining, crate up the dented unit, and send the whole thing back as damaged goods.

"Guess I can probably get through with a hacksaw," Billy said. "Might take a little while."

"Just do your best," Moss told him. "The Waxmans aren't coming in for the private ceremony until Saturday morning. As long as we get him in the ground before the weekend, we should be fine."

"Okey-doke."

Joel thought he saw Carl Rosen roll his eyes as he kicked off the wall. Hands still in his pockets, Rosen ambled back out the way he'd come in.

After a pause, Billy Guilder shrugged agreeably and followed along behind. On his way out the door, he turned back one last time.

"By the way," Guilder said. "I don't think we got no more of them coppers in stock."

Joel had already stopped listening. He was gazing out the window dreamily. "What was that?"

"That Ambassador. You want me to order one overnight air?"

"Mm," Moss told him. "I suppose." He scooped up a pen and tapped it against his teeth for a moment or two. "No, wait. Let's put him in one of the DuraLites. I think there's still a whole row of the butterscotch in the basement."

Joel knew darned well there were. Since his father's death earlier this year, Moss had maintained a perpetual overstock of the cloth-covered value caskets, and he was sick to death of seeing them sitting there, taking up space. Joel was forced to keep the things in his inventory, in the rare event a customer knew enough to ask for one. But unlike his dad before him, Joel never kept the economy models on the display floor. Oh, they looked fine. And in all honesty, they served the purpose as well as anything else. But you only had so much room for markup with a DuraLite. The per-unit margins were for the birds.

Billy Guilder looked perplexed. "Didn't you say you told Mrs. Waxman…."

"I know what I said. Trust me, it's fine."

"But…."

"Billy, please," said Joel. "We're just covering the darned thing up with dirt anyway."

QUINCE BISHOP didn't make it home from
the cemetery until almost three in the afternoon. He parked
his rusted hatchback on the street and dragged himself up
the walk, feeling like he'd been beaten with a sack of dimes.

As usual, he found his landlord, Arlen, puttering around
the yard in golf shorts and garden gloves. Arlen Maxwell
was a retired stage actor, a widower of nine years, who had
lived in this same tidy Spanish bungalow near Douglas Park
for nearly six decades now. Arlen and his wife had bought
the place together in the forties, just after their honeymoon.
Maxwell now lived alone in the house, sharing his seventies
with a rheumatic old Pomeranian who had gone blind years
ago.

Quince rented the converted storage walkup above Arlen's
garage. The apartment was drastically small, but Quince liked
the neighborhood, and Arlen let him have the place for only
$300 a month plus half utilities. In return, Quince mowed
Arlen's yard twice a week. He also looked after Vladimir the
dog whenever Arlen went to visit his daughter in Monterey.

At the moment, Arlen toted Vlad in the crook of one arm.
When he saw Quince, he held up a gloved hand.

Quince waved back and grabbed the mail, sorting as he climbed the wooden stairs.

The rains from the last few days had left the air in the apartment musty and stale. Quince opened up the windows for a cross-breeze and flipped on the television for noise. He tossed his dirt-caked jacket into the bedroom—an angled dormer that housed the futon and a reading lamp—and took the mail with him to the kitchenette. He tabled the bills, trashed the junk, and plucked out the only item of interest.

A postcard. Proud parent update from his brother Paul in Chicago. Quince flopped into the sprung sagging depths of the couch with it.

The front of the postcard featured a great, drooly color photocopy of Quince's six month-old nephew. Somewhere in the back of his mind, Quince connected trivial dots of irony: the card had been postmarked the previous Saturday, the same day Wax had run out of days.

He grinned in spite of his mood. Wallace, they'd named this unfortunate child, after the maternal grandfather. Wallace Theodore. Quince had tried to warn them; he'd done his level best to assure them that for young Wally, the playground chants were simply waiting to be coined. They hadn't listened.

Poor tyke. Hands down: the ugliest, most adorable little mutt Quince had ever seen.

It occurred to Quince that it might be possible to find something meaningful in a moment of juxtaposition like this. A funeral, an infant. A tragedy for a joy. Here was the ultimate binary pair—each an integral counterweight in the same balanced wheel.

Quince just wondered if the gods of wasted time were trying to tell him something. He was still looking at the photo when a nap sprang up and mauled him. He didn't attempt to defend himself.

Later that evening, after Quince had showered and changed and wandered over to the house with two pairs of beers, Arlen Maxwell imparted a nugget of perspective that, as usual, caught Quince Bishop off guard.

"You're a good kid," said Arlen. "Now please—grow up."

"Huh?"

They were sitting in lawn chairs on Arlen's back patio, looking out over the yard while daylight faded, bruising the sky purple and orange. Arlen sported his regular evening wear: boxers, flip-flop sandals, and an old T-shirt stretched out of shape at the neck. The man was practically all clavicles.

He said: "Exactly. See, that's exactly what I mean. For a half hour now, Vladdy and I have been sitting here listening to you pop-philosophize—and don't get me wrong. I understand. Believe me, I do. You've had a heck of a day. You've lost a good friend, and that's a rotten thing. But for heaven's sake. Enough already."

"What?" Quince said. "Enough with what?"

Arlen sighed. "With this useless existential angst routine! 'Why do bad things happen to good people?' 'What does it all mean?' 'Is there really some kind of finicky old God up there letting these things happen?' Lord, kiddo—do you really think I'd know?"

"I thought actors were supposed to have an expressive personality," Quince said.

"Piddle," Arlen told him. "You need to quit being so Byronic about everything. Your friend Waxman had as good a reason to die as anybody."

"How so, exactly?"

SEAN DOOLITTLE

"The man's heart stopped beating."

Quince leaned over and grabbed another beer from the cooler Arlen had brought out from inside. Arlen, with blind Vlad on his lap, wasn't quite halfway through his first. He tilted the bottle gently; Vlad turned his head, found the bottle's mouth, and lapped lethargically at the rim. Arlen scrubbed the dog's ears and took a small sip of his own. Vlad eased himself down onto the patio and padded over take a leak on a nearby banana tree.

"I'll say this, though," Arlen said. "You looked pretty good on the news. Get a suit on you, you know what? You don't cut a bad line."

"Gee, thanks."

Arlen kept his television on a wheeled cart; he'd strung out a fifty-foot, heavy-duty extension cord so they could watch the six o'clock broadcast out on the patio. And there Quince had been: mud on his face and a weed in his hair, giving some incomprehensible quote to an athletic-looking reporter in khakis and photogenically-trimmed goatee. The TV reporter was five years younger than Quince if he was a day.

"I mean it," Arlen told him. "What you've got, that's classic. Gary Cooper stuff. Get a haircut, you'd make a decent leading man."

"Arlen?"

"Mmm?"

"Can you fix it so I still get the apartment cheap after they take you to the home?"

Arlen only grinned, scooping the freshly relieved Vlad back into his lap. "Listen, kiddo. Can I tell you what I think is really bothering you?"

"I know what's bothering me," Quince said. "But go right ahead."

51

"This business of your friend? Having his clock punched for him this way? I think that all of a sudden, you're hearing the clock ticking just a little bit louder than you did yesterday. And do you know what's happening? Somewhere, deep down, you're beginning to face the fact that none of us really knows how many of those little ticks we might have left. And you're wondering to yourself: am I *really* getting the most out of my time?"

"Pondering my own mortality, you don't say."

"Perfectly natural," Arlen said.

Quince took a long pull from his beer.

"Then again," Arlen said, "you could just be one of those disillusioned coffee-house youngsters Vladdy and I keep seeing on the television sitcoms. What is it they call your age group? Generation slouchy-mopey-something?"

"Sorry? I wasn't listening."

Arlen laughed. He reached across the cooler, patted Quince on the knee. "Hang in there, kiddo. You're in a slump, is all."

Quince had to wonder if that were really true. For if this current state of affairs qualified as a slump, Quince wasn't sure he'd actually know how to recognize a groove.

Over the past few months, Quince Bishop had come to suspect that one of two things was true: either something important in him was broken, or his problem was nothing more complex than a naturally apathetic personality. He didn't know when it had started, or how it had accrued to such an unmanageable size. At some point, he'd simply found himself overrun by his own inertia, the way kudzu enveloped barns.

School? Skated through it, wound up with a graduate degree he didn't need. Jobs? Never had much trouble finding

SEAN DOOLITTLE

them, never found one he could endure for long. Even in the few years since college, he'd tried everything from corporate PR to installing bathroom tile. Each time out, Quince started with the very best intentions; on time every day, ready to rock, pumping with ideas and go-get-'em energy.

And each time out, it all ended up the same sad way. Over time he simply lost interest. Once that happened, the pointlessness of it all became undeniable. And once *that* happened, it was never long before Quince found himself phoning it in—shambling through a bad pantomime of the motions, ever descending toward the inevitable. Some-times, his downward spiral occurred so rapidly that his supervisors became convinced he was actually in need of professional help instead of a simple firing, and Quince was forced to quit out of sheer altruism.

Hobbies? Didn't really have any. Hadn't ever really been able to find one that didn't seem like a waste of time. Sometimes he told people he was writing a screenplay, but it was a lie.

Melanie took the view that *everybody* had an inherent passion for something; he just hadn't found his yet. Of course, Mel also believed that people had to look hard for their place in life. His habitual lack of effort was the one trait of his that she could neither comprehend, remedy, nor abide.

Couldn't blame her, really. But lately, Quince had started to wonder if his shiftlessness didn't go deeper than that. Maybe all the way down to the base pairs. He wondered if some chromosome, hard-coded for slackerhood, hadn't simply skipped generations, missed his older brother, and wormed its way into his DNA.

Mel certainly found the comparison troubling. Both he and Paul, upon turning 25, had received money from trust

53

funds their parents had established before they'd died. Paul had already been to the Culinary Institute and started a family by the time he hit the mark; he'd used the money to start his own restaurant on Michigan Avenue, and he'd opened two new locations since.

Quince, on the other hand—after paying off his school loans, thereby fulfilling the original intent of the trust—had stuffed the substantial remainder of his own grim windfall in a low-yield savings account for most of the last four years.

He hadn't wanted to touch it. Probably would have given it away, if the idea hadn't seemed disrespectful, somehow. It was a horrid bonanza, as far as Quince had been concerned at the time. A wrinkled monkey's paw. Playing the markets, or putting a down payment on something, or calling it "start-up capital" had once seemed like a rung below grave robbing on the karma ladder.

Funny how convictions faded and viewpoints changed— but the money still stayed green. He'd started dipping last May, while he'd been looking for yet another new job.

Sometimes it alarmed him, just how quickly he'd grown accustomed to subsidized living—but somehow, these days, not so much that he couldn't bring himself to face the ATM machine. Meanwhile, he'd stopped pretending he was looking for work altogether around mid-June or so.

"I'll tell you what you need," Arlen said. "You need to find yourself a nice girl. Somebody you can build something with. Like that Melanie—I always liked you two. You make a cute pair."

"I'll be sure and tell her."

"Go ahead and laugh. But take it from me. I was a God-awful wreck before I met my Rosalie. I mean it. Couldn't even find a good reason to get out of bed, some days. You find a partner like that, you hold on for dear life. They'll keep you on your feet, I promise you."

Arlen. Lord, but the man was worse than Wendy, Quince's sister-in-law. Personally, Quince was opposed to this idea that people couldn't manage to live without some kind of companion or other to prop up their days. What was so unbearably horrible about a little emotional self-sufficiency?

If for absolutely no other benefit, at least you'd never find yourself on the receiving end of what Rhonda Waxman would now be facing every single morning for a long time to come.

Quince was still struggling for a droll, topic-killing spike point when they both heard the sound of a car door slam in the driveway.

Quince looked, half expecting Melanie. Arlen turned himself in his lawn chair. In another moment, they both saw the stranger coming up the walk.

From this distance, partially obscured by Arlen's almond trees, all Quince could see was a shoulder-length spill of very dark hair. The young woman held a piece of paper in her hands. She looked at the paper, then up at the number on the garage. In another moment, she folded the paper and mounted the stairs that led to Quince's door.

"See there, Vladdy?" said Arlen. He had a silly gleam in his eye. "This is what I'm talking about. Life. It gives us little signs each and every day."

"If you say so," Quince said. Thinking: *not another one*. He'd talked to enough reporters in the past eight hours to last him all the rest of his days.

"Come on, now," Arlen said. "A little optimism. And get yourself together, you've got company. Not an unattractive visitor, I might add."

"Oh, what does that have to do with anything?"

Arlen smirked and scratched Vlad's ears.

As the delayed thump of the stranger's knocking reached the patio, Quince finished his beer in two big gulps and hauled himself resignedly up from his folding chair.

"Remember, kiddo," Arlen called to his back. "Life's for the living!"

On his way across the side yard, Quince thought: *and every day's a gift.*

Joel Moss was enjoying the first sip of his second gin and tonic when he heard a rhythmic pounding from somewhere downstairs. It was almost ten o'clock and gently raining again outside. A full twelve hours had passed since the Waxman funeral, and he'd only just begun to unwind.

Some days never seemed to go away.

Joel turned up the television and tried to ignore the racket, but the pounding only grew louder the longer it continued. He finally gave up, grabbed his robe, and made his way through the dark and down the carpeted stairs.

It was this unusual wet season they were having, Joel knew; rains like this always drove in the bums from the beachfronts and the piers. Sometimes they came around looking for a place to spend the night, knowing Joel's father, who harbored a notorious soft spot for the destitute, had probably left instructions with the night shift to let them sleep in one of the empty viewing parlors. It was aggravating.

But when Joel reached the grand foyer, his annoyance quickly faded to disbelief. He hustled to the front doors.

"What the hell are you doing here," he hissed. "Are you *impaired*?"

The kid gave him the finger and stepped inside, dripping water all over the tile in the entryway.

"I wad by bunny," he said.

I want my money. Joel couldn't believe this. Idiot!

In the dim light, he could see the adhesive tape running like a root system around the bandages covering the kid's nose. He'd wrapped gauze around the back of his head to hold the whole sorry, lumpen dressing in place.

"Get away from the windows," Joel told him. "Jesus. What's the matter with you? Do you have any idea how stupid this is?"

By concentrating carefully, Joel was able to mentally translate the kid's blunted, nasal mumbling on the fly.

"Hey listen, asshole," said the kid, who worked as a delivery driver for one of Joel's favorite nearby sandwich shops. "Don't yell at me."

"I told you I'd get you your money in a few days. I told you we'd meet later. That was the plan."

"Oh yeah? Maybe you should have told me about the rest of the plan. You dick."

"I don't know what you're talking about."

"I should kick your ass, is what I should do. You never told me you were going to sic that freak on me. That was bullshit, man."

"Listen, that was none of my doing. I was as surprised as you were." Joel looked at the kid for a minute. He sighed. "How's your face?"

"Throbbing."

Joel nodded his head, trying to project a sense of empathy. He finally gave up. "I guess you might as well come up-stairs, as long as you're here."

He moved without waiting for a reply, leading the kid up the stairs and down the hall.

Last February, after his father was buried and things had blended back to shades of normalcy again, Joel had sold his townhouse in Westwood and moved in here, above the mortuary. There was a one-room dormitory on the top floor; Walt Moss used to hire college students to work as night attendants in exchange for living expenses and minimum wage. The apartment sat vacant after Joel had finished paring down the staff.

He despised living at the mortuary, but it wasn't for much longer. In the meantime, Joel concentrated on minimizing his outlay to the extreme. Making use of the dorm, dismal as it may have been, kept his costs down. And he was tucking away an extra four grand a month of his own to boot.

Back in his room, Joel turned up the lamp in the corner and offered the kid a seat. There was a soft-core erotic thriller playing on Cinemax.

"Can I get you a drink? I have gin."

"I'll take a beer."

"Oh. Sorry."

The kid rolled his eyes.

"The money." Joel nodded. "I don't really keep a lot of cash. I can give you five hundred tonight, but you'll have to wait for rest."

"Tell you what," the kid said. "Give me the whole grand in the next two minutes, and I won't go tell the cops I know your ass."

Joel looked at him discouragingly. "I wouldn't actually advise that. In fact, I'd keep a low profile for the next few weeks if I were you. I hope you didn't let your pals in on any of this."

"They're not my pals. I found 'em at a pro-choice rally. And cut the shit, Moss. I did your job, so pay up."

Joel couldn't help himself. "You did the job, all right. Exorbilantly."

"Piss off. You typed it wrong."

"Did I really?" Joel thought about it. "I apologize."

"Mahogany loggers. I shoulda known this was a fucked-up deal. You think busting up some guy's funeral is my idea of a good fuckin' time, man?"

"Well, I guess you should have thought of that before you agreed to do it, shouldn't you have?" Joel said. "Besides. *You're* the one who had to get fancy. Jumping up on Mr. Waxman's casket like that. *That* was a little over-the-top, don't you think?"

"Whatever." The kid dug out his wallet and rummaged through it. He finally pulled out a wrinkled receipt and tossed it over.

"What's this?"

"Expenses."

Joel picked up the register slip. It was from a Rite Aid in West Hollywood: Neosporin, butterfly closures, Band-Aids, a roll of adhesive tape, and sterile gauze. The total came to $23.95.

If the kid hadn't looked so completely pathetic, Joel might have laughed. He took his drink with him to the bureau, opened the bottom drawer, and took out a safety box. From the lockbox, he counted out one thousand dollars in crisp new fifties. He put two extra twenties with the drugstore receipt and went back to hand over the cash.

"Keep the change," he said.

"Don't worry, I will."

"I guess that about does it, then." Joel clapped the kid

on the shoulder. "Nice doing business with you. Watch for infection, now."

"Go fuck yourself," said the kid, taking the cash and heading for the door.

"HE'S NOT HOME."

The stranger stopped in the middle of her knock and turned around. Seeing nobody, she peered over the railing. Quince waggled his fingers from the sidewalk below.

"Mr. Bishop?"

"What can I do for you?"

The woman shoved his address into her purse and descended the creaky stairs. From where Quince stood, she seemed roughly his own age. Faded jeans and a men's plaid shirt, untucked and unbuttoned, sleeves rolled to elbows. She wore a scooped white tank top underneath.

Touching ground, she approached him with her hand extended. "Mr. Bishop—hello. I saw you tonight on Channel 5."

"Right," Quince told her. "I saw that, too."

The woman smiled. "I really didn't think you'd be listed, but I tried information anyway. There you were."

"Got me fair and square."

He shook her hand. She had dark hair and dark eyebrows and deep, clear brown eyes. When she spoke, he caught a mild Hispanic lilt in her voice. Quince noticed a small silver cross, which she wore around her neck on a slender chain.

"I'm sorry to barge in on you like this," she said. "I should have called first."

"It's okay." Quince smiled. "Nobody would have been around to answer anyway. What's on your mind, Miss...."

"Casteneda," she said. "Maria Casteneda. I'm with the SoCal Valley Memorial Society."

At first, the name didn't register. Then Quince made the connection: the tree people.

He took his hand back and let it hang at his side.

"I'm probably crazy for coming to see you," she said. "But I was hoping you'd be kind enough to give me just a minute or two of your time."

"Excuse me." Quince stepped around her and headed for the stairs.

"Mr. Bishop...."

"Look, it's like I told you before. I'm not home. Thanks for stopping by."

Maria Casteneda followed him partway up the stairs. When he reached the landing and turned back, she stopped where she was and looked up at him—one hand on the railing, the other held forth. A gesture of assertion and entreaty at the same time.

Quince waited impatiently.

"I'm not quite sure what to say," she finally admitted. "But I feel sick about what happened at Palm Grove this morning."

"Congratulations. You have a conscience after all."

"Mr. Bishop, I'm going to be as straight with you as I know how to be, and I'll leave it up to you to decide whether or not you want to listen to what I have to say. SoCal Valley is in no way supportive of what happened at your friend's funeral.

I said it to the police, I said it to the reporters, and I'll keep saying it: this whole situation is just unforgivable. Whatever message these … people were trying to deliver, it's not what we're about. Not at all."

"Tell that to Rhonda Waxman."

"I wish I could," Maria Casteneda said. "But I'm not about to trouble that family at a time like this. If anybody deserves anything, those people deserve to be left in peace right now. That's why I decided to approach you."

"Look," Quince said. "What do you want?"

"I just wanted to talk with you for a minute," she said. "Would … would that be possible?"

"I don't have anything to *do* with this." Quince felt as though he were deflating, like a bad tire, a slow steady pound-per-square-inch at a time.

"Me either," said Maria Casteneda. "May I come in?"

Quince looked at her for a minute. He looked out across Arlen's lawn, toward the house. "It's been kind of a long day," he said.

"I promise. I won't make it much longer."

Maybe it was the tone of her voice. Or maybe he was simply too tired to sustain a defense. For some reason he couldn't quite fathom, Quince felt himself relenting in spite of his better judgment. It was beginning to sprinkle lightly again. He looked at her one last time. Sighed.

"Five minutes."

Maria Casteneda gave a single nod: *deal*. She climbed the last few stairs, and he held the screen door open for her, gesturing her in. He followed and flipped on a lamp. Maria Casteneda stopped in the middle of the room, next to his battered coffee table, and turned to face him. She didn't seem positive she'd made the right choice after all.

"What is it you want to talk to me about?"

"I wanted to tell you," she said. "For whatever it's worth—not much, I'm sure—but what you did this morning…. I think Mr. Waxman must've been very lucky. You must be a very good friend."

"Oh, I'm terrific," he said. "But that's not what you came here to say."

"No. No, it wasn't. Not entirely, anyway."

Quince left the front door open and closed the screen. The rain was beginning to put a tang in the breeze.

"Mr. Bishop, you're the one person who had any real contact with the people claiming to be with our group. I meant what I said before: SoCal Valley doesn't condone this sort of act at all. It's horrifying."

"That's one way of putting it."

"But I'm not naive," she continued, as though he'd said nothing. "One thing I've learned the hard way is that opinions differ in any organization. I can't imagine—Mr. Bishop, I just can't imagine any of my people doing anything like this. But I need to face the possibility that I'm wrong. If I am, I intend to take responsibility."

"I'm sorry," Quince said. "But I'm afraid I still don't understand what you're hoping to accomplish, here."

"I want to get to the bottom of this," Maria Casteneda said. "The cops, they wouldn't give me the time of day. I don't think they believed anything I told them, if you want to know the truth. But I understand that you got a good glimpse of at least one of the … perpetrators. I was hoping you might be willing to pass along any details. It would really mean a lot to me."

Quince listened with a mixture of empathy, wariness, and fatigue.

"Mr. Bishop?"

He finally sighed. "It's Quince. Look, I really don't know how much I can help you."

"Anything you can tell me," she said. "Anything at all."

So without stepping in from the doorway, Quince gave her the best description of Skull Punk that he could, which consisted mostly of the nose ring he'd yanked out of the guy's head. Quince found it interesting that despite their earlier proximity, he really didn't remember much else about the guy's face.

"Sorry," he said. "But that's about all I can tell you."

Maria Casteneda accepted this with a joyless grin. "Don't apologize. It's not you. I was wrong, coming here this way."

"Forget it." Quince looked toward the kitchenette. "Can I get you anything? Water? I think there's some beer left in the fridge."

"No," Maria Casteneda said. "I should go."

Which she did, almost as abruptly as she'd appeared.

There was only one difference between exit and entry. This time, on the way past, she stopped, stood on tiptoe, and kissed him on the cheek. While the spot warmed and tingled, he felt her place a business card in his hand.

"Thank you, Quince. I really am sorry to bother you. Feel free to call me at either of those numbers if you need to. And if you can find a way to do it—please, give my condolences to the Waxmans."

And while he stood there blankly, still unbalanced by her odd gesture, Maria Casteneda let herself through the screen door and walked out into the rain.

Ten minutes later:

Quince—still sitting on the edge of the coffee table, still

processing what had just transpired—heard footsteps coming back up the stairs, followed by another knock on the door.

Realizing he'd not heard the sound of Maria Casteneda's car pulling out of the drive, he sighed and prepared to stand. It was raining harder now, and he'd shut the front door. He'd just been sitting here, absently gazing at the postcard of little Wally, slobber king.

When the knock came, Quince put down the postcard and went to the door. He opened it, tripped the latch on the screen door, and held it open with his forearm.

"You're going to get soaked," he said.

The words had barely left his lips when he realized it wasn't Maria Casteneda standing there.

"Bishop, huh?" said this visitor. "Hey, man—I saw you on the news."

The light from the apartment spilled out onto the landing, just enough so that Quince could see the rain-drenched mound of gauze bandages in the middle of Skull Punk's face. There was a seepy red stain just left of center. The eyes above: twinkling.

Quince stood frozen by the surprise for just a moment too long. As if in slow motion, he saw Skull Punk execute a sleight-of-hand maneuver. Thumb and forefinger poised a few inches apart, the guy in the doorway held up a paper-wrapped cylinder. Quince was able to make out the object just as it disappeared into a fist.

Roll of quarters?

Quince didn't understand.

"You forgot your change, asshole," Skull Punk told him.

A smile.

And before Quince could move, the fist was speeding forth.

Out of sheer limbic reflex, Quince managed the unfocused beginnings of a flinch.

Then the world exploded, cool light filled his head, and he suddenly felt himself floating down toward the dark hole that had opened somewhere behind him, near the floor.

ON A CLEAR Tuesday morning in mid-October, Quince Bishop got up earlier than usual. Day had broken anew; birds chirped in the trees. Quince awoke in the spot where he had fallen the night before.

With a dog licking his face.

In the dream he was having, his little nephew Wally was drooling on him from a big picture postcard, which hovered like a shimmering hologram above Quince's face. Quince moaned and swatted at his cheek—where in the waking world, Blind Vlad rigorously anointed him with smelly doggie spit. When Quince's knuckles brushed cheekbone, dull electric flowers bloomed behind his eyes.

Quince moaned again. He rolled up on an elbow, then flat on his back once more. He tried to open his eyes, found that a serious case of monocular vision had set in. As the cobwebs cleared, he understood why: right eye wasn't opening. Tender probing revealed it to be sealed shut, swollen hot and tight. Quince noted that he was supine in his own doorway: top half inside the apartment, dew-soaked stocking feet still hanging outside. His head pounded like a subwoofer.

"Vladdy! For god's sake, *heel.*"

Vladimir was lifted from his field care efforts. As Quince managed to bring his sole functioning eyeball into focus, he saw Arlen standing over him. His landlord had a worried expression on his face. And now a wiggling Pomeranian in his arms.

"Quincey?" he said. "Good grief—can you say something, son?"

"Not right now," Quince murmured. Just moving his lips made his head feel as though it might crack open and ooze.

"Just stay right there, kiddo. We're going to get you something for that eye. Okay? Don't you move."

Arlen stepped over him and shuffled into the kitchenette. Quince heard him banging around in there for what seemed like weeks. The next thing he heard was the sound of a plastic baggie, parachuting open on the downswipe. Then the freezer door opening. Ice cube trays being twisted, their contents crackling free.

A few moments more, and Arlen returned with a rudimentary ice pack wrapped in a hand towel from the sink. Quince had managed to haul himself up into the couch, where he now sat semi-upright, arms at his sides, head resting uncomfortably against a big button in the ratty upholstery.

"Kiddo? How do you feel?"

"Million bucks." Quince accepted the ice pack, touching it experimentally to the portion of his bloated eye socket that seemed most consumed by the throb.

"You look horrendous. What on earth happened here?"

"At which point?"

"I think you should go see a doctor," Arlen said. "You could have a concussion. That girl might have broken something in your face."

At this, Quince turned his head so he could look at

Arlen with his good eye. If he hadn't felt so awful, he would have laughed. Arlen let Vlad down onto the couch. The dog curled up against Quince's hip, gave his bare leg a sympathy lick. Quince pulled in his free arm and scratched Blind Vlad between the ears.

"I called your friend Melanie," Arlen told him.

"You didn't."

"Oh, sue me. I didn't know what you'd want me to do, and she was the only person on your speed dial."

Before Quince could file another protest, footfalls were already thrumming up the steps outside. Mel appeared on the landing and pushed her way in through the screen door.

"Oh my God." She doffed the leather softsider, which carried her notebook computer, on her way to the couch. "What happened to you?"

"Hey," Quince said.

"Talk to me. What did you do?"

"I told him he needs to see a doctor," Arlen said. "And we should call the police. That girl. She looked so sweet! What the heck did she clobber you with, anyway? The television?"

"Guys," Quince said. The sound of their voices was beginning to clang in his skull. "Let's just everybody calm down. Please."

"I'm perfectly calm," Arlen said. "And I'm serious. Doctor and a cop. That's what we need."

Melanie said, "What girl?"

"It wasn't her!" Quince pleaded.

Melanie moved over to his other side, sandwiching Vlad between them. Gently, she lifted the ice pack away from his face. He heard her suck in a quick breath.

"What?"

"Nothing," Mel said quickly.

"Oh, come on. Is it really that bad?"

"Shh," Melanie told him, lowering the ice pack gingerly again.

"I need aspirin," Quince said.

Holding the ice pack in place with her hand, Mel nodded with him kindly. She asked: "Her who?"

Too much; this was just getting to be too much. Before Quince could say anything more—something to defend himself and his manhood in some definitive way—they all heard yet another ascension of footfalls on the landing outside.

Quince replaced Mel's hand with his own and swiveled his head toward the door, ice bag and all. Mel and Arlen looked. Vlad whuffled laboriously, struggling from where he'd become wedged between the sofa cushions.

"Bishop?" said the delivery man, speaking through the screen. He pulled up his manifest, which hung from a belt loop of his company-issue shorts. "Got a fruit basket here for a Quince Bishop. That you?"

Quince held up the ice pack, as if answering roll call.

"Whoa," said the delivery guy. Even through the rusty screen, Quince could see him wince. He propped open the door with his foot, leaned in, and raised the mammoth, cellophane-wrapped cornucopia with both hands.

"Listen, brother, don't get up," he said. "I'll just leave it right here inside the door."

One thing about this new guy, Rosen: Wasn't much of a morning person. Billy Guilder could tell.

Tuesday, Billy picked him up at the halfway house around seven-thirty. He didn't mind doing it. Kind of enjoyed the company, actually. So far, Billy hadn't gotten to know the guy very well—but all in all, he figured he liked Carl Rosen okay.

Quiet? Sure, the guy was quiet. No harm in that, at least not as far as Billy Guilder was concerned. But Billy generally liked people; he liked the little differences in personalities. Got along with pretty much everybody, really. One of these days, he figured Rosen was bound to look up and uncork something interesting.

Tomorrow, maybe.

So far, this morning wasn't much different from the mornings before. Billy rolled up in the cemetery pickup, sat there at the curb for a second or two, then tapped the horn one time with the heel of his hand. Rosen waited in his usual spot: out front on the cracked concrete steps, smoking a Camel, elbows on his knees. When he heard the horn, he just tossed his butt into the scraggly front yard, which was mostly just a dirt receptacle for cigarette butts anyway. Then he hauled himself up into the truck and stared out the passenger window all the way to Palm Grove.

While they punched in at the mortuary and headed downstairs, Billy Guilder tried a joke to break the ice. Maybe lighten the dude up a little bit.

"So there's these two gravediggers," he said. "Like, in Europe, wherever. Anyway. They're walking in the cemetery, and all of a sudden, they hear this music coming from somewhere. So they're looking all around, and one of them finally figures out it's coming out the ground. So they look at the headstone, right? It says, Ludwig van Beethoven, 1770–1827. And the first digger says to the other, you know what? That's the ninth symphony. Backwards, though. Pretty weird. Next day, they're walking in the same place again, and they hear music. So they go over. And the one says to the other—now that's the seventh symphony. Backwards, same way as before. These guys don't know what to make of it. Next day, you know what happens? Same damn thing. Only this time, they're hearing Beethoven's fifth. Backwards again. And the other gravedigger finally snaps his fingers, like he's figured it out. The first guy says, what? And the second guy tells him what's going on. That's Beethoven, he says. He's decomposing."

Billy said it and laughed. He looked at Carl Rosen.

"The fuck you talking about?" Carl Rosen said.

Billy decided to let him alone for awhile.

They went to the break room and stowed their lunches in the fridge. Billy stowed his, anyway. Like usual, Rosen didn't have any gear at all. Billy had actually started packing an extra sandwich for him, just to be a guy. Today, Rosen wore basically the same thing as yesterday, except for camouflage pants with big cargo pockets. Also, he had on those sandals Moss hated again. No socks.

Billy didn't know what to say.

He'd been dreading this ever since Moss took him aside about it yesterday. Asking him if maybe he could mention something to Rosen about the way he dressed. Like the guy would listen more, hearing it come from another con.

Billy didn't know if that would work as well as Moss seemed to think it would. Though for helpfulness sake, he did consider telling Carl he at least might want to look into some boots maybe, something comfortable he wouldn't mind wearing all day. Billy liked Timberlands, himself. Steel toe. Sure, they cost a little more, but they lasted a long time. Plus which, you didn't get the blisters with a better kind of boot like that. Worth your money right there.

But at the moment, looking at Rosen, Billy Guilder

decided maybe now wasn't the best time to get into the whole touchy issue of personal footwear.

So they went to work. Billy showed Carl the clipboard down in the basement, where Moss would put a list of things they had to do. Sometimes you'd see him and he'd talk to you himself, but if not, you just worked off the list. Some days he'd have you stop what you were doing and go out on a pick-up somewhere—but most times there'd be nothing happening and you just worked off the list.

First thing today was getting that guy Waxman situated.

So Billy showed Carl the basement storage room. He had him help pull out one of the DuraLites and get it on a roller, so they could wheel it down to the embalming room. It wasn't a matter of it being heavy; these guys were just fiberboard, covered with fabric to make them look nice. It was just easier with the cart, was all. Key to the job, he told Rosen, was you had to pace yourself. Though it didn't look to Billy like pacing himself would be Carl Rosen's biggest problem.

While they hoisted the box, Billy finally got around to filling Carl in on some of the prime cuts he'd missed yesterday, while he'd been in the break room filling out some leftover employee paperwork for Moss.

"So I'm over by the crematory, I showed you yesterday, right? I'm just pulling some weeds, killing time, since I can't run the tractor while there's a funeral. All of a sudden I hear this noise, people yelling, I don't know what it is. Next thing I know, Moss comes running up. He's in his thousand dollar suit—and he's panting, he can't get his breath, he's jabbering about what, man, I don't even know."

They were pushing the box down the hallway now, Billy going into detail about the granola munchers that showed up at the funeral.

74

"Oh, you shoulda seen. Seriously. They're all decked out in these little ninja suits, wearing these hood sorta mask things, look like skulls? With friggin' road flares, I swear—you saw the empties, you know what I'm talking about. And they're all yelling about Pygmies or something. Nobody knows what's happening. Moss is telling me, go after 'em—so here I am, trying to walk up on this douchebag swinging a flare in my face." He showed Carl one of the burns on his wrist; it was already scabbing over nice.

"Then the one guy, he actually gets on top of the casket. On the casket! No shit. And of course he knocks it over, and everybody's going crazy, it's a big damn mess. So I'm standing there thinking, now, what am I supposed to do, go get a fire extinguisher and hose these fools? And next thing I know that guy, Bishop, now here *he* comes, flying by. You shoulda seen this cat. Thought I was gonna crack a rib, I wanted to laugh so bad."

By now they'd reached the body room, or what Joel Moss called "the facilities." Bright overhead lights, kept clean and cool, with a counter and a sink and lots of stainless steel. There was a tile floor, with a drain in the middle. It was where they did the embalming and other things needed to be done. For some reason, the smell of the place always reminded Billy Guilder of that time he went to the dentist when he was a kid.

Waxman was waiting for them in there, still in the dented-up box from yesterday. While they wheeled in the new casket, Billy noticed that Carl seemed a little more interested in his surroundings, all at once. It was his first time in the place, and he looked around the way he did whenever he came into a new room—moving his eyes but not his head, taking everything in without looking like he was noticing anything in particular. Carl wandered over, checked out the steel table and the embalming machine.

"That's the guy?" He nodded toward Waxman's casket.

Billy said, "Yep."

"Just out in the open, huh? Don't have to keep him cold or anything?"

"Nah," Billy told him. "He's fixed up. That machine you're standing next to, with the tubes? That's how they do it, usually. These great big needle things, I can't remember what they call 'em—but these big honkin' needles go on the ends of the tubes. Then you just hook the dude up in a couple places, hit the button, wait a few minutes, and there you go. Got yourself a fixed-up dead guy."

"Push a button, huh?"

Billy nodded. "It's pretty slick. I mean, he ain't gonna last forever, now—but the way they do it, he'll be good for a few days. Moss'll prolly let you watch one if you want."

Rosen didn't say much, but Billy could see he was curious. Couldn't blame the guy. It really was kinda cool, first time you saw how it all worked behind the scenes.

"So, what. We're taking him out of there?"

"Gotta put him in the new box. On account of his is all beat to hell now—check it out."

Rosen looked where he pointed, while Billy rolled the DuraLite next to the trashed Ambassador.

"This one here," he said, nodding at the bigger casket, "Moss sells 'em for like, I don't know. You and me could buy a car for less. And not a shit car, I mean a decent used automobile."

"That a fact."

"Oh, yeah," Billy said. "Anyway—you gotta figure, the wife, she doesn't want to think about the whole ordeal every time she comes by with a pile of flowers to put on the grave.

So Moss tells her don't worry, we'll put daddy in a new box, just like nothing happened. Not like it matters to our boy here. But it makes the wife feel better."

Rosen nodded at the Duralite. "That ain't the same."

And Billy grinned. "Nah. It ain't."

Carl waited for him to say more.

"See, Moss can get his money back on that big boy," Billy explained. "Send it back like it was banged up when we got it. This other little buddy here? These only cost him like two bills apiece. So he figures, hey, she won't know any different. Be in the ground before she sees it, right? He thinks we don't know what he's doing, just groundskeepers, we don't do any paperwork. He's kinda slick that way."

"No kidding," said Rosen. He seemed to think about it. "So how much do you see?"

"How's that?"

"You're doin' all the extra scut on this, right?"

"Oh, I dunno," Billy said. "I guess you could say it that way."

"So that's what I'm wondering. The bossman kick a little extra your way?"

"I see where you're going." Billy shrugged. "Hey, you know. There's not, like, formal profit sharing, you know what I'm saying? But Moss, he's okay. He pretty much takes care of us, different ways. Let you come in late one day. Give you an afternoon off, you need it for something—cover your ass with the parole officer, he happens to call. You know how it goes."

Rosen listened to this. "So how much you think he's skimming on the deal, total?"

"Hey, what do I know?" Billy grinned. "I'm just a groundskeeper."

And Carl Rosen nodded again, cool as cool could be. Billy let him mull it over while he walked around the cart and unbuttoned Waxman's box.

Billy had to work on the latches a little, then found out that the lid didn't open straight. He put some arm into it, got it pried open most of the way.

Waxman was laying on one shoulder, facing the hinges. His head had slipped off the pillow a little; there were peach-colored streaks here and there on the white satin, where the rouge Moss used on him had rubbed off. Billy went around to the other side and gave the casket a jolt with his hip. Did it again. Waxman finally sort of slumped onto his back like he was supposed to be.

Now Billy came back around; Rosen stepped up so he could see. They stood together for a couple minutes, looking at the body.

Hadn't been a bad looking guy, probably. Kind of like a Peter Fonda, if Peter Fonda was younger and dead. Standing close, you could smell the perfume Moss used to cover up the smell of the fixer and antiseptic. They also used these caps underneath the eyelids—so they didn't look all sunk in, for one thing, and also to keep them pasted shut. Moss must not have used enough cement this time. One of Waxman's caps had popped out, and that eyelid had come open. The eye was blue. A little shriveled and cloudy, just staring up at the ceiling.

That part was freaky.

Otherwise, Waxman was basically in okay shape. Just a place on his cheek where the skin had torn, showing a slick pink-gray patch underneath.

"That can happen, getting knocked around inside there,"

Billy told Carl. "A guy's been dead a few days, the skin gets really soft and papery like that. It'll just rip, you rub too hard."

Carl Rosen listened, making a sound like he thought that was interesting information to know. After a minute, he said, "He needs to know what time it is, I guess."

"Huh?"

"Why they bury him wearing his watch?"

Billy shrugged. "Probably liked it, I don't know. Maybe the wife gave it to him for their anniversary. You see all kinds of things. We had one lady wanted to be buried with all her stuffed animals. Kitty cats and bears, like that."

"No shit."

"I guess on account of she used to sleep with them when she was lonely sometimes." Billy looked at Waxman's wrist, where his suit cuff had bunched back. He checked out the watch and nodded. "That's a nice one, though. Tag Heuer. I hawked a couple like that one time. Three bills apiece."

"That a fact," Rosen said.

"Grab his legs, will you? Help me haul him out."

"Yeah, right."

Billy grinned. "Aw, it ain't that bad. You can't get germs, really—he's preserved."

"That's nice," Rosen told him. "I still ain't fuckin' touching him."

"What. Seriously?"

"I look like I'm kidding?"

Rosen didn't look like he was kidding as far as Billy could see. Billy stood for a second, not quite sure what to do. He thought about saying, look, you may as well get used to it, right? Around here—we run into dead folks from time to time.

But he didn't say that. Instead, he said, "Hang on. I got something might help you out."

He went over to one of the cabinets, rummaged around for a minute or two. Billy found the surgical gloves, the kind that were powdered on the inside to help you slip them on. He almost brought a couple pairs over, then thought about it. Put them back. Got some of the heavy rubber ones instead—the long ones that went way up past your wrist.

"Try these," he said, handing a pair to Carl.

Rosen stood there with his hands in his pockets. He didn't reach. He didn't really do much of anything. Just stood there and looked at the gloves.

So Billy finally gave it up. The guy needed some time to get used to the idea, hey. Billy could relate. He decided to put on the gloves himself, as long as he had them out. He tossed the spares onto the steel embalming tray next to Carl. Then he went back around to the front of the Ambassador, spread his feet a little for balance, and worked one arm under Waxman's shoulders and the other under his knees. Hoisted him a little, to get a better grip. After a few hours, they weren't stiff anymore—just kind of rag-dollish. Like anybody asleep, except colder. A lot of people didn't know that. It was another one of those things you learned.

While Billy was getting situated, he happened to glance down at Waxman's wrist again. It caught his eye.

Being bare all of a sudden, the way it was.

Billy did a double-take. Without making a big production out of it, he leaned over and checked Waxman's other arm—just to make sure he wasn't remembering backwards or something.

He wasn't.

No watch. Just a watch-shaped space pressed into the skin, where that Heuer had been.

Billy looked up at Carl Rosen.

Rosen looked back. "Problem?"

And Billy didn't say a word.

Nope. No idea how to handle this one, boy. Billy looked at Waxman's wrist again, then back at Carl.

"I said, you got some kind of problem I can help you with?"

Billy Guilder decided to do what seemed like the smart thing.

"No problem here," he said. "But if you wanted to open up that other box while I hoist this guy, that'd be okay."

DESPITE QUINCE'S rigid protests, Mel
called the paper to say she'd be coming in late. It was mostly
Arlen's fault. The man wouldn't stop hounding Quince about
calling the police and reporting the situation. Finally, Quince
had crumbled, telling them he had other plans.

Which had actually been a lie, until the moment he said it.
He'd only wanted the both of them off his back.

So much for strategy. Mel did more than just pounce on
the idea. She told him she'd drive.

According to Maria Casteneda's business card, SoCal
Valley's office was on 20th and Wilshire, near Saint John's
Hospital. In the car, Quince and Mel discovered they had
information to trade. Quince gave the nutshell version of the
events that had led to his getting his ass kicked in the manner
which caused him to be found sleeping on the floor.

At a stop light, Mel reached into the back seat and
grabbed that morning's *Times*, already folded back to the
Metro section.

Mel's story took up three short columns beneath the
fold. Short slug, no photo. Quince scanned it with one eye,
lingering briefly on a few paragraphs about halfway through.

Quince Bishop, the Waxman family friend who disrupted the attack, declined comment. Other witnesses reported that the protest group fled when one member fell onto the casket, knocking it to the ground.

"The whole thing is appalling," said Palm Grove's owner, funeral director Joel Moss. "These people are hoodlums. They should be ashamed."

But Maria Casteneda, founder and president of the SoCal Valley Memorial Society, denied the group's involvement with the mahogany protest.

Casteneda described the Society as a not-for-profit organization designed to provide information and support to those dealing with the burdens of losing a loved one. Often, Casteneda said, this support takes the form of consumer advocacy.

"But protecting the bereaved against exploitative sales practices in the funeral industry is one thing," Casteneda said. "What these so-called activists are doing is unconscionable. We disapprove in every way possible."

"At least you spelled my name right," he said.

"So what do you think?"

"It reads really smooth. Nice lead."

"Not that, dumbbell. I mean, what do you think about this SoCal Valley outfit?" She glanced at him. "I keep thinking about that bit from Casteneda's quote, 'exploitative sales practices.' And what I keep wondering is: so what's *she* trying to sell, anyway?"

Quince folded the paper over his knee. "Don't ask me."

"You believe her, don't you?"

"I never said that."

Mel rolled her eyes without taking them off the road.

"Why?" he asked. "Don't you?"

"Yesterday? Yesterday, I could've gone either way. She's convincing, I'll say that for her."

"She seemed sincere to me."

"Don't they all."

"You sound like Woodward and Bernstein's love child."

"And you're the biggest sucker for a pretty face I know."

"Give me a break, Mel."

Mel smirked and faded into a gap in the adjacent lane. "You know it's true."

"Please," Quince said. "A little credit. It's the tits I look at."

"Now don't be a baby. I wasn't criticizing."

Quince said nothing. Instead he checked himself for the fifth time in the visor mirror. It was strangely difficult to keep from looking; fascinating, really, in a clinical way. His right eye had pulped and fattened to positively Balboa-like proportions. The socket and cheekbone looked like a sausage casing filled with hammered plums.

"All I'm saying," Mel continued, "is that you should consider the possibilities. You ever stop to think that maybe this Maria chickie just dropped by to make sure you were home?"

"Get me off guard," Quince said. "Divert my attention while she gives Captain Nose Ring the all clear?"

"Something like that. It's possible, you know."

"That's very dramatic."

"But not impossible."

"Then why leave the business card?"

"Interesting question," she said. "I'm looking forward to hearing the answer to that one myself."

When they arrived in the parking lot of the memorial society office, Quince tried to lay ground rules. "Let me do the talking. Okay?"

Mel nodded. "We'll see how you do."

Though he almost couldn't believe it himself, after only a couple weeks on the job, Carl Rosen was beginning to think he could learn to appreciate working at a boneyard after all.

On his lunch hour, he went to see a guy he used to do business with from time to time. Carl talked Billy Guilder into letting him borrow the truck; Billy tossed him the keys and told him to watch the clutch, which needed fixing as soon as he got some part. Carl said okay. On basic image principles, he took the rakes and the rest of the lawn jockey shit from the bed of the pickup and dumped it out back of the crematory before he rolled.

King's Pawn was down on Venice Beach, on Ozone Avenue. The entrance to the shop faced a garbage-strewn alley between a tattoo place and a Greek sandwich stand. Carl actually felt a little nostalgic as he pulled open the grimy, unmarked steel door.

Nine years since he'd been here, but some things?

They never change.

Behind the counter in back, Gerald Kinghorn sat on a tall stool, just the way Carl Rosen remembered him: Gyro sandwich in one hand, *Hustler* in the other, fat sweaty gut blobbed against the glass of the display case in front of him. The place even smelled the same: old dust, mildew, and body odor hanging in the warm stale air.

"Hey, read the sign," Kinghorn yelled, spraying soggy flecks of pita bread into the pages of the stroke magazine. "It's lunch. We're closed."

"Say your what hurts?"

Gerald looked up with a scowl. Out of habit, he picked a greasy strand of hair off his forehead and pasted it back against his moist bald scalp. "Hey listen, jerkoff…."

Then he stopped and blinked, a slow recognition building in his eyes.

Carl stood with his hands in his pockets.

"Well look at this," Kinghorn said. "I *will* be Goddamned."

"How's business, Gerald?"

"Carl Rosen." Kinghorn grinned. "Now, let's see. Last I heard, you were rolling a hard eight up in the Bay."

"Came up nine," Rosen said.

"How's that?"

"They gave me an extra year for good behavior."

Gerald Kinghorn twisted his mouth, expectorating a deep wet gurgle of a laugh. "Same old Rosie," he said. "Just older and uglier. Goddamn, you know what? It really is good to see you. I'm touched you came by."

"Yeah. Looked like you were just getting ready to touch something, 'bout the time I walked in."

"That's a good point," Gerald Kinghorn said. "Thanks for reminding me. Now why don't you state your business and let me get back to my quiet time?"

Carl stepped up and put his hands on the counter. "Need to check out some hardware."

Kinghorn nodded along. "That's what I always liked about you, Rosie. Man who don't waste any time getting back to work. What you got cooking?"

"Nothin' particular. Like it's your fuckin' business."

A shrug from Gerald. "Just being conversational."

"What's on special?"

The president and CEO of King's Pawn and Porn licked

cucumber sauce from between his fingers. What remained on his palms, he wiped on his stained undershirt. Gerald Kinghorn nodded down at the cracked, cloudy display case. "What you see is what I got. Little picked over right now, but hey. Browse away. And get your hands off my glass—you're getting it all finger-printy."

Carl kept his hands where they where, stepping back so that he could survey Kinghorn's merchandise. He ran his gaze along the runty, haphazard selection of firearms lining the shelf by his knee. Gerald Kinghorn displayed the guns on a swatch of mangy, grease-matted velvet.

"This is it? You kidding me?"

"Hey, I already told you," said Gerald. "Summer clearance sale. Look, let's do this the easy way. Why don't you tell me what exactly you're looking for?"

"Nine millimeter," Rosen said flatly, for no other response applied.

"Beretta, I suppose."

"There any other kind?"

"Yeah, well, sorry, Mr. Specifico," said Gerald Kinghorn. "You and everybody else in town. I swear—ever since that last Tarantino movie came out? Don't even matter what brand. Beretta, Glock, Sig—hardly ever see anybody bring one in. They do? Hell, I can't keep 'em on the shelves."

"What's a Tarantino?" Carl said.

Gerald Kinghorn didn't seem to hear the question. "The shame of it is, it was just getting to the point where I could sell a good old American forty-five around here again. But it ain't like when you were workin' the turf, Rosie. These punks we got around here now? Shit—they hear Mr. Samuel L. Jackson say it, and all of a sudden everything's nine millimeter this and nine millimeter that again." Kinghorn reached down behind the counter and came up with something wrapped in a single sheet of newspaper. "Gotta be a nine. And they gotta hold the fucker sideways, too, just like in the movies. I swear."

While Carl listened impatiently, just about bored out of his skull, Kinghorn unwrapped the newspaper and handed the contents across the counter. "Lucky for you, I just got this in yesterday," he said. "Ain't had a chance to clean it up yet."

"The fuck's this supposed to be?"

"Hey, what'd you ask for?"

Rosen hefted the oily semiautomatic in his hand. "I asked for a Beretta."

"That there's just as good. It's a Taurus, now. But see, your Taurus is basically just a Beretta come outta Brazil. Same frame, same mechanics—I'm telling you, it's the same damn gun. But I can give it to you for … oh, let's say, hundred-fifty off the sticker price."

Rosen thumbed down the hammer and handed the Taurus back. He had to admit, it felt okay in his hand. But in a pinch? Some quick situation where you had to choose between living, dying, or going back to the can? Carl Rosen just could not see pulling out a gun with the same name as a family four-door.

"Hey, whatever," Kinghorn said, wrapping the Taurus back up in the financial page. After the bundle disappeared behind the counter once more, Gerald nodded toward a dinky little chrome-plated thing with pearly lavender grips. "I got a zippy little .25 here you might be interested in. Little more your speed, maybe."

"Fuck you."

"I'm serious—look here. See how cute it is? Really brings out your eyes."

SEAN DOOLITTLE

"Just show me the Smith," Rosen told him, pointing. "Mr. I-can't-sell-no-forty-fives."

Now Gerald grinned fraternally and pulled out the one decent piece on his shelf. "A man with an eye for gunmetal," he said, racking back the slide. He handed over the Smith and Wesson with the chamber open, a stubby inch of barrel exposed. "This? For this here, I'd normally want three-fifty. But seeing's how you're breaking parole and all, I'll give you the friends and family discount."

"Which is?"

"Two seventy-five."

"Wrap it," Rosen said.

"Congratulations on your purchase," Gerald said. "That be cash or trade?"

Putting the Smith down on the counter between them, Carl held up his right arm. He slipped out of the Tag Heuer he'd palmed off the dead dude.

"Here's three," he said. "Throw me in a box of rounds, we'll call it square."

Gerald Kinghorn looked at the watch. Carl placed it on the counter next to the .45.

Kinghorn looked at him for a long moment, as if debating whether to verbalize his thoughts.

Then he picked up the Smith and Wesson and put it back in the case again.

"Hey," Carl said. "The fuck you do that for?"

"Rosie." Gerald pointed toward the other end of the counter display. "Look yonder, child. Tell me what you see."

Carl followed Kinghorn's grimy finger all the way to the watches. At least five rows of them. There were Citizens, Rolexes, a couple Movados, and three other Heuers, just like the one Carl Rosen now held in his hand.

When he looked back at Kinghorn, Gerald had pulled up a shoebox from somewhere below. He dropped it on the counter with a metallic rattle. Inside: a tangled ticking jumble, more upon more of the same.

"Rosie, as maybe you can see, I got watches comin' out of my ass over here." He shook one free from the top of the pile and held it forth. Gold Rolex. "Here," he said. "You need one? It's a welcome back gift. Take it home."

"Don't *even* give me that shit," Rosen said. He pointed at the Heuer. "This fucker's waterproof. And see here? This little dial moves."

"Oh, shut up. You poor sorry asshole, shut up. I can't stand seeing you this way."

"You wanna repeat that?"

"Hey. You gotta plug in, my man. You're out of prison now—start acting like it. And quit givin' me the eyeball, Mr. Stone Cold Badass. I'm saying this as a friend."

"Listen, you fat fuck. Bring that Smith back up here."

Gerald Kinghorn looked at him sympathetically, released a heavy sigh. "Rosie, you and me go back a ways. I wanna help, you know?" He bent down and rummaged a minute, farting delicately as he straightened his back. "Here. Here's what I can do."

In his hand, Kinghorn held a revolver that looked like it had been buried for a couple years and dug back up again. Black electrician's tape held the grip together. The bluing had worn off the trigger and parts of the barrel, and the trigger guard was missing altogether.

"You gotta be kidding me," Carl said.

"Look, pal, this ain't Free Shit Day at Sears. I gotta put my son through vocational school, okay? I mean this kid of mine, he's a complete fuckup—but for once, his instructors, they're telling me he's a natural. So what am I gonna do? Deny the fruit of my loins a big career in heating and air conditioning so the cons come in here with ripped-off watches don't get mad at me?"

"Put it away, Gerald. I want the Smith."

"Sorry, Rose," Kinghorn said. "No can do. But this here's a classic rod. Thirty-eight Special. And I filed the serial number off personally."

After staring Kinghorn down for a full minute, Carl finally took the gun and tried to balance it in his hand. He turned it this way and that way, tried sighting it in. When he popped the cylinder, something rattled loosely in the hinge.

"This is bullshit," he said.

"Yeah, well take it or leave it. Best I can do."

Carl looked at the piece-of-shit gun one last time, glared at Kinghorn.

"Well?"

"I'm thinking," Carl said. "I'm thinking I oughta cram this thing up your ass and dry fire it a few times."

"Aw, Rosie. You always were romantic."

While Carl watched, his old pal Gerald Kinghorn picked up the Heuer in two meaty fingers and dropped it into the shoebox with the rest.

"Tell you what," he said, in an unbending but fatherly tone. "Bring me in a coupla DVD players sometime, maybe we can work something out on that forty-five."

THE HEADQUARTERS of the SoCalValley Memorial Society occupied a tiny corner slice of strip mall, its presence indicated only by a narrow stencil on the front door. Inside, the office itself was scarcely larger than the U.S. mailbox on the sidewalk out front. The whole of the place could be appraised from the entryway: a single twelve-by-fifteen room crowded with file cabinets and a battleship-gray aluminum desk. A folding table held a coffee pot, hot plate, and microwave; crooked stacks of papers rose up Seuss-like from every surface available.

When Quince and Mel made their entrance, Maria Casteneda was sitting behind the desk with a telephone receiver tucked between shoulder and chin. Taking one look at him, she quickly rang off and scooted back in her wheeled office chair.

"Mr. Bishop?" Her eyes widened. "What happened to your eye?"

"Interesting that you should inquire," said Melanie. "We came by to ask you the same thing."

"Dammit, Mel," Quince said.

Hurrying around the desk, Maria Casteneda glanced at

Melanie Roth with what looked like surprise. But if she wondered what Mel and Quince were doing here together, she didn't stop to ask. Instead she dodged a leaning tower of manila folders stacked in the middle of the floor and made her way toward a dorm-sized refrigerator in the corner. Maria stooped and rummaged a minute. She returned offering an unopened bag of frozen mixed vegetables.

"Here," she said. "Put this on your cheek. Careful—oh, ouch."

Quince took the bag and thanked her. Beside him, he could have sworn he felt Melanie rolling her eyes. The vibe in the room was palpably circumspect. He thought: *this was a terrible idea, coming here.*

This morning, Maria Casteneda had traded last night's collared button-down for a snug USC T-shirt. She wore it with what looked like the same faded jeans, clean white sneakers, and a ball cap turned backwards on her head. Looking quickly between Quince and Mel, she finally stepped back and asked the obvious question.

"Miss Roth?" she said. "Quince? I … I don't like the looks of this. What's going on?"

"Don't ask me," Melanie replied. "I'm just the reporter."

Quince gave her a look. To Maria Casteneda, he said: "Then you really don't know?"

"Please," Maria said. "Tell me why you're here."

Pressing the cold veggies gently against his eye, Quince sighed heavily. "Benefit of the doubt, I guess."

"Both of you," said Maria Casteneda. "Please. Sit down."

The best she could offer was a pair of dented folding chairs that looked like they'd come with the desk. Quince and Melanie accepted. To his relief and mild dismay, Mel did as promised, shifting into observer mode and leaving him to take the floor. Casteneda listened quietly until he'd finished telling her the short tale of the visit he'd been paid, the ending of which had already been as much as revealed by his hammered visage.

"And you haven't called the police yet? Quince—you need to report this. You've been assaulted. This is serious."

"I keep hearing that," he said. The cold from the Green Giant first aid kit, which had ceased to be a soothing thing, was now sending icepick stabs from cheekbone south, all the way down into his neck and upper arm. He took the bag away and let the contents thaw on his knee. "To tell you the truth, I don't know if I'll bother. I really haven't decided yet. But either way, I thought I should at least let you know first."

"Why?"

"I don't know," he said. "If you really are in the dark on this, I guess I figured you deserved that much. And if I'm wrong, well, hey. Unless your boy's hiding under the desk there, I don't guess it makes much difference one way or another."

Mel looked from him to Maria Casteneda, who contemplated the big calendar blotter that covered the surface of the desk in question.

"Don't worry," Maria finally said. "Nobody under here. Whoever this creep is, he's never been with our group, I promise you."

Mel said, "Suddenly you seem awfully sure."

"Oh, I was certain yesterday," Maria said. "I'm afraid I wasn't being completely honest with either of you. I apologize."

Mel said, "Not completely honest, how?"

"Listen," said Maria Casteneda. She offered a weary smile.

"We're not exactly a national advocacy, here. The SoCal Valley Memorial Society?" She gestured around the office. "Want to know who keeps this magnificent nerve center functioning? Me and two volunteers. We used to have four; one had a baby, and the other left to do post-graduate work at Miami-Ohio. And the two wonderful people I've got left? One is the sweetest 70-year-old grandmother you'd ever want to meet. The other is a great 16-year-old girl. She has a degenerative palsy that keeps her in a wheelchair most of the time. Neither of them wears a nose ring, to the best of my knowledge."

Mel looked at Quince. He didn't know what to say.

Mel stepped into the silence. "Maria, why didn't you mention this yesterday?"

"These people are volunteers," she said. "They give up their personal time, and they work very hard, week in and week out, for no other reason than because they care enough to do it. I didn't tell you—or anybody else from the media—because I wasn't about to reward their efforts by sending a bunch of reporters after them. No offense."

"None taken," Mel said.

Maria turned to Quince. "And I didn't tell you because, believe it or not, I truly didn't want to involve you more than you already were. I just thought there might be a chance you'd be able to tell me something that made sense. And I did want to send my concern along to the Waxman family. Quince, I really do apologize. It wasn't the right thing to do."

"I don't understand," Quince told her.

"If it wasn't one of your people," said Mel, "then who was it? Why would somebody do a thing like this and claim to be part of your group?"

To this, Maria Casteneda offered no immediate reply. For a moment or two, she leaned back in her chair and watched her hands, which remained flat on the desk in front of her. Quince and Mel looked at each other again. With his eyes, Quince said: *huh*? Melanie replied: *Dunno. Shh*.

"Melanie, I liked your story in the paper today," Maria finally said. "I thought it was even-handed. Thanks."

"That's nice of you to say," Mel told her. "But don't thank me. It wasn't a favor. Just relating the facts."

"Yeah, well. The facts are however you present them, aren't they?" Maria leaned back in her chair. "The broadcasts made us sound like a bunch of crazies."

"TV for you."

Maria grinned. "I guess so." She got up from the desk and went to the folding table, where she poured herself coffee into a huge chipped mug with permanent prior stains. She offered styrofoam miniatures, which Quince accepted and Mel declined. Maria came back with the coffee for Quince, filling Mel's request with a Diet Coke from the mini-fridge.

"As for facts," Maria told her, "as far as I could tell, you only got one wrong."

Mel eyed her over the rim of the soda can. "Oh?"

"The quote from Joel Moss. When you attributed that statement, you identified him as the owner of Palm Grove. That's not actually true. Not anymore, anyway."

"Really," Melanie said. "The company profile I pulled was current."

"Oh, I'm sure that's true." Maria Casteneda waved her hand. "It's a marketing tactic. To find out otherwise, you would have had to dig a lot further than the company brochures. And I know you didn't have any reason to do that."

Melanie kept watching her. "Marketing tactic?"

"Sure. When one of the big conglomerates buys out a smaller independent funeral home like Palm Grove, a lot of times what they'll do is, they'll keep everything a customer would see the same as it was before. It's like product branding. Stick with the name and the faces folks already trust."

While Maria spoke, Melanie rooted around in her bag. She emerged with a pen and her notebook. Quince watched her scribble the word BUYOUT on the first page.

"Whatever the company literature says is about nine months out of date," Maria went on. "Palm Grove was owned and operated by Joel's father, Walter—that much is true. I knew Walt Moss, oh, maybe four years? A sweet, wonderful man. He died of pancreatic cancer last February. It was quite an awful shock, actually. Anyway, Joel sold out to KBH a month or two after Walt passed on."

Quince watched Mel print the initials KBH in the margin of the page.

"The funeral care industry as a whole is pretty much dominated by a handful of big national chains now," Maria explained. "KBH—they're maybe number four, sizewise, out of the major conglomerates. Knox, Burke, and Hare, Incorporated. They're based out of Galveston."

"I guess that's interesting," Mel told her. She rested her pen on the notebook. "But I'm not sure what you're trying to say."

Maria Casteneda shrugged. "I'm not trying to say anything. Not for sure. But I'll tell you this: SoCal Valley's only purpose is to protect consumers as much as we can. We don't work for a profit, and we certainly never see one. All we do is provide information, and in some situations, we help arbitrate grievances. I'll admit, we don't necessarily make many friends out of people like Joel Moss—but we don't show up at funerals with masks and road flares."

"You're saying you think Joel Moss has something to do with this."

"I'm not saying anything," Maria repeated. "But where grievances are concerned, let's just say we've run across some folks who have a few with Palm Grove. For about three months now, SoCal Valley has been trying to see these complaints … resolved."

When he looked at Mel, Quince could almost hear the gears turning in her head. He looked at Maria. They met eyes for an odd, private moment. Then Maria addressed them both once more.

"Listen," she said. "I don't have any idea what's going on around here. I don't know why somebody's running around punching people in our name. But Melanie? If you want a good follow-up story? There's a meeting being held this evening you might be interested in."

"What kind of meeting?"

"The unfortunate kind. Between myself, a few of our clients, and the attorney who until yesterday was handling our potential class action suit against Palm Grove."

While Quince moved the soggy bag of vegetables to his other knee, Melanie clicked her pen and did just exactly what he'd known she would.

"This meeting," Mel asked. "Where and when?"

IN 1939, an earnest but floundering young man
named Thomas Walter Moss flunked out of seminary and
started looking for a regular job. Tom Moss was no theologian;
he wasn't even a very good aspiring one. He was perhaps
too questioning by nature to excel as a pupil, and he was
uncomfortable with the craft of ministry. Where he needed
faith, he could muster only cautious optimism; where he
needed confidence, he found mostly self-doubt. He harbored
no fundamental sense that he was qualified to guide others
spiritually. What he did have was an unfocused but deeply-
felt yearning to somehow be useful to the world.

Like many useful people, Thomas Walter Moss came to
find his true calling largely by accident. Penniless, he went to
work as the keeper of a churchyard for a non-denominational
chapel near his home—and it was here that Tom Moss
developed a profound and everlasting sense of purpose and
place. He found a quiet nobility in caring for the dead; in
comforting the grief-stricken, he found important fellowship.
He carried a rare gift of empathy, and he was lucky enough
to discover it as a young man.

So when the church dissolved in 1942, he used his

savings and a modest inheritance to buy the small rattletrap building and the land on which it sat. By 1943, he'd cleared the pews, refurbished the chapel with sturdy new lumber, and converted the structure into a small but operational full-service funeral home.

Thomas Walter Moss went on to marry and produce a son. Esther Moss died in childbirth. When Thomas finally joined her—years later, in 1967—his adult son Walter took over Palm Grove Parlor and Cemetery. Walter married in 1968, producing a son of his own.

And as far back as he could remember, Joel Thomas Moss had known he too would follow his father's footsteps one day.

For Joel, this was never so much a calling, or even a conscious decision, as it was an intrinsic sense of eventuality. Unlike virtually every other child his age, Joel grew up with a natural understanding of the nuts and bolts of death. His early exposure to the family trade infused a unique awareness of the overall scheme of things. So during the unfettered, magical stage when most kids dreamed of becoming astronauts and detectives, cowboys and movie stars, Joel dreamed hardly at all. There just wasn't any point in it. By the age of seven, he'd already known what he was going to be when he grew up: an undertaker.

As a matter of course, Joel learned early in life to cope with solitude. He'd actually been allotted, in almost every other respect, the standard set of qualities that help a white middle-class kid fit in with the crowd: normal growth rate, average intelligence, acceptable looks, basic athletic ability. But these things weren't enough for a young mortician-to-be; he grew up without many friends, being invariably considered freakish by his peers. He'd never known his mother, who had divorced his dad and moved to Orlando with a PGA golf pro when Joel was six months old. The neighborhood kids thought he was creepy. Most of his teachers regarded him as sweet, unfortunate, and mildly strange.

But somehow, it never really occurred to Joel that he should feel short-changed. Alone, his dad raised him with all the love and encouragement imaginable. Walt Moss was a hard-working, compassionate man who taught Joel the inner rewards of independence, empathy, and pride.

When he was old enough, Joel began earning his weekly allowance by helping out around the mortuary. On Saturdays, when the other guys his age took Little League practice and learned how to cut back on a breaking wave, Joel weeded headstones and vacuumed carpets in the viewing parlors. As a teen, he worked summers at Palm Grove while his classmates took jobs as life guards and grocery baggers and record store clerks.

During the tempestuous hormonal years of adolescence, Joel felt infinitely more comfortable around certified embalmers than he ever did around girls. He learned to drive behind the wheel of a midnight blue '72 Cadillac hearse. At seventeen, he was already handling simple pick-ups from the morgue at Saint John's Hospital.

It really wasn't until college that Joel felt the first glimmers of doubt about his path. Maybe his outlook shifted with early adulthood, or maybe his curiosity just flowered later than some. Whatever the case, the color and diversity of campus life hinted at worlds he'd never considered before. For the first time, Joel realized that nothing was ordained; he could explore any lifestyle he chose.

But by then, Joel had no interest whatsoever in disrupting the momentum he'd attained. Because he'd never actively set any goals, it seemed pointless to re-evaluate them. So he continued with his mortuary science program at San Francisco College; he received his state embalmer's license, working his apprenticeship during the summer months at Palm Grove; and while he never once felt saddled by expectations, he took comfort in his father's quiet pride.

In spite of this, or perhaps because of it, Joel Moss gradually came to recognize the basic difference between him and his dad.

Walt Moss had considered the funeral business to be a historic and noble trade. Spiritually, he was shaped by the values he'd absorbed from his own father: dignity, humility, and a deep sense of fulfillment in serving humankind.

Joel, on the other hand, felt driven by almost none of these things. For Joel, automatically graduating into an established business concern was not so much about upholding family tradition as it was a good way to avoid the significant emotional strain of forging his own path. In truth, he had little in the way of passion or ambition of his own.

This was not necessarily a dooming quality in and of itself. Many professions tend, for many reasons, to be handed along family lines. Joel once read a *Fortune 500* article which claimed that there were two industries about which, statistically, this was most often true: waste management and mortal aftercare.

On some level, he'd always considered the two to be variations of the same basic thing. It just wasn't until late in his twenties that Joel felt he understood the reason why these statistics held.

Because almost nobody else would want to make a living at either profession, otherwise.

As a licensed and practicing funeral director, it didn't take long for Joel to become miserable. He loved his dad too much ever to say so, but over time, his mounting dissatisfaction took its toll. Dealing exclusively with those in mourning depressed Joel beyond words. Spending hour upon intimate hour with corpses warped his spirit beyond simple repair.

Worst of all was the unspoken social stigma associated with his trade. While his father had been respected by everyone who'd ever met him, nobody in the normal world ever feels truly comfortable around a person who handles the dead. Even proctologists are practically rock stars by comparison. To make matters still more torturous, Joel's interest in the opposite gender finally set in with a crackling intensity, yet finding dates was an exercise in rejection; the nubile young L.A. women who most enchanted Joel would sooner have sex with a registered pedophile. For the first time, he realized the significance of his mother's flight nearly three decades before. And all the things that meant nothing to Joel as a teenager suddenly seemed unendurable.

After just two years in the business, Joel began falling apart at the seams. He actually reached the point where the scent of tissue builder gave him esophageal cramps. He couldn't even look at antibacterial soap without two pairs of latex gloves. He developed a psychosomatic reaction to pancake makeup; for months, every time he touched the stuff, he broke out in a weeping rash.

For many of his colleagues, the downside of the trade was vastly ameliorated by its more lucrative characteristics. And Joel grew to envy them fiercely, with every molecule. For while a modern, profit-savvy funeral director can enjoy a spectacular income, Joel's father cared absolutely nothing for personal gain. Walt Moss ran Palm Grove with all the fiscal strategy of a social services program. As a result, Joel felt continually deprived of the fruits which, he was sure, might validate his labors somehow.

Without them, he sank further into a swampland of depression, until his permanent, day-to-day personality could only be evaluated clinically.

Joel trudged into his thirties crutched almost entirely by weekly therapy sessions, prescription antidepressants, and mail-order pornography. He worked hard to hide his malaise from his father, yet resented him for not noticing. It was an unhealthy time.

The bitter irony? Accessible only in hindsight.

For while Joel had been so absorbed in his own afflictions, he'd never even realized that his dad was the one who was actually ill.

It unfolded with a crushing resonance. One day, Joel simply looked up and saw a walking cadaver where his father had been. Even after the pain dug too deep to hide completely, Walter Moss had quietly claimed ulcers—and nobody at Palm Grove suspected anything more.

But it wasn't ulcers, it was cancer, and it didn't let its host pretend for long. Joel discovered the truth just in time to watch his father die badly. There wasn't a thing anyone could do.

In February of this year, the man who had spent his entire life upholding dignity for others was ultimately robbed of his own. His final slide was fast and slow and ugly, and it was over before Joel had even accepted it was happening. Walt Moss passed with a labored rattle—matting his sheets with frothy yellow diarrhea, pumped full of morphine and emptied by pain.

People come to terms with grief in a thousand ways. Ceremonies and observances, support groups, pop spirituality in trade paperback: all are designed not for the deceased but for those left behind. And ultimately, all provide only as much comfort as their subscribers can afford. In the end, some people filter their grief through a sense of greater meaning; some ignore it as long as possible; some actively learn to live with it in various ways. And some simply let it eat them from the inside out, until their capacity to feel anything is gone.

But the grief is real. Everybody experiences it one way or another.

At first, Joel didn't think he could withstand the weight of his own. He felt numbed by shock, wracked by guilt—and above all else, pulverized by the loss.

And yet—even in the midst of these feelings—somewhere underneath he knew implicitly that the ultimate antidote to his suffering had already been administered.

Joel first became aware of the healing sensation within a few days. At first, he honestly tried to deny it, if only out of respect. But as horrible as it seemed, this feeling was as real as the grief. And sometime during the hours he spent preparing his own father's body for the ground, Joel acknowledged the truth.

He felt relieved.

Even the shame of it faded quickly, sluicing like magic with Walt Moss's bodily fluids into the trocar and away. If he'd had the power then, Joel was certain he'd have granted his father the long and healthy life he deserved. But nobody could do that, ever; it was the one truth Joel had understood his whole life long. And while the act of embalming his dad was the most somber and loving task he'd ever performed, it was also the single most powerful moment of emancipation Joel had experienced before or since.

Walter Moss had given his son many gifts, and his last was

the greatest of all. For the first time ever, Joel felt as though he were in control of his own future.

For in dying, his father had liberated the both of them from their respective hells.

"Now that's enough of that, Joey," said the voice on the other end of the line. "I'm not even listening to that kind of talk. As far as we're concerned, you handled the whole thing like a pro."

Joel sat at the desk in his office, sipping a double-tall latte while he talked to Bryce Brenner on the speaker phone. Brenner was the regional VP of marketing for KBH, and he'd called first thing this morning to get the scoop on yesterday.

"I appreciate that, B., I really do. It's just … I don't know." Joel stifled a yawn with the back of his hand. While he spun out the words, he flipped through the November *GQ*, which had arrived in the morning's mail. "A situation like that—you just stand there, thinking, how does this happen? You know what I mean? I mean, what's *wrong* with this world?"

"I hear you," Brenner said. "I hear you loud and clear. And you know what? You want to know the worst thing? We've got no way to defend ourselves! That's the long and the short of it, my friend. Every hairy-pitted, Birkenstock-wearing, Jessica Mitford-wannabe in Bawlbaby Land can run around taking all the ludicrous potshots at us they want. But tell me you'll ever see *60 Minutes* doing a three-part bash piece on *them*. Mahogany loggers, my sweet ass." Brenner spat out a vitriolic little laugh. "So, what? They're going to start attacking *funerals* now? I'm telling you: don't beat yourself up on this one, Joey. You can't duck a sucker punch. All you can do is roll with it."

"I suppose you're right."

"Atta boy." Over the speaker, Joel heard paper shuffling. Bryce Brenner's voice grew distant as he spoke to somebody in the background. Another shuffle, then he returned to the line. "So anyway, big guy, here's the news. Your plane and hotel are booked. My secretary is going to email you an itinerary and a programming schedule today."

"Right," Joel told him. Brenner was talking about the NAAP convention this weekend in Seattle. "I'll look for it."

"How's the presentation coming?" Brenner asked. "All ready to knock 'em dead?"

"You bet," Joel lied. The truth? He hadn't even started putting it together yet. Not slide one.

The National Assembly of Aftercare Professionals was the industry's big annual trade show, and this year KBH was flying Joel in for the event. Knox, Burke, and Hare, Inc. offered to bring in the executive directors from each of their franchise locations nationwide.

By all accounts, KBH threw one hell of a company party. He'd even heard rumors of high-class call girls, and other gentlemanly diversions. Joel had been struggling to quell his hopes that this were true. But not mightily.

The only visible downside to next weekend's impending bacchanal was that Joel had been hand-selected by top KBH brass to deliver a lecture on optimizing the service/ profit relationship in "new millennium" funeral home management.

The whole assignment was just another clear confirmation, as if one were needed, of Joel Moss's underlying life philosophy:

Even when you win, you lose.

His eight-month business partnership with KBH was a perfect case in point. They, like their primary competitors, had been approaching Palm Grove each and every quarter for the better part of the last seven years. Like clockwork, each and every quarter, Joel's dad had turned them away.

Walt Moss had considered the conglomerates to be evil incarnate: carrion eaters, the whole pack of them. Where Joel saw a stunning corporate model, his father perceived some virulent air-borne spore.

It wasn't until Joel finally found himself with complete sell-out authority that he began to recognize just how perceptive his father had been, in his own misguided way.

At the table back in March, KBH had presented such a lucrative offer that Joel had scarcely been able to contain his joy. It would have taken a rifle-fired tranquilizer dart to keep him from signing on the dotted line.

But the original number, Joel soon learned, was merely the carrot. As soon as they knew they had him, Knox's team of negotiators showed him the stick.

They'd doubled their offer—with the proviso that he sign a prorated 11-month contract, wherein he agreed to stay on until year-end as managing director at Palm Grove. Their underlying strategy, of course, was to keep the acquisition as transparent as possible to Palm Grove's pre-paid and word-of-mouth clientele. In this manner, they could trade on the sterling reputation Joel's father and grandfather had established while Palm Grove made the smoothest possible transition to new management.

Attached to this contract was an additional performance clause based on quarterly earnings. The rider required Joel to meet an ascending profit schedule, to be reviewed at the 9-month point. The final asking price for Palm Grove Cemetery and Funeral Home would be derived according to a combination of fixed goal percentages, market fluctuations, and the decidedly less quantifiable brand of inflation KBH called "consumer mind share."

It was a devilish crossroads that stayed Joel's pen for nearly two indecisive weeks. His natural inclination was to take the buyout money and run, for he truly could not imagine enduring another eleven months in this prison that had cloistered his entire adult life.

On the other hand, he found himself looking at two scenarios: a comfortable retirement anywhere in the U.S. with a boat and possibly a summer home, versus a level of luxury he'd only dreamed of, complete with offshore and foreign accounts.

Plus a signing bonus.

In the face of this momentous decision, Joel found a stoicism within himself he'd never really known he possessed.

The bonus purchased a used silver Porsche Boxster, a closet full of Miuccia Prada, and a lifetime membership at the Riviera Club.

As for that nine-month performance review? His second presentation, Sunday power brunch, this weekend at NAAP. This one, Joel Moss had painstakingly prepared.

"That's our man," said Bryce Brenner. "Tell you what? We're gonna hate to lose you. That's a fact."

"Thanks, Bryce." Joel peeled out the free cologne sample from the center of the magazine and rubbed the tab behind his jaw. *Contradiction*, by Calvin Klein. "That means a lot."

"Hey, I'm just telling it like it is. Look, Joey, I got another incoming. We'll talk at you later, yeah?"

"Absolutely. You take it easy, B."

The speaker emitted a series of clicks, followed by a loud buzzing dial tone as Brenner rang off the line. Joel reached forward and tapped the button, squelching the empty noise.

Some days, it truly was a glorious thing to be alive.

Joel sat and finished his coffee while he picked through the rest of the mail. He took a moment to scan the *Times* article, lingering with satisfaction on the ring and flow of his own quotes. Brenner was right: he really was a brilliant son of a bitch, wasn't he?

The whole mahogany protest angle had played out even better than Joel could have anticipated. The idea had come to him in a shimmering vision, one afternoon at the embalming table. After debating for a day or two, he'd decided the plan was every bit as beautiful as he thought it was. And in a single elegant maneuver, Joel Moss had simultaneously muzzled his fiercest opponent and upped his own bargaining heft with Knox, Burke, and Hare.

Joel suffered no delusions that the stunt might cripple SoCal Valley permanently. Maria Casteneda would recover, of that he had no doubt. Bryce Brenner had been right about one other thing: over the long haul, the funeral industry had no hope of winning a PR war with these bombastic watchdog groups and their middle-class indignation machines.

But by the time Maria Casteneda wiped the muck of this off her face, Joel would be savoring early retirement in a beachfront condo somewhere. He looked forward to sending her a postcard.

Cruel? Perhaps. But cruel she had coming.

He only wished he could have seen the look on her face, the moment her holier-than-thou invective turned to bite her on her perfect little behind.

Joel was just about to log on to his PC and check for that emailed itinerary when Dolores, the morning receptionist, rang in on the intercom line.

"Another call for you," she said.

"Business or personal?"

"It's a Detective Timms? He says he has a follow-up question about yesterday."

Lord in heaven, Joel thought. *What now?* "Thanks, Dolores. Put him through."

When the incoming line began to blink, Joel tapped the speakerphone button again. "Detective Timms," he said. "Good morning."

"Bording, ath hoe," said the caller.

Joel's testicles retracted immediately.

Morning, asshole. He nearly climbed over the desk in pursuit of the receiver.

"What the hell is the matter with you!" he hissed. "What are you *doing*? How *dare* you call here on the phone!"

"Hey, tell me something. You check the mail yet today?"

"What?" Joel could hear his voice rising, matching the crescendo in his gut. "I'm hanging up. If you call here again, I promise you, the next phone conversation I have is with the police. Do you understand me?"

"Yeah, but seriously. You might wanna check the mail first," the kid said. He sounded like he had marbles shoved up his nose.

"I don't know what you're talking about," Joel said. "I'm hanging up. Goodbye."

And then he saw it, on the bottom of the remaining pile of mail by his arm. A small padded envelope. No postage, no return address. Only the words MR. JOEL T. MOSS printed in neat block letters where his own address should have been.

Joel cradled the receiver under his chin and tore into the parcel with fingers and teeth. Inside, he found a cheap mini-cassette recorder, with a white slip of paper taped to its black plastic shell. With numb fingers, Joel peeled the slip free. It was another Rite Aid receipt: same store, last night's date, this one for the recording device Joel held in his other hand.

"What…."

"Play it, Sam."

Joel did as he was told.

Already knowing, on some tilting plane deep within, precisely what he was about to hear.

He sat and listened to the replay of last night's conversation in his room down the hall: his voice clear as a bell, his name clearly identified. A feeling of odd detachment washed over him.

"Weird, huh?" the kid said. Joel noticed distantly that he was now speaking in a normal tone. Lower, more naturally resonant. The nasal muffle had vanished magically. "You never know how your voice really sounds until you hear it on tape."

Joel just sat. He didn't know what to say.

"I got a deal for you," said the kid, no longer bothering to disguise his voice. For now, of course, there was no need. "That tape you're holding? I made plenty of duplicates. But if you buy a few at regular club prices, we can talk about discount plans."

Joel heard himself say, "I don't … I'm not understanding you."

"Feel free to inquire about membership details."

Automatically groping for the Zoloft, Joel sighed into the phone.

Even when you win, you lose.

Some days, it truly sucked to be alive.

THOUGH HE'D reevaluated the opinion more than once already, Billy Guilder finally decided he liked Carl Rosen after all.

But he had to admit: this morning, for a couple of minutes there, he'd begun to have his doubts. Especially after he'd been a guy and lent Carl the truck, no questions asked. Rosen didn't even have a license as far as Billy knew. But hey. Billy knew what it was like, your first couple months outside again—trying to get used to a new job, cooling your heels in some crappy halfway house, parole officer dogging your ass every few days. So sure, he tossed the guy the keys.

Then what did he find?

All his gear, which he liked to keep organized, in a big pile where Rosen had dumped it outside on the ground. Three rakes, the gas-powered weed whacker, and two bags of Weed and Feed fertilizer, all tangled up in the garden hose.

Okay, so lifting some watch off a dead guy was one thing. Not exactly your most respectful way to operate, but hey. Billy had thought this one over, and when you really got down to it, he figured the watch thing probably fell somewhere in the "victimless crimes" category.

But leaving a man's tools in a pile, for no good reason? Normally, he didn't like to judge a guy—but shit like this was bordering on the rude side, in Billy's opinion.

On the other hand, you had to appreciate a man who knew how to pick just the right apology gift to say he cared.

The first thing Rosen did when he got back from his errand was reach into one of those deep pockets and toss Billy a little quad baggie of pot.

"Aww," Billy said. He peered in at the mix, noting the goodly number of fat, sweet-smelling buds. "My favorite. How'd you know?"

"Hunch." Rosen wandered over and fed some quarters into the break room soda machine. He punched the button with a fist, and the machine dumped out his Mountain Dew with a mechanical thud.

"So that was pretty quick, partner. Free world traffic better or worse than you remember it?"

Rosen tilted back the soda and guzzled until the sides of the can crumpled. "That truck of yours is a piece of shit. Clutch sticks."

"Yeah. It's like I told you. Gotta fix that."

Rosen tossed the empty can at the waste basket, missing a foot or so wide. The can hit carpet with a hollow aluminum clunk. Carl ignored it, shoving his hands in his pockets and leaning against the sink.

"But hey." Pocketing the weed, Billy picked up Rosen's can and dropped it into the recycle tub over by the wall. "It's good you made it back when you did. I got some good news."

"News is that?"

"I just talked to Moss. Looks like we get to go out on your first pick-up this afternoon."

"Pick up," Rosen said. "You mean like a stiff?"

"Might not be too stiff yet. Little old granny up in Holmby Hills. Keeled over in the La-Z-Boy, Moss says."

"Yay for granny," Rosen said. "Now what's the good news?"

Billy Guilder grinned. "The good news is, after we get her back here, guess who gets the rest of the day off?"

Rosen gave him a look.

Didn't like guessing games, Billy decided. He said, "You and me, partner. Long as you don't mind coming back in a few hours tonight. But you know what I'm thinking? They're playing old Eastwood flicks over at the New Beverly. I'm thinking maybe we could go chill with Clint, you feel like it. Get a burger after. You a burger man?"

"I'll eat 'em if I have to." Rosen folded his arms. "Back up to the coming in later part."

"See, they're having granny's funeral tomorrow."

Rosen kept looking at him: *and*?

"Come on," Billy told him. "I'll explain it while we go."

On their way downstairs to the garage, Billy told Carl how this kind of situation worked. Sometimes, when they were short-handed, which was pretty much all the time, Moss would send them out like this to pick up somebody from somewhere. That part was no big deal. Just moving freight, basically; Moss actually did the taking care of the body once they brought it in. All they had to do then was get things together for the funeral.

The way *that* usually worked was, the day before the day, Moss would have them pull a swing shift to get the place ready for the ceremony. They got paid time-and-a-half for the extra hours. Plus, for an extra bonus, Moss usually gave them the next day off. The way it happened to work out this time, the funeral being tomorrow, they'd be getting a day and a half for the price of one.

"It's kind of a sweet deal," Billy told him. "Like I was telling you before? Moss'll take care of you, different ways."

"What I'm saying is," Carl said, "I don't get the after-hours shit. What we supposed to be doing, again?"

"Got to open up the grave, a few other things."

"There's some reason we can't just do it during the day and go home?"

"Well," Billy explained, "there's what you might call an element of discretion involved. Moss, he's real big on discreet. Don't worry, it'll make more sense later. Check this out."

Billy pointed at a plain burgundy Plymouth Voyager with smoked windows sitting in the first stall. The hood was up.

Carl looked, didn't say anything.

"Normally, that's what we'd use. I mentioned discretion, right? Well, this here's, like, your more discreet mode of dead-people transportation."

"That a fact."

"Oh, yeah. These days, hearses, that's mainly just for show on funeral morning. Classier ride between the church and the cemetery. Pick-ups, now, that's something different. For that, you got your minivan. Makes folks feel less conspicuous, is the way Moss says it. You gotta figure that's probably true— but guys like you and me know what he really means is, the fat cats up in Brentwood and Bel Air, they don't want to be seeing the old corpse-wagon sitting in the driveway on a sunny afternoon."

Carl just stood and looked at him, like he was waiting for Billy to get to the point.

"Anyway," Billy said. "She's got a bad alternator. I gotta fix that. Come on, amigo—follow me."

He led Carl Rosen onward, across the spotless composite flooring of the vehicle bay. They passed by three gleaming, freshly waxed hearses lined up in a row: one white, one midnight blue, one dove gray. Billy waited until they'd reached the final stall, where he stopped and spread his arms before the big Caddy in front of them.

"This baby here," he said, "is what you and me are gonna use today."

The last hearse in the shop was a silver 1974 Miller-Meteor. It had a black crinkle top and a 3-way electric side loader. Personally, Billy would've taken a good used rear-loading Superior with low miles, like the one Moss got rid of last winter. But he had to admit, he'd grown to love the M&M after awhile. That big greasy 500 V-8 was just too much motor to resist—and he had a buddy down in El Segundo could get him parts for it next to free.

Billy Guilder did all the mechanical work on Palm Grove's machinery. In his spare time, he'd retrofitted the Caddy with an all-new, high-performance fuel system: electronic multipoint injection with an 870-horse pump, torque converter, and a knock control kit. He'd re-bored the cylinders, threw on a Holley four-barrel with Edlebrock intakes, put on some decent shocks and a competition ignition system.

Probably should have spent a little more time getting the alternator fixed on that Voyager. And the clutch in the pickup—he really did have to get around to that one of these days. But Billy just couldn't help himself; over the past couple of months, he'd fine-tuned the Caddy to a quiet hum. Billy Guilder took great pride in knowing he drove the only commercially-licensed hearse in L.A. that could squeeze NASCAR torque out of a tank of 85 octane and barely clear its throat.

But then you had Carl Rosen, who clearly didn't appreciate the artistry involved. Standing before this automotive masterpiece, the best thing the guy could come up with was: "You expect me to get in that thing?"

Billy just grinned.

"Come on," he said. "Take you for a ride in a fine American car."

"**I'M SORRY,**" said the attorney, for the third time. "But you have to understand my position."

"I'm trying, Jerry," Maria said. "I really am. Trouble is, now that you suddenly seem to be missing a spine, I just can't seem to make out what this position of yours actually *is*."

Quince watched Jerry's face twitch, as though Maria'd reached across the desk and flicked his ear. The attorney sat back in his chair.

"There's no call to be abusive," he said.

Maria looked away.

The attorney's name was Grundman; his firm consisted of two rooms worth of low-rent, street-level office space in Culver City. Quince and Melanie sat in vinyl chairs on one side of the cramped, windowless office. Maria, two middle-aged couples, and an elderly widow sat in front of the desk. Jerry Grundman, a small, harried, raccoon-faced man with round wire glasses and errant tufts of thinning hair, faced the row of them.

"Jerry," Maria said, an offer of truce in her smile. "Come on. These people have a case. So it's not a great case. It's still

119

as good a case as it was when you signed on, and you know it."

"Okay, fine," Jerry Grundman said. "If you're so interested in telling me what I know, let me return the favor. Does that sound fair?"

"Fair enough."

"You know the only reason you're here is because I'm the *only* one who signed on. And you know darned well why."

"Because you're a good man who knows a worthy fight when he sees one."

"Please," Grundman said. "Don't insult me."

"And you know a defendant with deep pockets when you see one, too."

Jerry Grundman leaned forward and touched an index finger to the tip of his nose. "Bingo. Thank you. That's precisely my point."

"You're not making sense, Jerry."

"People with deep pockets pay big judgments," Grundman said. "Do you know what else they pay for? Big lawyers. Great big teams of them. People like the people you want to go after? KBH Incorporated? They pay for the kind of legal representation that eats people like me on club crackers, okay? I'll be perfectly blunt with you all. I can't afford to take the kind of beating you're in for on this thing."

"Oh, Jerry," Maria said. "I can't believe I'm hearing this from you."

"Well, believe it," Jerry said. He sighed heavily, adjusting his glasses on the bridge of his nose. "I am not a particularly proud man. I know what I do for a living. And believe me, I know what I don't. I also happen to know that firms with twice my resources and thrice my case talent have already turned you down cold. There's a reason for that, Maria. And that reason is, as much as I believe these good people here deserve satisfaction, you stand a darned dim chance of ever getting it. I'm sorry to be so plain, but that's the truth. It's just the way it is."

"The way it is," Maria said, "isn't one bit different than the way it was yesterday! What's changed, Jerry? Tell me. What on Earth?"

"Are you going to make me come out and say it?"

"I wish you would."

Jerry Grundman looked at her and sighed again.

"Fine." He looked at each of the five clients in turn, but didn't meet their eyes. "This stunt you pulled? It's where I get off the bus, Maria. I can't say it any simpler than that."

From where he sat, Quince could see Maria grip the arms of her chair.

"You know better, Jerry," she said quietly. "You *know* better."

"Maybe I do," Jerry replied. "Maybe I don't. But you know what? My personal opinion isn't even a blip on the radar screen."

Maria sat still. She didn't say a word.

"Maria, how many times have you been to the state board with complaints against Palm Grove this year? Ten times? Fifteen? And of all the complaints you've filed, how many have been investigated and dismissed?"

"Jerry…."

"No, now, you just wait a minute. Let me ask it another way. Of the complaints you've filed, how many have led to Palm Grove actually being fined, or even reprimanded?"

"Every complaint we've filed is based on a clear Funeral Rule violation," Maria said. "Every one of them. Don't you get it, Jerry? This is part of the problem! This is why we *came* to you."

"Zero," Jerry told her, answering his own question. "Zero times. Not once has this state's Department of Consumer Affairs validated your complaints against Moss with any kind of disciplinary action at all."

"That's not a fair way to look at it."

"It doesn't matter if it's *unfair*, Maria. What matters is, it looks like you've been harassing the place. For months! Now this? This thing that's all over the news? Do you have any concept of the kind of field day Palm Grove's lawyers would have with us? Well, I do. I get an ache in my stomach just imagining."

"Then eat some Tums! Christ, Jerry, I can't believe you!" Maria took a deep breath, let it out in a slow stream. "Tell me something. Do you really think this is harder for you than it is for these folks sitting here? If you do, well, that's the saddest thing you've said so far. These people are willing to deal with some very real pain to see this thing through."

Jerry Grundman opened his mouth to say something, but he held back. He put his hands on the desk in front of him. Quince saw him glance at the couple at the end of the row. Then he lowered his eyes.

Maria saw it, too.

"What," she said. "What's going on?"

"We're out," said the man wearing khakis and a pressed plaid shirt. His name was Bill Jensen; he and his wife, Carol, had lost her mother to lymphoma several months ago.

Maria's eyes widened. "Bill?"

"I'm sorry you're hearing it like this," Carol Jensen said. "We wanted to talk to you before the meeting. For whatever it's worth, we believe you're telling the truth about that awful protest. We do. But we also think Mr. Grundman is right. This is already turning into a circus, and we just … we just can't participate. It isn't worth it. It isn't worth making some kind of spectacle out of Mom's memory."

As she spoke, Quince saw the couple next to them whispering pointedly to one another. They were the Rolands, Tom and Susan, whose twenty year-old daughter had been killed in a spring break boating accident up in Marin county last year. Tom appeared to be doing most of the whispering; Susan looked straight ahead, a tear-wadded Kleenex balled tightly in her hand.

Maria turned to them. She said, "Tom?"

"I …" Tom began, then just looked at her. "We haven't decided yet, Maria. We're still … discussing the whole thing."

"We're not discussing anything," said Susan Roland. Her voice husky and small. She didn't turn her head.

Silence filled the room.

It was impossible not to feel for Maria in the long, hollow moment that ensued. Quince could practically see her spirit fall. He watched her turn to client #5, the elderly widow. A silent, last-ditch appeal.

Helen Carlyle paused for a moment before offering a kind, sad smile in return. She didn't say anything, but no words were needed.

Maria folded her hands in her lap. "I don't know what to say."

But then, there didn't seem to be much left worth saying anyway.

From here, it didn't take long for the awkward meeting to reach its awkward end. Ragged closure was stitched with a final exchange of regretitudes, and within a few minutes, the Rolands and the Jensens filed out of Jerry Grundman's office in a quiet line. Grundman himself sat quietly behind the desk, as though he'd weathered a rain of blows and was simply waiting for the dull pain to fade.

Quince waited for Mel to collect her notebook and bag. Then the two of them joined Maria by the door. Helen Carlyle was just on her way out. She stopped to squeeze Maria's hand supportively.

"You hang in there, honey," she said.

"Helen, I'm so sorry."

Helen patted Maria's hand, smiling the apology away. To Quince, she handed a scrap of paper, on which she'd printed in pencil the following words:

For cut and swelling—dissolve three tablespoons Epsom Salts in warm water. Soak soft washcloth. Hold over eye twenty minutes each night before bed.

While he was reading the note, he felt her give his hand a pat, too. When he looked up, Helen Carlyle had already shown herself out the door.

Five minutes later, out on the sidewalk, Maria seemed to drift in thought, at an utter loss.

Mel broke the silence.

"That was a rough one," she said. "Listen. You did a good job."

Maria gave a distant grin. Then she straightened abruptly and said: "I need a drink. Anybody care to join?"

As far as Quince was concerned, that sounded like a perfectly great idea. He glanced at Mel—his ride home—and saw a polite decline coming on.

"Actually?" Mel glanced at her watch. "I've got somewhere I need to be."

Maria nodded amiably. Then she looked at Quince again. "How about you, Boom Boom? It's going to take more than one person to drown the mood I'm working on."

Quince said, "Hang on?"

"Sure."

He walked with Mel down the block to her car. When they reached the driver's side, he said, "You're bowing out?"

"'Fraid so."

"I figured you'd want to find out what that whole train wreck was about, in there."

"I do," Mel told him. She held up the fat manila-bound backgrounder Maria Casteneda had given her earlier. "But I figure I'll work my way through this later tonight. I'll give her a call tomorrow if there's anything worth following up on in here."

Quince nodded. "Where are you going, anyway?"

"I promised I'd meet some people. No big thing. But I'm already late. Listen—go with Maria if you want. Seriously. I'll be home by, what, ten-thirty? I can pick you up somewhere later, if you want to give me a call."

Quince looked back at Maria, thinking: *why not*? If anybody looked like they needed a little company, it was Maria Casteneda of the SoCal Valley Memorial Society. And if anybody had ever felt like a beer, it was most definitely Quince.

"Don't worry about it," he said. "I'll get a cab."

Mel nodded. "Either way. Look, I need to get out of here. Have fun."

"You too," he said, opening her door. "And hey."

"Yeah?"

"Say hi to Colin for me."

For a moment, Mel just looked at him, revealing nothing but the obvious.

Then she grinned at the piece of paper he still held in his hand. "Don't forget your Epsom salts. Twenty minutes."

Quince smirked and let her pull the door closed.

After Mel pulled away from the curb, he turned and walked back to where Maria Casteneda was leaning against a parking meter. It was a warm night for October, calm and humid, salty with the promise of still more rain later on.

Maria was looking at Jerry Grundman's office door as though retracing her steps back inside—through the meeting, back to the point where the whole thing had tanked before her eyes. When she saw Quince coming, she grinned pleasantly.

"I take it you're in?"

"Hope you're thirsty," he said.

Maria shouldered her purse and said, "Hope you can keep up."

They found a yuppie after-work place a few blocks away. It featured no place to sit, no place to talk at less than shout-level, but plenty of big, wall-mounted TV screens to go around. Quince swore all forty or fifty of them were playing the same baseball game. He and Maria stood at the end of the bar long enough to down a pair of cloudy amber microbrews, then they paid up and left to seek out quieter pastures and less crowded troughs.

Along the way, he found out through preliminary small talk that she was in fact his elder, at thirty-one years last May. Currently unattached, once divorced. The divorce she described as the good-idea dissolution of a bad-idea marriage at the no-idea age of nineteen.

They ended up taking refuge at a back booth in a little corner tavern a few streets over and down. It was a dim, hazy place, with peanut shells all over the floor and a scarce population of obvious regulars. Quince ordered a pitcher of the house draft, and over their next couple of pints he learned selected additional details.

Maria had been raised in Los Angeles, where her parents had legally immigrated from Oaxaca de Juaréz before she was born. In Mexico, her father had been a carpenter; in America, he'd worked as a furniture builder in his own shop in the East L.A. barrio where they lived. As was often the vocational tradition in his home city, Maria's dad also had built coffins in the back of his store for the families of the neighborhood.

By the time Maria was a teenager, her father had phased out the furniture business altogether, finding both a market and personal satisfaction in providing sturdy, low-cost caskets for those who lacked the means for elaborate burials of their deceased.

Lisandro Casteneda had continued this occupation for nearly thirteen years. When his mother became ill back in Mexico City, he and his wife, Isabel, closed out their lives in the States and returned to Mexico. Maria, twenty-seven at the time, had stayed in California.

"But I'm sick and tired of talking about me," she said. "Your turn."

Their first pitcher had been emptied and replaced. Quince took a long pull from his freshly-poured beer, wondering how best to follow her exotic, interesting narrative.

"I'm twenty-nine," he told her. "Thirty in November. Don't have a job."

Maria nodded at him over the rim of her glass, waiting for more.

"And I bruise easy," he said.

"That's it?" She smirked at him. "That's all I get?"

"The rest is pretty boring."

DIRT

"History is never boring," she said. She sipped, watched him. "What about you and Melanie? I get the feeling there's some history there."

"A long history." He grinned. "Of a doomed alliance."

"That's too bad," she said.

Quince was beginning to suspect that they might be on their way to getting thoroughly knackered. He raised his sticky glass.

"To Guinness," he said. "Patron saint of lost causes."

"Actually, I think that's Jude," she said. "But why quibble? *Salud.*"

They clinked, tipping back in unison. Quince poured the next round.

"So tell me about this doomed alliance," Maria said. "Or shouldn't I pry?"

"You know. Boy meets girl, girl dumps boy. Girl takes boy back, dumps boy—it gets kind of repetitive."

"And how would you characterize the … current situation with you two?"

"You know what? I can't think of anything I'd rather talk about less," he said. "Your stuff is better. Tell me about that meeting, earlier."

"You know what?" Maria answered. "Let's not talk about that, either. My mood is just starting to improve."

They clinked glasses again to seal it. While the search for mutually-agreeable new topics commenced, the foam level of their second pitcher slowly lowered to the base.

By the time the barkeeper announced last call, they were the only coherent souls left in the place. Maria didn't even bother digging for her car keys. Coherent they may have been, but clearly, it was cabs for the both of them.

They decided to split one upon Quince's pronouncement that he had more beer in the fridge at home.

Buzzes were already losing fizz by the time they got back to Quince's apartment. They set about remedying the situation with bottles of Bass Ale from his lettuce-crisper reserve.

Quince began and completed the nickel tour by turning in a circle while holding out his hand. Maria complimented his taste in art, which consisted almost entirely of movie posters in cheap black aluminum frames. Tour finished, they retreated to the beat-up couch with their beers. Quince anchored one end, Maria the other, facing each other from opposite arms, each with a knee on the cushions between.

At some point during the cab ride, Maria's mood had changed. It seemed she was ready to vent a little spleen about tonight's meeting after all. As emptied bottles accumulated on the coffee table, the topic of the meeting became a springboard and was set aside. Maria gradually fell into an impassioned narrative concerning what she considered the larger point.

"What we're talking about," she said, "is maybe *the* single-most disadvantaged consumer group in America. Think about it. Most people know more about buying a used car than they do about putting together a funeral. Who wants to think about it before it's time? But when the time finally comes, and they're stunned and hurting, they're at their absolute most vulnerable. All funeral directors know this. The Walt Mosses of the world would never exploit it. But you can bet your ass some do."

Quince didn't bother asking who she believed fell into the second category. Instead, he said, "When you say exploit…."

Her answer took the form of an anecdotal litany—stories of mischief perpetrated by the smallest family funeral parlor and on up the food chain. At the top of the ecosystem sat large national funeral service corporations like Knox, Burke, and Hare.

She told common tales of price gouging that rivaled the finest monopolies in history: caskets hard-sold to uninformed buyers at markups of several hundred percent beyond the retail norm; pre-paid funeral plans designed to sap client pocketbooks over time, under the soft-spoken guise of future security and peace-of-mind.

She outlined the classic bait-and-shuffle sales strategy employed by some funeral directors on the showroom floor: the arranging of caskets in such a way that grief-stricken clients could be steered from opulence to the bargain basement, and ultimately back to some over-priced middle ground. This tactic was easily extended to the corporate chain scenario: a high-end mortuary refers a client to a low-end alternative, who in turn refers to a happy medium—each establishment in the triangle owned by the same parent company.

As she described these tactics, Maria provided background about the federal regulations established to help protect consumers from the minor deceptions and the out-and-out frauds. Quince learned that in 1984, the Federal Trade Commission had codified a set of restrictions on funeral industry practices. The Funeral Rule, as it was known, had been overhauled and updated for its tenth anniversary—and Maria believed its presence truly had made a recognizable impact for the good.

But all rules had their effective limits, their built-in weaknesses. And according to Maria, the conglomerates had more ways around the stickier wickets than an in-dash stereo rip-off artist has around car alarms.

"I'm talking about a 25 billion dollar industry last year alone," she said. "Together, KBH and the top three conglomerates handle one funeral in every four. The two largest casket makers? Combined, they handle more than two-thirds of all casket and urn sales in North America. Now, you take this kind of market share, and think of it on the local level. I've seen *priests* make kickback deals with mortuaries, where they get a cut for referring their parishioners to a 'preferred care provider.'"

Quince sipped on this one, trying to think of something clever. At this point, the best he could manage was, "So what does an immortal soul go for, these days?"

Maria ginned. "Believe me—whatever the market will bear. Is that a computer I see over there?"

"I'm writing a screenplay," he said.

"Really?"

"No."

For some reason, it struck them both as the funniest thing in the world. Maria snorted beer suds and grabbed a sofa cushion, trying not to choke to death. Quince patted her helpfully on the back until she held up a surrendering hand, indicating that she was fine, much better now, he could stop pummeling her any time.

"Reason I asked," she said. "I see what looks suspiciously like a phone line plugged in the back there. Have you got AOL, or something like that?"

"I only subscribe for the porn sites."

Maria swatted him on the ankle bone. "Come on. I'll show you something."

They broke camp and relocated to the rickety computer

desk. By concentrating carefully, Quince was able to extract the manual coordination required to boot up and log on, after which he willingly turned over the driver's chair. Maria squinted at the screen for a full minute or more. They swapped intoxicated snickers while she worked at tapping in a cryptic address.

What she'd wanted to show him turned out to be SoCal Valley's Web site, which she maintained single-handedly. Quince listened to her talk while she clicked from one page to the next.

SoCalValley Online was an impressive collection of articles, links, and FAQs devoted to funeral planning. Maria had an entire section of topic-based message boards, where users could register free of charge; here people posted questions and answers, personal experiences, or just simple exchanges of condolence and support. Perhaps her most impressive offering of all: a searchable database of wholesale price lists for funeral products and services city-wide.

"This is incredible," he said.

Maria waved her hand. "I've got a crap provider, and the server crashes about every six minutes. But you get the idea. We try to put out a print newsletter every month or two. Mostly just bulletins, articles reprinted from the mainstream press, that kind of thing."

For the first time, Quince realized they'd never actually gotten back to tonight's meeting. Not specifically. He asked her about it.

"Sealer caskets," she said, draining her current beer.

"Pardon?"

"Sealer caskets," she repeated. "That's what that whole thing with Grundman was about. Caskets with gaskets. That was the main issue we were trying to build a case around."

Quince took her empty to the kitchenette, returning with fresh beers and big plastic cups of water for each of them. Maria put a moratorium on the ale but took the water appreciatively in both hands.

Then she explained that one of the Funeral Rule's restrictions concerned the type of caskets that were commonly sold with air-tight neoprene seals.

"Of all the scams," she said, "this one might be the most disgraceful. It's a real pet peeve of mine."

Quince noted her tendency to play with her silver cross pendant while she talked. "So they can't sell those."

"Oh, they can sell them," Maria said. "What they *can't* do is make any specific claims about their protective capabilities. But it's always implied. Look. Just look here."

She clicked a link on screen, which took them to a casket manufacturer's product page. "See this big copper monster, here? Check out this description." She read part of the text she'd highlighted; the paragraph wrapped a color photograph of a casket that looked to Quince like a lidded Roman coliseum.

"'Protective seal,'" she recited. "'Manufactured and tested to be completely resistant to the entrance of air and water'— oh, here's a winner. Listen to this: 'Constructed of the same enduring material as the Statue of Liberty.'"

"Sounds sturdy."

"You bet it does," she said. "Patriotic, too. See, the pitch is, you're spending all that extra money on a casket that's specially engineered to protect your loved one's body from the ravages of time. That bit about air and water? Completely typical. The word *water* is used a lot. *Insects* and *vermin*, too."

"There's a pretty picture," Quince said.

"Of course, if you're a smart funeral director, you never

actually *say* anything about how this protective, indestructible, totally air-tight box is going to protect against these elements. You just plant the images in a customer's head and let guilt do the rest. Or better yet: you merely extol the virtues of the 'protective' casket, which naturally implies the unpleasant alternative."

The way Maria said it, it certainly *sounded* smarmy as hell. Quince took a sip of water, watching his beer bottle sweat a wet ring into the mouse pad by her hand.

"So if you're a smart funeral director," he said, "you don't say how a protective, indestructible, totally air-tight box is going to protect Uncle Ralph because…?"

"Because it's a big pile of horseshit." Maria rolled her eyes. "No casket in the world is going to stop a body from decomposing. That's a biological fact. And the truth is, the process is much *less* pleasant in a sealed casket than an unsealed one. Everybody who's ever been within six feet of a mortuary science program knows that."

"Really?"

"Oh, absolutely. Sure. That's why, when somebody gets interred in a mausoleum? Above ground? You know the first thing any director with half a brain does, after the family leaves?"

"I give up."

"Props open the lid of that 'sealed casket' so air can circulate."

"You're kidding," he said. Thought about it. "Do I want to ask why?"

"Two words," Maria told him. "Anaerobic bacteria."

He sat for a few minutes and listened. Quince recognized some time ago that he was growing fond of the tone and cadence of Maria's voice.

Still, there was something about listening to her describe the putrefaction stages of dead human tissue that filled him with a peculiar discord.

She offered a gruesome little inverse of the Tupperware theory. The sealed casket: keeps the freshness out and the nasty rotting in.

Even when a body is embalmed, she explained, the treatment is really only designed for temporary cosmetic purposes. Eventually, even a commercially embalmed body decomposes.

But natural decomposition requires at least two things: oxygen and ventilation. Cool temperatures and low humidity also are optimal. When a body is sealed off from air, however, anaerobic bacteria begin to thrive. And so, instead of simply drying up and eventually disintegrating around the skeleton, bodies in air-tight caskets actually liquefy. Sometimes gasses filled torso cavities, bloating corpses until they burst. In some cases, she said, this gas pressure became great enough to actually pop the lid off the casket. In one particular instance—documented somewhere in the South, Maria said—a casket exploded with enough force to knock a 20-pound chunk of marble from a mausoleum wall.

Quince must have looked as green as he felt, because she stopped talking in the middle of the leaky details.

"Oh, gosh—I'm sorry. This is getting to you."

"Me? No, no. I'm just listening."

"Sometimes I get a little graphic when I've been drinking. Really—I'm sorry. Are you sure you feel okay?"

Quince nodded again as his stomach did yet another slow, sloshing roll.

He didn't know what was wrong with him. Maybe it was the beer. Maybe it was the beer combined with the skull-

DIRT

thudding throb in his eye. All he knew was that somewhere during Maria's lecture on rotting corpses, a hot salty wave of nausea had washed over him like an incoming tide.

"Quince?"

"Yep," he said.

Then he bolted up from his chair.

He barely reached the toilet before vomiting explosively. When the spasms subsided, Quince spat and panted, suddenly wracked by a case of the chills. His bad eye pounded mercilessly now, with the gravitational pull of blood to his head. He made the mistake of opening his nose and good eye to the fermented mess in the bowl below. Soon he was off again, heaving up his guts until they were emptied completely, practically turned inside out and tied in a knot.

Finally, Quince rinsed his mouth in the sink and emerged once again into the harsh light of the kitchenette. Maria waited for him with a hand towel, which she'd soaked with cool water.

"I'm so sorry," she said. "Here—try this. Are you okay?"

"I'm fine," Quince said. He took the towel and held it against his face, feeling like a ridiculous idiot. He picked up an empty Bass bottle from the counter. "Guess I should've known better than to mix the Irish and the English in the same belly. It just ignores history."

"Come over here," Maria said. She took his hand, leading him gently back to the couch. "Sit down."

She sat first, patting the cushion beside her. When he took it, she patted her lap. Quince looked at her. She smirked and patted her leg again.

He thought, *oh, what the hell*, and finally complied.

Legs hanging over the arm, Quince eased back with his head on Maria's warm knee, feeling silly and profoundly content at the same time. She took the towel from his hand and folded it. Then she held the cool wet square against his blackened eye, stroking his hair with her other hand.

So this is what it feels like to be Vlad, he thought.

"Feeling better?" she asked him.

"Will you move in with me?"

Maria smirked at him again and continued to pet his head. He closed his eyes, thinking: *what a weird week this is*.

Later.

Quince wasn't aware he'd drifted off. He didn't even know he'd been sleeping until he woke up. It was just after four in the morning, according to the clock on the VCR.

Somehow, he'd moved from Maria's lap to a sitting recline in the corner of the couch. The apartment was now dark; apparently, she'd gotten up at some point, switched off the lights, and returned. Maria now slept on her side, facing the room, a throw pillow bunched under her cheek and his afghan draped over her legs. He found that he was providing lap space this time, for her bare feet.

Blearily, Quince leaned down into the narrow space behind her. For some reason, in this surreal zone of pre-dawn solitude, it seemed like a perfectly natural thing to do.

Once he'd settled, the two of them were wedged in like mismatched spoons. Because there was no place else to put it, he rested his forearm on her hip.

The last thing Quince felt was Maria's hand covering his own. Her hand took his up, until both rested beneath her chin.

Then he drifted again, back to sleep, where sunrise and certain hangovers were still hours away.

AT TEN MINUTES past midnight, beneath a low dark starless sky, Billy Guilder licked his fingers and pinched the smoldering cherry from the joint he'd just rolled. He tucked the remainder behind his ear and lifted the worklight above his head. He continued to survey the ground in front of him.

Behind him, Carl Rosen said, "We gonna stand around out here all fuckin' night, or what's the deal?"

"Gimmee a minute," Billy said. He turned to his left. Thinking: *damn*.

They were back at Palm Grove, standing in a gentle valley at the south end of the grounds. It had showered a little, about an hour ago, so they'd had to wait for the rain to quit before they could get started.

Now the air was cool and heavy with the smell of damp earth. Thin clouds covered the moon and mist hung low to the ground; even with the portable worklight, Billy could only see twenty or thirty feet at a time. In the silence, he could hear the ground sucking and popping as the little bit of new rain soaked in.

Their current position wasn't far from the Waxman plot;

Billy noticed the rain tarp had come loose, and the big pile of dirt sat silhouetted beside the open grave.

"Hey, tell me something," Rosen said.

"Yeah?"

"You don't have any idea what the fuck you're doing, do you?"

This was embarrassing.

"Let's go in for a minute," Billy said. "I gotta ask Moss something."

"About time," Rosen said. "My feet are freezing."

As they walked back to the golf cart, which they'd parked on the paved tour path that meandered through the grounds, it occurred to Billy that now might be a good opportunity to bring up the subject of work boots to Carl.

Then again, maybe this particular moment wasn't quite the best time to mention it.

"Tell you what, we can stop by my locker," he said. "I think I got an extra pair of socks in my bag somewhere."

Joel Moss poured himself three more fingers of Beefeater, licking a splash of spillage from the back of his hand. He was just considering the wisdom of another Zoloft when he heard the soft knock at his door.

"Yes," he mumbled numbly. "I'm here."

The door opened an inch. Through the gap, Billy Guilder said, "Um ... coach?"

"Billy, you can come in."

Billy complied on tiptoe, looking like he'd just wrecked the family car. "Sorry. You were sleepin', I bet."

Joel answered by holding up his drink and swirling it. Melting ice cubes clinked musically against the sides of the glass.

No sleeping going on in here. For nearly three hours now, Joel had been sitting in his robe in the semi-dark, staring absently at the muted television. Turning this day's developments over and around in his mind.

Oh, the little bastard. The dirty little bastard and his little bastardly tape recorder. Joel Moss had never been the victim of an extortion before; he didn't have the first idea what the smartest way to handle one might be. That he'd never even considered this possibility was too depressing to think about. So he'd just been sitting here, getting quietly plastered while he considered the many possible angles contained in this disappointing turn.

"Coach? You okay?"

"Fine," Moss said. Then he looked up and regarded his groundskeeper with a sudden thoughtfulness. "Say, Billy. Can I ask you something?"

"Sure, coach. Fire away."

Joel wondered how best to phrase his question. To be honest, he wasn't even sure what to ask. *It's come to this*, he thought grimly. *I'm actually looking to a convicted felon for problem-solving advice.*

"Oh, nothing," Joel sighed. "Never mind. What did you need?"

"Yeah," Billy replied. "Um … could I get that master sheet from you, again."

"Honestly, Billy. Tell me you're kidding."

Billy Guilder looked sheepish again. "I swear, I thought I put my copy back in my locker last time. I dunno."

"We've talked about this," Joel counseled. "You really need to start keeping better track of these things."

"Sorry, coach. I know."

Joel waved it off tiredly and told Billy to follow him down

the hall. In the office, he unlocked the file cabinet and flipped through the contents of the bottom drawer. He found the folder containing the master chart and slipped off the rubber band. Then he pulled out one of the many copies he'd made, knowing Billy was bound to lose his again eventually.

"Here you go," he said. "And please, Billy, try to keep track of this one, okay?"

"Absolutamente. Sorry to bug you."

The chart in question was a detailed grid map of the south end of the grounds—a sprawling, 12-acre pain in Joel's ass, quite possibly the single greatest headache his dad had passed along.

Back in the early eighties, Walt Moss had set aside this corner section of the cemetery proper for special use, becoming a volunteer subcontractor with L.A. County to help defer the district's indigent burial load.

The hospitals and city morgues in Southern California were perennially flush with the homeless dead and the intestate—folks without families, assorted John and Jane Does. Joel's father had hated the grim reality of it, and he'd felt compelled to supply dignity where he could. So he provided plots, concrete liners, cheap but sturdy caskets, and simple flat stone markers for each poor soul he took off the public's hands. The county gratefully left record-keeping duties to Walt, which he was happy to fulfill. And in this manner, over the years, he'd managed to populate a sizable potter's field.

Which had immediately become the bane of Joel's existence, administratively. He'd never had the heart to oppose such well-meaning but vastly stunted business practices while his dad was alive—but once Joel had taken the helm, he'd drawn the bottom line deep in the soil. Square foot by square foot, cemetery ground was perhaps *the* most valuable brand of real estate anywhere; where else could you pack in such a dense population of long-term residents that needed no plumbing, no roads, and no emergency services?

KBH certainly needed no convincing. In fact, when Joel had presented his analysis of the situation, they'd praised his initiative. All agreed it was high time to convert as much of the south end as possible back into marketable inventory. KBH willingly put up the cash for an extensive "consolidation and beautification" campaign.

Once the funding was in place, however, Joel had come up with an even more brilliant idea. One that saved time, even *more* money, and ultimately yielded more saleable land.

Over three weeks in June, Joel had Billy turn up all the stone markers in the south end, then go ahead and tear up the under-watered, grub-riddled sod. Joel had rented a big commercial waste bin and had the whole mess carted away. Then he simply had Billy lay new sod over the top of the site, like carpet over a water stain. Billy had spent the rest of the summer landscaping the south end up to the aesthetic standards of the rest of the grounds.

Joel was actually darned proud of Billy Guilder; by September, the place looked better than he'd ever imagined it would. Twelve idyllic new acres, open for business. Moss could now sell each used plot at full price—and after a relatively simple and inexpensive removal operation, in most cases he could even use the concrete grave liner already in place. At $450 retail a pop, he'd be turning at least that much per burial in straight profit on rough boxes alone.

Of course, they'd needed a way to determine just exactly where in the hell all those old graves were. So before the razing commenced, Joel had drawn up a blueprint on graph paper. Using the crematory as a landmark reference point, the final treasure map indicated the location of each occupied plot on a five-feet by five-feet grid.

On this particular project, Joel had to admit, he'd actually impressed himself. It was better than brilliant; it was downright ingenious. As a reward, he'd quietly used what remained of the KBH front money to add a few hundred choice small-cap stocks to his personal portfolio.

"Thanks again, coach," Billy said. He folded the chart into uneven quarters and shoved it into the back pocket of his Dickies. "We'll get her done."

"That's my guy." Moss drained his gin. "And Billy?"

"Yepper."

Empty glass in hand, Joel pointed at the charred paper cigarette Billy had forgotten behind his ear. "Mind that, now. You know I don't approve of that kind of thing when you're operating the heavy machinery."

With the map, it only took Billy Guilder ten minutes to find the right spot. Using Waxman's hole as a starting point, he walked off the distance, then measured and staked out the exact place where they needed to dig. With the turf cutter and the little Bobcat skid loader, he got the unmarked, occupied grave opened up in about an hour. Carl Rosen spent most of this time in the truck, smoking cigarettes and listening to the radio.

But he must've finally gotten bored sitting there. As Billy was finishing up, he saw Rosen hauling over the big 75-pound bags of extra fill dirt from the bed of the pickup. The guy only had to make one trip, carrying a bag in each hand.

Behind the mesh cage of the Bobcat's cab, Billy made a mental note not to challenge Carl to an arm-wrestle any time soon. He raised the scoop, killed the engine, and climbed down from the tractor.

"Thanks, partner."

Rosen stood at the square edge of the new hole, washed in yellow light from the Bobcat's headlamps. He was looking down, big tattooed arms folded in front of him. He scratched his beard and looked up at Billy.

"I gotta hear this," he said.

Billy grinned, held up a single finger, and headed back to the truck for supplies. He returned with two pairs of heavy leather work gloves, a long iron pry bar, and a sack containing four blocks of wood.

"You remember I was talking about discretion, before?"

Carl said nothing.

"Well, this would be, like, where that part comes into play." He tossed the blocks and a pair of gloves to Rosen. "Help me get this lid off, amigo. I'll show you what I'm talking about."

Given the amount of help Rosen had been earlier, when they'd picked up the old gal out in Holmby Hills, Billy half expected the guy to tell him to screw off again. But this time, Rosen seemed just curious enough to play along. He put on the gloves and stood there, hands on his hips.

"Okay, here's what we'll do," Billy said. "Watch your fingers."

With the help of the pry bar and the wood blocks, they managed to raise the heavy concrete lid of the burial vault a few inches off its base. From there, they could get their fingers under the edge and lift it out the rest of the way. Without putting down the load, Billy jerked his head in the direction he wanted to go. They sideways-walked the cumbersome slab over to the truck and eased it into the bed.

Back at the grave, the two of them stopped side by side and rested a minute at the edge of the hole.

Rosen shook out a Camel, tore off the filter, and flicked it into the wet grass by his feet. Billy found the half-smoked joint behind his ear. He snapped his Zippo and held it over to Carl, cupping one hand around the flame. Then he fired up the J-bone.

"Question." Rosen said.

"Shoot."

"The fuck's there already another coffin doing in there?"

Billy barked laughter, stuttering a ragged shot of smoke through clenched teeth. He'd been trying to hold his toke, but looking at Rosen's face, he just couldn't hang on. He giggled and coughed hard, smoke scorching his throat raw.

"Casket, first of all," he said, roughly six times more stoned than he'd been a moment ago. "They don't call 'em coffins, really."

"Gee, that's so interesting," Rosen said. "You mind telling me why I'm lookin' at one?"

So Billy did, kind of getting a kick out of the way Rosen listened. Billy was getting so he could tell when the guy was actually interested in something.

"Next question," Rosen said.

"Wait. Let me see if I know what it is. Ready?"

"Be my guest."

"What are we gonna do with it, right?"

"Check you out," Rosen said. "You're like a mind reader."

Billy grinned, took one last teeny hit, and stubbed out the roach on the sole of his boot. "We're coming to that part, amigo. Here, help me haul up this box. What we're gonna do is, we're gonna bring it up, and then we're gonna head that way." Billy pointed ahead of him.

DIRT

Then he stopped, turned, and pointed the other direction—
behind them, toward the tour path. Had to give the Rose
Man credit; this was some primo herb. Billy corrected his
direction again, this time to the left just a shade.

"The truck?" Rosen offered.

Billy cocked a wrist, sprang out his thumb and index
finger, and gave Carl a finger gun. "Zactly. You with me,
partner?"

"Whatever you say."

"Rock and roll."

He left Carl standing on one side while he went around
to the facing edge. The casket was a simple pine job with
a slight bevel to the lid. There were dirt crumbs in the
routered grooves, and the wood was stained by time, but
Billy noted that there were hand-holds notched in on both
sides. Smooth operation; no problem at all. Carl followed his
lead. They got down on their knees, leaned in with one arm
each, and grabbed a handle.

"Okay," Billy said. "One ... two ... heave."

It was a smooth operation up until the two-count,
anyway.

The problem, Billy figured later, was about three inches
of muddy groundwater that had leaked into the bottom of
the vault. He'd noticed when they removed the lid. But he
hadn't really thought about it.

At least not until the rotted bottom of the wood casket
gave way with a marshy splitting sound.

Something splashed.

Then the bottom fell out completely and the weight
balance abruptly shifted; Billy lost his grip, Carl let go of the
other side, and the whole thing crashed to jagged pieces on
the vault's hard concrete floor.

"Aww," Billy said, resting on his heels and holding one hand over his eyes. "Shit."

Carl said, "Smooth move, boss."

"I don't even wanna look."

And after a quiet minute, Carl Rosen did something that Billy had never once heard him do before now.

He laughed.

"Well," he said, "I'll say one thing. Glad I'm not you."

"Oh, come on," Billy said. "Tell me you're gonna help me out a little, here."

Rosen just leaned back from the edge and rose to his feet. He came around and clapped Billy companionably on the shoulder. Then he looked back into the hole. Smiled again.

"I'll be in the truck," he said.

"Yeah," Billy sighed. "Thanks a bunch."

As Rosen ambled back toward the pickup, chuckling softly to himself, Billy finally stood up and peeked tentatively into the hole. Down there in the dark, beneath the twin beams from the Bobcat, all he could really see was a swirl of fetid dust still settling over a jumble of fractured lumber. He thought he saw some shredded fabric poking out of the mess.

Billy Guilder didn't even want to think about what might have made that splash a minute ago. Or whatever else remained beneath the demolished casket in a shallow, stagnant pool. But one thing was for sure.

He hoped it was really, really old.

Billy looked at the mess one more time and thought, *boy, am I glad I'm stoned.*

It was nearly 3 AM before Billy finally got a chance to grab a cushion and relax awhile.

He felt like he'd been thrown off an overpass onto a

embankment somewhere. His clothes were filthy, and he smelled. His brand new Wells Lamont calfskin work gloves? Going straight in the trash, as far as Billy Guilder was concerned. There were still dried, crackling streaks of mud and God-knew-what on his wrists, elbows, and arms. At the moment, he was in stocking feet, the soggy cuffs of his Dickies rolled up to his knees. His steel-toe Timber-lands were still outside. He'd had to spray them off with the garden hose.

"So how hot does that thing get, anyway?" Rosen asked. He was leaning against the wall a few feet away, watching the big stainless-steel cremation oven—retort, Moss called it—through a pane of curtained Plexiglas.

Billy stifled a yawn with the back of his hand. "Couple thousand degrees, you get it cranking."

"No kidding."

"Around there."

Rosen whistled. "And you're saying it takes how long to char a guy down?"

"Cremate." Billy yawned again. "The *cremation* process takes approximately two hours for an adult of average weight and build."

"Hey, just asking," Rosen said. "No need to get touchy about it."

Billy leaned his head back and closed his eyes.

They'd been here in the crematory almost an hour, kicking back in the furnished viewing area while they waited for the cooling cycle to begin. Moss had the room set up to feel kind of homey, with a couch and matching chairs, lamps on end tables in the corners, a few plants here and there. Nice carpet and wallpaper. Through the window, families could see into the clean tiled room where their loved ones were being returned to ash.

And while Billy appreciated the fact that Carl finally showed enough interest to ask a few questions about the work for once, honestly, at this particular moment, he wasn't much in the mood. He'd just spent an hour carting a wheelbarrow between the new gravesite and here. The wheelbarrow, he'd also had to clean out with the hose. Billy was totally wiped. Plus, the joint he'd smoked earlier had given him the munchies in the worst way.

"Sorry, amigo." He opened his eyes. "I'm just a little beat, is all."

"No kidding." Rosen came over and plopped down in the other chair, propping a muddy sandal on the coffee table. "You ask me, you work too damn hard."

Hey, you noticed, Billy thought, but didn't say anything. He just shrugged.

"Tell me something," Rosen said.

"Yeah?"

"You really like this job? I mean, hauling stiffs? Digging around in the dirt all day?"

"Well," Billy said. "I'll admit, you picked maybe not the best time to ask. But mostly I like it okay."

"You're shitting me, right?"

"It's kinda peaceful. And mostly you get to work outside."

"Man," Rosen said. "I'm sorry—but I just can't see it. You're telling me hanging around out here doesn't depress the shit outta you?"

Billy considered this. It hadn't ever really occurred to him until Carl asked.

"Hey," he finally said. "Overall, it ain't nearly as depressing as Burger King. At least you don't have to wear some stupid hat."

"Whatever you say." Rosen shook his head and kicked up

his other foot. "All I know is, Moss don't pay us enough for this shit here."

"Um, no offense … but so far 'us' ain't exactly the word."

"Damn right," Rosen said. "You ain't gonna get *me* down there muckin' around in some dead guy for minimum wage. That's what I'm saying. Shit, look at you. You look like I dug *you* outta the ground."

"Yeah, well." Billy sighed. He closed his eyes and laid his head back again. "Whatcha gonna do?"

Rosen didn't say anything for a minute or two. They sat and listened to the oven creaking and pinging behind the Plexiglas.

Then:

"Actually, since you bring it up," Carl said, "it so happens I might have an idea or two."

"Somehow I kinda thought maybe."

"You want to hear what I'm thinking?"

Billy yawned until his eyes watered. "Sure."

"I'm thinking about that granny we picked up earlier. Out in Holmby. That was some house."

Billy opened his eyes a crack, just enough to see Carl.

"Funeral's tomorrow, right?"

"Mm."

"And you and me, we get tomorrow off. Right again?"

Billy Guilder lifted his head from the back of the chair. For some reason, all at once, it began to dawn on him where Rosen might be going with this.

Granny's house. Day off tomorrow. Everybody Granny-related would be here for the funeral.

Which made sort of a perfect opportunity for a couple big bad wolves.

Tired as he was, he had to laugh. "You ain't *even* serious."

"Hey," Rosen replied, stroking his beard. "All I know is, for an old lady, she sure seemed to know a thing or two about putting together a quality home theater."

WEDNESDAY MORNING, Quince woke
up early for his third rut-busting day in a row. A cool breeze
drifted in through the screen door, bringing with it the scent
of bougainvillea and saffron crocus from Arlen's yard. Dawn
sunlight crept up the stairs and across the landing outside.
And Quince opened his eyes to something he hadn't seen
for quite a long time.

A bunk mate.

Maria barely stirred when he sat up; he lifted his hand from
her waist and edged off the couch, attempting to keep the
cushion-quake to a peaceful minimum. As she sagged back
into the indentation he'd left behind, Maria drew in a deep
sleepy breath but didn't open her eyes. Quince straightened
out the afghan over her legs. He watched her sleep for a bit,
pondering this strange but not unpleasant scenario.

He considered waking her, but she looked so peaceful
that he didn't have the heart.

Besides: why rush the inevitable? Given the circumstances—
hopefully not regrettable, but almost certainly not expected
or planned by either of them—that awkward first exchange
of morning greetings by the light of day and sobriety would

come soon enough all by itself. Quince was willing to postpone it awhile longer.

So he tiptoed into the kitchenette, trying not to make a clatter as he built the first pot of coffee of the day.

It wasn't quite 7:30. Quince stepped into the shower while the coffee brewed, last night's winding conversation still playing on a random loop in his head. A shmuckish twinge recurred at the memory of his illustrious concert yodel down the porcelain megaphone. At least there was a minor consolation to be reaped: it had probably been a hangover-saving performance, given the ample quartage of ale Maria's peculiar bedtime stories had relieved him of.

Had to sympathize with the fact that Maria wasn't likely to wake up quite so lucky. On the other hand, did it not serve her right? Exploding caskets, for pete's sake.

Quince made a mental note to offer Advil with breakfast anyway. In the meantime, he continued his own anti-swelling regimen by popping a few capsules himself. The heavy, bone-conducted throb of yesterday had been replaced with a tolerable radiant ache, and Quince didn't bother wiping the steam to check himself in the bathroom mirror.

Instead, he poured himself coffee and took the cordless phone with him to the landing outside.

It was mid-morning in Chicago, and his first guess panned out. He reached his brother Paul doing payroll in his office above the restaurant.

"Heeey," Paul said. "I take it you finally paid the phone bill. Or are you calling from jail?"

"That's funny," Quince said.

"How you doing, little brother?" There came a pause on Paul's end of the line. "Jesus—it's like eight o'clock in California."

"Yeah? So?"

"So I thought you slept until noon."

"Please," Quince said. "A little credit."

"Seriously. Everything okay out there?"

"Everything's fine, Paul. Relax. I can't call my own brother unless something's wrong?"

"Hey," Paul said. "I'm happy as hell to hear from you. You called more often, maybe it wouldn't seem so suspicious."

Touché.

"Did you get the postcard?"

"Still life of baby in drool puddle. It's a keeper."

"We thought it was cute."

"How's the chunky monkey doing, anyway?"

"Rolling over by himself this week," Paul said. "And stop calling him that, you asshole. You're gonna give the kid a complex."

"I thought that was what uncles were for," Quince said. "Wendy's good?"

"She's great. Wants you to come visit."

"Tell her I'll make her sorry she said so."

"Not likely. So, come on! Let's have some news. You find a job yet?"

"Nothing permanent." The half-truth came so easily, Quince figured he may as well just run it to ground and make it a full-fledged lie. "Picking up a little work here and there. Part time gigs. You know."

"At least you're not hanging around in that depressing damn apartment all day."

Quince said, "That's the way I look at it."

He waited a beat.

Then he said: "Hey, Paul. Listen. Answer a question for me."

"Ah. I knew there had to be one in there somewhere." In the background, Quince could hear Paul's fingers clacking on a keypad while tape cranked out of an adding machine. "What's the question?"

"Mom and Dad," Quince said.

"Yeah?"

"How much do remember about the funeral?"

The electric ratchet of the adding machine ceased on Paul's end. "I think I've got a vague recollection. Why?"

"No big deal. I was just wondering: did Mom and Dad have sealer caskets?"

"Did they have what?"

"Sealer caskets," Quince repeated. "You know, like sealed air-tight. Or did they just have regular ones?"

"What the hell are you talking about?"

"I just wondered if you remembered, that's all."

"I was thirteen, you weirdo," Paul said. "Why would I know something like that? Anyway, Uncle Pete and Aunt Caroline took care of that stuff."

"Kinda what I figured," Quince said. "Just wondering."

"Mind if I ask why?"

"No reason. Like I said. It's no big deal."

There was a longer pause on Paul's end this time.

"Okay, out with it. What's wrong with you?"

"Nothing," Quince said. "I told you. Let's move on already, can we please?"

"I'm serious," Paul said. "You're sure everything's okay?"

Quince insisted for the third time that everything was fine, wishing now he'd never brought it up the casket thing in the first place. He truly didn't know why he'd felt so compelled to ask.

Paul finally sighed into the phone. "Listen, little brother—

I keep telling you. You should think about coming back to Chicago, you know? You're all alone out there on the coast. Wendy wishes the kid could see you more. And I could use a decent nine-ball partner. I'm getting murdered in the Wednesday league."

"We've been over this a million times, Paul."

"And I mean what I keep saying. The places are doing great, bud. Gangbusters. We'll probably open another spot up on the north side next year. So I'm not talking about charity, okay? It's getting to where I could seriously use a full-time guy in house to handle advertising. Print, radio, television—you know all about that stuff."

"I told you," Quince said. "I'm writing a screenplay."

Paul didn't bother smashing back the feeble lob. As usual, he just tried the hard sell for another minute or two before giving in agreeably. At least until the next phone conversation.

"Well, look," he said. "The holidays are coming up. You should at least think about coming back for Thanksgiving."

"Maybe," Quince said. "I don't know if I can get away."

"Hey, I'll go half on a ticket. You want to ruin my son's brain, the least you could do is do it in person."

"I'll think about it," Quince said. "Promise."

"All I'm looking for." Paul punched some button, and in the background, the adding machine whirred again. "Anyway, don't worry," he said. "You can't make it, we can always mail you a nice envelope of leftovers."

Ten more minutes of chit chat, a little more of the usual trash talk volleyed over the line, and they rang off. Paul back to his bookkeeping. Quince back into the apartment to forage for food.

Maria was sitting up on the couch when he walked in.

Her eyes were bleary and half-lidded, dark hair a tousled mess around her head. One gravity-defying feather bobbed over her brow. He caught her in the middle of a cavernous yawn; when she saw him, she sat and blinked for a moment. Then she opened and closed her hand at him. A little wave.

"Morning," he said.

"Mm." He watched as she felt between her collarbones, finding the silver cross with her fingertips. As soon she'd located it, she let her hand flop bonelessly to the cushion again. It was a curious, automatic movement—as if she were just checking to make sure the pendant was still there.

She sat with her hands in her lap then, still blinking the slumber-vision away. She looked sluggishly to her left, to her right. Toward the coffee table.

Quince retrieved her water cup from the computer desk and handed it over. He'd guessed correctly; Maria took the big cup in both palms and drank deeply, tilting back until it was gone.

"More," she said, and he laughed, took her cup to the kitchen for a refill. Maria thanked him with great sincerity and downed half of the new glass before coming up for air.

"And how are we feeling?" he said.

"Like we were trampled by horses. What time is it, anyway?"

"Eight-thirty. There's coffee on."

"That might be the most wonderful thing anybody has ever said to me."

They looked at each other. He grinned. She grinned. He grinned again, feeling like an imbecile. Maria smoothed her hair. They looked at various nearby objects.

Quince thought: *mayday*.

For here it was. That so-here-we-are awkwardness he'd

been waiting for opened like a yawning chasm between them. They stood around, avoiding eye contact like crazy.

Then they accidentally glanced at each other at the same time and broke into pathetic chuckles.

Somehow, this seemed to be all that was needed. Morning After Canyon sealed itself and disappeared.

"Just so you know," Maria said. "I don't normally sleep with a guy on the first date."

"Don't worry. If anybody asks, I'll tell 'em you got me really drunk and begged me to have my way with myself."

She laughed. Quince decided he really did like how that sounded.

"So can I get you that coffee to stay? Or do you need to get back to the world."

"You had to remind me it was still out there, didn't you?" A little smile. She scratched her scalp vigorously with both hands, fell into another yawn. "But I really should go. You've probably got a hundred things to do."

"Can't think of one."

"Good," Maria said. "Because I don't think I can move."

Around ten—their first pot of coffee drained, a second put on to brew—Mel appeared on the landing and scratched on the screen with her fingernails.

"It's unlocked," Quince said from the couch.

But she was already on her way inside. Bloodshot eyes told him she'd researched herself to sleep again. At least part of him hoped that was why she looked so tired. The hopeless sap part.

Five minutes ago, Maria, galvanized by Advil and caffeine, had managed to boost herself from his upholstered sinkhole and retreat to the loo. In her absence, Quince had been letting his mind spin, listening to the sound of water running in the sink behind the closed bathroom door.

He marveled at the strange and interesting progression of the last twelve hours, from last night's meeting at the attorney's office to this morning's coffee and timeshare bathroom privileges.

Which naturally turned his thoughts to Rhonda Waxman and the kids. He wondered what they were doing right now. Wondered how this very same morning looked to them. Thought about calling, ultimately decided to leave them be.

He wondered absently if Martin had gone in for sealed or regular.

Wondered if, when all was done, it really mattered anyway.

"Morning," Mel said. She came over and held up the fat SoCal Valley backgrounder that Maria had given her before last night's parting of ways. "Guess what? There's some interesting stuff in here. You're up early."

"Morning yourself," he said. "Believe it or not, I'm starting to get used to it. Want some coffee?"

"Had my share already. Your eye's looking a little better." Mel examined him. "Another couple days, you might just have two again."

"Gotta love those Epsom salts." Quince tried to think if he actually even knew what Epsom salts were.

Mel grinned indecipherably. "So. How *were* the drinks with Miss Casteneda, anyway?"

Quince wondered how he should tell her that Miss Casteneda was currently using his spare toothbrush.

"We had a nice conversation."

"Really? That's good." Mel eyed him. "What's the matter with you, anyway?"

"How do you mean?"

"You've got a weird look on your face."

Before he could say anything more, the bathroom faucet came on again.

Mel cocked her head at the unmistakable pipe rattle, the tell-tale rushing sound. She looked at the closed bathroom door as though momentarily confused. Then she turned to him, eyebrows arching into high peaks of curiosity.

Moments later, Maria emerged from the bathroom looking rumpled but freshly scrubbed. She'd pulled her hair back from her face using one of his bandannas—holdover headgear from his lawn service days, still employed now and then when he mowed Arlen's yard. He sometimes left them hanging around on various doorknobs.

When Maria saw Mel, Maria stopped abruptly.

And the three of them stood there in a loose triangle— each looking from one to the next, three people passing around the same paste-on smile. No canyon of awkwardness, this time. This was a half-ton Liberty safe full of awkward crashing through the floor. Quince didn't have any idea what to say.

"Maria," Mel said. "Hi there."

Maria raised a wave. "Hello."

Mel laughed and looked at Quince. Her expression was casual. But her eyes said: *Nice conversation?*

He replied: *Oh, don't even start, Miss Gotta Go Meet Some Friends*.

By way of explanation, Maria said, "We had to get a cab."

Mel glanced at the city of empty beer bottles on the table in the kitchenette and grinned at Quince again.

Then she turned to Maria good-naturedly. "This is actually kind of handy."

"Oh?"

Mel held up Maria's press kit. "I was just heading over to your office to talk to you anyway."

"YOU'RE KIDDING," said Billy Guilder. "Right?"

"You gonna keep asking me that every three blocks?"

"Seriously, though. You don't you think maybe we could find someplace a little more outta the way?"

"That's what we brought the tarp for," Rosen said. "Pay attention. Guy up there's pulling out."

"But it's broad daylight."

"Thanks for the bulletin," said Carl. "Now park the fuckin' truck, will you please?"

Billy sighed. Not liking this at all, he pulled the pickup into the newly-vacated slot next to the curb on Ozone Ave.

"Wait here," Rosen said. "I'll go talk to my guy."

"Um ... hey?"

"What now?"

"Not to be difficult or anything—but like, I'd rather not be sitting here, if it's all the same to you."

Rosen rolled his eyes and got out of the passenger side. Billy locked up and followed him to the alley two blocks down. Usually Billy loved it down here when the beach was packed like it was today. He loved all the different kinds of people you could see—the junkies and punks and Muscle Beach jocks, skaters and tourists and girls. Normally, he liked listening to the street performers; he liked walking around looking at the crafts and all the other things people had made to sell. And he loved that guy with the turban—the one who played electric guitar on roller skates. Guy had been rolling up and down this strip as long as Billy could remember. He found this kind of comforting, in a way.

But today, the crowds and color and activity just made Billy nervous. When they reached an unmarked steel door, Rosen stopped in front of it, one hand resting on the handle.

"This better?" he asked.

"Much."

"Think you can hang out all by yourself for a second?"

"I'm cool."

"Glad to hear it. Gimmee ten." Rosen yanked open the door and disappeared inside.

After he was gone, Billy found a place on the other side of a nearby Dumpster and sat down against the brick wall. This time alone was a good opportunity to repeat the vow he'd made to himself earlier in the morning.

Never let a guy like Carl Rosen talk you into anything when you're stoned.

It was 11:00 now; they'd driven straight to Venice Beach from Holmby Hills. Billy still couldn't believe he'd gone along. And now that it was all but done, he was struggling with a powerful internal conflict over it all.

In terms of home invasions, this morning marked a number of milestones for Billy Guilder. For one thing, he'd officially come out of retirement, which for once in his life he'd honestly never planned to do again. And here it turned out to be both the low point and the sweetest score of his career.

Pulling this job had been almost too easy. Ten o'clock sharp, while Granny's funeral was just getting started at Palm Grove, he and Carl simply rolled into her secluded driveway and followed it around back of the deserted house. Amazingly, she had no alarm system; three or four seconds was all it took to jimmy the sliding glass door. And fifteen minutes later, they rolled back out again. With a Sony big screen, the five-disc DVD player, two VCRs, and a primo Bose surround sound system, all loaded in the back of the truck and covered with a big canvas tarpaulin.

Sitting here now by the Dumpster, waiting for Rosen to square things with his fence, Billy tried to think back through the pretzel logic that had made this seem like such a good idea.

It's not like she's going to need the stuff anymore. That was Rosen's first line of reasoning.

"Yeah, but that don't exactly make it okay," Billy had said. "I mean, you gotta have principles."

"So it's the *principle* you're worried about, I guess."

"All I'm saying is, it just don't feel right to me. Ripping off a dead old lady before she's even in the ground."

"Well, see, there's your problem right there," Rosen had said. "'Cause you already ripped her off. You just ain't looking at it clearly, is all."

"I must not be." Billy remembered laughing. "You mind explaining that one?"

And Carl had leaned forward and explained it this way:

"The way I see it, it's like these weasel dicks that turn back the odometers on cars. Moss? He sold this sweet old lady a bunch of used stuff like it was brand new. And he's already turning a sweet profit anyway—you said so yourself. But he sees he can stick it to Granny even more, and nobody'll never know the difference. You know why?"

Billy hadn't been able to think why at the time.

"'Cause he's got *you* out there, doing all the dirty work for him."

"I guess I never really thought of it that way."

"No other way to think of it," Rosen had said. "And what do you get out of it? A day off? Gimmee a fuckin' break. Now listen. I got a confession."

"Yeah?"

"That guy, Waxer."

"Waxman?"

"Whatever. Point is, I took that watch off him. Guess you probably figured that."

"I had a suspicion," Billy had admitted.

"But you notice what *I* did is, I gave a little back. Little something extra for your trouble. 'Cause that's the way it should be."

"Hey, it was a nice gesture," Billy had told him. "Ass-kickin' weed too, by the way."

"Not nice. Just fair. And it didn't hurt nobody, either. But this guy Moss? Now here's your guy with no principles. Moss, he's just trying to scam this Waxer family outta the expensive coffin they paid for—and he's havin' you do it for him. And the whole time, insulting your Goddamn intelligence. Thinking you don't know any better."

And Billy had to admit: at the time, Carl Rosen had started making sense, in a loopy kind of way. Especially after two hours scooping up muddy bones and some really not-so-pleasant mulch that he didn't want to think about anymore.

But now, by the light of day, Billy Guilder experienced a

misgiving or two. Rosen definitely had a point about Moss—and he was right about another thing. The Holmby score really was kind of a smart plan. If you were looking for a score, anyway.

But in that house, hauling out Granny's stuff like a couple moving men, Billy couldn't help feel like he was doing a shitty thing, somehow.

And more importantly:

This morning—restored by a hot shower and a few hours' sleep—Billy remembered with a clearer head just how decent life on the outside really was, overall. How much liberty and independence was involved in sitting down to a nice sticky breakfast cinnamon roll, warmed in your own microwave.

When you got right down to it, life on the outside was grand. Even your worst day was still better than the best day behind razor wire.

And when he thought of the pickup truck, now parked on the street and loaded with hot merchandise, Billy thought: *I must be totally stupid.*

When he heard the steel door open again, Billy got up and brushed gravel from the seat of his pants. Carl Rosen emerged from inside, holding a piece of paper in his hand.

"Next stop," he said, showing Billy the address.

Billy looked. "That's down by the airport. We're going the other way."

"Not yet, we ain't." Rosen said. "First, we're gonna go down to my guy's warehouse and unload. By the way: here. Little bonus from Gerald Kinghorn for early delivery."

Billy took the small object Rosen handed him, feeling the ounce-weight of it in the palm of his hand. It was a short little smokeless brass pot pipe; it had some little decorations carved into it, and there was a removable wire screen in bottom of the dime-sized bowl.

Billy looked at the pipe, looked at Carl, looked at the sky.

"Let's go," he said. "But can we, like, hurry it up some?"

Wondering if they had any chance of getting back to the mortuary before the boss realized they'd borrowed the utility carts from the storage room.

The warehouse turned out to be as quick a trip as Carl said it would be. No hassles, no holdups, no problems at all. They were back in the break room at Palm Grove by 1:00.

Billy sipped a nice cold Coke feeling much better about everything. Granny's funeral had broken up only a half hour ago, leaving plenty of time for him and Carl to get back, replace the borrowed gear, and stop up for sodas from the vending machine. He had eight hundred bucks in his pocket—their take from the warehouse split two ways. At this moment, it was getting harder and harder to remember exactly what he'd been so conflicted about before.

At least until he looked up and saw Moss standing quietly in the doorway, the coat of his dark, expensive funeral suit hanging over one arm.

"Enjoying your day off, fellas?"

Billy jumped. "Hey, coach."

"Billy."

Billy tried to grin but felt his lips trip over each other. "No tree freaks today, huh?"

"Not today." Moss looked at them. "What are you two up to?"

"Forgot something in my locker." Billy tried a little laugh.

Moss just nodded. Billy couldn't read his face at all.

"Carl," Moss said then. "I'd like to talk with you for a second, if you don't mind."

"Oh, yeah?" Carl said. "What for?"

"Why don't you step into the office for a few minutes?"

Rosen just shrugged, like it was no big deal.

But in that silent moment, Billy felt his heart drop like a stone. He looked over at Carl. Rosen didn't look back. He just ambled out, cool as anything, following Moss down the hall.

And Billy Guilder let a cold, numbing wave of paranoia flood his brain.

Shit, he thought. *Shit shit shit.*

Carefully, he crept to the hall and peered down at the closed office door.

Moss knew something was up; that look on his face said it all. Billy had seen the same look on school principals and cops his whole life long. And the principals and the cops had always done it this exact same way, too: swoop in, then divide and question. See where the stories don't match up. In a few minutes, that door was going to open. Rosen was going to come out. And Moss was going to look at him. *You next.* Billy Guilder knew it as sure as he was standing there.

All of a sudden, his mind swam with all the things he hadn't even thought of until now. Of *course* Moss knew they'd taken the carts. The guy lived here, for crying out loud. He knew everything.

And what if the police called here, after Granny's family reported the burglary? Moss had given Billy and Carl the day off, knew they had the truck. He'd put it together. Or he'd wonder, anyway. He'd wonder for sure.

What would he say? Normally, Billy wouldn't have

worried; Moss had covered for him with his parole officer for little things a couple times before. But with everything else that had happened this week, maybe Moss wouldn't want to risk it this time. Maybe he'd be a little suspicious himself. Maybe he'd start thinking some neighbor out in Holmby could have seen the truck somewhere....

Shit. What if the police had *already* called?

Billy closed his eyes tightly, repeating two key words to himself.

Shit. Shit. Shit.

Alibi. Alibi. Alibi.

He repeated them with increasing anxiety, watching the silent office down the silent hall.

When the door finally opened again, Billy ducked back into the break room. He hurried to the sink and leaned back against the counter, trying to look casual.

When Rosen returned—alone—Billy dipped his head and whispered: "Shit, man, what's going on?"

Carl was smiling. He had a weird look on his face, like he didn't know whether he was puzzled or amused.

"Hey," Billy repeated. "What'd Moss want?"

"Don't worry," Carl said. "You ain't gonna believe it anyway."

"Believe what?"

Rosen gave him a funny look that didn't tell him anything. As Carl turned and walked back out of the break room, Billy leapt from his spot and hurried to keep up.

"Seriously," he said. "What's the deal?"

Rosen was still grinning, heading for the stairs. "Looks like the bossman needs a little favor done," he said.

"A what?"

"A favor," Carl repeated. "You know. Somebody gets in a

jam, they ask you to help 'em out with whatever it is, then they owe you one. You maybe heard how it works?"

Billy sighed. He was starting to notice that sometimes Rosen had a habit of talking to him like he was stupid. He hoped it was a phase.

"What little favor?" he said. "What are you talking about?"

"Put it this way," said Carl. "You and me? Far as Moss is concerned, anybody asks for some reason, we been here on the clock all day."

QUINCE REMEMBERED clearly the first time he and Mel had realized they were all wrong for each other.

It happened in Mr. Pulaski's classroom at George W. Norris middle school in Palatine, Illinois. Eighth grade. He'd just gotten Mel her very first detention ever, after convincing her to skip fifth-period study hall to go make out with him under the bleachers by the football field.

Melanie Roth—honor student, captain of the junior debate team, editor of the student yearbook, and by far the hottest girl in morning gym—had been torn between two feelings: guilt over her own poor judgment, and disappointment in him for not appreciating the gravity of the situation.

And Quince Bishop—who focused his extracurricular energy mostly on comic books and who, although brighter than average, had never gotten better than a C$^+$ at any subject in his young academic career—had been equally disappointed in her for not sharing his personal belief that ten lousy detentions would have been worth it. Twenty. A detention a day.

At the time, the whole thing had seemed to Quince a

relatively minor philosophical impasse on a road otherwise paved with thrilling romantic possibilities.

Little did he know that this day of adolescent ups and downs would set the stage for a great many ups and downs to come. The two of them had been disappointing each other for over a decade now.

Love was never the problem. Or maybe it was their worst problem of all. For Quince couldn't imagine two minds more consistently divided where the same hearts were so obviously joined.

The trivial differences? They numbered in the hundreds. Mel lived for music first thing in the morning; jazz, classical, rockabilly, top-40—anything and everything, depending on her mood when she opened her eyes. Quince couldn't stand the racket right off the bat; it gave him a headache before his feet ever touched the floor. He liked to stay in and cook, she preferred sampling new restaurants. She liked meeting new people, he was antisocial on his best days. They both loved movies, but their tastes couldn't have been more polarized. She liked *cinema*, cerebral and subtitled; he just wanted lots of stylish suspense and a few bullets whizzing through the air.

Quince took too much comfort in routine; Mel feared stagnation so much that she could scarcely repeat a good joke.

Neither of them understood the other when it came to handling money, and trying to figure each other out sexually was like nosing through frequent pockets of clear-air turbulence.

Over the years, they'd broken it off over all these reasons at least once, and for any others that seemed good at the time. That Mel was more often the initiator was simply a function of her natural take-charge personality; that they invariably gave up on other people and gravitated back together again, Quince generally took as a sign that they probably belonged that way. It was Mel, after all, who'd sold him on college at UCLA after she'd been awarded a journalism scholarship at the school, even though they'd officially been quits at the time.

That had been six breakups and an adulthood ago.

Sometimes, it seemed to Quince that he and Mel were destined to remain part of each other's lives, if only to torture each other in perpetuity. He honestly couldn't imagine a life without her in it.

But then, love was never the problem.

For that matter, neither were the flashy but meaningless border skirmishes that continually divided their personal territories. Earlier this year—as they were poised on the brink of their most recent and long-lasting separation so far—Quince had told Mel exactly what he thought was their problem.

If we were in a lifeboat, he'd said, *we'd be rowing like hell. In opposite directions.*

And Mel had replied: *I'd be rowing like hell. You'd be asleep on your oar.*

"What do you think she's going to do?" she asked him now.

"Maria?"

"Huh? No. Rhonda," Mel said. She looked at him oddly.

He looked back at her.

And Mel sighed, fingering the handle of her coffee mug. "I can't even imagine. I can't imagine what she must be going through. I mean, the kids—God, it's bad enough for those two sweet little kids. But what on Earth is *she* going to do? She doesn't even have a college degree."

It was Thursday morning. They sat in their dress clothes, in his apartment, sipping coffee at the folding table in the kitchenette. They'd returned from Martin's private second ceremony at Palm Grove a half-hour ago. It had been a strange and disorienting morning, standing in the quiet cemetery around Wax's closed quiet grave, listening to Pastor Mike read some scripture about a river, while the eight or ten of them who'd been asked to attend stared down at the single wreath Rhonda had placed on the bare hump of dirt at their feet.

"She'll figure it out," Quince said. "Somehow she'll figure out a way to get up tomorrow, she'll figure out a way to make sure the kids know she's there, and then she'll figure out how to do it all over again the next day."

"I don't know if I could," Mel said. "If I was her."

"You would. So will she."

They sat quietly for a little while. Quince felt Mel pondering him.

"So I guess I don't need to ask what's on *your* mind," she finally said.

"How's that?"

"As long as we're almost speaking of Maria Casteneda. Couldn't help but notice you two seemed awfully comfortable, yesterday."

"I told you. We had an interesting conversation. Lots of booze. That's all."

"I'm only asking," Mel said. "You don't have to defend yourself."

"Who's defensive?"

Mel grinned over her mug. "You like her. I can tell."

"She's a nice person."

"To be totally honest, I get the feeling you're probably

174

right." She raised her mug to her lips. "Planning on seeing her again, then?"

Quince shrugged, as though he hadn't given it much thought one way or another.

In fact, he was meeting Maria tonight. Upon her request— a strange and interesting request, at that. One he still couldn't say he genuinely understood.

Not that he minded. The truth was that he'd been thinking about Maria almost constantly since yesterday, and he was looking forward to seeing her again. However peculiar the circumstance.

"What about you?" he said. "You and the stock broker getting along?"

"Colin's very sweet."

"Great." Quince finished his coffee. They looked at each other across the table for a minute. Traded smirks that were almost grins.

"Move to change the subject?" Quince offered.

Mel grinned. "Motion carries."

Quince sealed it by nodding toward the living room. Her softsider sat on the coffee table, bulging as though it had recently eaten something whole.

"I take it the research is going well."

"Spent all afternoon yesterday in the library," she said. "Plenty to read on the plane."

"The plane? Plane to where?"

"That's what I was going to tell you. I'm flying to Seattle tomorrow morning." Mel looked at the date counter on her watch. "Be gone until Sunday night—I'll leave a number where you can get ahold of me."

"When did this come up?"

"Just yesterday," she said. "Turns out there's a big industry convention going on this weekend—Maria told me about it, thinking I might want to check it out. She's being very helpful, isn't she?"

"Oh, give her a break, Mel."

"I'm teasing," Mel said. "Just wanted to see how you'd respond."

Quince smirked and said nothing.

"Anyway," Mel said. "I called the registration number this morning and set up a press pass. Even talked the paper into pushing a last-minute expense account through channels for me."

Yesterday, Mel had surprised Quince and Maria both with a piece of news. After looking over the background material Maria had given her, she'd gone straight to her features editor and sold a pitch for a weekend package about funerals. To Quince, Mel had later described the angle this way: *everything you need to know about the inevitable*. It was already slated to run as a special insert in the Living section.

"Mind if I make an observation?" Quince asked.

"Why would I mind?"

"You seem very into this thing all of a sudden."

"All of a sudden I am."

"I thought you wanted out of the human interest biz."

"All I ever said was that I was sick of the fluffy bunny pieces," Mel said. "This is a good story. Besides. You can't ignore the extras."

"Ignoring things is easy, Mel. You just have to put your mind to it. Like me."

"Mm. And you've got the black eye to prove it, right?"

"That's my point exactly."

She smiled a little. "Oh, boo hoo. Now look at it like a

normal person for a change. What about this whole corporate buyout thing? Don't you think that's kind of interesting?"

"Not really."

"Come on. It's practically a secret, for pete's sake! Doesn't that just sort of naturally pique your curiosity?"

Quince shrugged to indicate that no such piqueing had occurred. "Companies do that kind of thing all the time, Mel. What's the big deal?"

"Maybe it's not," she said. "That doesn't mean it isn't information people deserve to know."

"Still," he said. "You've got to admit. Compared to trapezing dog stories, it's pretty boring stuff, Mel."

She'd written that one last year. A circus-trained Schnauzer from Pasadena. This was one dog with tremendous upper-body strength.

"Allow me to quote the venerable Philly newsman Gene Roberts," Mel countered, "who said that basic investigative reporting is 'not so much catching the politician with his pants down or focusing on a single outrage, but in digging, digging, digging beneath the surface so we can help our readers understand what's really going on in an increasingly complex world.'"

"Well," Quince conceded, "I guess there's plenty of places to dig in a cemetery."

"Besides," Mel went on. "If it turns out Palm Grove really is pulling even half of the crap Maria alleges in the stuff I read? Like this one lady. Want to hear a quick one?"

Quince shrugged. "Sure."

"Maria has an older lady who says she was spreading her husband's ashes out in the flowerbed. Around the rose bushes. Which is what he'd wanted, apparently. Anyway. This woman claims she found a piece of metal in there with hubby. Didn't know what it was. Do you want to guess?"

"He was a cyborg?"

"Funny," Mel said. "But not so far off, actually. Turns out it's a little piece of a pacemaker. But you know what?"

"What."

"She says her husband never *had* a pacemaker."

Quince just looked at her. Mel grinned and nodded. "Yeah. You tell me."

"I don't get it," he said.

"Neither did the rose bush lady," Mel said. "Which is why she went to Maria, who took it to the state Cemetery Board in Sacramento."

"What happened?"

"Nothing," Mel said. "Maria says they haven't heard a word since. That was three months ago."

"And she thinks…."

"According to Maria, not everybody is comfortable observing the actual cremation of a loved one," Mel said. "So they just take the urn home afterwards. Maria believes that Moss is cremating people two or three at a time, divvying up the leftovers, and just wrapping 'em to go.

"You've got to be kidding. Why?"

Mel shrugged. "Who knows? Save time, maybe? I have no idea. Besides. I'm not saying that's what he *is* doing. I'm just saying that's what Maria suspects."

Quince just shook his head.

"But if it *is* true?" Mel said. "If you ask me, somebody needs to find a good public wall and nail that guy's ass to it."

"Let me guess. You'll be the one with the hammer?"

"Did I mention Moss will be attending this convention I'm going to?"

"You don't say."

"I figure, you know. Maybe we'll run into each other at the bar."

"You could've been a Bond girl."

Mel stuck out her tongue. "Hey. If this guy really does have any skeletons…."

"So to speak."

"Poor choice of clichés. The point is, I doubt your average funeral director is going to see any reason to feel especially threatened around their friendly local lifestyles writer." Mel tilted her head sympathetically and batted her eyelashes. "Especially if she all she wants is to give him a chance to talk about the business from *his* point of view for a change. Not like all those other dirt grubbers, looking to pull a Mike Wallace on honest, hard-working folks like himself." Now she grinned and sat back. "What do *you* think?"

Quince thought he could almost picture Mel grinning just that way while she bought this clueless conventioneering bundle of fun a drink. Sometimes, you had to admire the thought patterns at work inside Mel's brain. It really was sort of beautiful, in its own way.

"Okay," Mel said. "I need get out of here. I've got about a billion things to do before I leave."

He walked her to the door. She picked up her bag, then stopped and unbuckled the straps.

"I almost forgot." Mel dug around inside for a minute, then came out with a book. "Here."

"What's this?" He took the slim hardcover volume and turned it over in his hand. The book was titled *The American Way of Death*, written by a woman named Jessica Mitford.

"Maria loaned it to me. It was in with all the other stuff in that envelope. I finished last night."

Quince opened the book and leafed through the first few pages. The tome had obviously been around awhile; the pages had yellowed with time, and the brittle spine creaked when he opened the book. He checked the copyright: 1963. Which made this a first edition.

"What are you giving it to me for?"

"Careful with it," Mel said. "It came with one of those little yellow sticky-notes asking if I'd be gentle and not spill anything on the pages or tear any of them or fold the corners."

When he got to the title page, he noticed the book had been signed by the author. The inscription read: *For Maria. Keep the faith, dear. From one import to another: America needs more like you!* The note was signed: *Decca.*

"What am I supposed to do with it?"

Mel tossed back a sly grin on her way to the door.

"When you see Maria tonight," she said, "do me a favor and return it for me?"

He didn't take the book along.

But around six o'clock Thursday evening, Quince picked Maria up at the SoCal Valley office on Wilshire Boulevard. She met him at the car. For this date of sorts, Maria wore a light autumn dress and a small purse on her shoulder. In her hands, she held a big colorful bunch of flowers wrapped in a cone of green tissue paper.

"Hi there," she said.

"Hi. You look great."

"Ready to go?"

He walked around the car, jiggled the door handle, and wrenched open the passenger door, which had been tweaked months ago when somebody had backed into him in the parking lot of the video store. The hinge popped loudly, and flecks of rust sifted onto the curb.

"Last of the gentlemen," she said.

"I'm real smooth with the ladies. Be careful of the seat cushion—I think there's a spring poking through over there on the left side."

Fifteen minutes later, as they entered the Palm Grove parking lot, Maria said: "It's such a nice night. Why don't we walk?"

So Quince found a parking spot beneath the broad canopy of a stout, bearded shade palm. Side-by-side, they strolled along the winding pathway toward Wax's grave.

When Quince had asked her why she wanted to do this, Maria hadn't really been able to explain. But for whatever reason, it seemed very important to her that she come here and pay her respects personally. Quietly, and without intruding. Maria hadn't known Wax from any generic somebody she might have passed on a sidewalk somewhere. Still, she wanted to do this. It seemed to Quince almost as if she felt some kind of apology were necessary.

On his cue, they left the path together and cut across the lawn. They hadn't been speaking much, just sharing a comfortable silence in the pleasant October air.

But as they forged onward, Quince noticed Maria had a curious look on her face. She turned her head this way and that way; she looked back in the direction they'd come.

"Anything wrong?" he said.

"Oh … no." Maria looked over her shoulder. "Just lost my bearings for a second. I think."

"You sure?"

"I'm okay. Sorry. Never mind."

They walked along. On their way to Martin's resting place,

they passed a new grave Quince had noticed earlier today. Flowers covered the fresh mound. He saw brass tureens on either side of the headstone stuffed full of carnations in whites and pinks and reds.

He also saw somebody on one knee in the grass at the edge of the grave. As they drew closer, Quince recognized him as that groundskeeper from Monday morning. The one who'd helped him chase Skull Punk and the other tree people away.

"Evening," the groundskeeper said as Quince and Maria passed. Then he looked closer at Quince and said, "Oh. Hey there, man."

"Hi," Quince said.

The groundskeeper stood up and brushed dirt from the knee of his pants. He grinned. "Quince, right?"

"Good memory. Billy?"

"You got it." Billy stuck out his hand. "How you doing?"

"Not so bad." Quince shook with him. "This is my friend, Maria. Maria—Billy. He works here."

"Hi, Billy," she said.

"Howdy," Billy Guilder replied.

Quince noticed the groundskeeper had already glanced at her several times. He imagined almost any guy would. Billy gave her the same friendly grin and shook her hand, too.

Then he looked back Quince's way. "Some shiner you got there. That happen the other day?"

"Guess I stuck my nose where I shouldn't have."

Billy shook his head. "Man, you do a good deed. What a deal, huh? That was crazy. I gotta tell you, though—you were totally cool."

"Kind of a screwed-up situation," Quince said.

"That's a fact." Billy looked at the flowers Maria held. "Guess you're heading that way now, huh?"

"Thought we'd stop by."

"What about you, Billy?" Maria said. She nodded toward the headstone marking the grave. "Did you know her? Martha Reynolds?"

"Nah. Just an older lady we put down yesterday. Buncha grandkids. Nice old gal, lived up in Holmby—I don't know. Just felt like coming by for a minute."

"That's sweet," Maria said.

"No big deal."

Maria smiled. "Say, Billy—can you tell me something?"

"Sure," Billy said.

"It's been quite awhile since I've been here. But the place looks great. Have you renovated, or something?"

Quince glanced at her. The question seemed odd to him. Completely out of the blue.

But Billy Guilder seemed to know what she was talking about. "Yeah, a little," he said. He grinned, as though proud she'd noticed his efforts. "Been workin' on it, anyway."

"That's great," said Maria. She looked around. "Fantastic. You can really see the improvement."

"Hey, thanks. That's nice to say." He grinned at the both of them. "Guess I better get back to the shop. Let you two go visit your friend. Real sorry you got to, by the way. Condolences."

"Thanks, Billy," Quince said. "You take care."

"Same to you."

As Billy Guilder moved on, Quince turned to Maria again.

"Shall we?" he said.

"Hmm?" He'd caught her looking all around the area one

183

more time—the flowers she'd brought for Martin in one hand, her free hand upon her hip. She wore what seemed to Quince a contemplative squint.

He bent his elbow.

Maria seemed to shake off whatever was distracting her and smiled.

"Let's," she said, taking his arm.

"HEY," Billy Guilder said.

From the passenger seat, Carl Rosen sighed. "What now?"

"Not to, like, belabor a dead horse into the ground or anything—but what are we doing out here?"

Venice again, approaching midnight. They hung a ways down the beach, past the point where the street lights ended along Ocean Front, a few hundred feet beyond the pier. It was another dark sky tonight, heavy with clouds, and they'd been waiting here in the truck for almost half an hour. The beach and the boardwalks and the side streets behind them were deserted as far as Billy Guilder could see.

Deserted except for them: two guys sitting with the engine off and no headlights, windows down for air.

"Just, you know," Billy said. "Wondering is all."

There looked to be some kind of demolition project going on nearby during the day; the abandoned heavy equipment slept like hulking dinosaurs all around. Carl had told Billy to park behind a big stackpile of rusted water pipes—out of sight, but where they could still look out over the dark water with a clear view of the dark pier.

"I already told you," Carl said.

"No, you didn't."

"I didn't?"

"Nope," Billy said.

"Maybe I didn't." Carl raised his head now, eyes fixed straight ahead. "We're waiting for that guy."

Billy looked out the windshield where Rosen nodded, toward the slouching silhouette moving across the sand.

"Who's that?"

"You mean you ain't got it figured out by now?"

"Would I be asking?" Sometimes Billy wished Carl would just talk to him like a regular person for a change.

"That's our favor," Rosen said. "Cool out for a second. There he goes."

They watched the guy walk beneath the pier and disappear into the shadows. Carl didn't say anything for about five minutes. Billy was getting more and more anxious to know the score.

"Okay," Rosen finally said. "Let's hit it."

"Hit what? Listen, I'm not liking this. You gotta tell me what's going on."

"Relax," said Carl. "Just delivering a message. Come on."

They got out of the truck and set off across the beach. Carl ambled with his hands in his pockets, breeze flapping at his shirt tails. Billy wobbled and veered beside him, getting rotten footing with his work boots in the deep sand.

When they reached the midpoint of the pier, Rosen stopped at a fat, salt-crusted footing. He pulled a Camel out of his pack and lit it.

As the flare of the match chased away the shadows a few feet in front of them, Billy caught a quick glimpse of the guy they'd followed. He stood by another support post further in, like he was waiting for somebody.

"Nice night," Carl said.

"Yeah," said the guy in the dark. "Maybe you could take a hike and let me enjoy it in peace."

Carl stepped underneath the pier. Billy followed, too curious not to.

"Look, fella, occupado," the guy said. "Find another spot to blow each other, okay?"

"Hey," Billy said then. To his surprise, he recognized the guy's voice. As his eyes adjusted, he could make out the gleaming white lump of bandages covering the guy's nose. "I know you, you shit. You're that tree freako."

The guy stiffened against his post and said: "What is this?"

Billy came up next to Carl. Carl took one drag off his cigarette and dropped it to sand between them. The sand was damp and packed under here, where it was cooler, musty with the smell of creosote and sea-soaked wood. Beams criss-crossed over their heads.

"Glad you finally showed up," Carl said. "We was starting to wonder."

"And *you* are?"

"We're a coupla guys got a message for you," Carl told him. "Message is, Moss can't make it."

The guy looked at them. He stayed quiet for a minute or so. Billy could hear the bright echo of the water lapping against the pilings up ahead.

"Is that right," the guy finally said.

"Said to tell you he's real sorry. Prior commitments, you know how it is."

Billy heard the tree hugger snort.

"Should've known that guy'd pussy out," he said, kicking off the post. "Whatever. Toss the salad then, errand boy."

Carl looked at Billy. "Salad? Sorry, Mick—you're losing me."

"That's funny. You don't look lost to me."

Carl shrugged.

"You better not *even* be telling me Moss sent you dipshits without the money."

Now Carl frowned, like he was confused. He looked at Billy again. "You bring any money?"

"What money?"

"Moss didn't tell us anything about any money," Carl said.

"Didn't, didn't he?" The guy just kept looking at them. He shook his head, as though he were hearing the words, just not believing them. "Tell you what, you can give him a message from *me*, okay? Tell him the sale's over. Price just went up big time. See you two assholes around."

Billy didn't have a clue what had just happened. But he didn't say anything. As the guy tried to walk between them, Carl stepped into his path.

"What's your problem?"

"No problem here, Mick," said Carl. "You got any problems, Billy?"

Billy said, "I dunno."

"See?" Carl grinned. "No problems. You might say me and my man here are totally problem-free."

"Oh. Oh, *I* get it." The guy took a step back, looked back and forth between the two of them. He snorted again. "I guess you two must be the guys who are supposed to scare me off, huh? That it? That limp dick Moss is trying to go and use his head again, isn't he?"

A sharp-edged laugh.

"Sorry. Ain't gonna work. And you can tell him he better

get a fuckin' clue who he's dealing with, here. Next time he jacks me around, trust me, it ain't gonna be a pretty thing."

"We ain't here to scare you, Mick." Carl shrugged again. "I don't know about Moss's dick, though."

"Yeah, I bet. And stop calling me Mick. That's not my name."

"Why," Carl said. "You want me to call you Keith instead?"

"What are you *talking* about?"

Billy Guilder just listened, feeling like he'd walked underneath the wrong pier. None of this made a bit of sense to him.

But for some reason, he suddenly clicked on what Carl Rosen was playing at with the names.

"I guess you ain't a Stones fan," Carl said. "Shoulda known."

The guy just looked at him blankly.

"The Rolling Stones," Carl explained. "You know. The band?"

"I know who the Rolling fucking Stones are."

"Then you know what they say."

Another blank look from Mick. Or Keith. Whichever they were calling him now.

"Billy. You know what they say about rolling stones, right?"

Billy knew. And he guessed this was probably the right pier after all. He sighed and said: "No moss."

Carl pointed at him. *Bingo.*

"I'm outta here," said the guy.

But when he tried to make a wide arc around them, Carl's hand flashed out like a striking rattler. Billy didn't even see the whole thing; he just heard Mick let loose a quick, high little gurgle of pain.

From there, everything happened fast.

"Gotcher nose," Carl said.

Billy saw that he did. The knuckles of his first two fingers were clamped down hard on the guy's bandages. Billy winced.

"Leggo, you fucker!"

Carl twisted instead. The guy screamed once, tried to lean away, then dropped to his knees.

"Atta boy, Mick. Now whaddaya say let's bite some sand?"

This time the guy obeyed without hesitation. He flopped down on his belly, arms and legs spread-eagled. He looked like he'd just washed up that way, some bizarre mutant starfish left there by the tide.

Carl walked around behind him. Billy followed quickly. "Um … hey," he said.

"Yep?"

"Whatcha doin?"

Carl grinned and didn't say anything. He just started humming a little tune as he planted a sandaled foot in the middle of the guy's back. He stood up on that leg, as if testing his weight. The guy grunted heavily.

While all this was going on, Billy finally recognized the song Carl was humming.

It was that old Stones tune, which he swore he must have drank beer and played pool to about a million times. "Sympathy for the Devil."

"Okay!" the guy said. He panted into the sand. "Okay! You made your point!"

"You know what?" Carl said to Billy. "You're right. Work boots would be a lot more effective for this kinda thing."

"Guys! Hey, guys. Okay."

"Mick," Carl said, reaching behind his back. "Hush, now. You're embarrassing my man Billy, here."

And Billy couldn't say anything. Because all of a sudden he was frozen where he stood. One minute, he was just hanging out, wondering what Moss had gotten himself into, feeling maybe just a little hurt the guy had automatically gone to Carl about it instead of him. The next, he was watching Carl reach up under his shirt and pull a revolver out of his waistband.

"Hey," Billy said. "Carl. Jesus."

But Carl Rosen didn't say a word. He just hummed along and pointed the gun down at the back of Mick's head. When Mick heard the unmistakable double-click of the hammer drawing back beneath Carl's thumb, he started to wiggle, calling out: "Guys! Okay! Please!"

When Carl fired, Billy jumped and squeezed his eyes closed out of reflex, like somebody had lit off a firecracker by his ear. The sound of the gunshot echoed sharp and loud through the pilings beneath the pier. The powder-hot bite of cordite wafted to his nose.

Silence.

"I don't fuckin' believe this," he heard Carl say.

When Billy opened his eyes, Carl was still standing with his foot pressed hard in the middle Mick's spine. He was looking at the revolver in his hand like it had to be some kind of gag.

Mick was still alive; he'd covered his head with both hands, and he was trembling. Billy saw a dark stain spreading in the sand beneath him. At first he thought it might be blood. Then he realized it was just where Mick had let his bladder go.

Carl leveled the revolver and pulled the trigger one more

time. Billy jumped again with the sound. His ears were ringing and buzzing now. He felt like he was dreaming.

Meanwhile, Mick flinched like he'd taken an electric current from the ground. Wet sand flew, and a big divot appeared beside his right ear. But that was all.

"Unbe*lievable!*" Carl shouted.

Beneath his sandal, Mick began to weep quietly.

"Please," he sobbed. "Please. Okay."

"Yo, Carl," Billy said. "Hey. Ease up already, huh?"

"Can't you two fuckin' blabbermouths see I'm trying to concentrate?" In one motion, Carl lifted up his foot, straddled Mick, and leaned down to press the muzzle of the pistol firmly against the hard bone behind Mick's ear.

"Carl!"

Without a word, Carl Rosen pulled the trigger a third and final time.

This time, Mick spasmed. Then he shuddered. Then he laid still, fists uncurling one finger at a time.

Mick's head was still cocked to the side, facing Billy. Cheek against the sand. His eyes and mouth were open.

Billy just stared. He'd gone numb all over. The sound of the lapping water became a foamy roar in his ears.

"Fucking Gerald," he heard Carl say. "I'm gonna give that guy a piece of my mind. I can piss straighter than this fuckin' piece fires." A pause. "Hey. What's your deal?"

Billy looked at him. He looked back down at the guy laying there, at the pulpy mess near his head on the sand, then took his eyes away quickly. He felt his gorge rising.

"Earth to pothead," said Carl. He snapped his fingers. "Hey."

"He's dead," Billy said.

"No shit. Wouldn't you be?"

"Dude—you fuckin' *shot* him."

Carl Rosen rolled his eyes. "You're an observant son-ofabitch, ain'tcha?"

"What'd you *do* that for? Geez!"

Carl didn't say anything. He just lit another cigarette and prodded at Mick a little with his foot.

And all at once, Billy felt like he was waking up from a trance.

"Shit—we gotta get out of here." He slouched down behind the nearest footing and looked all around. Up the beach, down the other way. "We gotta get out of here, man!"

Carl just slipped the revolver back up under his shirt. "Take it easy, Dog Day Afternoon. We're going."

"What about *him*?" Billy glanced at Mick's body one more time and thought he might puke after all.

"What'd you think I wanted you to bring the plastic for? Shag ass back to the truck and grab it. I'll make sure he don't go nowhere."

Billy pressed his face against the scaly support post, no idea what to do. Briefly, he considered heading back for the truck, getting in, and tearing the hell out of there. But he was too scared to do it. He was too freaked out to do much of anything.

So he just watched Carl bend down and pick up something about the size of half-dollar from the sand. With a sick feeling, Billy realized it was a piece of the tree dude's skull. There was hair on it. Carl snorted and snapped his arm, skipping the skull fragment out over the shallow water between two pilings up ahead.

Billy groaned.

"You're still here?" Carl clapped his hands. "Chop chop, huh? We can't sit around *here* all night."

"I...."

"Plastic," Carl repeated. "Truck."

Billy didn't know what else to do.

He headed for the pickup in a running crouch, scanning the dark vacant beach in all directions every step of the way.

QUINCE WASN'T exactly sure how it had happened. He rolled onto his side and asked Maria if she had any idea.

"I attacked you, that's how." She smiled up at him, cheeks still lightly flushed. Her hair was a wild dark mess on the pillow beneath her head. She'd pulled the thin sheet up over her hips and stomach, clutched it just beneath her breasts.

The smile alone was worth losing a gunfight over.

"That's funny," he said. "I don't remember it that way."

"I was sneaky."

He laughed. She sighed and stretched, arching her back. Impulsively, he kissed her flat tummy through the sheet and put his hand over the spot to hold it there.

In truth, Quince honestly couldn't say who had made the first move between them; he couldn't remember that thrilling, pivotal moment at all. One minute they were chatting pleasantly. The next thing he knew, the two of them were just sort of … happening.

After visiting Wax at the cemetery, they'd stopped for a bite at a little deli nearby. They sat at a table outside, and conversation flowed.

Somewhere between the apple cobbler and dusk, the conversation finally dried up, and neither one of them had the energy to keep a new topic afloat. They were tired, both of them nearing the exhausted end of a exhausting week.

But neither of them admitted to being quite ready to part company, either. There was a video store nearby; Quince had suggested they rent a movie and spend a couple hours doing their best impression of sofa cushions back at his apartment. Maria had thought that sounded like a terrific idea. So they picked a flick and headed for his place, swinging by the SoCal office to pick up Maria's car on the way.

And somewhere between there and the microwave popcorn, they found themselves in a slow deep lingering kiss that just sort of carried them all the way to his futon and beyond.

"Personal question?"

Maria laughed. "Under the circumstances, I don't see why not."

"Catholic?" he asked.

For a second, she looked at him curiously. Then she seemed to realize that she was fiddling with her silver cross. Maria grinned.

"Lapsed, I think would be the term."

He nodded along. "But not fatally, I presume?"

"To tell you the truth, I've never been sure about that. Never say never, right? But it's definitely been shaky since I was nine or ten."

"Sounds like you got a good head start."

"My poor father. I think that was when he started losing his hair."

Quince smiled, trying to imagine Maria as a nine-year-old budding agnostic. He pictured this abnormally mature, headstrong little girl with a heart-melting smile and lively eyes and a crisis of faith on her hands.

"Personal question number two," he said.

"Why with the cross, right?"

"I know I'm prying."

"You're officially allowed." Maria lifted the pendant in her fingers so that he could see. It was small and hand-made, slim but sturdy, with a delicate filigree carved across its beveled surface.

"Beautiful," he told her.

"It belonged to my grandmother," she said. "Abuelita, on my mother's side. She lived with us, helped Mom take care of me and my brothers when we were growing up. It was my brothers she needed help with. I was an angel."

"Naturally."

"She made us kids all call her 'Abuelita' instead of 'Grandma.'" Maria smiled. "She was always afraid we'd lose our Spanish living in America. Now *she* was a Catholic. And stubborn!"

"You two must have made a pair."

"You couldn't even imagine. Around and around, we'd go. About anything and everything. Not even my brothers would get in the way; they'd just clear out of there and listen from under the porch outside." Maria's eyes gleamed fondly while she talked about it. "Then they'd all have this great time laughing at me when I had to sit in the corner or do extra chores."

"You loved your grandma a lot." He didn't know why he bothered stating the obvious.

"Oh, we loved each other," said Maria. "That part was

never in doubt. But I think there were times that woman would have strangled me, if she hadn't been so afraid we'd both go to hell if she killed me."

Quince grinned.

"My grandmother was definitely what you'd call *tradicional*," Maria said. "Very old-ways. She had no idea what to make of so many of the things she experienced here in Los Angeles— but that never mattered to her. Or to me. She was still just this great, tough woman who believed *unequivocally* in what she thought were the important things. Faith in God, faith in family. Doing right by others. And damn well holding your ground. That was what always impressed me about her, even when I was little. Her faith in what she believed was just so strong." Maria smiled. "You could always feel it. You felt safer, just knowing she was there."

"Must be in the genes," Quince said.

"I make you feel safe? That's so sweet."

"I meant the stubborn part."

Maria laughed and hit him. "When Abuelita died, my mother had all us kids come and pick out one thing of hers to keep." She fingered the cross. "I took this. To my Grandma, it was just another symbol of her religious faith, and she always wore it, every day. But it always seemed like more than that to me. It's everything I think of when I think of her."

He touched the cross once with a fingertip, then rested his hand on the sheet over her hip. "I'm glad I pried."

"Does that mean it's my turn?"

He grinned. "Fire when ready."

"Actually," Maria said, "in keeping with the theme of Catholicism we've established here … it starts with a confession."

"Now I'm definitely interested."

Maria pulled her pillow out and turned it lengthwise, propped it against the wall, and punched her fist into it a couple times. Then she sat up and scooted back, holding her side of the sheet in place at her waist with one hand. Quince thought he could probably look at her in just that position for days.

"Yesterday morning," she said. "You got up first, while I was still sleeping."

"I decided not to wake you."

"Technically, I wasn't asleep."

"Technically?" He tilted his head at her. "How would you actually define that? Technically not sleeping."

"Just sort of laying there with my eyes closed."

"You faker!"

"Well." She batted her lashes at him. "About *that*, anyway."

"If you think pumping up my ego is going get you absolved … actually, you're probably on to something. Proceed."

"I'm sorry." She covered her face in her hands, mock-shameful. "It was silly. But we hardly knew each other! I admit it: I was a little embarrassed to be waking up on your couch, wondering what you thought of me, not ready for that awful first few moments gawking at each other, first thing in the morning, trying to think of something to say … so I chickened out for an hour or so."

He drew a cross in the air in front of her. "Forgiven, child."

"That wasn't the whole confession."

"There's more?"

"A little." She held up two fingers, half an inch apart. "While I was lying there on your sofa pretending to be asleep, I overheard you talking on the phone outside. A brother? That was the feeling I got, anyway."

"Paul," Quince said. He'd forgotten all about the conversation until just now.

"I heard you ask him if he remembered something. About your parents' funeral."

Talk about a great way to eliminate that troublesome afterglow. Quince looked at her for a moment, wondering what he should say about the subject.

Fair was fair, he supposed. He'd tossed the religion card, after all. She'd seen it and raised him a childhood trauma. He figured it'd be rude to fold this early in the game.

"They died when me and Paul were kids," he said.

"Oh, Quince." She touched his hand. "I'm sorry. How did it happen?"

"Car wreck," he said. "Drunk driver on a bridge. They were coming home from an office Christmas party."

"How old?"

"Dad was thirty … five, I guess. Mom was thirty-four."

"I meant, how old were you?"

"Six."

"God." She pulled his hand up and kissed a knuckle. "You must have been devastated."

He shrugged.

"You don't like talking about it, do you?"

"I guess it doesn't very often come up."

A pause. She watched him.

"Are you mad that I asked?"

He squeezed her hand. "Why would I be mad?"

Quince could feel her studying him a moment longer before looking away.

"I felt guilty for finding out the way I did," she said. "It just didn't feel right, discovering this really personal thing of yours without you knowing. I thought about it all that day."

"No need to feel guilty," he said.

"Well." Maria smiled. "At the risk of swelling your head, to tell you the truth, mostly I was just thinking about seeing you again. But then tonight, at dinner, you said something that made me start thinking again about what I overheard."

"What did I say?"

"It wasn't anything, really," Maria said. "Just that line of yours—that bit about … how did you say it? Struggling to find the discipline to maintain your goal-free existence?"

Quince rolled his eyes. He said the dumbest damned things on dates.

"I got the feeling you were sort of kidding around, but not really."

"I was just blabbering. It was stupid."

Maria shook her head. "No—I thought it was funny. I really did. But it also made me think. And I realized there's something missing in this apartment. Something most people have, in some corner or other."

"A vacuum cleaner?"

"Pictures. I mean, photographs."

This caught Quince off guard. "How's that?"

"You know. Photos. Paul. Your folks. I just noticed that you don't really keep any around."

He shrugged. What was he supposed to say?

"It just made me think," Maria said. She snugged her hip a little closer to his leg. "I've been thinking about when my grandmother died. I was only fourteen, but I was crushed. Completely torn to pieces. I remember thinking: *this is so unfair!* And you know, I didn't even go to the funeral. It was like I decided it was up to me to play the conscientious objector, or something."

Quince listened, wondering why she chose to tell him this.

"I can't even explain to you how much I regret that now," Maria said. "There just aren't words. But at the time, you know, I was just *completely* unwilling to accept the fact that she was gone. Then I got really pissed off about it. I mean, I hated *everybody* for awhile, just for being alive and not being her. I flunked every class in school that next semester. I even got suspended once."

"For what?"

"Kicking a teacher."

"No kidding? Where'd you kick her?"

"Him," Maria said. "And you don't want to know. It wasn't my finest hour, let me tell you. My poor father. He thought I had a brain tumor or something."

Quince didn't say anything.

"It was a long time before I really, truly figured out how to deal with my grandmother's death," Maria went on. "Sometimes I think I'm still figuring it out. But back then— it's kind of funny, looking back now. All those pine boxes my father made for other people—and I never really even gave it a second thought. Abuelita was the first person *I* ever knew who died. The first person close to me, anyway. And for a long time after, I think I just walked around with this attitude like *oh, what's the fucking point?* You know?"

"You felt betrayed," Quince said.

"Oh, completely. A hundred percent. One day, there's my grandma making tamales, healthy as a horse—and then the next day … poof? She's just *gone*? I couldn't accept that. I just couldn't get my head around that one at all. That teacher— sometimes I still think I should track him down and send him a card or something. Here's this poor guy, he's just doing his job, and I'm like: *don't you get it? You could get smeared by a bus tonight, you stupid idiot! And you expect me to give a shit about* geometry?"

"Seems forgivable," he said. Wondering if that teacher of hers was still teaching somewhere. Wondering if he'd ever been punted in the balls over the Pythagorean theorem at any other time in the ensuing years of his career. "You had big things to deal with at the time."

"I know," Maria said. Looked at him. "And *I* was fourteen. I can't even imagine what it would be like for a six-year-old."

For a second, Quince just looked back at her. Then he said, "I guess I'm not sure what you're getting at."

"I'm not *getting* at anything." She jostled him with a shoulder. "I'm just saying that no kid should ever have to face that kind of reality at six years old. I can't imagine what it must have been like for you."

No. What she was saying was that he didn't keep any family photos around the house. That was what had started this whole side trip, as if family photos were some kind of prerequisite to talking to your damned brother on the telephone. *That's* what she was saying.

Implying … implying just exactly what, he didn't know.

"Quince? Did I say something wrong?"

Quince supposed that what he was doing must have been what Mel was talking about when she said: *now you're just sulking. Cut it out.* He looked at Maria and felt like a complete asshole. He didn't know why he was being so touchy about this all of a sudden.

"You didn't do anything." He tried a grin and kissed her hand, cupped both of his around it. "I don't know what's the matter with me. Sorry."

"For what? You don't have a thing to apologize about."

"I guess it's like you said. I'm not really very good at talking about it."

Silence for a minute. Maybe two.

"I'm the one who should be apologizing," Maria finally said. "I was digging around where I don't have any right. Forgive me?"

"Stop it. Of course."

"I just like you," she said. "A lot. It brings out my nosy side. What can I say?"

"Going for the ego again," he said. "Always a good plan." Taking her hand with him, he leaned his head back and looked at the ceiling. "But for the record?"

"Please," she said.

"Not everybody keeps pictures in frames. Some people have shoeboxes, you know."

Thinking to himself: *even if they never look inside.*

Silence again. Somewhere between awkward and comfortable—a truce where there had been no real battle.

"Hey," she said. She shook his hand. "You still feel like watching that movie?"

Quince was not amazed to find that—despite the residual heaviness of the moment—he most certainly did. It was one of his all-time favorites: *The Big Sleep.* Maria had never seen it before.

At the moment, he couldn't think of a better plan for finding their way back to the evening's earlier mood. So he found his cutoffs and popped the popcorn while Maria hopped in the shower, emerging ten minutes later in her rumpled dress with wet, fresh-smelling hair. They snuggled in the couch like teenagers, balanced a big bowl of popcorn between them, and rolled tape.

Maria hooted at the witty banter between Bogart and

Bacall, finally clapped with delight while the mono-recorded score swelled and the credits rolled.

Afterwards—to his surprise and dismay—she collected her purse and kissed him goodnight.

"You're leaving?"

"It's late."

"Exactly," he said. "Stay."

Maria stood on tiptoe and kissed him on the chin. "I had a wonderful time tonight. The best I can remember."

"Me, too."

"Which is why I think it's time we retreated to our corners."

"What for?"

"Call it a personal hangup—but after knowing each other only three days, I can't let myself wake up in your apartment for two of them."

Absorption time, if you please.

"Plus, I've got a cat that needs to be fed."

"I guess the last thing I need is a jealous cat to win over."

Maria grinned. "Do you eat breakfast?"

"Some days."

"Then it's my turn to make it. Be at my place at nine. And not at the office—I mean my apartment. I'll write down the address. Deal?"

"Deal," he said.

"Fair warning," she said then. "Over breakfast, I have another confession for you."

"Another one?"

"I should have told you before now—but honestly, I didn't expect things would happen quite this way."

"What is it?" he said.

"It'll keep until tomorrow."

"Hey," he said. "No fair."

She grinned and stood on tiptoe again. He kissed her.

She kissed him back. Then left him standing there, wanting more.

WHEN THE KNOCK he'd been waiting for finally came, Joel drained the last watery dregs of his gin. He wobbled to his feet and used the dim blue flicker of the television to feel his way through the dark to the door.

"Coach."

"Billy," he said. "It's about time. What's the matter? You look terrible."

Joel's groundskeeper stood silent in the doorway. Even in the darkness, Joel could see the man was pale as a glass of milk.

"Billy?" Joel sagged. With Billy Guilder, there always had to be *some* kind of glitch. It was practically inevitable. "What's the matter?"

But Billy couldn't seem to focus long enough to verbalize his angst.

"Did you guys meet ... the party? Did he show?"

"He showed."

"Well did everything go okay? Billy? Talk to me."

"I think you'd better come with me, coach."

"What's wrong?"

Again, Billy Guilder failed to respond. He'd already turned his back.

Joel watched as his groundskeeper shambled back down the darkened hall.

Big problems. Oh, just huge.

As Billy reached the staircase and descended out of sight, Joel struggled into his robe and slippers, sloshed a neat puddle of gin into his empty glass, and took it along.

Maria Casteneda finally stopped kidding herself. Because it was either that or lay awake staring at her bedroom ceiling until dawn.

Leaving Quince's apartment after midnight really had been the last thing she wanted to do. But if she *was* going to give in to her cautious intellectual side—if she really planned to enforce this withdrawal to separate personal spaces—at least she wanted to enjoy the feeling she was taking with her. Maria wanted to bask awhile in the residual endothermic warmth of the evening's chemistry. She wanted to curl up with a pillow, maybe a glass of wine, and spend some time savoring this tingle of newness and possibility.

She felt entitled to savor it a little. It had been a depressingly long time since she'd felt anything remotely close. Too long. As far as Maria was concerned, she was due.

So much for indulging that underflexed emotional side.

Despite what she told herself she *should* do, Maria only stopped by her apartment complex long enough to check off the top three or four things on the list she'd formulated on the drive home.

First, she fed Annabella.

While the cat made a production of ignoring her, Maria logged on to her computer and fired off the quick email she'd already composed in her head. Then she headed for the bedroom, where she peeled out of her dress. Down to bra and panties, she considered her options, finally changing into her black jeans, a dark ball cap, and the darkest clean T-shirt she could find.

Dressed, Maria grabbed her camera bag from the hall closet. It had been so long since she'd used it that she paused long enough for a brief equipment check, finding plenty of juice in the batteries and plenty of film to spare.

Then she locked up, got in her car, and headed back to Palm Grove.

The place had been nagging at her all evening, ever since they'd gone to visit Martin Waxman's grave. At first, she'd tried to convince herself that her memory was flawed. But she knew it wasn't.

Less than a year ago, the area where Quince's friend was now buried had contained more than a decade's worth of maintained paupers' graves. Maria remembered perfectly. In fact, she'd personally nominated Walt Moss for the *Times'* annual "civic contribution" award for his volunteer efforts, which in her opinion had gone unheralded for too long. The paper ended up selecting Joel's father from an impressive pool of fellow nominees. Maria still remembered how Walter Moss, with heartfelt appreciation, had turned the award down.

And even though the groundskeeper had confirmed her suspicions earlier in the evening, he hadn't answered Maria's biggest question of all.

Because she hadn't heard a thing about the renovation. And she was sure that news of a project of this magnitude would have made its way into the papers. Not even Joel could dig up more than a hundred bodies without *somebody* catching wind.

Parking her Mazda two streets down, Maria boosted herself over the low perimeter wall and entered the cemetery grounds on foot. She took only her camera, a spare roll of Ilford black-and-white film, and the Mag-Lite she kept in the trunk for emergencies.

Working from memory, Maria confirmed what she already knew.

Everything she remembered about Palm Grove's south end had been transformed into something other than it was. Flat ground, once regimented by dignified ranks and files of simple stone markers, had been replaced by artfully landscaped slopes and valleys and gentle berms. There were several new flower gardens connected by a lush, slate-paved memorial path.

Gas-fed "eternal flames," currently the rage amongst the Ford Explorer crowd, burned here and there in the darkness. Shadows crept in tendrils beyond the random flickers of torchlight.

Maria remembered there had once been a short, rough granite slab out here, inset with a small cast-iron placard. The iron offered what Maria considered a touching verse of remembrance to the anonymous dead. She remembered that the *Westside Weekly* had run a photo of that very monument a couple of years ago, alongside a regular column featuring local family-owned businesses.

Maria saw now that the granite memorial had been replaced by an extravagant, rock-bordered serenity fountain, which drained down four long shallow tiers into a glassy reflection pool. Nearby, she saw that Joel also had added a trio of large new rose-marble columbaria, each wall flanked by two clusters of slender young palms.

Maria hiked all around the area, soaking her sneakers and

cuffs in the damp grass. She wondered how much dough Joel had managed to sink into this serendipitous new fleece-yard of his. Knowing Joel, it couldn't have been more than a fraction of what he expected to yield.

She completed three full circuits around the new and improved south end, growing increasingly bellicose with each round. Maria used the flashlight only when absolutely necessary, hoping to minimize the possibility of getting rousted by some night attendant making rounds.

Along the way, she snapped quick flash-photos of the new gravesites dotting the remade landscape. Martin Waxman. Martha Reynolds, where they'd run across the grounds-keeper earlier. Three or four others.

After an hour, Maria was tired and depressed and ready to go home. She was just preparing to break down her camera and pack it away when she heard what sounded like voices.

She listened. Heard nothing. Then voices again, soft in the distance.

Maria had always noticed that night in a cemetery played odd acoustical games with sound. She stood quietly and drew shallow breaths. She focused on the stillness all around; it was nearly a sound itself, trapped and batted about by the monuments, muted by the absorbent earth.

In another moment, she saw the beam of a flashlight bobbing toward her. The voices were clearly audible now, rising as they neared. Two of them.

For some reason she couldn't pinpoint, Maria had a powerful gut reaction. She shrank behind a nearby headstone, tilted forward on her knees, and peered off into the dim ambient moonlight.

Under cover of darkness, two figures made their way across the lawn. The first person she thought she recognized, if only by his stride. It had to be Billy, the groundskeeper she'd met with Quince earlier.

Several feet behind him tramped a man in heel-slapping house slippers and a billowing silk lounging robe. With Chinese dragons on it, for pete's sake. He carried what looked like a highball glass in his hand. Maria didn't need good light to know who she was looking at. Everything about him was familiar.

She watched them all the way to their destination. A pickup truck, parked behind the crematory.

There they joined a third person who waited by the tailgate of the truck. Maria followed her gut again.

She swapped out her lens for a telephoto, shouldered her camera by its strap, and broke position.

Cloaked in the same graveyard night, she slipped from her hiding place and stole across the lawn, to the shelter of the next-nearest mausoleum.

"Sweet mother of Jesus," said Joel Moss.

Standing there in the cool misty night, girded only in pajamas and his open robe, he looked at his groundskeeping staff disbelievingly. Gaining nothing from their blank, workmanlike stares, he turned his back on the both of them. Drink in hand, Joel stood and peered once more into the bed of the pickup, feeling his stomach pitch and plunge.

"Billy? What *is* that?"

Behind him, Billy Guilder didn't say anything.

But Carl Rosen said, "Guy in your line of work has to ask?"

Joel stared at the object Billy had dragged him all the way out here in the middle of the night to see: a large, oblong, plastic-wrapped bundle with shoes.

"No," he said. "No, no. Oh, no."

"Yup," said Billy Guilder.

"Tell me," Joel muttered weakly. "Tell me you didn't do what I think you did."

"Piece a cake," Carl Rosen said. "Problem solved."

For a minute, Joel Moss worried that he might finally have over-medicated himself. Because he was almost positive that this couldn't be happening.

"You ... you *killed* him?"

"Didn't exactly take a pulse or anything," Rosen admitted. He squinted one eye while he took a drag from his cigarette. "But if he ain't dead, he needs a motherfuckin' doctor, I'll tell you that much. I mean STAT."

Joel stared blankly. The tip of Rosen's cigarette brightened; the muted orange flare cast shadows over his craggy bearded visage.

Suddenly, a dizziness came upon Joel. He felt as though he were losing himself in that single burning focal point of the cigarette. It was as if his damp slippers had lifted from the cold dewy grass; Joel felt minuscule, as though he were floating toward that burning ember, into the ash.

Distantly, he heard Rosen say, "Don't mention it."

The sarcasm in his voice snapped Joel back to his warping reality.

"Is this your idea of a joke?" He gulped his gin so quickly it spilled over his cheeks and dripped from his chin. He began to pace a short, erratic path.

"Gotta admit, it's kinda funny."

Joel looked into the back of the truck again and squeezed his eyes tightly closed.

"What have you done?"

"What I said I'd do," Carl said.

Joel had no words. Desperately, he looked to Billy Guilder. But Billy had retreated from the conversation entirely. He now sat a few feet away, at the edge of the halogen pool cast by the flood lamp overhead. Billy leaned back against the stucco wall of the crematory, sucking earnestly on a short metal pipe while he held the flame of his Zippo to the bowl.

"This isn't what we discussed," Joel hissed. "*This* isn't what we discussed at all!"

"Um ... yeah," Carl Rosen replied. "Correct me if I'm wrong, but did you or did you not ask me could I help you out of this little jam here you got your dumb ass into?"

"I didn't ask you to *kill* anybody!"

"Take care of it for me," Carl said. "That's what you said. I'm basically quoting, now."

"I didn't say kill him! Jesus! What's the matter with you?" Joel began to pace again. "Oh, God. This is ... oh, good God."

"Don't worry about God," said Rosen. "He wasn't in on it."

Joel's mind spun. Internally, on some fear-sick, booze-muddled level, he recognized that he needed very badly to think. Joel struggled to collect himself enough to assess this horrific new turn of events in a clear and rational fashion. But one more peek over the tailgate of the truck was all it took to shut down his brain like a bad fuse.

"Carl," he said. "Listen to me very carefully. This is bad."

"Is if you're that guy," Carl agreed. He flicked his cigarette butt out into the wet grass, where it died with a sizzle. "Real bad night to be *his* punk ass."

Joel tried to maintain focus by taking even, measured breaths. "Carl. You don't understand. We've got big problems, here."

"Who?"

"We've got to think about evidence." Joel could feel his panic level rising.

"Don't worry," said Rosen. "Ain't any. No witnesses, that's for sure. Gun's clean. And the rest of it here's gonna fit in a shoebox in a couple hours." He grinned. "You know, you got yourself a real nice setup here for this kinda thing, by the way. I gotta admit. This is almost fun."

"Oh, really?" Joel wheeled on the man. "Well, you've just got it all figured out, don't you? You've just thought of *everything*. Is that it?"

Rosen winked. "Little secret? Case you didn't already know? You ain't exactly dealing with an amateur."

"Oh? Oh *no*? Well tell me, Mr. Big Shot. Mr. Big Shot Professional. What did you think he was *blackmailing* me with?"

"Okay, now, see, this is the point where you seriously need to chill." Carl folded his thick tattooed arms. "I can recognize you're maybe a little agitated here, little boozed up, so I'm willin' to let some shit slide. But I got a tolerance level, now."

"No wonder you two brain surgeons keep getting put in jail!"

"Okay. Now one of us just ain't listening."

"Troglodyte!" Joel shrieked.

To this, Carl said nothing more in reply. He merely stood with his arms folded, gazing toward a truck tire thoughtfully. In a minute, he scratched at his thick Civil War goatee with the fingers of both hands. Then he lit another cigarette and shot twin streams of smoke from his nose.

"I'm not, like, what you'd call a word expert." He gestured vaguely with the cigarette. "So I'll give you the benefit of the doubt on that last one. But starting now? Asshole, you better think real careful about the next word comes out your mouth."

"Tapes," Joel said. "There's a word for you."

"I'm supposed to know what the fuck you're talking about?"

"*He ... had ... tapes!*" Joel cupped his hands around his mouth, enunciating each syllable as though speaking to a dimwitted child. "That's what I was supposed to pay him for. Tapes with *me* on them! Okay? Tapes that *somebody*, at *some* point, is going to *find!*"

From over against the wall, Billy Guilder leaned his head back against the chalky stucco and let out a quiet moan.

"Tapes, huh?" said Carl Rosen.

"That's right." Joel let out a long breath. "Tapes. God knows how many of them."

"You're right," Rosen said. "That's a bitch."

"It's a nightmare," Joel corrected. "That's what it is."

"Guess you shoulda been a little bit more detail-oriented when you asked that favor, huh?"

Joel blinked at him. With dim amazement, he thought: *This bovine thug actually has a point. He's actually right.*

And in that moment of realization, all Joel Moss could do was stand in his PJs in the middle of his grandfather's cemetery and let the enormity of the situation wash over him. In a moment, an odd calm followed.

Even in his compromised state, Joel could visualize a damage control plan assembling itself in his mind. The strategy appeared before him in the form a bulleted list.

Priorities.

"His wallet," he said. "What was in his wallet?"

"Please," said Carl Rosen. "I look like the kinda guy steals off a dead man?"

"Driver's license," Joel said, mentally checking off the points on his growing punchlist. "We can find out where he lives from his driver's license. Carl—you and Billy. You've *got* to go find those tapes for me."

Carl Rosen had lit yet another cigarette, upon which he now pondered thoughtfully. "That'd be smart," he agreed.

"Okay," Joel said. "Okay."

"Only problem," said Carl.

Joel waited, as Carl Rosen grinned through a cloud of smoke. Somehow, the look on his face alone was enough to resign Joel to what he somehow knew—intuitively—was coming out of Rosen's mouth next. But he asked anyway.

"And that is?"

"Me, I'm fresh out of favors," Rosen said.

"What does that mean?"

"Means this one's gonna cost you."

"Oh, you're a piece of work," Joel said. "You really are."

"That's what I like, working for you. We understand each other."

Joel sighed. "Let's just cut the crap, Carl. How much are we talking about?"

"Haven't really priced it out," Rosen said. He shrugged, nodding toward the truck. "How much was he charging, outta curiosity?"

And Joel—who liked to think of himself as a man who had developed, over the years, a unique ability to absorb life's many cruel jokes with a kind of serene fatalism—wished he could truly appreciate the numerous poetic ironies at work before him now.

What he was, however, was a man who instinctively plunged a hand into his robe pocket and chased down his bottle of pills.

From the wall, Billy Guilder said, "Coach?"

"What is it, Billy?"

"Think I could borrow a couple of them?"

"You most certainly may not," Joel said. Without looking at Billy, he shook a capsule into his palm. He swallowed it dry, capped the bottle, and dropped it back into the pocket. "And by the way? Billy?"

"Yeah?" Billy sounded glum as glum could be.

"I," Joel informed him, "am *extremely* disappointed in you."

Ball cap turned backwards, one eye glued to the viewfinder of her Canon 35mm, Maria thought: *Oh, that's cute, Joel. We're wearing Gucci slippers, now?*

The three-hundred-millimeter lens she'd attached to the camera body had plenty of reach to bring her three targets into crisp close-up from her hiding spot a hundred feet away: Joel, Billy, and a man she'd never seen before. The third man looked to Maria like either an outlaw biker, a carnival ride operator, or a middle-aged philosophy grad who might or might not have been emotionally stable.

Maria stayed in her crouch, knees and hips screaming bloody murder. For awhile she tried individual close-ups, thinking she could try reading lips through the view finder. A wasted effort. Billy merely sat off, a mute and distant third point in the triangle, with what looked like worry in his bloodshot eyes; the other guy, the taciturn tattooed one, wore a shaggy goatee that obscured what few words he seemed to utter; and Joel just pranced around flinging his arms like a maniac, rarely turning his face to the lens long enough for Maria to decode a word. Periodically, he looked in the truck—an act which seemed to renew his distress all over again.

Maria widened her angle, picked a slow shutter speed, and snapped off a few frames. Thinking: *What in the heck have you got in there?*

Maria continued to shoot the three of them where they'd gathered around the tailgate of the pickup truck. She couldn't risk using a flash, and she had no Earthly idea if there was enough ambient light from the quarter moon and the crematory floods for the photos to turn out. She remembered enough from the beginning photography class she'd taken at the local community college to know that even small movement would develop into little better than a blurry smear at this shutter speed, so she steadied the lens atop the chunky square headstone to cut down the camera-shake as best she could. After a few frames, she opened the aperture a bit and tried a quicker shutter, hoping to cover her bases enough to get at least a couple legible shots.

For she was willing to bank on that original gut instinct, which intensified by the minute. Joel was up to something. She knew it. She knew him too well.

Interesting, under the circumstances, that she'd decided to bring the camera along. A one-time fiancée—initially prone to sweet but somewhat overly-zealous displays of woo—had set her up with the gear in the first place. Once, Maria had made an off-hand remark about taking up photography someday, and he'd run out and bought her this pro-grade Canon body, both lenses, and a bag full of accessories as a surprise. Personal policy would normally have dictated that she box up the extravagant gift and mail it back to him after the relationship had ended. But for some reason, Maria never had gotten around to it.

At the moment, she couldn't help but ponder the irony. The shutter snapped beneath her finger and the auto-wind hummed quietly in her ear.

Soon, she saw Joel stalk out of the frame, his slinky silk robe trailing behind him. She took her eye from the view finder and watched him stride back across the grounds. She thought: *Where are you running off to now, you little weasel?*

Then she heard a bright wrenching of metal and looked back toward the crematory. She watched Billy Guilder and the other one lowering the pickup's tailgate. Maria quickly snugged the camera to her eye again.

Her pulse quickened while she watched through the lens. She watched like the camera: frame by frame.

Two men hauling a body wrapped in plastic out of the truck and onto the ground. The tattooed one going back to slam the tailgate closed again. Billy Guilder sinking dolefully to his knees. Putting his hands on the bundle.

Maria watched as Billy rolled the package along the ground in front of him, unwrapping the figure like a grisly tamale. When she zoomed in, Maria had to bite her lip until she drew blood to keep from gasping out loud.

Blood. Crimson spatters and smears of it—on the plastic, on the ground. Glistening in dark slick matted hair.

She zoomed in tighter still.

The young dead man had a ragged purple crater just above his left eye. The eye itself, open and staring, was so dark that Maria first thought it was gone; after fine-tuning the focus, she realized that the eyeball was intact. It was dark because it had filled with blood.

Maria had fired off a string of frames before the vision truly sunk in. It was as if the camera lens filtered the reality of the scene. The single thin clear pane of the view finder provided just enough detachment for Maria to observe, marvel at, and finally experience what felt to her like an oddly clinical epiphany.

In all her time on the periphery of the business of death and dying, she'd never once seen an actual corpse in the raw before.

Certainly not one that had been produced by whatever violence had occurred here.

That was when it truly hit her, and Maria found she couldn't look anymore. Not another moment longer. She sank behind the headstone, pulled her knees in close, and tried to catch her breath while she waited for her pulse rate to decline.

After a moment, she heard the two men arguing about something. She looked. Billy Guilder stood in the middle of the plastic, over the body, while the tattooed guy smoked a cigarette. She could make out snippets of the disagreement at hand.

The fuck you unroll him for?

You said....

... wrap his ass back up. We'll do it plastic and all....

... but ...

Jesus. Move over and let me do it, then.

Leaning around the headstone, Maria zoomed to a medium angle and locked focus. Then she ducked back and rooted in her camera bag for two items: the mini-tripod and the cable release. Quickly, she attached both devices to the camera body and positioned it atop the headstone directly above her head. She checked the view to make sure she had all three subjects in frame.

Then she pulled back again, out of sight, remote shutter button in hand, wondering what could possibly be the matter with her. She should have bolted the minute that tailgate slammed; she should be in her car now, trying to forget everything she'd seen here.

Instead she leaned against the cold marble, elbows on knees, and squeezed off several more exposures. In a minute, she popped up to check the position of the subjects.

Ducked back and fired off a few more.

Maria continued in this manner, trying to ground herself in the chill of the stone at her back. The voices rose and fell silent. Plastic rustled. She pressed the button with one hand and fingered her cross with the other, keeping her eyes closed all the while.

She thought absently of Quince. She wondered what he was thinking about right now. She wondered if he was asleep. She imagined him sleeping.

Tried to focus on thoughts like these. The image of the dead man with the open mouth and the blood-filled eye pushed them away.

Joel, she thought. *Oh, Joel. What have you done this time?*

And that was when she heard a scrape and felt the wire of the cable release snap taut in her hands.

Before she could react, the shutter button zipped from her grasp. Maria opened her eyes, disoriented. And she knew, somehow, before she even looked up, that her situation had taken a very bad turn.

The man with the beard and the hard frightening eyes loomed over her. He held her camera in one blood-smeared hand.

"Evenin'," he said.

Maria opened her mouth silently.

The man smiled.

Many thoughts raced toward her lips but clogged on the way. Before she could scramble to her feet, her apprehender had already drawn back his arm.

"Say cheese-doodles," he said.

Mind blank, Maria managed to press her body back against the headstone as she watched her own camera swinging in a hard downward arc toward her head.

She thought: *Nuts.*

And had just time enough to raise one hand before a great invisible lens cap descended, blacking out everything in view.

"YOU KNOW, you could be right. I'm startin' to think this place does maybe have its advantages."

Three AM again. And here they were.

Carl Rosen had just come around from the other side of the glass. He shut the door to the furnace room and joined Billy in the comfier furnishings of the viewing parlor. Rosen actually seemed pumped for once. If Billy had been paying closer attention, he probably would have been amazed at the personality change. The guy had turned into a regular chatterbox.

But at the moment, it was all distant static to Billy Guilder.

"Seriously," Rosen was saying. "Coupla guys like you and me could capitalize on this setup for real. Think it through." Rosen leaned up against the wall by the curtained observation window and folded his arms. Thick cords worked in his wrists and forearms; jailhouse ink-work danced. "You got the East Coast out here, workin' the Hollywood biz. You got the Asians, expanding the Frisco trade. Hell, you even got the gang bangers doin' whatever the fuck it is they do. Pumpin' each other fulla bullet holes.

224

Whatever, right? Now, say we float a little 411 out there, get a little word-of-mouth kicking around the management level? We could be workin' a serious disposal business out here."

Billy wasn't really listening.

Rosen kept on anyway. "I'm gonna say, you figure in labor, we could go two grand a pop. Easy. Handle the pick-ups. Charge extra on weekends, emergency situations...."

Silence.

Then: "You *still* playing around with that thing?"

Billy Guilder looked up from his chair and blinked his hot red eyes.

Rosen just shook his head. "You're baked."

"Baked," Billy repeated, thinking of the furnace, and giggled until he coughed.

"I swear, you are such a fucking stoner." Carl came over and reached out. "That's it, hand it over. You can't pay attention, I'm taking it away."

Billy tried sitting up and handing over the camera. But his thumb slipped, and he accidentally hit the button. He was staring directly at the flash when it popped off in his face.

Billy sank back into the soft chair cushions, blinking and giggling his head off, too blind to see.

"Dude, that is seriously fuckin' pathetic."

Billy felt the camera leave his hands.

He closed his eyes.

Time swirled around his head. Billy watched the electric flashbulb patterns turn from white to blue to red behind his eyes. He enjoyed watching the sparks and trails and curlicues. It was like a laser light show in his head. He watched the light show until he became aware that Carl was speaking to him again from the fog.

"I'll be Goddamned," he heard Carl say. "Now I'm *really* not believing this."

Another pause. Billy watched the lights and felt good.

Then:

"Hey. Slap Happy. You want to hear something *really* funny?"

Billy opened his eyes and waited for the spots to disappear. He didn't want the colors to fade, but they did, one at a time. His head felt like it weighed several hundred pounds.

When he finally managed to lift it from the back of the chair, he saw Carl holding the camera up for him to see. The camera was open. The back swung on its hinges.

"How 'bout that?" Carl ran a rough thick finger around inside the camera. "Bitch didn't even have any film."

Billy Guilder looked at the empty camera. He looked at Carl. Then he closed his eyes and tripped off with the giggles again. Billy couldn't breathe, he giggled so hard. He giggled so hard that tears squirted. He giggled so hard he thought he'd never stop.

Friday morning went something like this:

The birds didn't tweet. They warbled arias. The sky? Blue enough to make you fall upon the ground and weep helplessly. The crisp autumn air drew fresh in the nose, sweet as cinnamon sticks, zesty as lemon peel.

Quince supposed it could have been the euphoric early-stage effects of sleep deprivation he was experiencing.

But if the cool October sunlight insisted on following him around, puddling about his feet like this all day, really—who was he to argue? Even his bad eye had opened. He could wink in code again.

Quince couldn't help but think about the fact that somewhere, this same morning, Martin's family was still picking up the jagged pieces of their broken world. Part of him felt guilty about how far from his mind Rhonda and the kids were right now.

But the rest of him couldn't help it. For the first time in as long as he could remember, Quince honestly looked forward to the day ahead.

Around 8:15, when Arlen and Vlad came out for the morning newspaper and caught him scissoring a big bushy handful of hydrangea blossoms from Arlen's six-foot hedge, Quince waved, extricated himself from the shrubby network of branches, crawled out, stood up, spat out a leaf, and greeted them cheerfully.

"Look in my eyes," his bathrobed landlord replied, gazing into Quince's pupils. "Kiddo? Can you hear me?"

"Of course I can hear you. I'm right in front of you."

"It's Arlen. Vladdy's here, too. It's morning time. Do you remember what you took, son?"

Quince laughed and scrubbed Vladimir behind the ears. "Just your advice."

"Lord." Big yawn. "What did I say now?"

Quince chucked Arlen lightly on one knobby terry-clothed shoulder. "Life's for the living, right?"

Arlen made a twist with his mouth which could have been a grin. He looked at Quince with a morning-dim gaze, thin white hair still standing out from his head in wisps and bed-mashed sheaves. He narrowed his bleary eyes. "Who are you?" he said. "And what have you done with Quince Bishop?"

Quince merely grinned. He stooped and scooped up Arlen's newspaper, handing it over with the garden scissors he'd borrowed from the greenhouse cradled in the fold.

"Love to stay and chat, fellas," he said. Another pat for Vlad, who looked like he might be asleep. "But I'm going to breakfast. Hey, Arl—you want me to cut the grass when I get back this afternoon?"

But his landlord never answered the question. Arlen was already heading back toward the house again—bathrobe, slippers, sagging black socks, newspaper, blind Pomeranian, and all.

"Earth to Maxwell. This afternoon okay, or should I wait another day?"

While Quince watched, Arlen Maxwell raised the newspaper over his head in vague acknowledgment.

"Whatever works, kiddo," Quince heard him say through another yawn. "You kids have a nice time."

Maria lived down in Mar Vista, in what she'd described as "one of those gross prefab super-plexes that's supposed to look like San Juan Capistrano." To cover the rent, she worked as a freelance grant writer for a local community college. Two nights a week working a checkstand at a nearby grocery store, she'd explained, generated enough additional income to pay the monthly bills on a strategic rotating schedule that prevented any one utility from falling more than 60 days past due. This left her free to devote the remainder of her time to SoCal Valley, which really was the only work she cared about doing anyway.

Quince made the drive in thirty minutes, found her door a few minutes before 9:00. He positioned the flowers between his face and the peep hole, knocked, and tried to think of a good opening line.

By 10:15, he was pretty sure that one of three things had happened:

a) Maria, who unlike him led a busy life and who, also unlike him, probably had a million other things on her mind, had forgotten about their breakfast date (mild sting there, but certainly forgivable).

b) Something unexpected had come up. In which case, a message from Maria was probably waiting for him on the answering machine back at the apartment right now (no problem at all).

Or,

c) He was an unbelievable stud, and the poor exhausted thing had simply slept through more than an hour of intermittent knocking (he shoots, he scores!).

Whichever the case, by 10:30, Quince finally decided to pack it in and head home. He left the decanter stuffed with hydrangea in the hallway outside Maria's door, #302. He checked the address she'd written for him one more time, just to make sure he was in the right place. Was.

Her Mitford book—which he'd already started reading— he took with him for safekeeping and later return. He'd been up with it all night, curious to discover its contents, wondering what insights the material might offer into the person to whom the book had been signed. He'd been too juiced to sleep anyway.

Now, standing there in the carpeted third-floor hallway of her apartment building, a fourth scenario occurred to him:

Maria had come to her senses and was having an attack of the Mels.

While he considered this possibility, Quince hefted the book and enjoyed a sense of confidence he'd never felt with Melanie. For here was the one ace every dating person should have in the hole.

Ransom.

Still disappointing about breakfast, though. He grudgingly quit his post and headed for the stairs at the near end of the hall. Rounding the second floor landing on his way down, Quince passed another guy coming up, who looked him over and said, "So what's the other guy look like?"

"Poor bastard," Quince said gravely. "Talk about the short end."

As they passed each other, Quince heard the stranger snort from above, as if to say, *Sure, pal. Whatever you say.* The echo of their footfalls parted, until a door slammed in the stairwell high above his head.

Grinning to himself, Quince found his own exit and emerged into the bright glare of the apartment complex parking lot.

Only on his way out did he think to check parking slot #302. Maria's little Mazda indeed was there. Briefly, he considered turning around, going back up, and trying the door again.

Then he decided: *nah.*

All of a sudden, he was liking the idea of heading home, running the mower around Arlen's big yard, maybe reading another chapter or two, and waiting for Maria to call. For at the moment, despite being stood up, Quince felt happy and invincible. Truly, he was a man among men.

And if it *wasn't* option C at work here, at this particular moment he was perfectly content not to know.

Carl Rosen was convinced. He could've been a damn detective, he'd gone a different way.

Take Mick's place. Most guys, what would they do? Go in and toss it, throw shit all over the place, make a big production. Just like they saw on TV. And then what? Real life, you practically never found shit that way. What you did was, you ended up standing around with your thumb up your ass. Kind of tuckered out. With nothing to show for it and an even bigger mess to sort through.

Unlike most guys, Carl Rosen understood the fact that your average dumbshit just wasn't that hard to figure out. Not if you really stopped and thought about it for a second or two.

Early this morning, he'd taken the pickup down to Mick's

place, a shitty little one-bedroom unit in one of those low rent Venice bungalow courts. Fucking place looked like it had been tossed already, months ago, and never cleaned up. But ten minutes inside that mess, Carl found a shoebox full of cassette tapes, like Moss had told them about. Found it first place he looked, just where an average dumbshit like Mick would've kept it. Under the bed.

First problem solved. And he hadn't even had breakfast yet.

Then, on his way back to Palm Grove with Moss's tapes riding shotgun, what happened? Carl just happened to drive by a lonely Mazda parked under a walnut tree a couple blocks from the cemetery. He didn't even know why he looked twice.

But on a crazy hunch, he'd parked the truck. Tried the key from that hot little Chicana's keyring.

Bingo. Her car.

Carl even surprised himself a little, on that one. He knew he was a smart cookie—but talk about being on a roll. You got right down to it, being a cop would have been a tragic Goddamn waste of skills.

Carl stopped by Palm Grove long enough to stash the blackmail tapes in his locker, unload the stereo system he'd taken the liberty of hauling out of Mick's shitty bungalow, and grab a Mountain Dew from the soda machine. He thought about hiking out to the crematory and waking Guilder's stoned ass up. Guy was still sacked out on the couch in the viewing parlor, where he'd passed out the night before.

But after he thought about it, Carl decided he was enjoying the peace and quiet too much. So he finished his soda and took the pickup back to Maria Casteneda's car alone.

Purse was on the front seat. He dumped it. Found

her driver's license, some makeup, a pen and a notepad, a checkbook, and a pink plastic wheel of birth control pills. Nothing that gave any clues about what the girl had been doing out here, shooting pictures in the middle of the night. Call it a personal curiosity, but Carl Rosen just had to know.

So he got behind the wheel, lit a cigarette, and followed the address on her license.

No reason why not. It was still early, he didn't have anything better to do, and it'd save him the trouble of getting rid of the car later on.

Down in Mar Vista, Carl found Mission Place Apartments on Lamanda Street. He rolled in, followed the numbers around the side of the first building in the complex, and parked the little Jap-made five speed back in space #302 where it belonged.

A few minutes later, on his way into the building, he passed some asshole on the stairs. It just so happened Carl Rosen was in the right kind of mood to shoot the shit with some asshole in a stairwell.

So he asked about the other guy.

"Poor bastard," said the asshole with the knuckle marks on his face. "Talk about the short end."

What a faggot, thought Carl Rosen.

He went on up to #302.

Figuring, the roll he was on today, he'd know soon enough if the hot little Chicana shutterbug was just your average dumbshit, or something more.

IN THE DREAM, Billy Guilder walked along a beach.

He wore his favorite pajamas. His favorite pajamas from when he was a kid. They had dinosaurs on them. Little Triceratopses and Stegosauruses, Tyrannosaurus Rexes, all manner of dinosaurs. His Dinojammies.

In the dream it was night, and the moon was full. There were stars. The light from the moon and stars was silver, and the sand glowed white all around. Dark water lapped at Billy's bare seven-year-old feet as he walked along in his Dinojammies, hunting for seashells by the light of the moon.

In the dream, he saw a glint and ran over to it. He bent down to pick up a gleaming white shell. Billy rinsed it off in the water and held it like a coin in the palm of his small hand. The shell felt strange, and he turned it over.

It had hair on the other side.

In the dream, Billy was frightened. He didn't know why. He looked at the weird shell with hair growing out of it, and he felt warm pee soak through his pajama bottoms. He couldn't hold on to the shell anymore. He wanted to throw

234

it as hard as he could out into the sea. But he knew the tide would just end up washing it back onto the beach again.

In the dream, Billy stood still. His bare feet sank slowly into the cold sand. He looked down at his Dinojammies. For some reason, the dinosaurs had all started to move. They unfroze, and moved around, and while they were moving they lost their shape. They turned into little black blobs, like spreading ink blots. The ink blots changed color.

One by one, each dinosaur was changing into a red question mark. He grabbed at them and tried to make them stop changing.

Soon he was covered with question marks. All the dinosaurs had disappeared.

He started to cry.

Not knowing what else to do, Billy took the shell and put it in his mouth and swallowed it. It got stuck and he swallowed harder, hard as he could, feeling it scratch his throat on the way down.

He swallowed the shell and started running, but he couldn't move his legs fast enough. On his feet, he now wore red galoshes. The boots sucked and slurped in the wet sand. The sand didn't want to let him go. He couldn't run in his boots.

Billy fell down. Before he could get up, the tide came in and washed over him. Saltwater soaked his pajamas and pulled off his boots. He tried to get up. Dripping water, he made it to his hands and knees.

Then the tide came again. This time, it lifted him up. It pulled him out. Billy tried to swim for it, but the current had him.

In the dream, the tide pulled him into the cold dark water, away out to sea.

★   ★   ★

Billy Guilder woke up gasping for air on the hard carpeted floor of the crematory viewing parlor. He opened his eyes and flailed unconsciously with an arm. Gradually, he rose from the depths of sleep, kicking hard for the surface until he could breathe again.

Reality filtered in slowly. Billy leaned up against the base of the couch until the dreamy panic subsided.

And he found it wasn't a relief to be awake after all.

Billy felt like he'd been buried alive. He was dizzy. His head felt packed with cotton, his mouth was furry and sour. A greasy, low-grade nausea pulsed in his bowels.

Which only deepened as he continued to shake off the dream and the events of the night before slowly reassembled in his mind.

Billy rose quickly, stumbled down the hall to the rest room, and threw up in the toilet. He rinsed his mouth at the sink. He drank water from his cupped hands until his stomach sloshed.

When he couldn't drink another drop, Billy stood and caught his breath. He looked at himself in the mirror and hardly recognized what he saw.

Billy stood on tiptoe and pushed open the high bathroom window. Then he hunched down in one of the toilet stalls, loaded his pipe, and smoked a little helper bowl.

Some little while later, Billy Guilder emerged from the crematory into the bright sun of a new morning. All around him, it seemed just like any other day. He could hear the clack and ratchet of the automatic sprinkler system. He breathed in familiar smells: the green smell of grass, the dark smell of moist earth. Everything looked and felt just like any normal morning at work. Back in the basement of the big building, there would be a list of all the things he needed to do today.

That was when Billy remembered what was in the basement of the big building, and his heart sank.

He looked both ways. He looked all around. Nobody out here but him and dead people.

So Billy got on the path. Got on it and stayed on it. He ran all the way back to the mortuary.

Quince stopped at the Chevron near Maria's apartment complex to gas up for the drive home. He was distracted as usual, anxious to get back to the apartment before she called. But as he was standing in line at the counter, Quince happened to notice a flyer for a boat show this weekend down in Marina del Rey. It made him think of Martin.

From there, his morning took a short detour. Before he'd even realized he'd made the decision, Quince found himself cruising south on the 405 instead of north, toward home.

He made one stop on the way. A Gelson's Market. Quince went to the deli counter and bought an armload of stuff in carry-out containers: pasta salad, baked chicken, scalloped potatoes, steamed vegetables. Stuff you could pull out of the fridge if you had hungry kids but found you couldn't face the kitchen without losing your mind.

Twenty minutes after leaving the store, Quince was back in the familiar environs of the South Bay, where he'd once worked and often visited. Martin and Rhonda lived in an eclectic charter-controlled subdivision on the Palos Verdes Peninsula. Quince carried bulging plastic grocery store sacks up the Waxman's flagstone front walk, mounted the steps of the portico, and used his elbow to ring the doorbell.

After a few minutes, Rhonda answered wearing an old

sweatshirt and faded jeans with a hole in the knee. Quince recognized the sweatshirt as one of Martin's. Her hair was pulled back into a quick gather that had come loose over one shoulder. She held Katie on her hip.

For some reason, seeing them together like that, the first thing that struck Quince was how big Katie was getting. Almost too big for her mom to carry anymore.

When Rhonda saw it was him, her face opened. "Quin," she said.

He held up the sacks. "It's not a covered dish, but you can eat it. I think."

She grinned a little and stepped back, saying, "You didn't have to bring anything. Just come in. Come inside."

Quince pulled the door after him with his foot. Katie said, "Hi, Bob."

She couldn't pronounce his name. Couldn't quite get that "Q" sound out. Joking, Martin had once instructed her just to call him Bob. Katie seemed to be able to work with that.

"Hiya, sweetie," Quince said. Went for her tummy. "How you doing?"

Katie pointed at his eye and told him he had an ouch. He told her it was almost better and didn't really hurt very bad. She didn't seem to believe him.

With a shallow groan, Rhonda put Katie down and patted her on the behind and told her to go find Nate and tell him to come see Uncle Quince.

As Katie took off into the house with a thumping of size four-year-old sneakers, Rhonda straightened and pantomimed an aching back. Then she came over and gave him a hug. He put down the food and squeezed her tight.

"I'm so glad you came by."

"Sorry to just drop in."

"No, stop it. I've been meaning to call you all week, but ... I don't know. It seems like the days just blend."

He broke the clinch and leaned back and looked her in the eyes. They looked like they'd been through a workout. "How are you?"

"We're managing," she said. "My parents are here until next week. That helps." She touched his bruise lightly, wincing. "How about you?"

"It's not as bad as it looks," he said.

She looked at him much the same way Katie had a moment ago. "You shouldn't have just waded in there like that, you know. Who knows what could have happened?"

Quince waved it off. "The funny part is, he'd have loved it," he said. "Wouldn't he? Martin would have thought the whole damned thing was hysterical."

And Rhonda nodded, her eyes suddenly brimming. "Please don't make me cry," she said. "It's all I've been doing. I can't take it today."

He squeezed her hands and she tried to grin.

"I swear," she said. "They say the body is eighty percent water? If that's true, you should be able to see right through me by now."

Quince just squeezed again. There always seemed to be lots of squeezing during moments like this. Probably because nobody was ever sure what to say.

Rhonda squeezed back and let him go and used the heels of her hands to wipe her eyes. "Come on," she said. "Let's get this stuff in the fridge before it grows germs."

She'd been going through boxes of pictures that had never been put into scrapbooks. Rhonda told him she'd been meaning to do it for two years now, but for some reason she just kept putting it off. Never seemed to find the time.

The photos lay in scatters and piles on the living room floor. He sat amongst them on the carpet with her. They drank coffee together and picked through the piles.

"Here," Rhonda said, handing one over. "He'd want you to have this one."

Quince took the photograph and looked at it. It had been taken on a windy, sunny afternoon last year. He and Wax had taken the Bertram out fishing off Flat Rock Point. In the photo, they were posing together on the starboard deck: Quince mugging for the camera, holding up a puny sea bass, while Martin dumped a beer over his head.

Quince smiled. And felt like bawling. Ten years from now, they should have pulled out this picture and laughed over it together.

"One minute," Rhonda said, "I still think he's going to come inside from the yard. The next ... it's almost like he was never here at all."

Quince said nothing, for there was nothing to say. They sat and sipped their coffees and picked up random photos from their various piles. Traded them, put them back again. The piles shifted between them on the floor.

After awhile, Katie came in the room with tears in her eyes. Rhonda took her on her lap and asked her what was the matter.

"Natey yelled."

Rhonda glanced at Quince—only briefly, just long enough for him to see her own eyes filling again. She blinked hard and hugged Katie and told her Nate wasn't mad. He probably just wanted to be by himself for a little while. Katie fussed for a minute, then crawled off Rhonda's lap and went over to a pile of toys in the corner. Took an armload with her to her room.

When she was gone, Rhonda looked back at Quince. And that was all for her. She covered her face with her hands. Her shoulders began to bounce, and quiet sobs followed. Quince put down his mug and went to sit beside her, put his arm around her shoulders. They sat like this for a long time.

Until Rhonda finally drew in a ragged breath and lowered her hands. "Tell me they're going to be okay."

Quince kept his arm around her and took a hand in his. They leaned back against the couch and sat for a little while more.

When it seemed like the right time, he spoke. Not really sure what he'd say until he was saying it.

"Our folks used to be out of town a lot," he told her. "On business. They had their own public relations firm, and they traveled all over, meeting with accounts. Paul was quite a bit older, so it didn't affect him as much. But I didn't do so well with it, them being gone all the time. So whenever they'd go on a trip, they always sent me a postcard from whatever city they were in. Addressed to me personally. Just to say they were thinking about us and telling me when they'd be home."

He paused long enough to reach back for his coffee and take a sip. Rhonda broke away and wiped at her eyes again.

"When they died, my aunt and uncle tried to explain it to me," he said. "I was about Nate's age. It just didn't compute for me at all. I checked the mailbox every single day, looking for that postcard—waiting for them to tell me where they were and when they'd be coming home."

Rhonda sniffed and wiped her hands on her jeans. Looked at the floor.

"After about a month," he said, "the postcard finally came. It said that they were going to be away for a long time, but they loved us, and they'd be thinking about us every day. And if I ever wanted to talk to them about anything, I could write it down and give it to my Aunt Caroline. She'd make sure they got it."

Quince grinned at nothing. "It was signed, 'M&D.' A couple of years later, when I was a little older, I found out Paul had written it and put a stamp on it and stuck it in the mailbox for me to find. By then, I sort of had it figured out for myself. But Paul ... that's what he did."

He looked at Rhonda. She was crying again. Not sobbing this time. Just sort of welling back up and spilling over.

"They'll be okay," he told her.

Rhonda looked back at him, and smiled, and let the tears fall. She didn't seem surprised to find she had more after all.

"What about me?" she said.

Quince reached out his hand. She took it fiercely and leaned back into him. He held her close and felt her tears soak his shirt.

"Just cry for now," he told her. "You're not going to disappear."

Dolores the receptionist smiled from behind her desk.

"Good morning, Billy."

"Hey, Dolores." Billy tried the grin he usually used when he showed up late. "Moss ain't here yet, is he?"

"He's in Seattle, remember?"

"Oh. Oh, yeah."

"Billy, you look awful." Dolores glanced at her wristwatch. "You went home and slept in your clothes again, didn't you?"

"I guess."

"Honestly." She smirked. "You need a mother."

"Yeah," Billy said. Shrugged. "Better punch the clock."

"Okay, Billy." Grinning, Dolores went back to her magazine. Without looking up from the page she was on, she said, "I brought in Friday donuts, if you're hungry. They're upstairs in the breakroom."

"Right on."

Billy moved along, hoping he wasn't coming off too strange. He didn't think so.

Behind him, Dolores called out: "By the way—Schuler's looking for you."

Schuler was a certified independent-contract embalmer who Joel brought in whenever he needed an extra hand around the place. Nice guy, Schuler. The only Jewish embalmer Billy Guilder had ever heard about. Billy remembered now: Schuler was supposed to work this weekend while Moss was out of town.

Billy liked the guy okay, but he just didn't think he could handle running into Schuler right now. He tried to walk quietly and keep his eyes peeled, hoping he could punch in and get on his way without being seen.

But to get to the time clock, he had to pass through the lounge, where Moss kept a television and a VCR and some board games for when it was slow.

Schuler was in there in one of the Barcaloungers, drinking from a box of apple juice and watching a *Matlock* rerun on the big screen. Billy hardly recognized him in the suit; usually, Schuler had on a rubber apron. But today, he was wearing this dark brown three-piece job. From the look of it, he hadn't tried the thing on in about 15 years.

Billy tried to duck out quickly, but it was too late.

"Billy boy!" Schuler cried happily. He got up out of the leather recliner and came over; the sleeves of his jacket pulled halfway up to his elbows when he spread his long skinny arms. "Hey, sweetheart. Long time no see."

"Yeah. How you been?"

"I could complain, but it wouldn't do any good. Now, you." He pointed. "You're staying out of trouble. Tell me you are."

For some reason, Billy's voice caught in his throat. "Uh huh."

Schuler laughed explosively, like an asthmatic jack-hammer pounding cement. "That's what I thought. Say, Billy. I was doing a quick once-over, just checking around…."

Billy felt his heart freeze.

"… and it looks to me like we're running low on germicide and Flotone. Ligature, also."

"Oh," Billy said. He let out a breath he didn't even know he was holding. He felt himself unclench from scalp to toes. "Yeah. Right. Might be some more downstairs in the supply room."

"And I couldn't find any putty or mouth formers, either." Schuler shook his bony head. "What the heck does Joel use to prep these people, anyway? Spackle and spray paint?"

"Yeah, I dunno. Been slow, I guess. I'm on my way down there anyway, I can check for you."

"That'd be great, Billy. Thanks a million." Schuler found his plastic straw and sucked on his apple juice until the box gurgled. "Say, while you're down there, see if Joel's got any Cavity 55 sitting around, will you?"

"Roger."

"Thanks, Billy. You're good people."

Billy didn't know what to say to that. He just said, "Okay."

SEAN DOOLITTLE

All the way downstairs, Billy listened for Schuler to come running after him with a list of more shit he needed. Nothing. The coast was clear.

When he got to the supply room, he stood outside the door for several minutes. Still no footsteps anywhere above his head that he could hear. Dolores would be sitting at her desk, reading her magazine. Schuler was back with Matlock. Slow day ahead, probably. For some reason, nobody ever seemed to die on a Friday.

Billy waited another five, just to make sure.

Then he took a breath, dug out his key ring, and unlocked the supply room door. He slipped inside, flipped on the light, and shut the door quietly behind him again.

The supply room was plenty roomy, though it was usually pretty short on supplies. What they had was on flimsy aluminum utility shelves. Some stuff usually sat around the floor, still in boxes or shipping crates. More shelves, mostly empty, lined the walls all around. Over in the corner sat the row of DuraLite caskets Joel kept trying to get rid of. Newer caskets sat here and there, wrapped in bubble plastic.

One of them was unwrapped. The plastic was still laying around in shreds on the floor.

The box they'd unwrapped was a Conquistador. It sat where Carl had made Billy leave it, on a wheeled cart in the middle of the room. Big burnished steel job with a pearl satin lining, adjustable innerspring mattress, and SureLok seal.

SureLok seal. Which Rosen didn't even stop to think about. Or maybe he did. Billy didn't know.

He'd tried to explain.

Padding, was all Rosen had said. *Bitch does wake up, she can holler all she wants in there.*

Billy had tried telling him she'd run out of breathing

245

room in there, but Carl wouldn't listen. Billy hadn't known what to do—except to sneak back in later with the DeWalt high-speed and drill six or seven air holes in the lid.

Which he'd done while Carl was busy loading Mick into the oven.

Now, Billy hurried over and unbuckled the casket, tingling all over with dread.

Inside, Maria Casteneda lay on her back, still in the black jeans and black long-sleeved T-shirt she'd been wearing the night before. Eyes closed, hands folded across her chest. Heavy rubber tubing bound her wrists. More tubing held the wadded-up pillow case in her mouth, cruelly bunching her dark pretty hair.

It gave Billy a jolt, seeing her. The sight of bright red against the white satin made him go numb. The pillow under her head was all smeared with it. Her dark pretty hair was wet on that side.

The way she looked, laying in there like that … when she opened her eyes, it gave Billy a chill deep in his bones.

When she saw him, Maria's brown eyes filled with tears that spilled over and ran down her cheeks. She blinked hard and made a quiet sound. Clear snot bubbled out of her nose.

Billy hurried to undo the tubing from around her neck and pull the silky pillow case out of her mouth. He unwadded the pillow case and folded it dry side out, and used it to wipe her nose for her, gentle as he could. He asked her if she wanted to sit up.

Helped her when she nodded that she did.

He'd officially changed his mind again. That guy Rosen was an asshole after all.

Billy helped Maria lean against the open lid. When she was situated, he left her sitting there and ran out of the supply room. At the door he stopped. Listened. Looked both ways down the hall.

When he saw nobody, and heard nobody, he ran down to the water cooler, filled as many little paper cups as he could carry, and hurried back again. Locked the door once more behind him.

Maria Casteneda sat up in the casket with her shoulders hunched forward. Bloody hair hung in her face. She'd started to sob. When Billy came in with the water, she squeezed her eyes tight and drew in a deeper breath, and it was like she just clamped down and stopped herself from crying before she'd even got good and started. She opened her eyes.

He supported her with his arm and held one of the water cups to her swollen lips. She drank a little.

"Thank you, Billy," she said softly.

Billy wasn't as strong as Maria Casteneda. Or maybe he was just too stoned to get a grip. He started to cry himself.

"I'm so sorry," he told her. "I'm sorry you got hurt."

"Billy, where's Carl? Is that his name? The one who hit me?"

Billy nodded. He was starting to lose it now, like some kind of little kid. He tried to get his act together.

"Billy."

He noticed that Maria's words sounded slurred. When he looked at her, he could see there was something wrong with her face. The right side of it, anyway. Her cheek looked strange, kind of limp. And the corner of her mouth sagged a little. He noticed the water she drank trickled out that side.

Noticed how that eye sort of wandered on her.

He thought: *oh, God*. Billy remembered the sound he'd heard when Carl had smacked her with the camera, and his

bowels loosened. He thought, *Oh, shit. He hit her too hard …
she stroked out in there or something…*.

"Is he here?"

"No," Billy said. "I don't know where he is. Truck's gone.
He could be … he could be back any time."

"Billy. I'm hurt."

Billy squeezed his eyes shut and nodded.

"My scalp is badly cut. It needs stitches. And something…."
She paused, and the look on her face was like a slice on
Billy's heart. "Something is *wrong*, Billy. I need a doctor."

Billy nodded again. "I'll get you some ice for your head.
And there's donuts. You want some donuts? I can bring you
some."

"Billy…."

"But I'll definitely get you some ice. And I think we got
some Band-Aids. Sit tight, okay? I'll bring some down here.
Okay?"

"Billy…."

"I'm so sorry," he blurted. "I never killed anybody."

"I know, Billy," Maria said. "I know you didn't."

He felt like he couldn't breathe. He felt like he was
drowning. "I couldn't ever kill nobody."

"I know."

"I'm so sorry. I'm so sorry you got hurt."

"Billy."

Billy held her there with his arm and squeezed his eyes
closed again.

"Holmby," he muttered. "That poor little granny's house
… that was his idea, man. I didn't even *wanna* rob that poor
woman. I never even … I didn't know he'd…." Billy was
babbling now. He couldn't help it. He made himself stop.
"I'm so sorry."

"Billy, listen to me. Please listen. You've got to let me go."

Billy opened his eyes now and looked at her. "I … Carl. Oh, shit. He could be back any time."

"It doesn't matter, Billy. Please. You've got to help me." She reached forward with her tied-up hands and grabbed his shirt. "I can't hurt you—Carl took the camera, remember? I promise, I won't say anything to anybody. But you've got to help me. You're the only one who can."

"He caught us, he'd cap us both." Billy tried to think, wishing he hadn't smoked that bowl. He tried to think.

The truck was gone. No alternator on the van. He thought of the M&M, sitting all alone out in the garage. But where could he go?

He sure as hell couldn't come back here. Couldn't ever go to his apartment again. Rosen? Rosen would find him and kill his ass dead, that's what Rosen would do. He'd shove him into the oven just like Mick. If Maria slipped those tubes on his watch, he'd have to drive that M&M all the way to Mexico. Because he wouldn't ever be able to show his face anywhere near here again, not as long as there was a chance Carl Rosen might see it.

"He's not going to let me go, Billy. You know he won't."

"That cop," he said. "That cop who was out here—Timms. Maybe…."

He froze before he could finish the thought.

Keys. In the door.

Maria Casteneda sucked in a quick breath beside him.

The next second, Carl Rosen came in. He was eating a Croissan'wich wrapped in Burger King paper. With his foot, he kicked the door closed behind him. Maria jumped a little when it slammed.

"Hey," Carl said to Billy. "Nice you finally decided to wake

249

your dead ass up." To Maria Casteneda, he tilted his head and waved. "Mornin', shutterbug."

Maria let go of Billy's shirt and didn't say anything.

"Um," Billy said. "Hey. Hey there, Carl."

"You two getting all acquainted, I see." Carl grinned and wagged one finger at Maria. "I know something about you-hoo." He winked. "We need to have a little talk."

"May I get out of this casket?" she asked him. The one side of her mouth sagged even worse when she talked. "Please?"

"What, you ain't comfy?" Carl came over with his Croissan'wich. He put his free hand between her legs. Slow. Winking again while he reached down. Billy saw Maria hold her breath.

But Carl only patted the mattress a couple times. "Seems to me like it'd be nice in there."

"Please," she said.

"Promise you won't holler?"

"I promise. Please. I won't make a sound. Just please, don't keep me in here."

"Hey, come on, partner," Billy said. "Can't hurt to let her out awhile, huh?"

Carl Rosen shrugged. "Don't make any difference to me." But he looked at Maria sternly. "You yell, though, you're going right back in. For keeps. You hear what I'm saying?"

Maria nodded.

Billy held out his hand. He helped her out, got an arm around her waist. He helped her move over against the wall between two stacks of boxes. When she was situated, he went back and got the water cups and brought them over. She thanked him.

Very quietly, he whispered, "Hang in there, sis. Okay?"

Having just discovered the bulge in his pocket, which he'd forgotten all about until just now.

Maria nodded so that you could barely see it. Her eyes were wide. They were so brown.

Billy stood up and tried his best to look cool.

"I gotta go," he told Carl. Hating the idea of leaving Maria alone with him. But knowing he couldn't do anything from here. Knowing he couldn't just hang around and wait for Carl to do something first.

"Go where?" said Rosen. "Get a manicure?"

Billy shrugged. "That time of the month."

"Get the fuck out of here. You gotta go meet the PO? Today?"

"'Leven o'clock sharp," Billy lied. In fact, he didn't go see his parole officer for another two weeks. But it was the best he could come up with on the spot.

Only he was a terrible liar. Billy knew it. Always had been; it was one thing that always did him in eventually. Carl Rosen looked like the kinda guy who probably knew when somebody was lying to him. Even a good liar, which Billy wasn't. Billy held his breath and waited.

But Carl just laughed. "Man, you better find somebody to piss in the cup for you, is all I can say."

Billy tried to chuckle normally. It was difficult to do with his heart pounding his throat.

Rosen finished his sandwich in one huge bite. He crumpled the wrapper in a fist and tossed it. "Well, shag ass back here, huh? I wanna take that camera and some other stuff down to Gerald later."

"Yup," Billy said. "Later."

He tried to make eye contact with Maria one last time.

But Carl Rosen had already pulled up a crate and taken a seat in front of her.

"So tell me something," Billy heard him say. "I just gotta know."

Billy scooted out of the supply room. He left them there.

His brain was flooded. There was a loud buzzing in his ears. He plunged a hand into his pants pocket. He fingered the small, hard, cylindrical object that was making the bulge down there by his keys.

Billy hurried down the hallway, trying like hell to figure out what he was going to do with it.

AT THE PAPER, there was a reporter named
Corcoran who had been working the crime beat for fifteen
years. He knew all the cops, all the snitches, and all the DAs.
He'd been around the track, as he liked to say. Corcoran was
a blowhard and a horndog, but one thing was certainly true:
if you wanted a good joke, a grisly anecdote, or the straight
scoop on virtually any newsroom rumor—present, past, or
coming soon—you went to Corcoran.

Unless you were a woman, of course, in which case
Corcoran—a likeable scoundrel with three divorces and a
fourth in the pipes—was generally too busy to be of much
help, distracted as he was with trying to sleep with you.

The closest thing to professional advice Melanie Roth had
ever gotten from Corcoran came yesterday as she prepared
for this morning's early flight to Seattle. She'd poured a
couple coffees and swung by Corcoran's disaster area of a
cubicle, hoping to shoptalk the interview she was trying to
put together with Joel Moss.

Corcoran just looked up with a cagey Zen-master
expression and said: *get yourself a tape recorder.*

She supposed he'd been trying to help.

253

Seriously, he'd told her. *One of those little handheld jobs. It'll cover your ass one day.*

It wasn't that she necessarily disagreed—though she'd seen enough lazy reporters sporting tape recorders to mount an argument, even if Corcoran himself wasn't one of them. It was just that, in certain areas of life, Melanie Roth still considered herself a pen-and-notebook kind of gal.

So on Friday morning, while the hotel shuttle jockeyed for position amidst the multicolored clog of competing hotel shuttles, all waiting to belly up and deposit their cargo in front of the Herman K. Showalter Convention Center in downtown Seattle, her pen and notebook were the tools she dug from her bag.

She shared the ride from the hotel with four other conventioneers. Up front, in the shotgun seat, half-turned toward the goings-on in the back of the van, sat a quiet middle-aged fellow from South Bend, Indiana. He wore a trim dark suit with a green-and-gold GO IRISH tie. The back seat was taken by a talkative but pleasant couple from Omaha, Nebraska.

And finally, swiveling gamely back and forth in one of the captain's chairs, the guy who had been hitting on Melanie since the hotel: a young, tan, lean, side-burned, muscle-toned stud from Houston. He wore silver earrings and bracelets, black jeans, black cowboy boots with stainless steel caps on the toes, and a tight black T-shirt with white block lettering: MORTICIANS MAKE IT LAST.

"Y'all sure you don't want someone to keep you company?"

"I think I can manage," Mel told him.

"Now that I *do* not doubt." He actually winked. "Still, you should think about it. I'm real quotable."

"It's a tempting offer," Mel said. "But I really think I'm set."

Tex clucked his tongue as though that were just a dadgum shame. "Suit yourself, cutie." He stretched his arms, yawned luxuriously, patted out a quick rhythm on his corrugated abs, and flashed another grin. "But y'all can be sure it's a standing invitation."

The woman from Omaha rolled her eyes and slipped Mel a sisterly smirk.

Melanie grinned back and flipped to the first clean page in her notebook. While the shuttle slipped into an open gap and made for the curb, she scribbled a title at the top of the page and began making entries from there.

NAAP
Day 1

9:30 AM
Am officially dying for coffee. Bad pun (fear the
atmosphere here already is rubbing off). Knott's
Berry Farm has shorter lines than this registration
table. But probably fewer comedians.

These funeral people are much funnier than
expected. (Then again, a healthy sense of humor
would have to be an asset in this line of work, yes?)
Novelty neckties seem popular. Look out, Seattle.
These folks are here to par-tay.

Parking lot: Saw guy in L.L. Bean and aviator
shades driving mango-orange 'vette convertible
with vanity plates. Tag: #1 MBALMR.

There's some sort of tournament?
★ Abandon all assumptions. ★

—Day Plan—
* Find coffee
* Lecture at 10:00, Sierra Room ("Autopsies and
  the Open Casket: Your Local Morgues and Why
  You Should Be Nice To Them")
* Check out "Vendor Pavilion"
* LUNCH—CALL Q RE: MARIA C'S EMAIL. PALM
  GROVE DISINTERMENT PERMITS???
* Panel discussion at 1:00, PeachTree Suite
  ("Tradition and the Not-So-New Age")
* Competing 1:00. Lecture, Sierra Room
  ("Helping Clients Understand Their Dignity
  Options") ?? Must hear this.
* Troll pavilion
* Lecture at 3:00, PeachTree (J. Moss's "Tightening
  the Links in Your Service/Profit Chain")
* Pavilion again? Play by ear.

Don't forget tonight's special mystery performance
by as-yet-undisclosed celebrity entertainer. Main
auditorium, 8:00. Word around the lobby is Aaron
Neville. Party on.

10:00 AM
Autopsy lecture: what a hoot. County M.E. from
Tacoma delivering. Definitely must remember to tell
Q this guy's ice breaker:

———————

A professor is giving first year med students their
first lecture on autopsies. He decides to start by
presenting them with two key principles. Professor

says: "You must be capable of two things to do an autopsy. First: you must have no sense of fear."

The professor sticks his finger into the dead man's anus, and then he licks his finger.

He asks all the students to do the same thing with the corpses in front of them. After a couple of weird minutes—total silence, everybody looking back and forth at each other—the students finally do as the professor says.

Then the professor holds up his hand.

"The second thing is that you must have an acute sense of observation," he says. "I stuck my middle finger into the corpse's anus, but I licked my index."

———————

You gotta love these guys.

11:30 AM
A few of the products I hope will never be used on me:
* Mort-o-Cide (A disinfectant for "advanced cases.")
* Jaundice Blend 2000 (Embalming fluid for jaundiced deceased. From the bottle: "Provides the softest, most natural tone possible for all severity levels." Apparently, per sales rep, regular embalm. fluids make the subject turn Ghoul Green.)
* Maggot-X (Gawd. An insecticide. Enough said.)
* PerfectaWax (From the jar label: "A pliable yet sturdy compound; expertly repairs surface irregularities caused by most common traumas. Perfect for gunshot wounds [entrance or exit].

Recommended for use with PerfectaTone color
foundation and PerfectaRouge finishing blush.")

12:30 PM
Lunch.
Forget about it.

12:45 PM
Sudden flurry of activity on Pavilion upper level.
Followed a herd of morticians up the escalators
toward the excitement. What can it be?

It's a company from L.A. selling air brush
makeup systems (covers bruises and other unsightly
discolora-tions lickety-split). They are doing
demonstrations on a live model in an extremely ·
skimpy flesh-toned thong bikini. She has blonde
hair down to her round little ass, legs up to her
perky little chin, and one seriously great pair of tits.
(Not a bruise on this girl that I can see.) There's a
crowd around this booth like you wouldn't believe.

Note to model: Honey, you must not be sleeping
with the right people. I mean what kind of gig is
this? Posing as a corpse? Fire your agent!

At least she looks like she died happy. Big bouncy
smiles for all the funeral fellas. The wives look like
they truly hate this chick.

Listen to me.

1:40 PM
—1:00 lecture—
Dignity Options? Was not aware there was a base
model.

This appears to be the point. Makes sense when you think about it. Who's going to feel good about sending grandma on The Long Trip in a Plymouth Neon after they've imagined her in a smooth-rolling Cadillac with heated seats, in-dash CD changer, and all-leather interior?

No better way to express yourself than through purchasing power. Quote from lecture: "Most people would never dream of cheaping out on their daughter's wedding. Why should they feel it's acceptable to cut corners on her funeral?"

Observation: these funeral people would have a better image if they hired MasterCard's PR firm.

2:00 PM

Speaking of dignity options, there's a company here selling shotgun shells.

Now this I like. Say you've got a big hunter in the family. Wanted to be cremated? Wanted to have his ashes scattered? Just send the "cremains," as they are called, to this company, and in two days they send you back a box of shells loaded with loved-one (name, dates, and a 72-character message of your choice printed on the shell casing). Boom! Send him right out of his favorite duck blind!

(Available in 12- and 20-gauge. I asked the guy the difference. He said: "Mostly, we use the twelves for the boys. The ladies usually like the smaller 20-gauge load. Last year, we even did up a box of .410s for a midget gentleman down in Arkansas. His family was extremely pleased. In a case like that, of course, the personal message is limited to 36 characters.")

$45 bucks a box, and the guy tells me they're
selling 'em as fast as they can crimp the shells.
Particularly in the "upland game bird belt"
(wherever that is).

Note: the urn people seem to genuinely despise
the shotgun shell people.

Also talked about this to a woman selling
jewelry. Her take on higher honor through superior
firepower: "extremely distasteful, if you ask me."
For $950, however, you can purchase from her a
handmade cameo brooch in solid silver, inside
which you can carry a smidge of your dear departed
"forever near your heart." Birthstone insets optional.

3:30 PM
PeachTree. Main event: "Tightening the Links"

Interesting development. No speaker.

Big turnout, but no Joel Moss. Fifteen minutes
of nothing, it's official: he's not showing. Some exec-
looking type from KBH steps up to the lectern,
apologizes for the confusion, and sends everybody
to the bar for a complimentary beverage.

What a gyp.

6:30 PM
There can't be anyplace else in the world quite like
happy hour in a bar full of undertakers.

So far have lost six rounds of darts, two games
of eightball, and turned down 12 drink offers. Also
have met some nice people in here.

Observation: there may be a fundamental
difference between me and Maria Casteneda.

Is this what Q sees?

Okay, the girl's heart is in the right place. No argument there. Probably her efforts, too. Think she's a good person and glad there are some like her out there.

Maria C's only problem: she believes people are victims. In Maria C's world, all sellers are predators and all buyers are prey.

Always another side to that coin. Think about it, Maria. Would there really be the supply if there wasn't a demand?

Twain said: "In order to know a community, one must observe the style of its funerals."

Caveat emptor? Fine. Absolutely. Let the buyer beware. Just remember that we are a culture that drives safari-class Range Rovers to the video store.

They say nobody wants to pay for a service. (Even a funeral service—ha. No more puns.) Any plumber would tell you it's true. So can you blame the funeral people for selling products instead, to make up the difference?

For the last hour, been sitting here at a table chatting with the Nebraska couple from this morning. Three months ago, this man (Tom) cared for the body of a two-year-old boy. The boy had been kidnapped, killed with a claw hammer, wrapped in plastic garbage bags, and left for two weeks in a drainage ditch. This was July. Two weeks. The boy's body was found first by raccoons. Then by a passing cyclist, who called the highway patrol.

While Tom talked about it, his eyes were sad. His wife (Marjorie) had to excuse herself from the table.

You ask me, he *deserves* to be paid. This is a man who deserves to be paid for what he does for a living.

Wonder what happened to our boy Joel M.?

* Call PG tomorrow and see if they'll give his hotel. Request breakfast interview?

* Call Q tonight. (Replied to Maria C's email with questions, 10:45 AM. No response yet.) Maybe Q hasn't talked to her either (yeah right).

BREAKING NEWS FROM THE RUMOR MILL: buzz for the 8:00 show now says Dana Carvey. Now that would be funny. Wonder if he's ever heard the one about the professor and the autopsy lecture?

Not so funny: here comes Tex.

Too late. Already saw me. On his way over now. Two drinks: one in each hand. Doesn't he know a strut like that just doesn't work without the spurs?

Here's what he said to me earlier today: "Darlin', the dead ain't so bad. It's the live ones give you the pain in the ass."

He's quotable, all right. Somebody help me.

BILLY GUILDER made a list in his head and
started at the top.

First, he found Schuler. Still where he'd left him, hanging
out in the lounge, eating a jelly donut and watching some
kind of daytime soap. Billy told him the truth: they were
short in the stock room. Then he lied and said he was on
his way out now to see what he could pick up from the
wholesaler down in El Segundo. Asked Schuler if he needed
anything else. Schuler thought about it a second, wiped some
red donut filling off his cheek, and said he couldn't think of
anything.

So Billy went up front and told Dolores he'd be back in
an hour or two. Dolores flipped a page in her magazine and
said okay.

Billy took off out of there. He headed for the truck first,
then changed his mind and went down to the big garage.
Billy got in the Miller-Meteor and sat behind the wheel for
a second or two. He took a deep breath and tried to get his
head in gear. Then he rolled down the windows, turned her
over, and drove.

Out in the world, it was a sunny day. Not quite lunch

traffic yet. People going places. Doing things regular people did.

All except Billy, who just drove. He wasn't going anywhere. Never had been.

Story of his life, so far.

Billy tried to block out the noise and the other cars; he tried to focus on the smooth, heavy rumble of custom automotive goodness all around him. The M&M was practically the only place in the world where he felt like he could think right now. It was the only thing in his whole life he'd ever done that turned out worth a damn.

So he drove.

At the front of a hundred other thoughts spinning around in his head, Billy found himself thinking about Martha Reynolds. That sweet little old granny from Holmby. Probably baked cookies for the neighbor kids around Halloween time. Probably never hurt a fly in her whole life. He thought about the turnout he'd seen at her funeral, the day he and Carl got back from stealing the poor dead woman blind. Only yesterday. Yesterday seemed like a whole life ago.

And it was, at least as far as Martha Reynolds was concerned. Billy thought about all those people, all gathered around to cry for her. All the people who would miss her. All the people she'd mattered to while she was alive.

He thought about Bishop's friend, Waxman. The one whose watch Rosen stole. Thought about all the people who came that day, too.

He thought about all the people and all the funerals he'd been around to see since he'd started working at Palm Grove.

On his way through a green light, Billy thought about what would happen if a big truck, loaded with something heavy, ran the red and plowed into him and trashed the

M&M and killed him dead. He thought about who would come to *his* funeral. The people who would be sorry his life had ended.

He thought about that. Thought about it real hard.

And it was that moment when Billy Guilder realized that if that big truck plowed on into him and he died right here today, he'd be no different than any of those other poor vagrants and loners and losers buried out back in Moss's south end. The ones he'd been digging up like bad turnips and tossing on the fire.

Just another bad turnip, was all he was. Probably worse than most. And if he got even as good as they did, Billy knew it'd be better than he deserved.

If he died right here today on the pavement, Billy Guilder didn't know where he'd go afterwards. If there was a heaven, or a hell, or some ghosty limbo. Or just dirt. But for the first time ever, Billy knew one thing.

He wouldn't leave a damn thing worth remembering behind.

It only took him fifteen minutes to find what he was looking for: a one-hour photo place in the parking lot of a drugstore on San Vincente. The photomat was one of those little drive-through hut things, where some bored-looking college kid did minimum wage time behind the glass.

Billy pulled the big hearse around back and cut the engine. He got out and looked around the parking lot. Nobody nearby. He checked the bulge in his pocket. Then he went over and knocked on the little side door of the photo hut.

No handle on the outside. Billy had to knock for about ten minutes before the door opened a crack.

"Help you?"

Billy hated to do it. He honestly did. He wasn't any good

at this kind of thing; never had been cut out for it. This was what guys like Carl Rosen were for.

But he took a breath, looked around one more time, pumped up his nerve, and jammed his steel-toed workboot into the crack. At the same time he grabbed the edge of the door and yanked. The kid behind the door said "Hey!" and latched on tight. Billy threw his weight back, heard a yelp, and felt the resistance give way.

When he got inside the booth, the kid had backed against the tall machine in the corner. He was a shaggy-haired guy with droopy eyes and acne scars all over his face. Maybe twenty. The name tag pinned to his red vest said CORBIE. He was holding his hands up in front of him. Billy saw one of his fingernails bled a little, probably injured in the door scuffle.

"Sorry," Billy told him.

The kid held his hands where they were. His eyes were big. "It's in the register," he said. He reached over quickly and punched a button on the cash machine. The drawer popped open and slid out. "Shit. Take it, man."

"Easy," Billy told him. He was starting to get a little nervous now himself; he hoped nobody could see them through the windows. He went over and turned the CLOSED sign around, then pulled down the interior shades. "Geez—put your hands down, okay? I ain't robbing you."

"You're not?"

"Man, you ever heard of anybody knocking over a picture place?"

"We've been hit twice this year."

"You gotta be kidding me."

The kid shook his head. No joke. He still had his hands up, like he'd had the practice.

Billy couldn't believe it. He looked around the photo

booth. Back in the days, he wouldn't have ever thought about trying a place like this in a million years.

"Listen," he told the kid. "I need some film developed. How fast can you do it?"

Without taking his eyes off Billy, the kid angled one finger toward the sign that said "One-Hour Photos."

"That says color," Billy told him. "You can do black and white, though?"

"Um …" the kid said. He hesitated. Very slowly, he lowered his arms. "Is it C-41?"

"Forty who?"

"C-41." The kid backed up another step. He looked like he was trying to crawl inside the photo developing machine backwards.

"Look, you're gonna have to help me out here, man. I look like a guy knows cameras to you?"

"C-41," the kid said again, like it was the only thing anybody needed to know. He looked at Billy carefully and took a breath. "Um … do you have your film with you, sir?"

"Oh," said Billy. "Right. Yeah. This is it right here." He pulled the bulge out of his pocket and handed it over to the kid.

Carl Rosen had been wrong. Maria did too have film in the camera.

Last night, while he'd been monkeying around with it, Billy had accidentally shot off the last picture on the roll. The camera had started buzzing in his hands; after a few seconds, he'd realized it was rewinding. Just like a VCR at the end of a tape. When the camera stopped humming, Billy had slipped the roll out and put it in his pocket before Carl came back in from the oven room.

He still didn't know why he'd done it. It just seemed like

the thing to do. But then, he'd been stoned out of his gourd at the time.

One eye on Billy, still acting slightly nervous but seeming to feel a little bit more in his element now, the kid lifted up the film spool and read something along the side.

"Um … yeah," he said. "This is c-41 film. That means … it means we can process it using the same chemicals we use for color film."

"So you can do it in an hour, right?"

"I … I guess so. Yeah."

"Coolest." Billy reached over and patted the kid gratefully on the arm. "That's seriously great, partner. You're a real life saver."

The kid just stood there. He didn't seem to know what to say.

"Okay," Billy told him. "This is kind of what you might call a special order. Here's the deal."

While he talked, Billy pulled out a fat roll of bills from his other pocket. His $800 split from the Holmby job. Actually, more like $750 now; he'd gotten a couple burgers and seen a movie. And he'd put gas in the M&M.

When the kid saw the money, his eyes grew wide again.

"All you want is some photos developed?"

"Uh huh."

"Right … um, right now?"

"Man, do you see me sitting in the drive-through?" Billy pressed the heavy wad of bills into Corbie's free hand.

Corbie looked down at the money like he'd never seen cash before. While he looked at his hand, he continued repeating Billy's instructions. Like he was just making sure he had it all straight.

"But you don't want me to look at them."

"You can do that, right? I mean, what, you just stick the film in that machine there and wait for 'em to come out the other end, right?"

"Well it's not exactly … I mean, sort of. I guess."

They stood there and looked at each other. Billy felt like he wanted to say something more. He felt like he wanted to tell this kid what it had taken him so long to finally learn, personally. He wanted to tell the kid: *Pay attention. Think.* He wanted to say: *Live your life a decent kind of way. Do it while you're young, like you are now. 'Cause you only get one time around, kid, and I know you don't think so now—but trust me. You don't know when your turn's gonna be up. Could be today, for all you know.*

And when it's all over?

You're lucky, you'll have people who are sorry to see you go.

That's what Billy wanted to tell him. *You do it right, it'll matter you're gone.*

But Billy didn't say any of those things. Instead, he just held up one finger. He dug back into his pocket, pulled out what was left of his herb, and plopped that into the kid's hand on top of the film and the money. The little brass pipe Carl had given him was still inside the baggie.

"That there's a tip," Billy said. "Sorry about barging in like that before."

Corbie the photo kid looked down at the pile of stuff cupped in his two hands like Halloween treats: the roll of film, the roll of cash, and a mostly-empty baggie of killer bud. He sucked his bleeding fingernail for a second or two.

Then he looked up at Billy and said, "Did you want duplicates?"

WHEN THE GUY named Carl laughed, Maria Casteneda knew just what she was hearing. It wasn't the eulogy she might have imagined for herself.

"So don't tell me," he said. "Let me guess. You sprung that biological clock shit on him and he dumped your ass, right?"

"Something like that," she said.

It hadn't been anything like that at all. The irony of this conversation was not lost on Maria; for here, in what she left unspoken, was the same conversation she'd been planning to have with Quince this very morning. A piece of her history she'd omitted that night at the bar. At the time, it had been none of his business.

But that had changed. Now, Quince deserved to know the truth about her and Joel before things between them went further.

Current circumstances being what they were, gone so horrid and wrong and out of her grasp, Maria had neither the faculty nor the will to lay out the fine points now. Not here on the cracked and grimy floor of a basement storage room, wrists and ankles bound. Not to the man who held the gun.

"That's rough," he agreed. "I mean, kicked to the curb by *that* limp dick?" He pointed at her with the barrel of the gun. "I'd be pissin' fire, too."

Maria sat and said nothing.

The man named Carl looked at her. Even from several feet away, he smelled like cigarettes and body odor and cheap cologne. He shook his head again, slowly, as if musing over what she'd confirmed for him. Filling in the blank pages of a scrapbook he'd obviously found in her apartment.

She knew the one. She kept it on the top shelf of a closet and hadn't looked at it herself in years.

"True love," he said philosophically. "Fuckin' bitch, ain't it?"

"You said it."

"Guess it explains a few things, though."

"Guess so."

Carl sighed. "Well, I don't know about you—but *I* sure feel better." He tilted his head thoughtfully. "You know, it didn't conflict with personal interests of mine, hell—I might enjoy turnin' you loose on the little weasel-fucker. Guy deserves what he gets, you ask me."

"You know I can't hurt you," she said quietly. "I've got nothing. I'm no danger to you at all."

"Loose ends," he said. "It's nothin' personal. Besides. I got plans."

"Somebody will hear you." Grasping at anything, now. "I know there are people upstairs—I can hear them walking around. If you shoot that gun, they'll hear it."

"What, this?"

Carl looked at the revolver in his hand. Then he did something that surprised her.

He grinned. Slowly. Another wink.

"Okay, okay," he said. "You got me. I was just holdin' this for effect. Piece of shit barely works anyway."

Maria didn't reply.

But Carl must have seen something pass across her face, because he shrugged—not unkindly—and rested the pistol on his knee. "Don't worry, girl. You just stay chilly down here and don't make problems, this'll all go easy. You got my word."

Maria tried to shift her position enough to alleviate the ache in her hips and back. The headache that had woken her inside the casket had grown steadily worse through the morning. She hadn't thought it possible. It felt as though the pressure had nowhere else to build; if her skull split open like a ripe melon, it would be a blessing. She was dumb with hurt.

Except for a very occasional hot sting in her cheek—some nerve bundle twitching reactively, some phantom flicker in a scorched synapse somewhere—Maria couldn't feel the right side of her face at all now; it felt dead and useless, like she'd been spiked full of Novocaine. She couldn't bring her vision into focus, and it hurt too much to try. So she closed her eyes.

A bleak day indeed it was, when a probable head injury seemed the least of her concerns.

"Hey," she heard Carl say. "Makes you feel better, in a certain sense, this'll kinda be like your chance to help stick it to loverboy."

Maria leaned her head back gently as she could against the wall behind her, resting her cross-bound wrists in her lap. The rubber tubing had cut off the circulation in her hands hours ago. The tips of her fingers had turned gray.

"I don't know what kind of help you think I'm going to

be," she said. Anything to keep the conversation from ending. Knowing that, if nothing else, the longer she could postpone his exit, the longer she might forestall being put back in that casket to wait. Maria didn't think she could bear that.

So she marshaled what strength remained and opened her eyes. The sudden re-entry of light pierced her dilated right pupil like a nail.

"Don't you worry. I know all about guys like Moss."

"I take it you're planning on blackmailing him," she said.

"Blackmail?" Carl shook his finger back and forth. "Nah, see, that's the wrong way to think about it. You might say it's more like … a maintenance plan."

"So you're blackmailing him."

"You oughta try being more creative in your thinking, anybody ever told you that before?" He grimaced. "See, that's exactly what gets a retard like Mick in over his head: no long-term planning."

Carl gestured with the gun while he orated.

"Granted, now, a lot of it's just experience—but it ain't like it used to be. Not anymore. Nowadays? Competition's too heavy. Resale markets, they're all flooded. Everything's organized. You just *gotta* be ready to consolidate, you want to make it out there these days. Now, you take Mick. That'd be the guy you saw last night."

"I remember."

"Yeah, well that dumb fucker's a perfect example what I'm talking about. That lone wolf blackmail bullshit's for idgits, this day and age. You think that small? Lay it all out on the short score like that? You know what usually happens?"

"I think I get the idea."

"You get fucked, that's what. It's a big fish/little fish kinda thing."

Carl rested the gun on his knee.

"Other hand," he went on, "you got a guy like Moss, who's basically just too fuckin' stupid to live anyway. Guy like that *thinks* he's a big fish. But you know what?"

"Little fish?" Maria said.

"Fuckhead don't even know he's in the wrong pond." Carl winked. "'Bout to learn, though."

Maria closed her eyes. "I guess you've put a lot of thought into this."

"Hey, you know how it is. Guy my age has to consider future security."

Big fish. Little fish. She thought: *more like birds of a feather*.

But for some reason, Maria also felt her heart start beating again. Something in what Carl said had flashed briefly, illuminating an unexpected foothold.

She tried to sit up a little. The effort made her head pound and her vision bend and her stomach turn.

"Not that it's any of my business," she said, not sure what she'd say next until she said it. "But … well, how far in the future are you thinking, anyway?"

"You could say I'm in the process of developing a set of long-term goals."

"See, that's where I'm not sure I get where you're going." Simple speech was a struggle, and she was flying by the seat of her pants besides. But Maria kept on spinning out each maddeningly mush-mouthed word on the thread of the last. "I'd think you'd be … well, on a *time* schedule. Wouldn't you?"

"Don't know why that'd be," he said. Clearly he was humoring her. Out of boredom, Maria supposed. "Tell you the truth, I think this place is starting to grow on me."

"Great," she said. "But I'm not sure I'd want to get too attached, if I were you."

"Oh, no? And why's that?"

"Please," she said. "You *know* Joel is out of here as soon as he closes the deal."

Maria felt her heart beat faster still. She feared, if the silence lasted, Carl would be able to hear the pounding in her chest.

"Okay," he finally said. "I'll bite. Deal you talking about?"

"The whole KBH thing. You know."

Silence again. Longer this time.

Carl had become unreadable. His eyes had gone dull and hard.

But Maria felt a quick hot rush of adrenaline. The foothold was bearing weight. She put her bound hands to the floor beside her and boosted herself up another inch. "You don't know, do you?"

No answer.

"I should have supposed," she said. The more she talked, the faster her thoughts came together. "He hasn't told you, has he? That's really perfect. Classic Joel. I don't even know why I'm surprised."

"Fuck you talking about?"

"Put it this way," she finally said. "Maybe you shouldn't count out the little fish too soon."

Carl chuckled flatly at that. Then he sat forward on his crate. Reaching over with his arm, he pressed the muzzle of the revolver up underneath her chin, into the soft hollow part of her throat.

"I thought you said that didn't work," she said.

"Works okay up close like this."

"Listen," she said. "Joel? Joel sold this place months ago. I don't know what your 'long-term' plans are, but I'll let you in on a little tip: the clock is ticking. Big time."

"That a fact." Without blinking or changing his expression, Carl pulled the hammer back with his thumb. Maria could feel the cylinder rotating against her chin.

Maria tried to crane her neck away from the sharp pressure of the sightpost on the gun's barrel. "You don't believe me? Let me tell you what he's doing up in Seattle this weekend."

"Do that."

"There's a big sitdown with KBH, for starters. That's the company buying him out. Joel's contract is almost up—that's what the meeting is about. At the end of the year, Joel takes a big payday. And if I know Joel, he's on the first plane to Grand Bahama after the check clears."

Carl looked at her.

"Say hello to the new boss," she said.

After a long moment, Carl finally took the gun away and sat back in his chair. "Stones fan, huh?"

With the departure of the gun from her throat, Maria released the breath she'd been holding. "Some of their early stuff was okay. But I think you're thinking about The Who."

Carl grinned. "Funny how you seem to know an awful lot about an awful lot. How's that, exactly?"

Maria tried the best return grin she could manage. But the results were pathetic. Only half her mouth moved. Suddenly, she was afraid she might cry.

But she didn't. "You said it yourself, right?"

"What's that?"

Maria folded her bound wrists over her heart. "True love. It'll bite you on the rear every time."

It probably hadn't ever been true, though she hadn't known it at the time. Looking back, she doubted it had even been love. At best, her relationship with Joel had been a logical attempt, and little more.

Joel's father, Walt, first introduced the two of them. Walt Moss and Lisandro Casteneda had developed a deep friendship over the course of several years. It was a camaraderie that grew out of a business relationship; after being approached and agreeing to a few very simple terms, Maria's father spent nearly a decade supplying Palm Grove with durable, well-made discount coffins for the unclaimed souls Walt Moss buried in the south corner of his cemetery.

The two men naturally had hoped for a match between Joel and Maria, who both were unmarried and eligible and roughly the same age. Maria supposed it was the admiration she felt for her father and for Walt, their friendship and their work together, that made it so difficult to recognize her true feelings for Joel. For so long, anyway.

Three years and four days, to be exact. Four days after Joel had proposed.

When the stunned thrill cleared, and she'd come to her senses and handed back the ring, even her father had been mystified.

But somehow, Walt Moss seemed to understand. He seemed to know. Maria had always suspected that somewhere, deep in his core, Walt knew just how broken and hollow his son had allowed himself to become.

Maria believed he'd died thinking it was somehow his fault.

"Question?" she said.

"Aww, sure. We're practically pals."

"What would you say if I told you I could help you with those long-term goals?"

Carl seemed to ponder this. "I'd say you're trying to bargain your ass outta that box over there."

"You're damned straight I am," she said.

Carl looked at her for a long moment. Maria looked back. She tried to seem indecipherable.

It wasn't hard. She'd played her hand, such as it was, as far as she could. She was out of ideas, and didn't know how to freshen the bluff. For the first time, it occurred to her: *he was at my apartment this morning.* She wondered by how many minutes he and Quince had missed each other. She wondered if Quince was annoyed with her for breaking their breakfast date.

Somehow she doubted it. He didn't seem the type. She wondered what he was up to now.

Wondered what Billy Guilder was doing this minute.

Drawing her bound wrists to her chest, she took Abuelita's cross in her numb fingertips and prayed to Whomever might be listening that whatever it was, he was hurrying.

Exhausted from trying to keep her eyes open long enough for Carl's response, Maria finally closed them.

And was almost shocked when she heard the man with the gun say, "I'm listening."

QUINCE FOUND no message from Maria when he finally got back to his apartment at half-past noon. He decided he'd call her and leave a scathingly witty message, if he could think of one.

But first, one thing.

From the top shelf of his only closet, Quince pulled down the shoebox he kept in the back corner. Its edges and corners were scuffed and dented from once-frequent handling. But there was a dose of candor in the heavy rubber band that held the lid down tight; the rubber band had grown so brittle since the last time he'd been inside the box that it just crumbled apart when he pulled.

The box always had been too large for its contents. For all the hours he'd spent rummaging around inside when he'd been younger, there really hadn't ever been much he kept in there.

There were a couple of photographs. One had been snapped around Christmas time in the snow-covered parking lot of a tree farm near Crystal Lake. He and Paul, in hooded parkas, rode the felled family tree like a sled; Dad—gripping hold of the cut end of the trunk with one gloved hand, carrying the bow saw in the other—kicked white powder up from the snowpack as he pulled them toward the car. The other photo had been taken in the summer; Mom, Dad, Paul, and him, all holding corn dogs in front of one of the roller coasters at Six Flags.

With these, he'd kept the postcard Paul had scribbled full of the thirteen-year-old handwriting that had fooled Quince so completely for a while. The postcard, plus a dog-eared copy of the program from the funeral. He'd kept a couple of newspaper clippings about the accident, which he'd copied from microfiche at the Palatine Public library one afternoon when he was supposed to have been doing research for a sophomore English term paper.

Quince pawed through the old stuff for a few minutes. He indulged himself, if only for these few moments, allowing the maudlin nostalgia to play.

Then he placed the picture of him and Wax inside with the rest.

But before he lidded the box and returned it to its place, he paused long enough to take out the one other object inside. The only thing in the whole box heavy enough to make a rattle.

The object was a red Swiss Army pocketknife—much smaller than Quince remembered, holding it now. His parents had gotten Paul one just like it for his twelfth birthday. Quince, only five at the time, had been heartbroken, filled to the eyeballs with left-out kid brother jealousy. He'd pouted and moped about it so much that Mom and Dad finally had gone back to the same sporting goods store and gotten Quince one of his own. Just like Paul's, down to the accessories: two blades, a corkscrew, a can opener, and the little mini-toothpick and tweezers that fit into the handle.

They'd told him he was too little to carry the knife around. They'd explained that Paul had to wait until he was twelve before he'd gotten his own pocketknife, and that Quince would have to wait for his, too. But they wanted him to know he had one waiting for him, and it was just like Paul's.

Quince couldn't help but smile, holding the pocketknife in his palm. He opened one of the blades and tested the edge with the pad of his thumb. After a minute, he closed it and put it back into the box again.

The pocketknife had always depressed him. More than the pictures. More than any other single memento in the box, really. It was the pocketknife—so much more immediate and three-dimensional than frozen images or words typed on a page—that seemed to contain the most painful energy of all for him. When he was a kid, sometimes he used to imagine, ludicrously, that if they'd had the knife with them at the time, maybe they could have cut through their seatbelts and helped each other crawl to safety before the car blew.

Even as a kid, he knew that was crazy, knew it wasn't true. The car hadn't even exploded; he just imagined it that way. But there was an odd mental association with the knife just the same. For some reason, that pocketknife always made Quince think of his parents dying together in a wadded ball of steel.

But for some other reason, today the knife only carried with it the memory of the day Mom and Dad had sat him down and explained that Paul got certain things because he was older, not because they loved him more.

For some reason, today, the pocketknife made him remember the smell of Mom's shampoo, of Dad's cologne. Holding the knife, for the briefest of moments, it was almost as if their spirits hung in the room.

DIRT

The cross insignia on the knife's handle made Quince think of Maria and the cross she kept with her. He thought about how near she wore that pendant, never beyond a fingertip's reach. He thought about something Maria had said, the other night as they'd walked together out to visit Martin's grave. Something her grandmother used to tell her.

Death is the reason God gave us a memory.

He thought about that while he put the box back on the shelf where it belonged. Or where he kept it, anyway.

Quince was still thinking about it while he hunted for the receiver to the cordless phone. First he called Maria's apartment. No answer. He tried her at the SoCal Valley office and got no answer there. He left messages on both machines.

Wondering where she was, what she was doing and why she hadn't called, Quince wandered back into the dormer and found himself taking his box down from the closet shelf again. He slipped his hand beneath the lid, then put the box back once more.

Why not, he thought. He was old enough. He had pockets.

Wondering if Paul still carried his, Quince headed outside to mow Arlen's yard while he waited for Maria's return call.

Billy Guilder didn't make it back to Palm Grove until almost two in the afternoon. He came in the basement through the garage access to avoid running into Dolores or Schuler on the way. Billy unlocked the door and flipped on the light and closed the door behind him.

When he turned around, his heart took a plunge.

No Carl. No Maria. The storage room was empty.

All he saw were the same empty shelves as usual. The same stacks of boxes and crates. The only thing out of place in the room was the Conquistador, still sitting on its cart amidst clear ratty sheets of torn bubble wrapper.

Billy noticed the lid was closed again. From where he stood he could see bright flanges of bare metal poking up here and there, where he'd drilled in those air holes. He set down the armload of stuff he'd been carrying and went over. Flipped the latches and lifted the lid.

And felt much better when Maria Casteneda opened her eyes and looked up at him. As soon as the box was open, she wiggled and rolled onto her side and struggled to push herself upright.

She mumbled something he couldn't make out. Carl had re-gagged her again.

So Billy reached out and untied the rubber tubing and pulled the satin pillowcase out of her mouth for the second time today. Supporting her with his arm, he said, "What you doin' back in here? Where'd Carl go?"

"Joel's office," she told him. "Come on, we've got to hurry."

"Huh?" Billy tilted his head, not liking the sound of this. Thinking of Carl stomping around upstairs with Dolores and Schuler made him nervous. "What'd he go up there for?"

"Billy—just untie me, okay? I'll explain after we get out of here."

"Don't worry," Billy told her. "I got help on the way. We just gotta hang tight for a while longer, okay?"

"Billy!" She grabbed his shirt again and looked him straight in the face. "What's the matter with you?"

Billy tried not to look at her. Since the photomat, he'd been starting to feel a little more confident, a little more in control. He'd been starting to feel like maybe there was still time to fix things after all. But all of a sudden, looking at her

eyes and her sagging mouth and her pretty hair all crusty
with dried blood on one side, Billy was afraid she was going
to make him lose it all over again.

"Listen to me," Maria Casteneda said. "You're not like
Carl, Billy. I don't even know you, and I can tell that much. I
can tell you're a good person. So don't just stand there, okay?
Help me."

"I ain't so good," Billy said.

"Please. Untie me before that psychopath gets back."

"Help's comin'," Billy said again, without quite as much
conviction as the first time.

"We don't need to wait for help," Maria said. "We can go
to the police ourselves, together," Maria said. "Right now."

Just the thought of going to the cops made Billy queasy
with anxiety. And the added vision of what might happen if
Carl happened to walk in while he was untying her didn't
help calm his nerves all that much, either. "Um, yeah, okay.
I'm not sure that's such a good idea."

"No, just think about it," she said. "Carl's been to my
apartment. He's been to … to the other boy's. The one who
was killed. I'll bet you anything he's been leaving fingerprints
all over the place. That's got to be worth something."
She nodded at him like he ought to see that for himself.
"Somebody's bound to notice that guy is missing soon."

Billy figured she was probably right. About the fingerprints
part, anyway. He'd been thinking about the exact same thing
when they went out on the Holmby job, which was why he'd
taken along the heavy rubber gloves from the embalming
room for both of them to wear. Carl had just looked at him
like Billy was some kind of idiot trying out for a dishsoap
commercial. Later, Billy had understood Carl's thinking:
they'd had the perfect excuse already for any fingerprints of

theirs that might be found, considering they'd already been inside granny's house for legitimate purposes the day before. Which was one of the things that made Carl's plan so smart, according to Carl.

Still, Billy figured Maria was right. Based on what he'd seen so far, he didn't figure Carl Rosen for a rubber glove-wearing kind of guy.

"He practically told me that he has property from the boy's apartment here right now," Maria went on. It was like new stuff just kept coming to her the more she thought about it. "And he said something about having tapes, too. Something he was going to use on Joel."

"I don't...."

"And the crematory!" Maria said, shaking his arm a little now. "The retort. Did you guys clean it after? What did you do with the ... with the remains?"

"We ... I dunno," Billy said, wondering how she knew so much about this stuff. Of course they hadn't cleaned out the oven yet; between the two of them, he was the only one who knew how. Normally, they used this machine to crush down what was left of somebody when the cremation was finished, since what was left was usually pretty chunky still and didn't really look like ashes at all. More like a pile of cinder and bone pieces. So what they did was run a big magnet over it to lift out any jewelry or fillings or surgical hardware that made it through. Then they ran it all through this pulverizer, which looked about like a stainless steel washing machine, and made the remains come out nice and powdery so people could scatter them if they wanted to, or whatever they wanted to do.

Carl wouldn't know about any of that. He hadn't even seen Billy use the pulverizer on anybody yet; they never bothered using it with the south end disposals, since there wasn't really much point in it.

Billy started to get nervous as he thought about all of this. Why couldn't he think like Maria? Why couldn't he ever figure out this stuff for himself?

Maria asked him the obvious question. "If you haven't cleaned it yet, then there still could be some evidence of the murder, right? Bone fragments, teeth … you know the furnace never gets everything." She looked at him seriously. "We'll drive straight to the cops, figure out something to tell them, get our stories straight on the way. I'll vouch for you. I'll tell them you found out the protest was a sham, that you found out what Joel was doing and tipped me, just trying to help. I'll say Carl and Joel caught me snooping, and you helped me again. Billy, I promise you, if you trust me and we work together it'll be okay. We'll get through this."

Billy shook his head and tried not to listen. He felt so guilty he almost couldn't stand it. Guilty and getting scared all over again. He didn't know what to think—but he knew if he listened to Maria too much now he'd end up wrecking this for them both.

If he hadn't already.

How he wished they'd had more time to put their heads together on this before Carl came in before.

Not knowing what to do about it now, he rubbed Maria's shoulder a little, trying to be soothing. Billy felt like an idiot. He felt like he was trying to pet a cat.

He told her, "Listen, we're gonna do all that stuff, okay? I swear. But you don't know Carl, man. Shit, I don't even know Carl. Anything went wrong—I don't even know, okay? All I know is, we gotta do this right the first time, or … or I don't even wanna think about it, you know what I'm saying?"

"What's going to happen?" Maria asked him.

"What's gonna happen is, you and me, we're just gonna hang tight and play like everything's normal and wait for the good guys to show up. Okay?"

What he didn't tell her was that he actually had no idea what was going to happen from here. He didn't tell her that he'd never had a plan, not really. Just a dim 40-watt bulb of an idea, and all his fingers crossed.

Somehow, Billy didn't think that was the kind of thing Maria really wanted to hear.

So for her sake, he didn't mention that her only hope of getting out of here and getting to a doctor and getting some help was a dumb con who'd bungled pretty much everything he'd ever tried to do, mainly due to the fact that whenever he got nervous he just seemed to go stupid in the head. Normal circumstances, when nothing went wrong, Billy liked to think that he generally got by okay. But when it came to high-stress situations like this, for some reason he couldn't seem to think his way out of a wet paper sack.

It wasn't an excuse. Only the truth, that's all. It was one of those things you start to figure out about yourself, you go to jail enough times.

And speaking of jail: frankly, Billy feared cops even more than Carl Rosen, which didn't help matters.

Billy didn't mention any of that.

He didn't tell Maria that the more he thought about it, the more he considered the idea of getting in the M&M, and hopping on the 10, and driving it east. Driving until he got out into the desert, and then driving some more. Years ago, at Chino, he'd been celled up with a guy who lived on a little patch of ground outside Nogales on the Arizona side. Nachez, was the guy's name. Always told Billy that once they were both outside, he could come on down and visit any time he felt like it. There were big empty canyons all around his place where they could go and camp and drink beer and shoot off some guns some weekend, just for laughs.

They'd kept in touch off and on since Nachez made his paper way back when. As far as Billy knew, Nachez still lived his days down there, sun-drying his own peppers and repairing Harley bikes, occasionally renting out storage space in the dry arroyos around his place for certain kinds of merchandise. Maybe helping a few items back and forth across the border from time to time.

Maybe now was a good time to go see his old buddy Nachez. Matter of fact, the more Billy thought it over, maybe that seemed like just exactly what he should do.

He didn't want to go back to jail.

But he didn't mention any of that, either.

What he did was help Maria down out of the casket. With her ankles tied, Maria lost her balance, and when she tried to catch herself her knees buckled. Billy threw his arm around her and helped her over to the wall, where she could sit down and lean.

"I brought some stuff," he said, and jogged back over to the pile he'd dropped. On his way back from the photomat, he'd stopped to pick up rubbing alcohol and bandages, three different brands of over-the-counter painkiller, and some girl-type magazines he thought she might enjoy if her head didn't hurt too bad to read. He'd also stopped in the breakroom and grabbed the box of donuts Dolores had brought in. What was left of them, anyway. He'd thought Maria might be hungry.

"Billy," he heard her say. "Let's think this through. Together. Okay?"

But before he could answer, Billy heard keys in the door. Carl came in, looking aggravated.

"Carl," Billy said, too loudly. "Yo."

He could practically hear his own voice in Carl's ears; the way Billy heard himself, he sounded like some pimply kid who just got caught whacking off to the bras and panties section of his mom's Sears catalogue. He squeezed his eyes closed and thought: *try to be cool*. Billy stood up with his armload and turned to Carl.

Carl looked at him questioningly. Billy braced himself for whatever was coming.

But the question surprised him.

"Who's that goony lookin' motherfucker upstairs, anyway?"

"Huh?"

"Freakshow with the suit don't fit."

"Who, Schuler?"

Carl just looked at him.

"That's just Schuler," Billy said. "He's okay."

"Fucker gives me the creeps," said Carl. Billy saw that he had the pistola that didn't shoot straight tucked in the front of his waistband, up under his shirt. "That's the first thing that's wrong with him."

From over against the wall, Maria Casteneda said, "What's the second thing?"

She had her head back and her eyes closed. She looked like somebody waiting for a bus on a hot day.

"Fucker's been up in the office playing some kinda damn card game on that computer for an hour." Carl shrugged. "So everybody listen up. Plan's changing."

Maria opened her eyes. Arms full, Billy looked at her. He looked at Carl.

"What plan?" he said.

And for the first time, Carl seemed to really notice him. "Yo, what took your ass so long gettin' back here, anyway?"

Billy shrugged and tried to seem natural. "They always make you wait, man. You know the drill."

Carl snorted. "I hear that." He glanced at the donut box Billy was holding and came over. Carl pried the lid open and took the last two.

Billy sighed and let the empty box fall to the ground. "What plan?"

"Okay, here's the deal," said Carl. "I ain't gonna be able to poke around that office until tonight at least. Meantime, there's too much fuckin' traffic around here. So what we're gonna do is, you're gonna go get the pickup and back it up into the garage. Me and chickyboom here are gonna meet you out there and we're gonna put her in the back. Then you're gonna go up and make sure Freakshow and that secretary ..."

"Dolores," Billy said.

Carl gave him an exasperated look but didn't stop talking. "... ain't looking out any windows. I'll take shutterbug out to the barbecue hut where it ain't so crowded. Anybody got any questions?"

"I have a question," said Maria. She sounded tired to Billy all of a sudden. Slurring her words kind of bad.

"How come I ain't surprised? Let's hear it."

"Why didn't you just put me out there last night to begin with? Seems like it would've been easier."

And Carl just looked at her, looked at Billy, and to Billy's amazement, grinned.

"You know, I'm seriously starting to like you," he said. "Almost kinda hoping me and Billy here don't have to shoot your ass."

Maria didn't say anything to that. When Billy looked at her, he saw that she'd kind of slumped against the wall. But then he saw her chest rising and falling. Still breathing. She must have either fallen asleep or passed out. Either way, he was glad for her. Maybe even a little jealous. Part of him wished he hadn't given away all his pot to the photo kid.

Billy looked at Carl and raised his hand.

"The fuck you got your hand up for?"

"I have a question."

Carl gave him the same exasperated look and said, "Well spit it out already. Jesus."

"What plan?"

Carl had shoved a donut into his mouth. There were colored sprinkles and flecks of sugar caught in his beard.

"Let's just say," he mumbled around the donut, "I got some shit I gotta do. Gimmee the keys to that muscle buggy of yours. I ain't driving that truck no more. Fucker's dangerous."

"You want the M&M?" Billy asked, feeling his heart sink again. "You're leaving?"

"Little while." Carl winked. "Don't worry, I'll be back soon as I see if a couple things are like the shutterbug says they are."

"What about me?"

Carl pointed at him with the last donut and then stuck it in his mouth. "You're babysittin'."

When Arlen got up out of the lounge chair and waved, Quince couldn't tell what he wanted at first. He was edging around Arlen's almond trees while Arlen watched from a chaise lounge on the patio, Vlad in his lap and a Long Island Iced Tea in his hand. Arlen was not characteristically a drinker by day; when Quince had asked him why the mid-afternoon cocktails, Arlen had smiled distantly and informed him that today was his anniversary.

Quince wished he'd known.

He lifted one side of his headphones and leaned over the push bar; the roar of the lawnmower drowned out the sound of the new Lounge Lizards CD that had arrived in the morning mail.

"What!" he yelled.

Arlen made a sawing motion across his throat and pointed out toward the driveway.

Quince cut the engine and immediately heard what Arlen was pointing about. Repeated blasts from a car horn punctuated the sudden silence.

Just as Quince began to hike toward the garage to see what was going on, a sudden squeal of car tires arced through the air. Quince could hear the high whine of a reverse gear winding tight as the car backed out of the drive, banged its front bumper on the curb, then shifted, laid rubber again, and tore off down the street.

Quince took off running. He got to the driveway just in time to see the car's back end disappear around the tree-lined corner.

He caught neither make nor model, and the car was already too far away to apprehend the license number. But what Quince did glimpse seemed odd indeed.

He wasn't positive. But he could have sworn it was a hearse.

Panting, he turned and looked back toward the house. Arlen and Vlad were making their way across the yard.

When they joined him, Quince said, "It isn't Girl Scout cookie season, is it?"

"Not to my knowledge."

"Any other ideas?"

Arlen shrugged and pointed. "I'm sure I don't," he said. "But it looks like they left a calling card."

Once again, Quince looked where Arlen pointed—this time, toward the wooden steps leading up to his apartment. There was a large manila envelope on the first riser. Quince went over and picked it up.

Scribbled on the front in black magic marker: BISHOP

He held it up and showed Arlen.

"It isn't ticking, is it?" Arlen asked.

"Gotta hand it to you, Arl," Quince said. "You serve a dramatic eviction notice."

"Open the bloody thing already," Arlen said. "You know Vladdy's got a bad heart. The suspense isn't good for him."

"BY THE WAY," Quince said. "Happy anniversary."

Arlen nodded absently and said nothing.

The three of them sat around the small rickety table in Quince's kitchenette: Quince, Arlen, and Blind Vladimir, nobody saying much of anything. Quince still had grass clippings from the yard on his shoes.

Moments ago, Arlen had drained what remained of his Long Island in a gulp. Quince retrieved the bottle of Dewar's he kept in the cupboard above the refrigerator, returning to the table with the bottle and two short glasses. He poured a couple of liquid amber inches into each. Arlen gazed at something beyond Quince's head. They drank without comment.

Between them, spread out on the table like a bad news tarot hand, were the contents of the mystery envelope, its mystery revealed.

The envelope contained six photographs in all. Grainy black-and-whites, all shot at night in bad lighting. The focus was fuzzy in most of them, but the face of any one of the three subjects was clear in one shot or another. The one in the silk Chinese robe Quince was sure he recognized as Joel

Moss. He'd only seen the guy twice, at Martin's funerals, but Moss had a face that stuck. Or maybe it was just the fifty-dollar haircut.

In another photo, Moss was motion-blurred, but Quince could make out the person to whom Moss spoke. This face was familiar also, but Quince couldn't place it. He swore he'd seen the guy before, but he couldn't think where. Pocks, tattoos, Charlie Manson beard.

But for Quince, it was the face of the third person that brought out the Scotch from the cupboard. Laying on a broad sheet of dark-smeared plastic, staring at nothing, this figure was the most familiar of the three. The bandages on his face were impossible to forget.

The only difference between the face as it appeared in the photo, and as it had looked the last time Quince had seen it, was that the bandages now covered the far lesser of two wounds.

A note accompanied the stills. It looked like it had been scribbled quickly, by a hand that didn't write many notes. The note said:

> *I'm giving you these to you becuse a frend of mine*
> *told me you are a smart guy. SO I guess you will no*
> *what to do. They (the picturs) are from Palm Grove*
> *from last night (Thursday night). My frend says you*
> *shoud show these to a detective Timms and to hurry*
> *because there is still evidence at PG if you hurry.*
> *Please call timms and show him these right away.*

The note was signed, *Anonomous*. There was a post script:

> *My frend says to tell you again hes sorry about your*

frend. Please call det Timms. Tell him to check the
storage room and also tell him to HURRY!!!

Vladimir yipped once from across the table, chasing whatever blind Pomeranians chased in their sleep. Arlen stroked the dog's head and said, "Hush, Vladdy."

Quince stared blankly from across the table. He felt like a sudden breeze might sweep him off his chair.

"Kiddo," said Arlen. "Oh, kiddo."

"This is crazy," Quince said. He didn't know what else to say.

"I'll say one thing for you," Arlen glanced again at the photographs and looked away. "When you break out of a slump, you don't mess around."

"Jesus," Quince murmured, and was interrupted by the phone warbling in his hand. He cut it off in the middle of the first ring and said, "This is Quince, hello?"

"Timms," said the deep voice on the other end of the line. Quince heard commotion in the background. "You paged me?"

"I … yes. That's right."

"Better be good. I'm at my kid's soccer game. Who is this?"

Quince spoke quickly, reminding the detective who he was, telling Timms that he needed to meet with him as soon as possible. Timms cheered loudly away from the phone, then returned to the line.

"Yeah, okay. I remember you. What's up?"

Fiddling with the corners of the card Timms had given him earlier in the week, Quince gave the detective an abbreviated version of everything he'd just explained to Arlen. Adding: "I think … I think somebody's been killed."

Without pausing, the detective told Quince to sit tight and asked him for his address.

Quince took one look at Arlen, who stroked Vladimir while he gazed at the tabletop with a deeply troubled look in his eyes.

He said, "I'd rather come to you, if you don't mind. Can I meet you somewhere?"

Timms recited the address of a soccer field not far from Arlen's neighborhood. Quince told Timms he knew the place; Timms told Quince he'd meet him out front. Parking lot for Field B.

So Quince hung up and scooped up the photos and put them back in the envelope with the note. He looked at Arlen. "I've got to go."

Arlen nodded. "Can I do anything?"

"Would you stay here until I get back? In case Maria calls?"

"Of course," Arlen said. "Kiddo?"

"Yeah."

"Be careful, okay? Rent's almost due."

Envelope in hand, Quince tossed a salute, tossed back his Scotch, and grabbed his car keys from atop Maria's book on the coffee table on his way out the door.

Carl Rosen finally understood why Billy Guilder had such a chub for this ugly-ass car.

Driving this growler reminded Carl of the time back home in Flagstaff when he'd boosted this tricked-out '68 Camaro from out front of his neighbor's trailer. He'd only been sixteen at the time. To tell the truth, for a teenager he'd never really given much of a shit about cars, and the only real reason he'd jacked the damn thing was because it was

the middle of summer, most of his buddies were in juvie, and
Carl had been just about bored out of his skull.

But that Camaro took him by surprise, making him
wonder if all his gearhead buddies were right. Maybe he
really *was* missing out on something. Carl had loved the
way all that steel surged forward when he stomped the gas;
he loved the way the fat speedway tires howled when he
cornered, couldn't get enough of the deep heavy growl that
rumbled out from those oversized cams. He'd planned to
just take that Camaro around the section a couple times and
bring it back, but Carl had gotten such a charge driving it
that he'd ended up cruising all the way to the other side of
town and robbing a gas station just to see if he could get
some cops to chase him for a while.

Guilder. Jesus, that guy was a pothead, and he wasn't
necessarily all that bright the rest of the time, but Carl
had to admit: the man knew his way around a motor. This
meatwagon made that Camaro look like an ice cream truck.

And now that he thought about it, a hearse really was
kind of badass ride. Carl liked the tie-in. Paint this bruiser
all black, have the front windows tinted dark like the ones
in back, maybe get some vanity plates with a skull and
crossbones? Carl could definitely see it. Things worked out
like he thought they would back at the boneyard, a car like
this could make a stone-cold signature for a guy in his line.

For now, he rolled it on down to Venice with Mick's stereo
equipment loaded in the back. When he got there, Gerald
pissed about the gear being three years old, moaned about
it being JVC and not Pioneer, griped about there not being
any user manuals. Pointed out how the shutterbug's camera
was all dented in on one side.

He'd finally offered to trade up after Carl told him hey,

fine, you greasy bitch, I'll just take it down the street from now on.

They shook on a deal, and Carl got what he'd come for. He then backed the hearse up into the alley and used the automatic lift to pass the goods out the side, where Kinghorn could unload the merchandise without stepping out from the doorway of the shop.

Happy with the feel of the new .45 in his waistband, Carl got back to business and steered the meatwagon north again. Following the directions Casteneda had given him, he took Ocean Avenue back up to Wilshire, then headed east, eventually pulling into a parking lot with several businesses all bunched together in the same strip. The door marked "SoCal Valley Memorial Society" was the last one on the corner. He pulled the hearse around the side into a vacant stall, went up to the door, and dug in his pockets for Casteneda's keys.

"Suit yourself," she'd told him. "But I don't think I'm the bargaining chip you seem to think I am."

"I was you," he'd told her, "I don't think I'd be tryin' to convince the dude with the gun he didn't need me."

"I never said you didn't need me."

"That's a good point," he'd agreed. "You just said Moss wouldn't give a shit whether you lived or died. So why should I?"

And she'd looked up at him and replied: "Because I'm the one who knows where all the bodies are buried."

He'd kind of liked that one. Made a mental note to use it himself, sometime.

And when he'd called her bluff, she'd told him she had proof. Could back up everything, she'd said.

Her office. Big gray file cabinet, top drawer, left side. Said she had a copy of some kind of permit, something she'd gotten from state records herself, and it showed proof that Moss had transferred ownership of Palm Grove to another company earlier this year

"Hey," she'd told him. "If you want to take your chances and see how far those tapes of yours get you, go right ahead. But just remember: you aren't exactly holding all the cards, here."

By this point, Carl had been willing to play along. He'd said: "And how's that?"

"Well, you've got something on Joel, right? But he's got something bigger on you."

"Think so?"

And the girl had surprised him by bringing up something that he hadn't fully considered before. If what she said was true, it just hadn't been an issue until now.

"Tell me," she'd said, "that it'll take Joel more than one phone call to have your parole jerked all the way back to whatever hole they let you out of."

There she was, her face all fucked up, hair all scabby, eyes wet and red. Couldn't even talk right. He'd just about caved in the side of her head a few hours before, but there she was—down there on her ass on the floor, still thinking on her feet in a situation where most women Carl had ever known would be bawling and carrying on and offering to suck his dick for him right about now. Carl had to admire the girl a little: she had brains. And she damn well had balls. Made Guilder look like a retard, if you really wanted to compare.

"See," he'd told her, "that's where you gotta start thinking in terms of negative reinforcement. It's like with little kids. Sometimes you just gotta be willing to apply a little tough love."

"Like?"

"Like you help a guy understand how it's kinda hard to dial a phone when all your fingers are busted," he'd told her. "One example I could name."

"This from the same guy who was talking about the finer points of long-term planning a few minutes ago?"

"Hey, that's business, right? Sometimes you gotta resort to the hard sell."

"I'm sure that's what your friend Mick was thinking," she'd told him. "But I don't know. Still sounds like the same basic thug mentality to me."

"Yeah, well. Shows what you know."

And she'd looked at him like some kind of career counselor. "Listen, the way I see it, you're the one at the disadvantage here. You want to talk business? Let's talk like people who know how business is done. Joel's in complete control of the playing field. You've got no idea when the deal closes and no idea how much you stand to make or lose. Joel could screw you over so many different ways I don't even know where to start. It could all be over by the time he comes back, for all you know. He could have the whole jackpot in an offshore account and cut your cord before you even knew the fix was in." She'd shrugged. "What good are me or those tapes going to do you then?"

Carl hadn't said anything to that.

"Or maybe," she'd went on, "he's been setting you up from the beginning."

"Now you're reachin', girl."

"Maybe," she'd said. "Maybe not. Think about it. How long have you been here now, a few weeks? A month, tops? And what does Joel *really* need you around here for, anyway?" She'd looked at him carefully. "Kind of a funny coincidence, isn't it? How all this stuff just happens to be happening *now*?"

And he hadn't said anything to that.

"But like I said," she'd told him. "I'm sure you know what you're doing."

"Careful."

"All I'm saying is that when you're doing business, you should never underestimate a guy who thinks he has everything to gain and nothing left to lose."

"Hey," he'd told her. "Everybody's got something left to lose." He'd glanced over at the casket, then looked at her meaningfully. "Ain't that right?"

"That's exactly my point," she'd said. "Why else do you think I'd be offering my services?"

"I got a partner already."

"Tell you what," she said. "Since I'll already owe you, you and Billy can just go ahead and have my shares."

"That wouldn't be the smartest business move I ever heard," he'd advised.

"What can I tell you?" she'd said. "I'm not very entrepreneurial."

Carl didn't impress easy. He figured the girl got points for that much, at least. And to be totally honest, they had a few hours to kill anyway. Moss had cleared him with the halfway house until tomorrow noon. He'd also left some bullshit with the staff about Guilder having unsupervised status now, being so close to making probation and everything.

Still, it'd be awhile yet before Freakshow and the secretary cleared out and left him and Guilder alone on the night shift.

So he'd told Casteneda he'd make her a little deal.

He found the paper trail she told him he'd find, right where she'd told him he'd find it, maybe he'd come back and they'd chat a little more.

He didn't? That'd be okay, too. He didn't really need any new partners anyway.

The phone on the big gray desk was ringing when Carl let himself into Casteneda's rathole of an office. He ignored the phone and flipped on the fluorescent lights overhead. One of them flickered for about thirty seconds before finally giving up and staying dim.

Looking around at the bare walls, dirty windows blocked by file cabinets, gray metal all around, Carl seriously had to wonder about anybody who wanted to voluntarily spend time in here. Between the ringing phone and the piles of work papers and the depressing buzz coming from the lights above, Carl thought, if it were him stuck in here all day, he'd probably have to go ahead and beat somebody to death before too long. Back at Quentin, at least you had your own toilet. Got to go work out in the yard a couple times a day. For entertainment, maybe you got to see some dumb asshole get shanked in the chow line from time to time.

He was just on his way around the desk, heading for the big file cabinet she'd told him about, when the answering machine picked up and cut the phone off in the middle of a ring.

Carl didn't listen closely at first. He pulled open the top drawer of the file cabinet and started poking around for the papers she'd described.

But then he stopped what he was doing.

Maria, the caller said. *It's me. I've been trying you at home all day—thought you might be here. Listen, something ... something's come up.*

Carl listened.

And as the guy talked fast into the answering machine, it was as though Carl Rosen could see his whole business plan changing right before his eyes.

By the time the guy hung up, Carl had his name and number from the caller ID unit by the answering machine. He started pulling drawers.

A half minute later, Carl was on the move, the page he'd ripped from the phone book's residential listings clutched in his hand. Somewhere behind him, the phone had started ringing again.

Just as he busted out the front door, Carl heard the same guy come back on again. Something he'd forgot to tell her the first time. Very important. Listen to me very carefully.

Carl didn't stop to listen very carefully. He just cut a swath toward the meatwagon.

Figuring if he punched it, nearby as the address was, he might just get there before the asshole hung up the phone again.

JOEL THOMAS MOSS awoke disoriented from a troubled sleep.

In the dream he was having, Joel wore rags: a filthy shirt, torn gabardines, mud-caked brogues with wide cracks in the soles. It was past midnight. He sprinted down a misty cobbled street lined by gaslamps on both sides.

In the dream, Joel had been working for a professor of anatomy at the local medical college. The professor was known to pay well and ask no questions; Joel had worked for him before.

Now he was being chased. Each lamp flickered and extinguished as he breezed past it, one after another down the street. Joel ran on, pumping his arms like a madman, wheezing with fatigue.

But each time he looked over his shoulder, he saw that the constable who had roused him from his task had gained ground. The constable gripped his short wooden baton in one hand; with his other hand, he held his whistle to his mouth while he ran. The repeated blasts of the whistle were shrill and accusatory.

Joel ran. And still the constable gained.

Panic washed over Joel.

And as he bolted awake, the sound of the constable's whistle dissolved into the sound of a ringing telephone.

Joel groped awkwardly and fumbled the phone to his face. He turned the receiver earpiece-up, disentangled his wrist from the cord, and croaked: "Yes."

"Joey?"

"Yes."

"It's Brenner."

Heart still thumping, Joel rolled onto his back and sat up. As he absorbed his surroundings, Joel gradually remembered where he was.

Hotel room. It was Friday. He was in Seattle.

"Bryce," he said. "Hey. Hey there."

As he spoke, Joel felt a distant, muddle-headed relief in finding that he was not wearing godawful ratty gabardines after all. In fact, he wore no pants, period. A quick survey of the room found his trousers hanging where he'd left them. On the back of a chair, keeping their creases.

Joel breathed. No soiled, foul-smelling, badly-tailored clothing of any kind. No dirt on his face or under his nails. He had woken up wearing just what he'd been wearing when he'd fallen asleep: his favorite boxers, charcoal dress socks, and a $150 Dolce & Gabbana shirt.

"Hey there my ass," Brenner said. "What *I* wanna know is, Hey Where?"

Joel tried to clear his throat, which was coated with a thick sour film. "Pardon?"

"As in hey, where the hell were you? You know you're my big star, right? You're making me look bad over here."

"Pardon?"

"New word, Joey. You used that one already."

There came a sudden flash of comprehension, and Joel felt his heart go racing again. He checked his watch but didn't believe what it said; he fumbled for the clock radio on the bedside table and saw that it agreed.

"Bryce," he said, "what time do you have?"

"Little hand's on the four, sweetie pie."

"Oh, shit," said Joel. He ran a hand through his hair. Pinched the bridge of his nose. Drew in a deep breath and said, "Shit, shit, shit."

The marketing VP from Knox, Burke, and Hare began to chuckle on the other end of the line.

Joel sat and blinked away the last clinging threads of sleep. The last thing he remembered was sitting down on the edge of the bed and calling for a shuttle to the convention center. That had been a little before 8:00 this morning. It was now 4:30 in the afternoon. He'd slept through his own lecture.

"Joey? You still there?"

"Shit," Joel said.

"Give yourself a kick, Joey. You're stuck on the same word again."

"B," Joel said. "I'm so sorry. I don't know what to say."

Bryce Brenner was laughing now. "Rise and shine, punkin'. Everything okay?"

"I wasn't feeling well," Joel told him.

"Oh, no?"

"B, I don't know what to tell you. I think I must have gotten some bad calamari at dinner last night."

"Ooh. Been there and ate that," Brenner said. "Got it coming out both ends, huh?"

Joel closed his eyes queasily at Brenner's cheerfully eruptive imagery. "Hit me like a ton of bricks," he said, spinning out the excuse word by word. "I was up all night. And then the plane ride—B, I just felt like a whipped dog when I got in this morning. Thought I'd try sleeping a little."

Brenner was still chuckling. A good sign. Joel forged on.

"I guess I must have really conked out. Jesus. I just apologize like hell."

"Ah, forget about it," Brenner said. "I'm just busting your hump. Nobody comes to these things to sit through some boring goddamn lecture anyway. Main thing: you feeling better, big guy?"

"I … I think so," Joel lied.

"Good," said Brenner. "Then get your ass over here to the center. We're in the bar now, but I think eight or ten of us are heading down to the waterfront for dinner. Maybe hit a couple tittie bars after. What do you say?"

"That sounds nice," Joel said.

"Tell you what: we'll observe a no-squid appetizer rule just for you."

"I'm sorry again about this, Bryce. Truly. It's totally unprofessional."

"Do me a favor, Joey. Okay?"

"You name it."

"Shut your mouth, open the mini-bar, open your gullet long enough to down a couple quick-like, and get your ass in a cab."

Joel actually had raided the mini-bar already, early this morning, the moment he'd gotten his bags to the room. The stress of trying to pack, the hustle to LAX, the turbulent flight, the knuckle-clenching pre-dawn cab ride from the airport to the hotel—all these things, on top of everything else, had left his entire body singing like a raw nerve. He didn't mention any of this to Bryce Brenner.

He only said: "I think I can manage that."

"That's my boy," said Brenner. "And it's all on the company tonight, big guy. After the week you've had, I'd say you've earned yourself a night on the town."

Never had truer words fallen upon the ears of Joel Thomas Moss.

After Brenner rang off, Joel hung up the phone and sat in the dark and breathed the stale hotel room air. The heavy curtains were drawn against the light of late afternoon.

At least part of what he'd told Brenner was the truth. He hadn't been feeling well. Joel hadn't been feeling well at all. And he really had been up all night.

Nearly thirty hours straight, to be exact.

He just hadn't been able to relax long enough to doze. Ever since that mongrel Rosen had dragged home a carcass and laid it at his feet, Joel had been caught in a hyperphobic, consumptive, endlessly repeating mood loop. It came in five primary stages.

1. *Denial*
This was not happening. Everything had been going so well; he couldn't believe how quickly circumstances had slipped out of his control.

2. *Anger*
This was not fair. He'd worked too hard; he'd waited too long. And now this! Just as a bit of sunlight was about to brighten his dreary morbid existence—just as his years of toil and personal sacrifice were about to pay off—suddenly, the future he'd so painstakingly arranged depended on the two commonest criminals that ever lived. He didn't deserve this. It just wasn't fair.

3. *Bargaining*
Okay, God, let's just be up front about this. I've never

much believed in you, and you've damn sure never believed in me. We both know it. But if all good souls really go to heaven … haven't I kept you in business all these years?

4. *Depression*

Praying was useless. And Joel should have known better in the first place. He should have known better because he'd been living in and around the hard cold truth his whole life long. Life sucked. Then you died. And in between? Even when you win, you lose.

5. *Acceptance*

For what was done was done. All that was left now was damage control.

It was during this final stage that Joel would succumb to a deep, soul-squeezing anxiety that slowly escalated to a howling windstorm of generalized paranoia.

Which eventually broke like a fever, and the whole cycle began again.

Joel tried to take comfort in the knowledge that he was prepared for the worst. He'd pre-planned, in a manner of speaking. He was equipped to handle unexpected contingencies.

Because if necessary, he could always go to Michael.

The one person in the world he knew he could trust.

The one person Joel knew would always be there for him.

If the situation reached critical mass, Michael had the power to fix just about anything.

Michael Ward was a 32-year-old homeless junkie. Three years ago, he had died in a needle-strewn alleyway from an overdose of black tar heroin. The only information that had been found on his scarred, scabbed, and wasted body was a photo library card. Through the vital records office, authorities had been able to determine that Michael Ward had been born in L.A. County. But no family was ever located, no driver's license or criminal record ever found. Michael Ward had never been treated in a hospital, and he'd never filed an income tax return. When Michael came to Palm Grove, nobody had even been able to determine with certainty that the young man had ever been enrolled in a Los Angeles public school.

Personally, Joel had been in a particularly dark place himself at the time. During one especially despairing session, several weeks before Michael arrived, Joel's therapist had talked him down from a tangent by suggesting he try to imagine himself living the life he wanted instead of the life he lived. She'd suggested he imagine himself the person he *wanted* to be, not the person he was at this moment in time. She told him to be realistic but honest. She told him to imagine everything he could about his fantasy scenario, down to the last detail.

He'd done as she asked. And while he laid there with his eyes closed, imagining his way into a calm, she'd said: *Now there. There are your options.*

It was a perspective Joel had never achieved on his own.

She'd told him to practice this technique between sessions. She told him to remind himself of his options every day.

As corny as it sounded, Joel had found the technique intensely powerful. He found it so useful, in fact, that he'd taken it one step further.

Instead of copying the death certificate his father had signed for Michael Ward—filing one copy at Palm Grove and submitting the original to the county records office, as was his responsibility for all other south-end burials—Joel had pocketed the document and hidden it amongst his things.

Over the next several weeks, he'd augmented his "identity visualizations," as his therapist called them, with an exhilarating hands-on reinforcement exercise.

Joel obtained Michael Ward's birth certificate by calling in a favor from a vital records clerk he knew. He told the clerk a story of lost parents, private investigators, and uncollected disability benefits; the clerk had FedExed a certified copy of the original and wished him lots of luck.

A few days later, Joel used the birth certificate to obtain a replacement Social Security card.

From there, Michael Ward became such a fascinating diversion that Joel simply extrapolated the project to its various natural endpoints. He used the birth and Social Security documentation to obtain a valid California driver's license. Then a credit card. A post office box and a savings account. He signed Michael up for a year's subscription to *George*, *Entertainment Weekly*, and *Oui* magazines.

On his darkest of days—days when he felt so low and smothered by life that he seemed barely able to breathe— Joel reminded himself of his options by getting Michael Ward an international passport. A video club membership. A price shopper card at the local grocery store.

At the time, he'd honestly considered the whole project to be metaphoric. Michael was merely a symbol—a symbol of Joel's ability to change his lot. To conjure an alternative identity from the air. To start a life over again from scratch, leaving behind its sorrows and mistakes and failures to dry and disintegrate like a shed skin.

Michael was a symbol. The butterfly from the cocoon.

But then, in a certain sense, he also was as real as anyone.

Joel had been keeping Michael Ward in a fireproof lockbox for two years now. After his father had died, and the deal with

KBH went through, and his accounting strategies gradually became more creative as circumstances necessitated, Joel had begun to think of Michael less as a symbol and more as a potential disaster recovery plan.

A hundred times since last night's nightmare at the cemetery, Joel—pinwheeling for balance on the short edge of yet another moment of dread—had to force himself not to give in to his own flight reflex.

A hundred times in the past several hours, he'd actually considered killing Joel Thomas Moss. Just putting the poor sorry shmuck out of his misery and resurrecting Michael Ward for real.

But that wouldn't be fair.

It wouldn't be fair to either of them. To bail out now would be a weakling's play, and Joel Thomas Moss had played the weakling for too long. He'd invested too much to be denied the deliverance he deserved.

And Michael Ward?

Joel considered Michael Ward his contribution to the cosmic reimbursement system. Why shouldn't Michael Ward have, in his second life, all the comforts and triumphs he himself had been denied the first time around?

The trick now was to keep things together long enough to make it all happen. Joel had made it this far; he had only a little while longer to hang on. This was the home stretch. This was nothing a little crisis management couldn't cure. This was gut-check time.

So for the moment, Joel coped with his most paralyzing moments the best way he knew how. In a carry-on bag, he'd packed the most reliable stress combatants in his arsenal. A quart flask of gin for ameliorating the corrosive effects of Stage 2. His Zoloft for Stages 4 and 5. A short bottle of mixed leftovers from old prescriptions for Xanax, Prozac, and Klonopin, just in case he needed to throw those seratonin receptors a little curve ball along the way. To counteract the libido-draining effects of the mood stabilizers in case after-hours circumstances required, he'd thrown in a foil sample packet of 100 milligram Viagra tablets, which he'd scored from a urologist who'd lost his mother to natural causes six months ago.

Finally, to sharpen himself for Sunday's negotiations with KBH, Joel had tossed in a little something he'd recently read about in *Men's Health* magazine. A surefire cocktail for boosting the mental faculties: Ginko Biloba, B-12, and Zinc.

Even when you win, you lose. Maybe so.

But Joel had been in the business of loss for long enough to understand the truth forever residing on the other side of that coin: some lives just weren't worth living in the first place.

Sometimes, death was kind.

A toast, then. To the imminent demise of Joel Thomas Moss. A simple raising of the flask seemed all the ceremony required; Joel didn't bother with the standard funerary platitudes he'd delivered so often for others. *Ashes to ashes, dust to dust; gone to a better place; departed in spirit but alive in memory; life everlasting, amen.* As far as Joel was concerned, none of them was worth drinking to.

Especially since Michael Ward intended to spend the rest of his afterlife disproving the most commonly-spouted one of them all.

For even when you win, you lose. But that didn't necessarily mean you couldn't earn out in the end.

And sometimes you *can* take it with you.

★　★　★

In the dream Arlen Maxwell was having, it was 1947 again. He and Rosalie were doing *Menagerie* together at the Pantages Theater on Hollywood Boulevard. It was the summer before the autumn they'd slipped away to Tahoe to be married.

Rosalie had played Laura. And she'd shone.

In the dream, it was curtain call. He and Rosalie stood side by side at the apron of the stage. They held hands and bent at the waist together, and all around them, the house came down.

Somewhere amidst the applause and the whistles, Arlen could hear an odd whooping cheer that rose above the rest. He squeezed Rosalie's hand, and she squeezed his. They stood together and looked out across the dark faces, into the lights.

The applause faded, but the whooping grew louder. It became a high bark.

And Arlen opened his eyes, still sitting in the middle of Quince's awful davenport where he'd drifted off in front of the television, half in the bag in the middle of a Friday afternoon. The glass of Scotch Quince had filled for him sat within reach on the arm of the couch. The cordless telephone rested in his lap, along with Vladimir.

Who was barking his yap off at the empty far corner of the room, roused by some sinister presence only he could sense.

"Vladdy. Hush. There's nothing there."

Vladimir growled at the corner. Arlen stroked the dog's head.

And as Vlad sniffed the air, Arlen turned his eyes to the actual source of the dog's distress: the bearded man in sandals and camouflage pants sitting on Quince's rummage sale coffee table, smoking a cigarette and letting the ashes fall.

Though he had no idea how long the man had been sitting there, somehow, Arlen knew immediately who he was looking at. The tattoos.

"Cross-eyed rat for a watchdog," said the man from the photograph. "Can't say I seen that one before."

Perhaps it was the mellowing effect of the alcohol. Perhaps it was the residual melancholy of his anniversary dream. Arlen was dimly amazed at how calm he felt, under the circumstances.

An old stage actor's trick for rescuing an unplanned moment: he yawned instinctively, hoping the gesture masked the glimmer of recognition no doubt visible in his eyes.

"Oh," Arlen said. He scratched Vladimir behind the ears. "He's not a watchdog. This is Vladimir. And he isn't cross-eyed. Vladdy here is blind."

The man squinted, smoking his cigarette. "Blind, huh?"

"I'm afraid it's congenital." Arlen found a smile and put it on. "You must be a friend of Quincey's?"

"Something like that," said the man. "Guess he's not home, huh?"

"I'm sorry."

"Guess you don't know when he's gonna be back, either."

"I'm afraid I wouldn't," Arlen said. "I'm only the landlord, you see. Quince lets Vladdy and me come over and watch his cable from time to time. He gets the Turner Classics."

"That a fact."

"A wonderful tenant," Arlen said. "Extremely conscientious. Can I pass a message along?"

The man with the killer's eyes dropped his cigarette to the carpet and ground it beneath the sole of one sandal.

He said: "Sure."

MARIA CASTENEDA slept with her head on his lap.

They'd been in the viewing parlor for an hour and a half. At first Billy had tried keeping her awake, thinking maybe letting her sleep wasn't such a great idea. But he didn't have the heart to keep poking and prodding, and eventually he'd just let her close her eyes. He'd loosened the tubes around her wrists and ankles for her a little while she slept. Otherwise he just sat on his end of the couch—the satin pillow from the Conquistador on his leg, Maria with her head on the pillow. Every once in awhile, Billy moved a piece of hair out of her face.

Rosen had said he'd be back in an hour. Billy didn't want to know what was taking him so long. He was nervous enough just waiting, and he couldn't stand thinking about all the possibilities.

In fact, Billy had almost taken off out of there several times. At first, he'd stayed because he wanted the M&M back; he just didn't feel like he could bring himself to leave without it.

But then he decided the car didn't matter. It was only a damn car anyway. He could take the truck, bad clutch and all. Just hop in and go and figure it out on the way.

Once, he'd gotten so close to doing it that he'd lifted Maria gently, scooted off the couch, eased her down, and went to the door.

But when he got there, a rush of sick guilt stopped him. Billy Guilder made the mistake of looking back, back at Maria curled up there on the couch, hurt and stuck here to wait this out alone. He'd made the mistake of thinking: *just another bad turnip. All you are and all you're ever gonna be.*

And then he couldn't do it. A few steps the other direction and he'd have been on his way, but for some reason, Billy just couldn't seem to take himself through the door.

So he'd gone back and lifted Maria up and sat down again. In his shirt pocket, he found half a leftover joint he'd rolled last night and forgotten about, so he dug it out and fired it up and sat there and smoked.

Waiting.

That was awhile ago, now. Billy wasn't sure how long. Didn't really matter.

He recognized the sound of the M&M's big motor long before it neared. A few minutes later, he heard the front doors of the crematory bang open.

And in another moment, he looked up and nodded at Carl, who came into the parlor with a dark stormy look in his eyes.

"Hey, partner," Billy said.

Rosen just looked at him. Didn't say a word.

Maria stirred on Billy's lap. She murmured something. Billy couldn't hear what it was.

He said, "What's the matter?"

Again, no answer from Carl. Instead of speaking, Rosen reached around his back.

At first Billy didn't understand what he was doing. Even when he saw the big steel-plated gun appear in Rosen's hand. Even as he watched Rosen rack the slide.

"Carl?" Billy felt calm. "Hey, man."

And Rosen held the gun up in front of him. He said: "You see this?"

Billy nodded. Maria shifted on his lap.

"This'n here works just fine."

That was when Billy understood. It just settled over him.

He didn't know what had happened, what had gone wrong, but it didn't much matter now. He sat there on the couch in the viewing parlor of the crematory, feeling surprisingly mellow, thinking clearly for the first time all day. Billy thought of the furnace in the other room, and for some reason—instead of jumping up or saying something or trying to bargain or plead—Billy just thought of the saying Rosen had used once before. The one about the rolling stone that gathered no moss.

Now he thought about another saying. The one about turnips.

Understanding that it was wrong. Billy guessed a guy like Carl Rosen could probably get a little blood out of one if he really wanted some.

In the dream Maria Casteneda was having, she snapped Polaroid photos of a collie dog that had been run over in the road. The animal had been laid open and turned half inside-out by the impact that had killed it; fat flies buzzed around the carcass and landed in the slick colorful pulp that bloomed there. She didn't know why she was photographing the collie. She felt atrocious and ashamed. But for some reason, she couldn't stop herself from pressing the shutter button. The flies buzzed, and the camera hummed, and the blank gray photos fed out and fell to the ground around her feet. She tried to look at them, but they weren't developing properly; the hard sunlight bleached them and turned them white as bones.

At some point, Maria woke up to the sound of voices. Her head pounded. She sat up, riding a wave of dizzy pain.

And opened her eyes to find herself still in the parlor of the crematory. Just in time to see Billy Guilder sitting on the couch next to her.

Just in time to watch Carl Rosen extend a tattooed arm.

Point a gun at Billy.

And shoot him in the face.

The sound of the gunshot was deafening; for a moment, it blanked her mind. Maria watched some dark wad leave the back of Billy's head. She watched his head snap back and roll to the side and then hang, facing the opposite wall. Billy's arms flew out to either side of his body, as though he were bracing himself for a sudden stop.

Maria wasn't aware she'd closed her eyes until she opened them again. A cool numbness draped her like a sheet. The air all around smelled sharp and sulfurous. One of Billy's hands had flopped to rest on her knee. It was warm.

Carl Rosen looked at her.

"Deal's off," she heard him say.

Then the sheet covered her, and she felt everything in the world begin to merge with the ring in her ears.

QUINCE CLIMBED the stairs to his apartment exactly forty minutes after he'd descended them with the envelope of photographs. His cheek throbbed, and he had a headache, and he felt like he could sleep for a year.

But at least he'd managed to beat the blue-and-white home.

The car had been the Detective's idea. Photos in one hand, a no-nonsense look in his eye, Timms had produced a tiny cell phone and dialed a SMPD dispatch operator from the parking lot of his daughter's soccer field. Timms told the dispatcher to send a squad unit to Quince's apartment. Then he'd told Quince to head home and sit tight until he called.

So Quince had hustled, hoping to get back in time to save Arlen the added stress of meeting the cops alone.

Now, trudging his way up to the landing, Quince marveled at how the events of a single day could warp your sense of time. He thought about his visit to Rhonda and the kids this morning. This morning seemed like a week ago. A week ago, Martin had been alive. Quince thought about something Rhonda had said: *sometimes I still think he's going to come inside from the yard. The next, it's almost like he was never here at all.* He thought about the simplicity of a hot shower. A cold beer.

Then he saw the screen door, and thought stopped.

But Quince moved.

The door hung wide, disjointed by its bottom hinge. The screen had been torn from the center out; it looked like a rusty exit wound.

Inside, his television sat on its back in the middle of the floor, a jagged crater where the screen had been. The bookshelves had been pulled over; their contents lay scattered across the carpet, spines broken, pages torn out and flung. His computer lay in dented pieces, monitor screen shattered, the desk reduced now to a fractured pile of particle board. The couch had been flipped. The coffee table lay with its legs in the air. There were holes in the walls.

For a moment, Quince stood in the doorway, unable to process the scene.

Then he saw Arlen in the kitchenette, and his blood chilled. He plowed through the mess, glass crunching underfoot.

"Arlen!"

Arlen lay sideways on the floor, tied to an overturned chair with telephone cord. His eyes were open, and he appeared to be conscious. He looked at Quince without expression. Quince grabbed the chair and heaved up, righting it and Arlen together. The man weighed about as much as a bird.

"Arlen," he said. "Christ, Arlen, are you okay?"

Arlen said something that made no sense to Quince: "Sink."

Quince knelt down in front of Arlen's chair, trying to gauge the lucidity in the old timer's eyes. He remembered the Swiss knife in his pocket and dug for it, dropped it, picked it up again. He snicked the blade open and sawed through the cords around Arlen's ankles and wrists.

Freed, Arlen didn't move. His thin arms hung.

"Arlen," Quince said. "Talk to me. What happened here? Are you okay?"

"The sink."

Quince stared at him a moment, not understanding. Arlen looked past him. Quince followed his eyes.

For some reason, he noticed a single droplet of water, hanging suspended from the lip of the leaky faucet. Quince watched it. Suddenly he could hear the ticking of his own watch on his wrist. The drop fell, and Quince heard nothing.

He stood.

In the sink he found Blind Vladimir. The dog's neck had been wrung. Vlad's cataract-clouded eyes stared backward, toward his tail.

A crumple of paper had been stuffed into Vladimir's narrow muzzle. Numb, Quince reached down and pulled the wad free. Unwadded it.

Palm Grove, the note said. *Second building out back. You know what to bring. Anybody comes along, you get to count the ways you wish you hadn't fucked up while you watch her burn.*

Behind him, he heard Arlen say: "Son."

Quince looked. Arlen was holding out his hand. Misunderstanding, Quince reached over and took it—but Arlen only squeezed once and shook his head. He pulled his hand away from Quince's grip and extended it toward the sink.

"He's gone, Arl."

"Just hand him to me, son. Please."

Quince didn't know what to do. He watched Arlen, feeling disoriented and useless. Arlen didn't lower his hand.

Finally, not knowing what else to do, Quince turned back to the sink, reached down, and took the dog's still-warm body in his hands. He picked Vlad up. Closing his eyes, Quince took a queasy breath and turned the dog's head right again. Then he pivoted and stepped forward and handed him to Arlen.

Arlen took Vlad in his lap. He looked down and sighed and stroked Vladimir's limp coat. "Bloody hell."

Quince stood silent. He stared at the note in his hands. Time stopped, then accelerated.

He grabbed up he phone.

"Arlen," he said. "Arlen, listen to me. Are you with me?"

Arlen nodded without looking up. He petted his dog. Quince handed Arlen the note while he dialed.

"The cop's name is Timms," he said. "Read it to him. Okay?"

And Arlen finally raised his head. "Kiddo. You wait."

But Quince was already out the door. He barged his way past two uniformed officers on their way up the stairs. The three of them looked at each other for a split moment. Then Quince juked once, slipped a grab, and ignored their shouts as he made the sidewalk and sprinted for the street.

One of the cops was ten steps behind him when Quince reached his hatchback parked at the curb. He jumped in and locked the doors and put the keys in the ignition and started the car. Through the driver's window, he shouted the word "Apartment" at the cop, who pounded on the glass with one hand and drew his revolver with the other.

No windows shattered as Quince dropped into gear and pointed the car toward the place where he seemed to be spending all his time this week. The place where almost everybody winds up eventually.

"Okay, Joey. Here we go. One after the other ... atta boy."

"I can walk by myself."

"We already tried that, remember? Out on the sidewalk? You remember when you tore your pants on the sidewalk?"

"I had these pants tailored."

"They're great pants, Joey. Look like a million bucks on you, even with those bloody holes in the knees. Ron, you got his key card?"

"Yup. Hold him up."

"I am holding him up. And he's breathing on me. Open Sesame before I pass out over here."

"Bryce?"

"Yeah, Joey."

"I want you to call me Michael from now on."

"Sure, Joey. I'll call you Michael."

"Promise!"

"Cross my heart, okay? Damn, son, you are definitely gonna hurt tomorrow ... hey. Joey. Hey."

"I think he passed out."

"Joel baby! Up and at 'em, hoss."

"I told you. My name is Michael. Michael Ward."

"Sure, Joey. Michael Ward."

"I am the master of my own density!"

"Did he just say he was the master of his own density?"

"Yeah. And he's gettin' denser by the minute. The door, Ron. The door."

"Voilá."

"Okay, Mikey my lad, here we go. In the door ... that's it ... wait! ... oh, you gotta be kidding me."

"Hey. Way to hold him up, Brenner."

"Some help you are."

"My name is Michael, I got a nickel ..."

"Now this is just sad."

" … I gooott a nickel … a nick-nick-nickelll…."

"Look at that, B. Grown man singing into the carpet. Isn't that the most adorable thing you've ever seen in your life?"

"Ron, I worry about you."

"Awww. Look at how his wittle hiney is sticking up in the air with his face all buried in the rug."

"Yeah. Reminds me of my ex-wife. Now would you please shut up and grab his feet before I start laughing too hard to hoist this lummox?"

"Think I should I take his shoes off first?"

"Sure, Florence Nightingale. Maybe you'd like to go ahead and give him a little hand job while you're down there?"

"Well … those are some nice pants he's wearing."

"Just help me get him on the bed already, you lunatic."

As Bryce Brenner shut the door to room 1031 behind him, he turned to his division sales manager and sighed.

"That," said Ron Jurgens, "is a guy with problems."

"Without a doubt," Brenner agreed. "But nothing a stomach pump and a good treatment facility couldn't cure."

"Think we should leave him?"

From behind the door they could hear Joel Moss begin to bellow mournfully. After a moment, Brenner thought he recognized the inebriated meanderings of a tune.

Ron cocked his head. "Is that 'Bridge Over Troubled Waters?'"

"Jesus, what an idiot."

"Well," Ron said, tapping his watch, "on the bright side, it's not even 10:00. Rest of the guys are probably still at the Flamingo."

Bryce Brenner clapped him on the shoulder. "Come on. That redhead owes me a lap dance."

"Hey," said Jurgens, hurrying to catch up. "I saw her first."

As HE ROLLED through the front entrance of Palm Grove Cemetery for the fourth time since Wax was buried and buried again, Quince Bishop suspected he'd probably found the quietest place in Los Angeles, at a quarter of rush hour on a Friday afternoon.

He got on the winding tour path and drove out into the green. He drove out amongst the monuments: stones, flat markers, statuary. Stout Doric mausoleums. He passed intermittent deposits of flowers, some of them recent, others wilting. He passed decorative, shielded installations of abiding memorial flame.

A hundred yards from his destination, Quince put the car in neutral and twisted the keys, cut the engine and coasted the last gentle slope. He took the path down and around toward the low white stucco building with the red clay tile roof and the silver hearse parked in the rear.

Quince yanked the brake and got out into the quiet. He walked up the rough slate path. Pulled open the glass double doors. And went inside.

He didn't know what was about to happen. He didn't have a plan.

Somewhere in the back of his mind, it occurred to him that he should probably be much more concerned about what waited around the corner of the coming moment than he seemed to feel.

But nothing happened when he entered the tastefully-appointed foyer. He stood and gathered his surroundings; he saw plants in the corners, gentle art on the walls, frosted glass wall sconces sending soft light toward the ceiling. Nobody stepped out to meet him. Nobody threatened him menacingly. Nobody clubbed him on the back of the head. He heard no voices. Only silence, all around.

Then he heard a series of mechanical noises coming from somewhere further inside. Hinges and rollers, a motorized hum. A hard metallic slam.

Quince headed toward the sound.

When he entered what looked like a waiting room, he saw Maria sitting in an upholstered chair. She was bound and gagged.

Her eyes flew wide when she saw him. Maria sucked in a breath through her nose, moving her eyes urgently to a long curtained window in the wall.

And Quince's calm dissolved. He hurried over, seized by a sudden panic, scanning the otherwise empty room. From the other side of the window came another heavy clang.

Maria winced as he pulled what appeared to be heavy rubber hospital tubing down over her chin. The folded fabric gag fell into her lap.

"Hurry." A hard whisper. "Hurry."

The sight of her almost stopped him. Maria's hair was dark and matted around a wide swollen gash below her crown. Her eyes were red and full of matter. Her face had a limp, wrong look.

But he forced himself to move. While Maria kept an anxious eye on the window in the wall, Quince dug the Swiss Army knife out of his pocket and used it to slice through the tubing at her wrists. He glanced briefly at the sounds behind the glass window, then started on her feet. Frantic with hurry now, he slipped once and gouged her ankle bone with the point of the blade. Maria let out a yelp; Quince cursed and jerked the blade back hard, severing the tubes.

"Come on," he whispered. "Can you stand?"

Maria shouted the word "No!" so loudly that it startled him. He looked up at her, and saw her eyes had gone wide again. She looked past him, over his shoulder.

Quince turned just in time to see the familiar man with the beard and the tattoos raising his hand. In the hand, there was a gun.

The gun came down hard.

When the worst of it passed, Quince felt almost glad that he'd never quite lost consciousness. He would have hated to sleep through his first pistol-whipping. Even as he felt something solid in his cheek pop and give way, some daft distant part of him was thinking this would all be great stuff to work into that screenplay he meant to write one of these days.

First, a bomb went off in his head. Hot yellow light blotted out the room. Some long moment later, he found himself looking at carpet, weakly braced on hands and knees. He couldn't bring his vision into focus, and his face burned. It felt like somebody had lodged a hatchet in his skull.

The first words he heard, somewhere in the thick warm fog: *You bastard*.

Then the same voice, clearer this time:

"Quince."

Soft in his ear.

"Oh, God. Come on, sweetie. Here we go."

Then he was sitting back against the base of the chair. Maria leaned over him. She stroked his hair with one hand.

Squinting, hurting, emasculated, muddled, Quince opened his eyes again. The guy who had clocked him sat on the couch a few feet away, one arm tossed across the back of the couch, gun hand resting on his knee.

"Considering the situation," he said, "you gotta be thinkin', maybe the other guy got the better end of it after all."

At first, Quince had no idea what he was talking about. Then, all at once, he knew why the face was so familiar. It was a mental fingersnap: the stairwell of Maria's apartment building.

"Oh," he said. "I knew I remembered you from somewhere."

The guy with the gun grinned. "Small fuckin' world, huh?"

Quince touched his cheek. A bright new flash of pain strobed behind his eyes. "I swear," he said. "This is never going to heal."

"Where's the Kodak Keepers?"

Quince looked at Rosen blankly. He saw two beards. Then three. Then one.

"Okay," Rosen said. "Just so you know, you're about this close to pissin' me off."

"They're in the car," Quince lied. "I left them in the car. Front seat. Outside."

"Now why'd you go and do a thing like that?"

"Stupid, I guess."

"Guess you must be," Rosen said. He stood up and wagged the gun. "Okay, kiddies. Up we go."

They stood like walking wounded. Maria helped Quince to his feet, propped him when the dizziness buckled his knees. Then her own balance teetered, and he caught her.

"Aww," Rosen said. "Sweet. Now move."

Maria glared at him. "Why don't you just go to hell?"

Rosen snorted, knocked Quince half off his feet with a hard shove, and marched them back into the foyer and out the front doors.

Outside, Rosen prodded Quince in the spine with the gun barrel and said, "Keys."

Quince dug in his pocket and handed them over. They marched up the slate walkway to the edge of the tour path. When they got to the car, Rosen handed the keys to Maria. He told her to unlock the passenger side, get the pictures, and pass them on back.

Maria threw the keys back at him. She appeared to be aiming for his head, but they hit his shoulder and fell clinking to the slate between them. "Get them yourself, you murdering asshole."

Rosen pressed the muzzle of the gun against Quince's temple and pulled the hammer back, as if by way of punctuation. "Me, I'm busy."

Maria said nothing. She only looked at Quince. Then she picked up the keys from where they'd fallen and went to the passenger door.

To Quince, Rosen said, "Hope you remembered the negatives."

The two of them stood by—Rosen with the gun in Quince's ear, Quince trying not to pass out from the throbbing hurt that seemed to gather and swell in cycles. He tried to think of what he was going to do when Maria emerged from the car.

He hadn't come up with a plan by the time she finally turned back to them, empty-handed.

"Now what?" Rosen said.

"Maybe they fell under the seat," Quince suggested.

Maria looked like she was struggling not to lose hold of whatever it was that was keeping her on her feet. She didn't look at Rosen. She kept her eyes fixed on Quince, as if trying to establish a connection, and hold it, if only from a distance.

"Or maybe I forgot them at home."

Rosen said, "You're gettin' stupider by the minute, you know that?"

Quince was still thinking of a reply when Rosen flung him aside, stomped a few steps the other direction, and grabbed Maria by the hair.

Back inside they marched.

It must have been a viewing parlor. Which would mean it must have been the cremation furnace Quince heard clanking and pinging behind the glass. He was thinking about Billy Guilder when, his first few steps back into the room, he noticed a dark wet smear of gore on the carpet behind the couch. The slick patch led his eyes to a pattern of red on the wall. Quince was gazing at it when he felt his feet leave the ground, and then he was flying.

He hit the arm of the couch hard with his hip. The couch skidded with him several feet, and then he went over, bounced off the cushions, and hit the floor.

"No!" he heard Maria shout.

When Quince looked back, he saw that she'd gone berserk; she clawed at Rosen's face with her nails, going for the eyes, her face twisted and feral.

Rosen just twisted her hair in his heavy fist and jerked her head back. Maria let out a furious scream and spat and swiped at him. Rosen jerked her again, harder, dragging her across the room with him.

Quince took the first kick full-force with his ribs; he felt his lungs empty, then noticed he was looking at the ceiling. Black-and-white spots danced there. The second kick caught him in the opposite ribcage; he felt a dull crack in his side, and then he was looking at carpet again.

The next few blows came and went and blended into each other. Maria screeched banshee curses in the background; English blended with Spanish, and soon the words blended, too. When the kicks stopped coming, Quince lay curled in a tight ball on the carpet, facing the chair Maria had been sitting in when he found her.

Above him, Quince heard Rosen panting a little, and he thought: *maybe he'll get tired and give up.*

Quince drew in an experimental breath, and it was like an icepick in his lung. His stomach felt knotted, tight as a charleyhorse. He forced himself to breathe again. The next breath came easier still—at least until a mild convulsion snuck up on him, making him cough. With a disconnected curiosity, Quince pondered the few bright speckles of crimson that appeared on the carpet in front of his face.

Into the carpet, he mumbled, "You had enough yet?"

Above him, Quince heard a pair of clicks. He didn't move. Didn't know if he could, or if he even wanted to.

"You know what that is?" Rosen said.

"I don't guess it's a complimentary Palm Grove ink pen?"

"Don't guess it is."

"You know," Quince suggested, straightening his legs to a fresh series of happy stabs from the phantom icepick, "It'd be counter-productive to shoot me *before* I tell you where I stashed the photos."

"That's why it ain't pointed at you, fuckhead."

"Quince, don't," Maria said. "Don't make it easier on this murdering asshole."

"You already called me a murdering asshole once already," Rosen commented. "You should try some variety. Spice of life, right?"

"Okay," Quince said. "Okay. Just give me a minute."

Above him, Rosen said, "Sure."

At first, from his worm's-eye view, Quince hadn't even recognized the object he'd been looking at, a scant several inches away, beneath the chair.

Now, he took a shallow breath, rolled onto his stomach, and swept out his hand just an inch or so wider than necessary. The pain in his cracked ribs zigged one way; the pounding throb in his head rolled back the other. He lay there and rested for a second.

Then he pushed up onto hands and knees and rested there a few seconds more. Another cough stitched him like a hot needle. He spat a bloody stringer to the carpet between his hands.

Footsteps moved around behind him; Maria cried out. Rosen deposited her roughly in the chair, then came back around again. A low hum emanated from behind the window in the wall. Quince listened to it. Something about the tone seemed to resonate deep in his center, both alarming and soothing at the same time.

Rosen came to stand directly above him, one foot entering his view of the floor.

"Time's up," he said.

Quince nodded, and pushed back on his heels. He sat there. Closed his eyes.

And thought: *here goes nothing.*

When he opened his eyes, he drew a bead on the top of Rosen's sandaled foot. Using one hand to cover the other, Quince gripped the handle of the Swiss knife he'd palmed from beneath Maria's chair. He focused on the skeletal fanwork of long thin bones running just beneath the skin behind Rosen's toes.

Then he raised up the pocketknife, lunged, and brought it down point-first as hard as he could.

The sound Rosen made seemed almost more animal than human: a throaty, wounded bellow. Then a roar.

As Rosen did an odd hop back, Quince struggled to his feet and went for Rosen's gun hand. Dizziness descended like a hood; Quince stumbled and almost went down again.

But somehow, he managed to grab hold of Rosen's thick wrist with both hands. He got his feet under him and tried to twist, got nowhere, actually felt his own grip breaking against Rosen's pure bull strength.

Rosen had already recovered his balance. Desperate now, feeling the tide of the moment already turning back against him, Quince did the only thing he could think of to do.

He picked a place on Rosen's wrist, went in with his teeth, and clamped down hard. Rosen roared again and began to pound the top of Quince's skull with his free fist, bleating: "Ah! Bitch!"

Each blow felt like a falling sledgehammer. Quince fought the blackness creeping into the corners of his vision by grinding down until his gums tingled. He bit until he tasted blood, warm and rusty and strange on his tongue. He tried not to swallow. He tried to make his top teeth and his bottom teeth meet in the middle.

The gun went off, and his left ear went quiet, and stinging hot grains peppered his cheek. The long curtained window shattered and rained out of the wall in thick shards; the sound of the furnace became a low pulsing rumble that seemed to fill the room.

Quince bit down until he could feel his head quaking, and to his dim amazement, the gun thudded to the carpet and bounced. Flushed with triumph, Quince kicked at it and missed. He tried to stomp back, behind him; he visualized the pocketknife still vertical in Rosen's foot and tried to imagine stomping a tent stake into the ground. But he missed again.

And then, somehow, he found himself gnashing at empty air. Some hard invisible blow to his ribs doubled him over, and then he thought he saw Rosen's knee coming up fast.

Then the rumble of the cremation oven thundered over him and the lights went out again.

Maria barely tracked the moment until it was over. It happened so fast.

First, Quince was down. Then he was up. Then he was down again. Along the way, the gun went off. Then Carl Rosen had a look on his face that seemed caught somewhere between rage, pain, and surprise.

Then he picked up his gun from the floor and everything slowed to a dreamy crawl.

Before Maria could react, Rosen pointed the gun at Quince's back and pulled the trigger.

She was screaming before she realized that she hadn't heard a bang.

By the time she collected herself, Rosen was hopping in a circle on one foot, shouting, "Fucking Gerald, you fat fucking piece of shit!" He wrestled the gun with both hands like he was trying to strangle it.

For some reason, Maria understood what had gone wrong.

She didn't know anything about weapons, not a thing at all. But it made sense, visually. The gun just *looked* jammed.

Maria was out of the chair and on the ground at his feet before Carl had turned to face her again. She found the handle of the knife in his foot and grabbed it. When she twisted, she felt the blade scrape against bone.

Carl made a sound like a volcano erupting.

Maria made a last-moment decision, gave up on the knife, and was clawing at his belt when he backhanded her. It was an awkward, off-balance strike; still, the force of it rocked her, and she fell back.

But not without reward.

Quick as she could, Maria scrambled to her feet. She double-handed the revolver she'd snagged from the front of Rosen's waistband and pointed it at the center of his broad chest.

"Okay, girl," he said, panting. "Don't be stupid."

She pulled the hammer back like she'd seem him do it.

"You better be fuckin' ready to shoot me, that's all I got to say."

Maria spoke to this by taking a breath, closing her eyes, and squeezing her finger toward her palm.

The gun bucked, but not as hard as she'd expected. The bang was loud, but not as loud as the one from Carl's gun before. When she opened her eyes, Carl was looking at a small red hole in his shoulder. He appeared more curious than injured.

"Guess maybe I should rephrase," he said.

Before he could, she squeezed the trigger again. This time, she kept her eyes open.

So she was able to see just how badly she missed. Carl ducked his head and looked back over his shoulder at the lamp that popped, sizzled, and fell off the short table in the corner.

"See," he said, "I told you that gun was a piece a shit."

She used both thumbs and pulled the hammer again.

"Careful, now. I ain't loaded that heater since I wasted Mick's dumb ass. Way I count 'em, you're down to your last round."

"Guess I'll have to make it count, then."

Wincing as he poked his own bullet wound, Carl limped over to the couch and dumped himself into it—jammed gun in his left hand, bullet hole in his left shoulder, right wrist torn and bleeding, Quince's knife still in his foot. He bent down and grabbed the knife and yanked it free with a low grunt. He looked at the thin blade for a moment, as if considering possible uses. Blood welled up in the wound and spilled over, running freely now.

The furnace in the room beyond the broken window must have finished some stage in its cycle, for its tone changed, shifted gears, turning higher but quieter. Somewhere, a fan kicked on.

"Wonder if ol' Billy's done yet," Carl mused to the pocket-knife.

"Is that supposed to be funny?"

"You wanna know what's funny?" Carl looked at his bleeding foot. "That poor goofy asshole kept tellin' me I oughta get some boots. Guy must have said it a hundred fuckin' times."

Maria kept the gun on him. She didn't say anything. Beside her, Quince started to move. He moaned once, rolled to his side. Sat up and leaned forward on his knees, cradling his head in his hands.

"Gimmee a sec," Carl said. He looked at his gun for a

minute. Then he put the knife down, gripped the top of the gun firmly, and began to jerk and wiggle it. "Be right with you."

"Stop," Maria said. "Stop it. Put the gun down."

"What are you gonna do, shoot me? From all the way back there?"

Maria tried to map the gun's sight pattern in her head. First shot: she'd aimed dead smack dab in the middle of his sternum. And got his left shoulder. Second shot: she'd aimed in the exact same place, and the round had hit the lamp. Over his right ear.

It was no good, and she knew it. She couldn't take a chance. Not from where she stood now.

"Fuck!" Carl spat. Disgusted, he threw the gun across the room. "I swear, guy sold me these is gonna hear about this." He picked up Quince's pocketknife again and leaned forward, elbows on his knees. His hair hung in his face. "Well?"

"Why don't you move a little closer?" Maria said. "We can talk better."

"Nah." Carl beckoned with the small bloody knife blade. "I'm tired. Why don't you come over here?"

"Think you can touch me before I get close enough to be accurate with this thing?"

"Hey," Carl said. "You said it yourself, right? Never underestimate a guy who's got nothing to lose?"

"Everybody has something to lose," Maria reminded him.

Carl laughed. He grabbed the casket pillowcase he'd used to gag her, wincing hardly at all as he tied it tight around his foot.

"Well look at us," he said when he was finished. He leaned back, checked his shoulder, and shook his head. "I swear, this is the dumbest damn Mexican stand-off I ever heard of."

"Does anybody besides me smell something burning?" Maria heard Quince say.

She looked at him. At first, she thought he was joking. Then Quince raised his head, and she knew he couldn't be. Not looking the way he did.

Carl seemed to sense it next. He cocked his head like a wolf.

Maria looked up. She didn't know why.

And above them, over in the far corner, a small section of ceiling burst into flame.

"The hell?" Carl said.

They watched the ceiling, the three of them, each momentarily transfixed. The flames spread flat across the smooth white surface, already blackening the corner from which they'd sprang.

They watched. Quince from the floor, Maria standing beside him, Carl Rosen bleeding on the couch a few feet away. It was such a strange, hallucinatory vision that they couldn't help but share it momentarily.

Then the bonding moment ended.

"I swear," Carl Rosen said, as the sound of approaching sirens drifted through the walls. "I'm startin' to wish I never got out of bed today."

There were several things Carl Rosen didn't know about the proper operation and maintenance of the TherMAXX 2500 Human Reduction System.

Though an older-model, entry-level appliance, the 2500 exceeded basic industry performance standards for the incineration of human remains. The furnace featured a dual chamber design with an integrated fan system and fume hood, ensuring the operating location remained within stringent state and federal health and emissions regulations. The high-resilience composite hearth lining had been engineered and manufactured to withstand extreme temperatures and rapid heating/cooling cycles. Internal stack brushes cleaned the TherMAXX-patented "Breath of Fresh Air" exhaust system after regular use.

Palm Grove's ten-year-old cremation furnace featured simple two-button functionality; with brief instruction, practically anyone above the age of five could operate the incinerator with relative ease.

However, the TherMAXX 2500 lacked the full complement of automated functions and computerized diagnostic controls found on newer, more advanced models. A series of external gauges, for example, monitored internal conditions during the incineration process. But in case of malfunction, system overrides required manual intervention by the operator.

Certain general maintenance functions, such as cleaning cycles, required user initiative as well.

Billy Guilder had been meaning to run the stack scrubbers for several weeks, but his daily workload around the grounds kept him busy doing the work of two or three full-time people as it was.

The external fire started first in 2500's suet-coated ductwork, and was accelerated by redline temperatures caused by an overload of unremoved material in the primary chamber.

Carl Rosen didn't know anything about that. He didn't really care.

The important thing was knowing how to read life's little warning signs. As the sirens neared, and a flaming chunk of ceiling fell to the carpet several feet away, Carl took it as an omen and made what seemed like the smartest business decision under the circumstances.

The way he figured it, it was just the basic law of survival in the marketplace. The unexpected just hit you head on sometimes. Sometimes, you had to be ready to ride it out. And sometimes, you had to know when it was time to cut your losses and bail.

Carl hit the back door and made the M&M just as the first car—a big brown unmarked—came tearing down the tour path toward the crematory. Two wailing cruisers followed, lights strobing. They took the curves hard, single file.

Carl gunned the M&M and headed the other way around the building, churning up chunks and clods of cemetery turf in his wake. He cranked the wheel a heartbeat too late and lost the muffler, the manifold, and most of a tail pipe on a jutting grave marker. He uprooted a rose-colored headstone with the front bumper, and then bore down, bouncing the big silver meatwagon across the grounds.

Carl aimed for the tour path behind the first two cruisers. Gravestones and statues blurring past his windows on either side.

He made it before the blue-and-whites could figure out a way to turn around. He gunned the motor again, fishtailed, and laid a long black smear of rubber behind him as he straightened the wagon and put the pedal to the floor.

Without the muffler, the M&M sounded like a bulldozer. Huge, nasty, powerful. Carl let out a war-whoop and felt the noise rumble his bones.

Up ahead, two more cruisers had wedged themselves nose-first across the entrance to the grounds. Two cops took position in front of the blockade and drew down on him— one crouching on a knee, the other taking a three-point stance. The sight almost made Carl feel nostalgic for the old days.

Each of the cops got off a few shots, missed, and then had to dive. Carl whooped again and aimed for the V where the two cruisers touched bumpers.

They might has well have put a pair of aluminum cans in his way. Carl had plenty of runway. He hit his mark full bore and crashed through the blockade.

The momentum took him across the street, through oncoming traffic, over the median, across traffic again, finally up and over the opposite curb. Carl banged his head on the ceiling, yanked the wheel back the other way, and went hard for the brake.

When his foot skidded off the pedal, slippery with blood-soaked satin, he had just enough time to think: *Seriously shoulda listened to that dumb pothead con.*

Then he hit the oncoming light pole, center grille.

Carl felt a pleasant, floating sensation. The next time he opened his eyes, all he saw were misty white clouds. At first, he thought: *what an unbelievable break this is.*

But then, instead of angels, a bunch of guys in black appeared in the radiator steam.

All of them standing around with guns they probably hadn't been dumb enough to buy off that asshole Gerald Kinghorn.

WHEN THE SMOKE finally cleared, Melanie Roth would look back on the final progression of events and ponder the irony. For as hard as she'd worked to create her own opportunities, and as generally successful as she'd been in doing so, it was Quince—slacker extraordinairre—who ultimately led her to break what would end up being the biggest story of her career so far.

After all. If he hadn't called to warn her away, she might actually have given up on Moss and come home.

Mel, the message he'd left on her hotel voice mail had said. *Listen to me, okay? Something's happened. I'll explain later. For now, just stay away from Joel Moss. Are you listening? This is serious. Just steer clear. Forget the story. I'll fill you in the minute you get home.*

The timestamp said he'd called early Friday afternoon; Mel hadn't even checked her messages until she glanced at the phone on her way to the bathroom Saturday morning and noticed the blinking light. She considered calling him back. Wondered briefly if she'd find him at his number, or at Maria's.

Instead of finding out, she picked up the phone and dialed for a cab.

A few minutes before 8:00 AM, Mel exited the cab at Moss's hotel, which she'd tracked down the day before through the receptionist at Palm Grove by posing as a KBH intern.

She entered the overdone glass-and-brass lobby with no information to work with and nothing resembling a strategy. All she had was Quince's message. This, plus the cryptic email she'd received from Maria Casteneda yesterday morning before getting on the plane.

Disinterment permits. Without explaining why, Maria had told Melanie to check L.A. County health department records to see if any such permits had been issued to Palm Grove in the past year. Assured her she'd find none. Suggested she corner Joel and watch him lie.

All afternoon Friday, Melanie had been hoping to do just that. But as long as Moss wasn't going to come to her, she figured she might as well go to him.

So she got off the elevator at the tenth floor, hoisted her softsider, and followed the numbered arrows down the carpeted hall. Surrounded by early-morning hotel quiet, Mel tried to refine her opening line on the way.

She didn't even hear the voices until she neared her destination.

Rounding her last corner, Mel saw four people gathered outside a single door: two uniformed officers, a guy in plain clothes with a two-way radio, and what looked like the hotel manager with a fat ring of keys. The man with the radio wore a badge in a wallet hanging from the oustside breast pocket of his sports jacket.

One of the younger officers nodded politely as she approached, clearly expecting her to gawk a bit and keep walking. The officer seemed surprised when she stopped and joined them.

"Miss …" he said.

"What's going on, fellas?" Mel actually double-checked the room number, just to make sure this wasn't too good to be true. 1031. Just like the receptionist at Palm Grove had told her.

The plain-clothesman turned her way. He had a face that looked like it owned a boat but didn't get to spend nearly enough time on it. "Miss, please keep moving along."

"This is me." Mel nodded at the door, hoisted her bag on her shoulder noticing the word HOMICIDE on the cop's badge. Detective Petersen.

The two officers glanced at each other. The hotel manager looked like he needed a Rolaids.

Petersen studied her. "You are?"

"Melanie Roth," she told him. "*Los Angeles Times*."

One of the uniformed cops rolled his eyes. But Petersen just nodded. "Little off your beat, aren't you?"

"I was supposed to interview Mr. Moss for a story," she lied. "I'm in town covering the NAAP convention."

"An interview."

"That's right."

"At eight in the morning?"

"I thought it was kind of early."

She could see that the detective wasn't buying it.

"Miss Roth," he said, "I'm going to have to ask you to head back to the elevators at the end of the hall there. If you'd like to contact me later in the morning, I'll do my best to make a little time for you."

"What's going on?"

"Miss Roth, please."

"What if I just sort of stayed out of the way?"

"Would you like to be arrested?"

"For what?" Mel took a step back. "See? I'm completely out of the way. You won't even know I'm here."

The detective looked at her and sighed. Mel smiled at him winningly and took another step back, just to show him how out of the way she could be.

Petersen rolled his eyes and nodded to one of the cops, who reached out and knocked sharply on Moss's door.

"Mr. Moss," Petersen said, in an authoritative tone. "This is the Seattle Police Department. Please open the door."

After a couple of minutes, the cop knocked again. Harder this time.

"Joel Moss," said Detective Petersen. "Seattle PD. Open the door, please."

A few doors down, a man in a bathrobe poked his head into the hall. One of the officers told him to please remain in his room; the head ducked back inside and the door closed. Petersen nodded to the hotel manager. The manager stepped forward, selected a key, and used it to open the door.

The uniformed officers disappeared inside. A moment later, the one who'd first nodded at Melanie reappeared.

"What's the story?" Petersen said.

"Better call EMT," the cop said.

"Miss Roth," said Detective Petersen. "Are you going to make me shoot you?"

When she entered the room, she saw one of the cops kneeling on the carpet, trying to rouse Joel Moss by shaking him gently. The other cop had been sent on some coply errand. Petersen hung up the telephone on the bedside table.

"Buddy," the cop was saying, wearily, as if this was not the kind of thing he'd been hoping to spend his time doing after academy. He slapped Joel lightly on a cheek. "Pal. I mean sir. Hey."

Moss lay in the middle of the floor, wearing a dress shirt, one sock, and no pants. He was half-tangled in a sheet that trailed from his ankle to the bed. Mel noted a collection of pill bottles on the dresser, plus a colorful scatter of capsules on the carpet by the bedside table near Petersen. The room reeked of booze.

"Out," Petersen told her.

"Oh, come on."

The detective walked over, touched her on the arm, and steered her backwards, toward the open door.

"I'm only watching!"

"Watch from out here."

Out in the hall, a small group of people in various states of dress had gathered, blinking and curious. One man actually stood outside his door in a bath towel, a sudsy streak of shampoo still caught in his wet hair. Petersen told them all to give him a break and disperse already.

"You realize," she told the detective, "that you're striking an injurious blow to the whole idea of free press, don't you?"

The detective seemed about to offer his opinion on that particular issue when they heard the sound of violent retching from inside the room. This was followed by a high, disgusted exclamation from the cop they'd left behind.

"There you go," Petersen said. "You can report that the guy puked on one of my officers."

"Very funny."

"Doesn't sound like Officer Newton thinks so."

There came a shout. Another shout—louder this time, alarmed.

Followed by a gunshot.

Met by quick gasps from the crowd in the hall.

Detective Petersen had drawn his gun before Melanie had absorbed the surprise. He ducked back inside the room and slipped to the side, into the bathroom. Melanie heard Newton say, "Okay, pal. Easy does it."

From the bathroom, Petersen barked: "Drop your weapon. Do it right now."

And Joel Moss responded with an urgent, gargling cry. "Stay away from me! You stay away from me!"

"Sir! Drop your weapon!"

"If you come near me, I'm going to shoot myself. Do you hear me? I'm not bluffing! I'll blow my brains all over everybody!"

The onlookers in the hall had cleaved into two neat groups, one on either side of the doorway. Everybody chattered in hyper tones, tentatively craning for a view, nobody quite brave enough to break the plane of the doorway, lest they catch a stray bullet in the eye. Mel joined the group on the left, next to the hotel manager, who looked just terrible.

Petersen and Officer Newton emerged from the room once again. Petersen spoke quickly into his two-way; Newton looked like he wanted to crawl under the carpet and stay there a few days. He had dark yellow spatters on the legs of his trousers, a chunky wet coating of the same thing all over his shoes. His gun was not in its holster.

Petersen hissed at him. "What happened in there?"

"The guy puked on me!"

"Obviously."

From the room: "You stay away! I'll do it! I will! I have no fear of death whatsoever, do you understand me?"

Newton seemed deflated. Disappointed. Demoralized. "I just bent down to roll the idiot over so he wouldn't choke to death. Next thing I know, he's … ah, fuck." He looked down at his clothes. "I don't believe this."

Petersen just rolled his eyes again. He told Newton to clear the hallway, stepped to the side of the doorway and said: "Sir? Let's just take it easy. Okay? Nobody's coming in. You and I can just talk awhile."

But there was no talking. From Joel Moss, there came no answer at all. Melanie looked at the hotel manager. He looked back, one ear cocked expectantly. Behind them, the vomit-covered Officer Newton herded half-dressed guests down the hall. They complied willingly, seemingly repelled by the smell.

"Mr. Moss," Petersen said. "Are you with me? Everything okay in there?"

When the next gunshot came, Melanie jumped and felt her heart pause. The hotel manager jumped beside her. Newton whipped around, one hand reaching automatically for his empty holster.

Petersen was inside the room like a flash, gun pointed at the floor. Melanie couldn't help herself. She followed him in, three steps behind.

Joel Moss raised his head when they entered. He looked up at them, blinking drowsily. He was sitting in a chair, arm hanging limp, Newton's gun still dangling in his hand.

What had happened was so obvious that Mel instantly translated the scene into headline format: *Crooked Undertaker Shoots Self in Foot.*

"Mr. Moss," Petersen said. He leaned forward and carefully plucked the gun from Moss's hand. "I'm going to have a look at you, okay? Just remain calm. An ambulance is going to be here any minute. Okay?"

At the moment, remaining calm did not seem to be an especially tall order for Joel Moss. It took the man almost a full minute to notice his own self-inflicted wound. He stared at it for a moment, still blinking. Then he looked up at Petersen.

"I'm bleeding," he said.

Petersen glanced at Melanie. She just looked back. What was there to say?

"Yes," the detective told him. "Yes, you are."

ALMOST A WEEK passed before Quince finally returned to the apartment to begin the long task of picking up the mess that waited for him.

They'd kept him in the hospital only a day beyond the surgery. Once the docs seemed satisfied that he'd met most of the important items on his post-op checklist, they'd signed him over to Mel, who had arranged with the paper a week's working vacation to stay home with her laptop and play nurse.

He'd told her it was unnecessary, but she'd ignored him. So Quince gave in, spending the first several days of his recuperation at her place, availing himself of the bedside service and all the softer foodstuffs on hand.

All told, the worst of his trauma had occurred above the neck, which Mel rarely failed to acknowledge was the softest part of his anatomy anyway. He had three cracked ribs and a punctured lung, which the doc told him would knit themselves in time. But the spot in his left ocular orbit where Skull Punk had tagged him had been chipped and fractured by the blow from Carl Rosen's gun. A pair of surgeons had

353

repaired the injury with tiny stainless steel pins; with return trips and proper care, they'd told him, external scarring would most likely be minimal.

As for wound care, internal scarring seemed to have been left up to him. But in that area, Mel seemed optimistic about his resilience—and if not precisely that, at least confident in her therapeutic abilities.

Maria Casteneda had gotten off slightly less lucky, at least where hospital discharges were concerned; she'd been badly concussed, and they'd kept her for three nights' observation before finally giving the all-clear. Swelling in the temporal lobe caused the most concern initially, this being the culprit behind the minor facial paralysis she'd brought with her. But the doctors took her daily improvements to be an excellent sign, measured in leaps and bounds, and they expected the palsy-like symptoms accompanying her injuries to be temporary.

Quince had wandered down the hall to visit her twice in the hospital. And there was the morning Detective Timms had asked for a brief clean-up interview with both of them in the same room together before Quince's release. Beyond that, the general chaos of those first several days had kept their chances for private interaction to a minimum.

But they'd agreed on a date, to be met at an undetermined time in the near future.

So on the Friday after their ordeal together at Palm Grove—partially to prepare for Maria's eventual call, but mostly because the time had simply come—Quince left Mel to the day's deadline and ventured out alone for the first time in days. He took a cab from her apartment to the shambles above Arlen's garage, planning to spend the afternoon sorting through the damage, putting things back where they belonged, and throwing out what wasn't worth keeping anymore.

He'd only spoken to Arlen once, the morning his landlord had visited him in the hospital. The two of them found a twenty-minute window between cops and reporters, during which they'd shared idle chat and long quiet moments, ending with an agreement to meet on the patio for beers when Arlen returned from his daughter's in Monterey.

Quince took the stairs slowly, pausing to rest between throbs. By the time he got himself inside the apartment, the place seemed so wrecked and unfamiliar, and his energy reserves were running so low, that he decided the sorting and straightening would have to wait for another day.

For now, he took care of the only two things on his mind.

First, he searched the living room. Found Maria's book intact beneath the overturned coffee table. Pinned open, pages down, but without serious injury.

His closet hadn't come through as clean. But after a short reconnaissance effort, he'd collected the trampled contents of his shoebox from where they'd been scattered around the floor.

By the time he'd reconnected the phone line and called for a return cab to Mel's, Quince had restored the shoebox to very near the state in which he'd left it. If minus a small Swiss Army pocketknife, which had been impounded as evidence in an unrelated matter.

The call he'd been expecting finally came near the end of the following week. Maria said she'd wanted to wait until she looked more like herself, and less like the walking, talking tragicomedy mask she claimed she'd resembled before the nerves in her cheek and mouth started punching the clock again.

Quince suggested Italian. But Maria said she already had a place in mind.

So on Friday afternoon, they met at a back booth of a dim, hazy little corner tavern in Culver City, with peanut shells all over the floor and a scarce population of obvious regulars. Quince ordered a pitcher of the house draft. It was a ceremonial gesture, really. Neither of them felt particularly thirsty.

But sometimes ceremonial gestures served their purpose just fine.

They sat. They talked. They swapped still-painful smiles. Quince reached into the bag he'd brought and handed Maria her book. She took it and looked at him.

"What's this?"

"Overdue," he said.

She grinned and thanked him. They sat and chatted about nothing, about nothing important at all. They didn't waste time on the awkward or the obvious, for life was too short to bother, the company too agreeable to spoil.

Eventually, they only sat.

Quince wanted desperately to explain himself. He wanted her to know that what had passed between them had mattered. That it would not be forgotten. That he truly wanted to build upon it—even if they both knew the foundation they'd begun together had probably already been rezoned.

History is never boring, she'd told him, the last time they'd shared this booth. He wanted to know if she still felt that way.

Because somehow he couldn't help but sense that at the moment, Maria was pondering history, too.

Especially when she tilted her head and broke the silence with a question.

"The last time we were here. What was that toast you made?"

Quince tried to think back. It seemed like years ago. "Lost causes, I think."

Maria nodded thoughtfully. They sat together in the booth until she decided what she wanted to say.

When she finally settled on it, she smiled and found her beer. "To retrieval."

Quince raised his glass and said, "Cheers."

Authorities from the L.A. County Medical Examiner's Office, the California Health Department, and a Los Angeles Police Department Haz-Mat detail recovered an indeterminate catalogue of human remains from the crematory facilities at Palm Grove Cemetery and Funeral Home in Santa Monica. Six partially-calcined adult male teeth were matched to the prison dental records of **William Harold Guilder**. Guilder's remains were statused itinerant, shipped to a burial acreage maintained by the California Institution for Men at Chino, and interred at a total taxpayer cost of $41.79. Guilder's burial was attended by the prison chaplin, a janitorial trustee, and a young woman from Los Angeles. Only the young woman returned regularly to the site—once each year in mid-October, to leave a small floral arrangement on behalf of the SoCal Valley Memorial Society.

Shortly after being taken into custody, placed under suicide watch, and returned to Los Angeles, **Joel Thomas Moss** was found hanging dead by a bedsheet from the window of his ground-floor room at Saint John's Hospital. The young ward nurse and rookie officer assigned to monitor the funeral director, who had been placed under the hospital's care for detoxification and treatment of a non-mortal gunshot wound to the left tarsus, were fired without severence. They were married in a Catholic/ Judaic ceremony six months later and currently are expecting their first child.

Operation of the **Palm Grove Cemetery and Funeral Home** was assumed by the Cemetery Board of the California Department of Consumer Affairs, pending an investigation and complete financial audit of North American funeral service provider **Knox, Burke, and Hare, Incorporated**. A civil class action lawsuit, organized by Los Angeles attorney **Jerard Grundman**, seeks damages from KBH, Inc. for nine primary violations of the 1994 Funeral Rule, as established by the Congress of the United States and alleged by 24 complainants in the West Los Angeles area.

For the murder of Billy Guilder, **Carl Rosen** was convicted and sentenced to serve a life term without parole at the California State Prison at Folsom. Despite a wealth of circumstantial evidence, district prosecutors were unable to win a conviction for the alleged execution of 21-year-old **Curtis Albrecht** of Venice. Subordinate victories on felony counts of kidnapping, assault, miscellaneous weapons charges, parole violation, and fleeing to avoid arrest each drew individual sentences, to be served consecutively.

Gerald Kinghorn was acquitted on charges of receiving stolen property due to insufficient evidence.

In the spring, following a cross-department investigation of the Palm Grove homicides, **Adrian Timms** left the Santa Monica Police Department for a position in the Robbery/Homicide division of the LAPD. Detective Timms celebrated his new job with two weeks of salmon fishing in Puget Sound, where he enjoyed full run of a six-room furnished cabin off Gig Harbor. Keys to the cabin were loaned to him by an old college football teammate named **Raymond Petersen**, who was the newest Detective Lieutenant on the Seattle force and unable to get away.

After a difficult but survivable holiday season, **Rhonda Waxman** began attending certification courses in computer network administration. **Nathan's** progress during weekly half-hour sessions with a private practice family grief counselor has been encouraging. He enjoys reading and drawing and is looking forward to spring soccer. **Katie** is preparing herself emotionally for kindergarten.

Maria Casteneda continues to act as president of the SoCal Valley Memorial Society, with the help of a paid part-time office assistant and a new full-time volunteer. The organization remains not-for-profit.

A few short weeks after the events at Palm Grove, **Quince Bishop** arranged for a few days' sabbatical from his volunteer duties at the SoCal Valley Memorial Society. He and **Melanie Roth** spent Thanksgiving in Chicago with Quince's brother Paul and his family. On Friday morning, Mel, Wendy, and the baby ventured out into the year's largest shopping mob to catch a few sales, leaving the brothers to their own devices. Quince and Paul returned from their visit to Woodlawn Cemetery in Palatine by late afternoon. By Friday night, **Wallace Theodore Bishop** had spread his cold to everybody in the house. But a few germs never killed anybody.

Precisely one year after Vladimir's murder, **Arlen Maxwell** celebrated his wedding anniversary by returning to the stage. In doing so, Maxwell witnessed the realization of a long-forgotten ambition: to one day try his own hand at the fine art of play-writing. In keeping with the Halloween season, the production was patterned after the lurid and cheerfully-macabre tradition of the *Théâtre du Grand Guignol* (the Parisian equivalent, Maxwell postulated to a *Theater Watch* interviewer, of America's infamous pulp fiction movement). The play—essentially a series of interconnected satirical vignettes—was titled, "The Grim Trader's Memoirs." Arlen Maxwell himself played the title role of Mortimus Maximus, the bumbling undertaker. During the finale, while Mortimus orated in iambic pentameter and

wandered the house with a
collection plate, players on
stage tossed non-toxic foam
rubber human organs into the
shocked and delighted crowd.

Notices were mixed. The
Los Angeles Times pronounced it
"Wickedly twisted, wonderfully
wry … cold hands down, the
best argument for immortality
you're likely to find!" A critic
from *L.A. Weekly* dismissed
the production as "an
unapologetically dreadful
revival of drama's most
embarrassing moment in
history. Here lies proof, if proof
were required, that poor taste is
alive and well in America. May
it soon be granted the burial it
deserves."

EPITAPH

noun

An inscription on a tomb, showing that virtues

acquired by death have a retroactive effect.

Following is a touching example:

   Here lie the bones of Parson Platt,

   Wise, pious, humble and all that,

   Who showed us life as all should live it;

   Let that be said—and God forgive it!

                —*Ambrose Bierce*, The Devil's Dictionary

THE PUBLICATION of any edition of an UglyTown book is cause for celebration, and I'd happily write an Afterword for any one of them. But I hope you'll forgive me if my egalitarian front slips enough to reveal an extra shade of pride and gratitude for this edition of this particular UglyTown book.

Now pride can be a treacherous thing, particularly when directed selfward. This topic carries a helpful bit of synchronicity, as a good old friend completes a similar assignment for one of his books at the same time I begin this one for mine.

In the Foreword to a new deluxe edition of his 1992 novel *Deathgrip*, Brian Hodge (you may notice the blurb he authored for the novel preceding this essay, a source of pride in and of itself) writes:

Perspective is everything.
On one page, a rediscovery: *That's nice, I like that.*
Turn the page: *Who wrote this crap?*

It's a lot like that. I don't know any authors who can look back at previous work without the occasional flinch, maybe even a full-on scowl or two. I'm sure there are a few, and I'll bet they lead relatively normal lives, much like you or me. But I certainly don't live in their neighborhood.

Looking back on *Dirt* across even a comparatively slim margin of removal, I see a first novel with first novel problems, first novel indulgences, and, yes, a few triumphs that maybe you only stumble into the first time around, before you know any better.

But I can still allow myself the pride that comes from knowing that, for better or worse, *Dirt* was every bit the book I was capable of writing when I wrote it. The probability that I'll never write a book quite like it again is strangely reassuring and bittersweet at the same time.

Now. Turning pride outward? That's easy. And fun. And if you're me, writing this, this is the pride that comes with built-in hooks on which you hang a whole lot of gratitude.

Because I couldn't be prouder of my association with UglyTown, and the road we've traveled together since the summer of 2000, when we first came into each other's lives. UglyTown had published a few books by then—Tom and Jim's own intrepid Dashiell Loveless, Rodney Johnson's wonderful debut Rinnah Two Feathers book, a handsome BookSense 76 anthology of short stories. They've published a whole bunch of fantastic books since, with more on the way. But *Dirt* was the first adult crime novel by another author that UglyTown brought into the world.

I'm proud of that. I'm proud of the editorial work Tom Fassbender and Jim Pascoe did on the manuscript, and I'm proud of the beautiful—and sturdy!—final product. I'm proud that they don't have any more of 'em, and I'm proud that you're looking at this second generation. I hope you enjoy it.

I like to say that I was looking for an UglyTown at the same time UglyTown was looking for a … me. But let's be truthful. UglyTown would have gotten along just fine without Sean Doolittle. I can't make the reverse statement with nearly as much confidence. And so my gratitude couldn't be more genuine when I say: Thanks, guys.

Sean Doolittle
March 2005
Omaha, NE

Like most novels, this one owes a great deal to people other than the author.

Special thanks to Thomas Belford of the John A. Gentleman mortuary for his generosity, for the tour, and most of all, for being one of the good guys.

A lifetime supply of gratitude to Jessica, first reader for everything and a trooper if ever there was.

Salud to Scott Lindvall, Tracy Baker, Jill Richards, and the unsinkable Sheri Forman, for top-notch input and insight offered while this manuscript made its way through various stages of completion.

All the Ketel One in Schiedam to Tom Fassbender and James Dean Pascoe. Because beauty is in the eye of the beholder, but Ugly is a categorical imperative.

Thanks to Gerald Shapiro, Judith Slater, and Ed Baker for lessons still being learned. To Brian Hodge, for more than one refresher course. And to Roland, Mackie, and Alesis for invaluable homework excuses.

Finally, a bottomless tank of hugs and smooches to the home team: Mom, Dad, Seesta Jeel, Tobaz & Co., Casa Grasso, Wayne Edwards, Eric and Becky Rauch, Brian Hodge and Dolly Nickel, Clark Perry, Wayne Allen Sallee, Michael Okerlund, Daniel Higgins, Yvonne Navarro, all VonCon attendees, Norman Partridge, Dallas Mayr, and everybody who has ever overlooked my sliding into work late.

If this book were a corporation, you'd all own original shares. Which isn't the same as a cut of the royalties, but I'm sure you understand.